THE LAST CONFEDERATE FLAG

BY
LLOYD E. LENARD

AmErica House
Baltimore

First printing

ISBN: 1-58851-468-4
PUBLISHED BY AMERICA HOUSE BOOK PUBLISHERS
www.publishamerica.com
Baltimore

Printed in the United States of America

Dedication

This novel is dedicated to the thousands of valiant men in Confederate uniform who fought and died on battlefields of the Civil War. They were tired of the constant battering given them by "Yankees" who wanted only to dominate them. It is also a salute to the millions of Southerners who refuse to be intimidated into adopting a posture of shame and surrender to the forces of prejudice and historical ignorance who daily assault Southern heritage and culture.

Acknowledgments

I owe a debt of gratitude to my wife Sky. It is she who has done the tedious job of proofreading and editing and who never stopped believing in me. I would also like to thank John E. and Mary Blanchard and the other men and women who read the book and particularly my mother and father, who helped hack out this great land I so fiercely love from the daunting landscape into which they migrated as "poor people searching for freedom and a better life."

My literary agent, Brenda Bailey of Conway, S.C., on first reading *The Last Confederate Flag*, fell in love with the work. "I can sell this," she enthused, and promptly proceeded to do just that.

PROLOGUE

I was flying high, puffed up with my own delusions of self-importance and basking in the glow of public adulation. Suddenly, I crashed down to earth. When such a thing happens, the cause usually stems from a person's own peculiar make-up. Or an over-sized ego.

In my case, it was my make-up. The way I saw the world did not allow for the changes erupting with explosive force across the United States. The dim and distant call to remembered glories, the myths and legends, which color the Southern mind in hues of nobility and honor, stirred unceasingly within me. I was caught up in the Southern penchant, which finds us far too ready to fight for lost causes as a matter of principle.

When militant minorities and Southern turn-coat politicians launched a drive to haul down the Confederate flag flying over General Robert E. Lee's monument on city hall grounds, I was plunged into a raging controversy and marooned in the barren, pock-marked wastes of no-man's land. The enemy forces were very real. Their objective as the conflict escalated? Eliminate Stonewall Bedford; that's me.

If I were to survive, I had no choice but to fight my way out.

When the challenge came, I couldn't help myself. To me, not running from a fight, standing up for the things I believed in with every fiber in my body, were matters of personal honor. I would never run from those who wanted to pull me down. Perhaps I should have ignored their taunts, their sneers and their insults—and their threats of violence—but I simply could not. The price I paid in taking them on in a head-to-head battle was shattering.

My Southern heritage pulses through every fiber of my being. In my mind, I am there at Gettysburg on that fateful July 3, 1863. With Pickett's forces, I charged up Cemetery Ridge. To this day, I can hear the faint sound of the bugles urging us forward, ever forward. I find my feet wanting to march to the muffled roll of the drums. I'm caught up in the seas of gray as we charge toward the Yankee forces holding the high ground. The enemy rifles and cannons create a curtain of death through which we run. I hear them still. The screams of fallen comrades, their pitiful pleas for help, their final moans of death. My eyes grow misty at our failure to gain the high ground and rout the blue coats. Victory for us was so close . . . so close.

If only we had triumphed that day, the South would have won the war and we'd be a free and separate nation. If only . . .

If only I had turned and walked away from my challengers that dreary, gray day at City Council meeting in Forest, Georgia. If only I had chosen not to pick up the gauntlet they threw down and dared me to undergo the certain trial by fire. If only . . .

Chapter 1

"Something evil this way comes!"

In the dead of night, when I was a child and winter winds howled around our big old house, I often listened to the strange creakings and groanings and slid farther down under the covers in efforts to hide from the sinister terrors evoked by the unexplained sounds. In my imagination, the hooded wraith beckoned to me from the edge of darkness.

"Something evil this way comes!"

It was spitting rain. I watched the car's windshield wipers flick the rain drops away and, for a moment, again heard the strange creakings and groanings of long ago.

For reason I couldn't pin down, I dreaded going to the Forest city council meeting. The day was another one of those dark, depressing February days that made you doubt that the sun would ever shine again and I was feeling down.

The cold gray drizzle had oozed itself deep into my bones and aroused vague sense that something evil was out there waiting for me. My natural optimism had run away and was in hiding. I told myself that I was being silly and that today's council meeting would be like most of the others—another exercise in futility where the hot air of political posturing would leave me feeling empty and resenting the waste of my time.

It was one-thirty in the afternoon. I glanced at city hall as I drove into the parking lot with its wet, black asphalt surface. Like many other things in Georgia, the four-story building was old and spoke of history and days long past. Its crumbling yellow bricks had probably been pressed into crude wooden molds by black hands, fired in some primitive oven where the heat came from blazing hardwood logs that had been hauled into the clearing by horsedrawn wagons, driven by black men handling the reins that controlled the mules.

The lawn's thick grass of summertime was now brown, matted and wet. The spitting rain that had hovered over Forest for days kept the sides of the building wet and glistening in the low light. I thought of old men walking against the rain without a coat. The black green leaves of the huge live oaks that surrounded the building danced a slow minuet to the cold breeze. Shrouded figures seemed to coalesce from deep in their branches and dance toward me.

Professor Harris Woolford turned his Jeep Cherokee into the parking lot and motioned for me to wait for him. I stopped on the tiny porch of the attendant's booth and tugged at the brim of my black and gray checked hat. I shoved my hands deep into the pockets of my tan trench coat and hunched up my shoulders as a reflex action against the cold and dampness.

Harris locked his car doors and walked toward me. He was one of those intellectual college professors whose Italian mother had passed her dark good looks and flashing black eyes on to him. As he often reminded me, he'd inherited his mother's quick tongue and his father's piercing intellect, traits that pushed him into the public arena as a colorful, slashing combatant who was difficult to challenge and defeat in logical debate—of which there'd been precious little of late in council chambers.

"Man," he said. "This damn weather. Won't it ever quit?"

"It's got me feeling low, too," I said. "I keep glancing over my shoulder to see what trouble's following me." I was always looking down at the jaunty professor, since I was at least five inches taller than he was.

The professor rubbed his plastic ID card across the face of the courthouse security recognition box, then pushed the button that unlocked the basement door. He shoved his left hand against the long bar and pushed against the door with his shoulder. We walked along the empty basement corridor.

When the elevator stopped at the first floor, several people crowded in to push us close together. A tall, black man with acne-scarred face looked at Harris and me, grunted, and said, "Well, if it ain't two of our honorable city council members. The two who always vote against anything that helps poor people." A twitter of laughter ran through the others in the crowded elevator.

I shrugged and looked at Harris. I could tell he was biting his tongue to keep from tying into the rude bastard. On the fourth floor, the elevator emptied with a rush, leaving the two of us alone for a moment.

"What was that all about?" I asked as I stepped into the corridor outside the council chambers.

"Was he trying to tell us something? It was all I could do to keep from tearing into him."

It was slow going as we picked our way through the dozens of people standing around in groups. "All these people . . ." I said. "The agenda didn't show anything special. I did wonder about the name Abdul Karim listed under 'visitors.' "

"Yeah. I noticed that strange name. Who the hell is he?" The fire of his Italian mother sparked in his words.

The milling of too many people in the over-sized corridor, the babble of male and female voices, the air of surly defiance. A sixth sense told me this day would not be like most of our days for conducting the business of the city and coping with political issues in Forest, Georgia.

Woolford—in that hat with the brim turned down all the way around. You had to give him a second glance. The college professor always looked as though he should be smoking a Meerschaum pipe and discussing clues with Holmes and Watson.

As we walked toward the meeting room, we almost bumped into a short, fat man who glared at us and seemed determined not to move from our path. We stepped around him.

Three tall, broad-shouldered black men—they looked like those distinguished men from a *New Yorker* magazine ad with white shirts, red bow ties and black, expensively tailored, double-breasted suits—stopped the two of us there in the hall outside of the council meeting room.

"The meeting *does* start at two p.m., doesn't it?" one of them asked. He was smiling, as my mother used to say, "Like the cat that ate the canary."

"Yes, two o'clock," Harris said. "Why? You up here for something special?"

"You might say that," the questioner replied. His voice was precise, the pronunciation of words clear and clipped. He carried himself tall, above the crowd, his eyes aglow with a piercing cynicism that said you'd have to deal with him on his terms, like it or not.

"Say," the youngest of the trio said to Harris. "Aren't you a professor out at the University of Georgia branch here in Forest? Woolford? Harris Woolford?"

Harris raised his chin so that his eyes could look through the center of his glasses that perpetually slid too far down on the bridge of his Roman nose. "Yeah, I'm Woolford." He extended his hand to the questioner who pretended not to see it. The professor peered intently at the man's face with its inscrutable smile, searching for some clue as to who he was. "Who are you? Did I teach you in one of my government classes?"

"I'm Mueschle Jabbar. No, I've never been in any of your classes. I recognize you from your pictures in the Forest *Ledger*. It's in there quite often. You're always raising hell about something."

"You're right about that," I said, sticking my hand out toward him. He ignored it. I turned to the man who'd asked the question about the time of the meeting. "My name is Stoney Bedford. What's your name?"

I don't know why the man made me think of a silent hawk, swooping and searching for prey. "Just say I'm one of those Black Muslims that scare the hell out of people like you," he laughed. "The name's Malcolm the Fourteenth, but you won't remember it."

"Why should I be afraid of you?" I asked. I felt my face turning crimson.

There was no answer. The three laughed, did a high five, looked at Harris and me with mocking disdain, then walked into the meeting room.

"Well," I said. "I don't believe those three have come to today's meeting to take part in a Sunday school picnic. Something's burning their guts." My uneasy feelings intensified, why, I didn't exactly know.

"Black Muslims? Here for a city council meeting?" Harris' eyes swept the crowded hallway. "Most of these people here *are black*." His shoulders lifted and tensed as if to protect his neck. "Do you feel threatened somehow?"

The hairs on the back of my neck were standing up. "Something's not right up here. It's in the air." I moved my head slightly toward the tall trio who had questioned us. "Did you and I do anything to cause the ice I felt between us and those three?"

"Damned peculiar behavior." Harris answered.

I found myself stroking my chin, something I usually did when I was puzzled. "Black Muslims. The 'Merciful Ayatollah's' troops. Highly disciplined. Great leaders in the black community. I read that they call themselves 'holy warriors.' "

"I know one thing," Harris answered. "I certainly wouldn't want to cross one of those three. They look strong enough to tear you apart with their bare hands." He stood with his back toward the wall, a pensive look on his face. "Did you see the way they talk and carry themselves, as though they were on a mission with high, great purpose?"

I was nodding my head. "I see now why black people in their neighborhoods respect them, why they give them plenty of room."

Woolford raised his chin to look at me. The glasses had slid down on his nose again. "Dr. Elijah Smith, sociology professor at the university, says that even those blacks who are heavy into drugs respect the Muslims, including gang members. As I understand it, they are leaders who strive to get black people to take charge of their own lives, to quit blaming others for their problems, to stand tall and build self esteem—for themselves and other blacks."

The fat man was in front of us for the second time, his face and eyes cold as steel. He said nothing, just stood there with his arms folded across his barrel shaped chest. We stepped around him again.

"Someone has to help those poor, beleaguered people in our black communities," I said. "Blacks prey on each other like hyenas rushing in to finish off wounded stragglers. Drugs, robbery, rape, muggings, senseless murders, drive-by shootings." I sighed. "The good folks out in those jungles live in fear night and day."

The hall was dimly lit. The closely packed bodies moved almost in choreographed fashion, clustering in tight groups, unfolding, the dancers dancing away only to cluster again in a different group. I caught the smells of heavy perfumes, heard the deeper bass of male voices, saw the visual contrast of the women's long, white gowns against the dark colors of the men's suits. My fingers rubbed across the rough gray and black checked fabric of my hat as I placed it on the top of the coat rack I slipped my trench coat onto the hanger and noticed the drops of rain still clung to the coat's surface in tiny globules.

For some reason, a cold shiver ran down my back. As we stood in the alcove behind the meeting room and sipped the hot coffee, I remembered a vivid scene from last summer when my wife and I were in Philadelphia for a few days. We took a city tour on one of those air-conditioned coaches. In an area of palatial homes on wide streets, the tour guide stopped the bus and pointed to a huge mansion that covered an entire city block.

"That's our leader's headquarters," the young bus driver said, an air of pride in his words. "You know him as the 'Merciful Ayatollah.' You can't dismiss him and his Black Muslim movement. He's declared war on white people and boasts about it. The Ayatollah's turning things upside down and I'm glad. He's good for us black people."

Harris and I finished our coffee and moved back into the corridor. Several more black women in long white gowns and Muslim head dress got off the elevator, eyed the crowd and headed for the three imposing men who had talked briefly to Woolford and me.

"More Black Muslims," Harris said. Perplexed, he scratched the back of his head. "The other night on TV they showed the Ayatollah's Philadelphia headquarters. The camera took us inside the place."

"I missed that. Did it show his guards spaced along the sidewalks surrounding the place? Splendidly dressed young men that looked exactly like those three we just saw?"

"Nobody gets into that place unless the Ayatollah okays them," Harris said.

The fat man was blocking our way again. "We'll get you two sooner or later," he said.

"Get us for what?" Harris asked.

"You'll see," he snarled and rubbed his plump hands together as he moved away.

"That man's crazy," Harris said. "He's not smart enough to be one of the Ayatollah's men. Probably just a supporter who's trying to push others around."

The tall man we'd seen in the elevator, the one with the acne-scarred face, stopped us. "You think a black man might get a cup of that coffee back there? Or is that space 'off limits' to blacks?"

"Yeah, man," I said, pointing back through the door to the place where the coffee was. "Help yourself."

"Why do people seem so belligerent today?" I asked.

Harris scratched his head again. "Pisses me off, but I guess we have to consider the source. It's better we don't pay any attention to people like him."

"In our part of the country," I said, "people are too busy with their six packs of beer and television programs when they get home from work to be bothered with things like the Merciful Ayatollah."

Harris looked around again, shrugged and said, "I guess we'd better go on into the council chambers, although I'm not exactly looking forward to today's meeting. I'm expecting trouble."

The spectator's section of the paneled meeting room was already packed with people, male, female, black, white. Those who couldn't find seats stood two deep in lines around the back of the hall. Television camera operators from Forest's two stations leaned their heads toward each other as they talked. Two women TV reporters sat at the press table, along with Victor Allen, reporter from the *Ledger*, Forest's daily newspaper.

Allen stood up when he saw Harris and me enter the room. The short, chubby little man with his perpetually angry frown hurried toward us, a smug smile on his face.

"Here comes trouble," I said to Harris.

"Hey guys," Allen piped up. "What do you think about the demands that Abdul Karim and the other Muslims are going to make today?"

Harris frowned. "What demands, Victor?"

"Oh, you haven't heard?" Allen asked. "They're going to demand that Chief of Police Dennis Crowe resign."

"You've got to be kidding, Victor," Harris said. "On what grounds?"

"They say Crowe's not giving black people enough police protection. That he's a racist who deliberately neglects crime in the black community through assigning a greater number of police to patrol the white neighborhoods."

I couldn't believe what I was hearing. I knew that the Muslims were militant and that there was great unrest in the black community. But this about Chief Crowe. "Allen, you know that there's not a racist bone in Crowe's body. I've seen the figures. Seventy percent of the officers are regularly assigned to the patrol of minority communities. And most of the city's budget is spent on trying to protect citizens in the black communities from the criminals who terrorize innocent people. It's a terrible thing."

"Who knows?" Allen asked. "Perhaps the figures have been doctored just to make them look good."

"Oh, come off it, Allen. Those are trumped up charges," Woolford said. "The best thing the mayor ever did was to appoint Crowe as police chief of Forest. He's earned the respect of people in all corners of the city through absolute fairness and his tough stance on crime."

"Trumped up or not," Allen smirked. "It'll be front page news in the morning *Ledger*."

Harris struck back. "We knew we could depend on you and your newspaper to distort anything that comes up at our council meetings. Whatever happened to the supposed objectivity of the press?"

"My newspaper just happens to believe most whites have a hidden agenda to keep blacks pushed down in society," Victor said. "We're out to correct it."

"I'm glad to hear you admit it, Victor," Harris said. "Most people in this area know you're a bunch of biased, prejudiced bastards over at the *Ledger*, and that you use reverse racism against whites to push your own hidden agenda."

"Use your head, Victor," I said. "You know as well as I do that this is a slick trick, a disguise for something else the Muslims want to accomplish. It's not Crowe who's a racist. It's the three blacks we've got on this city council who are the racists. If we oppose any thing the three blacks on the council want, they point their fingers at us and yell 'racist.' They know the media will take up the hue and cry and print all their phony charges."

Woolford raised his chin again in an effort to peer through the center of his glasses, which were again riding far down on his nose. "Yes, sadly, Tolman, Cape and Dines try to define everything in terms of black and white." He finally pushed up his glasses. "And everything that comes up on this governing body cannot be defined in those simplistic terms."

"I've sacrificed a lot to serve on this government body," Harris said. "I base my decisions on the principle of the greater good. What's good for the majority of our citizens, not just for me and the people in the district I represent."

The newspaper reporter was disgusted with both of us. "You guys are mired in self-pity. You're trying to put an honorable face on your buried racism. Besides, I don't have time to engage in a philosophical debate. Or is it just plain old shit?" He laughed, his sarcasm plain.

Harris put his hand on my arm to encourage me not to plow into Allen again.

Allen turned to me. "Can I quote you on what you said about Chief Crowe?" Including your statement about the charges being trumped up?"

"I said it, didn't I?"

"Yeah," Victor smirked. "It's a typical racist statement by a member of the privileged group of whites who control Forest. I can always count on you for an inflammatory statement." The smirk came again. "It does liven things up though."

"One of these days, Victor . . ." Harris caught my arm. I stopped talking.

The reporter turned to scribbling in his short hand notebook. As he walked back to the press table, he was a rumpled figure in cheap, discount store clothes. That fact certainly never bothered Victor Allen.

We walked toward our seats.

Before the courts forced the city to redistrict, the seven members of the old council who had been elected "at large" worked together in harmony and accomplished much that benefited the citizens of Forest. The U.S. Justice Department forced the city to draw new district lines to insure the election of minority members in the three black majority, inner city districts.

That's when DeLong Tolman, Norris Cape, and Frank Dines were voted into office. The atmosphere changed immediately. Tolman, Cape and Dines held us at a distance and challenged anything we tried to do on the Council. They were intractable. No amount of persuasion could change them.

Bert Lampkins, the other white? Obviously, he had formed a coalition with the three blacks. Now, the vote usually came down 4–3, the three blacks and Lampkins against Woolford, Erling and me.

The three of us began asking ourselves what was wrong. Several times, Woolford, Erling, and I made concerted efforts to get to know Tolman, Cape, and Dines better with private dinners, retreats and telephone calls. It didn't work. They'd built a thick wall around themselves and we had not been able to scale it. It was "do it our way or it won't get done." Often, they laughed at our efforts and dismissed our suggestions with a curt, "You're wrong; we're right. And we've got the power to vote you down, 4–3."

Allen came sidling up to Woolford and me again. "You guys haven't been keeping up very well," he taunted. "You don't actually know the other big thing that's coming up today?"

I frowned and ran my right index finger around the inside of my shirt collar. For some reason that I couldn't exactly define, I found it difficult to like Allen. His face always showed a perpetual sneer that broadcast his distrust of any political office holder. "Well, don't keep us in the dark, Victor," I said. "Let us in on the secret."

Able Erling walked over to join us. "He won't tell me either," the balding, ruddy faced Erling laughed. "I think he's pulling our legs."

Erling's coat was always open, mainly I think so he could put both of his hands, with his fingers outstretched, across his belt line. "I love good food and good drink far too much," he was fond of saying.

"You just wait and see," Allen smirked. "It'll knock you on your conceited, conservative asses. I'll be watching your faces closely when it happens."

Chapter 2

I sensed that council chairman Erling didn't want to start the meeting. He was standing behind the podium, making out like he was busy, shuffling through and reading a stack of papers on the podium before him. His bald head glistened in the overhead lights. Occasionally he glanced at the clock in the back of the room and hitched at his slacks. One of his shirt buttons was open over his protruding paunch. The knot of his red tie rested at least an inch below the unbuttoned collar of his shirt.

Finally, he could delay no longer. He banged the gavel and called the meeting to order. After the invocation and the pledge of allegiance—none of the Muslims in the audience stood for the opening prayer, nor did they join in the pledge of allegiance to the flag—DeLong Tolman quickly moved that the rules be suspended to allow visitors to address the council. Citizen participation. It was both an acknowledgment and a bow to the democratic process.

Erling thumbed through the cards with the names of the people desiring to speak.

"Mr. Chairman," DeLong shouted. "Call on the visitor listed on our agenda."

The chairman shrugged and called out the name of Abdul Karim.

The tall and stately Karim rose slowly from his seat and made his way to the microphone and the speaker's stand. The perfect white teeth highlighted his gleaming black face. He turned his back to council members and bowed majestically to those in the audience. Applause and cheers broke out. Most of the eighty faces in the crowd were black. They began smiling and jabbing closed fists into the air. The black power salute. It signaled that any resemblance to orderly debate had disappeared.

Erling banged the gavel. Hard. "Displays such as applause and cheers are forbidden at council meetings. If you do it again, I'll have to ask the deputies to clear the council chambers."

Loud jeers greeted Erling's announcement. Karim turned back to face the seven council members. We sat in a horseshoe pattern, three on each side. The chairman and secretary sat on a raised platform at the apex of the horseshoe.

17

Karim leaned over to speak into the microphone. "That might not be advisable, Mr. Chairman."

Wisely, Erling did not respond to the taunt. I looked at Harris and raised my eyebrows and frowned. "Look at Lampkins," I whispered. "He's smiling like a Cheshire cat. He knows exactly what's been planned by this group, what they're going to spring on us. He's part of it."

Karim, in slow, measured voice, said simply, "We're here to demand that you fire Police Chief Dennis Crowe."

An audible gasp ran through the members of the audience. The forbidden applause and cheering broke out again. Clenched fists jabbed into the air. "Crowe has demonstrated that he's a racist and that he discriminates against black people," Karim said. "He doesn't furnish adequate police protection on a fair and equal basis to black people in Forest."

"Right on, brother," a loud voice yelled. "That's telling 'em!"

Karim continued. "Records will show that Crowe assigns more officers and patrol vehicles to the white sections of Forest and lets criminals terrorize the black neighborhoods. Our streets in the black communities are controlled by the drug pushers and gang members. We hide in our homes and pray that stray bullets from the drive-by shootings don't kill us.

"At any hour of the night, when we dare listen, we can hear gunfire. We have sat down with Crowe to discuss these things, but he does nothing. We have asked the U.S. Justice Department to investigate and they are here now, digging into the facts. Unless Crowe is fired in three days, we'll march on city hall and shut the business of government down completely."

The cheers and applause came again. The television cameras moved in for close ups of Karim, then panned the cheering crowd where many were jabbing clenched fists into the air. The two women television reporters and Victor Allen were vigorously scribbling notes for their news reports.

"We'll force you to listen to black people. A new day has come to America. We claim our birthright. The white man is no longer our slavemaster. We intend to war on our oppressors and seize power for ourselves." Karim was making a show of it for the media—and sending a clear message to us council members and citizens throughout the city. He turned again and bowed to the audience, then walked back to his seat.

Mueschle Jabbar, one of the imposing trio we'd met in the corridor before the start of the meeting, followed Karim to the podium. The muscles in his powerful chest made his suit coat fit snugly.

18

His voice cut through the air like a chain saw ripping through wood. His arms began windmilling as he denounced the police chief. His voice rose and fell in the hypnotic rhythms of a charismatic black minister. The man's strong voice chose the words that pierced deep into the buried hatreds of black people. Many of those in the audience chimed in repeatedly with rhythmic phrases such as, "Right on, brother" and "Amen. You said it right, brother."

Jabbar had unbuttoned his coat. Several times in his heated gyrations, he threw his arms skyward. I was startled to see the pistol in a shoulder holster under his arm as his coat fell open.

"Racism, racism, racism," he shouted. "White people practice this repugnant form of social power to keep us blacks pushed down as slaves. We will war to the death to force you to give us power and treat us as equals."

Five straight times Jabbar punched his clenched fist into the air, urging the spectators to join in the black power salute. He had helped to push the audience into a frenzy. Erling waited patiently for the demonstration to quiet down, then recognized the next speaker.

Jabbar was followed to the podium by one of the Muslim sisters in long white gown and jeweled headdress. She seemed seven feet tall; although I was certain that six or more of the inches were accounted for by the headdress. When she began speaking, she closed her eyes and intoned a rhythmic chant. Soon, most of those in the audience had lifted their arms above their heads to join her in weaving, rhythmic chanting. Though I could not understand the meaning of the moaning sounds, the effect was weirdly hypnotic. Suddenly, she opened her eyes, hammered her fist on the podium and said, "That's a call to arms for all of our black brothers and sisters."

It was a signal to the audience. Many of them leaped to their feet and punched their fists into the air as they chanted, "Crowe must go! Crowe must go! Crowe must go!"

President Erling pounded the gavel and yelled for order. The demonstrators paid no attention. The meeting was out of control and there was nothing to do but wait. "And this is a city council meeting," Harris leaned over and said to me. "It's awful, man. Shameful."

I shrugged in disgust. "I agree, but what can you do? Nothing."

Abdul Karim walked back to the microphone and motioned for his followers to come stand with him in rows. "This is the message we send to the council members of Forest, Georgia, our mayor—and all white people everywhere. We Muslims will not be denied. We have declared war on white people everywhere. We're armed, disciplined and motivated. You can either surrender now or face annihilation."

I couldn't control myself any longer. The gauntlet had been thrown down, the challenge made. It had become a matter of personal honor. I knew the value of dramatic action too. I began hammering on my desk and jumped to my feet.

"Karim," I yelled. "You can't come into these chambers and threaten council members in such outrageous fashion. You expect us to stand by and let you tear apart the democratic processes of this governmental body? You want us to meet your demands and sacrifice an innocent man like Chief Crowe to appease your thirst for power? Who do you think you are?"

I felt Harris Woolford's hand on my arm. I took a deep breath and called on my reserves of self discipline. My jaws were clenched as I looked out at the audience.

Karim was equal to the occasion. Calmly, he replied, "I know who I am. And I know who you are Mr. Stonewall Bedford." Acid etched his words. "Stonewall Bedford! That great statesman, descendant of Civil War generals and plantation owners with their hundreds of slaves. Let's see. One of those generals whose name you bear died at Gettysburg and another one met his death in the Wilderness Campaign."

He snorted. His face had molded into a livid mask. "I'm told you go into the library and the parlor of the old family mansion once a week and commune with your famous forebears. Oh, yes, we know that their portraits line the walls of that great house. Tell me, General Stonewall Bedford. Do you also listen to the moans and cries of the dozens of black people your family held as slaves until they died and were buried in that cemetery reserved for black people, now hidden under massive brush and weeds a mile from the plantation's big house? Well, last week, some of my brothers and I walked through the woods and clawed through the undergrowth to find their unmarked graves."

The television cameras suddenly appeared close to my face. I'd been through things like this so many times until I knew how to stay composed and avoid doing anything foolish. I summoned a broad smile to my face. "I see you know how to play to the gallery, Mr. Karim. And to the media, too.

"Tell me, Karim, wouldn't your people be better served if you spent your time and energies and used your armed troops in clearing the gangs and drug pushers off the streets in the black communities? Chief Crowe, with the help of many of us, is doing all he can. Why don't you help us instead of trying to intimidate us and fan the flames of revolution?"

He stood immobile, a statue with a frozen smile on an impassive face.

"Why no answer, Mr. Karim? I think each of us here know the answer. It enhances your power in the black community to engage in, what do black people call it, 'bashing whitey'? In threatening to take the law into your own hands, you've given militant blacks the vicarious thrill of punching us whites in the face with their fists. You ought to be ashamed. That is not conduct befitting the leader you are supposed to be.

"Crime *is* rampant in the minority communities, and Chief Dennis Crowe needs your help to fight and conquer the criminals, the pushers, and the shooters who kill for the fun of it. What he doesn't need is your demand that he be fired. For the sake of all of us, these slashing attacks on the very foundations of community peace and order must be halted. We in the white community extend the hand of friendship and love, not the fists of hatred and violence."

I sat down. I'd said far too much, gone too far, plunged too deeply into the maw of flaming hatreds. But dammit. This council didn't deserve to be bullied into rash, immoral, unjustifiable actions like Abdul Karim was demanding.

I had chosen to stand up to Karim and his assaults with my shoulders squared. I would not be cowered into meek submission. I knew there'd be hell to pay, but so be it.

Karim was not intimidated either. He stood there smiling. Deliberately, in mock solemnity, he nodded in my direction, then turned back toward the audience. "I want all the brothers and sisters who came here to support me to stand up, raise your right fist in mocking salute to these white racists who no doubt are members of the Ku Klux Klan, then follow me as I walk from this chamber."

The sisters in the long white gowns and the jeweled turbans were the last ones to reach the door. One of them paused, shook her shoulders and kicked backwards in contempt. Slowly she turned, her even white teeth showing in a smile of malice. She raised her right fist toward the ceiling. Suddenly, her middle index finger separated from the balled fist and shot into the air.

"This bird's for you, General Bedford," she said. "And both its wings are broken."

DeLong Tolman began yelling, "Mr. Chairman, Mr. Chairman."

Able Erling nodded to Tolman. "Yes, Mr. Tolman."

"I move for a ten-minute recess," Tolman yelled.

"I second that motion," Norris Cape shouted.

"The chair rules the motion out of order," Erling answered.

"I call for a division of the house on the chairman's ruling," Tolman said. "That's my right."

"All of those who support the chair's ruling that Tolman's motion for a recess is out of order, please stand," Erling said

I stood up. So did Woolford and Erling. Baxter Lampkins looked around the raised, horseshoe-shaped platform where council members sat, then slowly stood up.

"Motion to recess denied," Erling said. "Now, we move on to old business. Any old business to come before the house?"

No one said anything.

"Now, we move on to the section of the agenda for 'New Business,' " Erling said. DeLong Tolman's hand shot up.

"Yes," Mr. Tolman," Erling said.

"I want to make a motion and reserve the right to speak on it—if I can get a second." Tolman said.

"Make your motion," the chairman said.

"I move that this council direct the city attorney to prepare an ordinance for introduction at our next meeting to ban the flying of the Confederate flag in front of city hall."

"I second the motion," Frank Dines yelled, banging his fist on the table.

I was stunned. Pull down the Confederate flag over General Robert E. Lee's monument? Why, to thousands of decent citizens in Forest, that would be like cutting out a part of our hearts.

Harris Woolford leaned over and whispered to me. "So, that's the big surprise our friend Allen said was coming."

All I could do was nod my head. DeLong Tolman had launched into one of his tirades—as he so often did—and I decided I'd better listen closely. Many of us knew that with DeLong, as with many other black political leaders, that what he was doing was a practiced routine. They actually went to seminars and studied and rehearsed how to bully, intimidate and throw public meetings into disorder and confusion. Such tactics often allowed them to force through actions that otherwise would die in rational debate.

My blood pressure was near the boiling point. I'd have to debate Tolman and the others vigorously. *They'd pull that Confederate flag down only over my dead body.*

Tolman was a skilled orator, one who knew how to address and inflame emotions. He was nobody's dummy.

"For 350 years," he fumed, "you white Southerners down here in this Confederate prison stockade you call the South have kept black people stomped down into the dirt. The Emancipation Proclamation freed us from slavery. The North, in that holy war called the Civil War, whipped your asses. But that didn't matter to you. When the war was over, you put on the white sheets, mounted your horses and rode through the night with burning torches held high. You lynched hundreds of us and left us swinging in the public square as object lessons for blacks. Such things scared us, denied us of our rights and dignity as human beings. In your reign of fear, many times you abducted black people, tied them to trees and lashed them with whips until they died."

The room was so still until you could hear several of us shifting uneasily in our chairs. Tolman was using the familiar words and phrases demagogues always used to hammer at the South and its traditions.

"You white Southerners are so eaten up with racism until there's no hope for change. It's an integral part of the face you turn toward black people each day. You deny us equal opportunity, dignity, equality and freedom; You deny us jobs and the chance to claim our rightful places in society. You deny us the police protection we need to keep our neighborhoods safe."

The light glistened on his concrete hard face. He waved his clenched fists in aimless fashion, like a boxer waiting for the bell to start the next round. Dines and Cape were smiling and nodding approval.

Tolman took a deep breath and plunged into his fulminations again. "And that damned Confederate flag out there on the city hall lawn. You raise it daily above that stupid statue of your beloved General Robert E. Lee. It's a symbol of slavery."

Dines and Cape began pounding the table. "No more! No more! Things gotta change! No more! No more!"

The white-robed women who had filtered back into the spectator's section, had joined hands, closed their eyes and were swaying from side to side, moaning, "Oh, Lord. Oh, Lord. They gotta let us go. They gotta let us go."

Erling pounded his gavel to restore order to the meeting. Cape and Dines quieted down.

Tolman drank water from the glass in front of him. When he wasn't waving his arms and yelling, you could see how overweight he really was. "Each day you run that rebel flag up the flag pole, you're rubbing the noses of black people in the mud of your Southern culture based upon disrespect of black people as human beings who were once your slaves. Each time we see it, we're reminded of how you captured us as defenseless people there in Africa, chained us in the holds of those slave ships and brought us to America. We were your property, valued only for our capacity to work and reproduce. Slaves!"

"No more! No more!" Dines and Cape were moaning and swaying their heads back and forth. Their eyes were closed. "Slaves! Slaves! Chained us. Treated us like property. No more!"

"Oh, Lord. Oh, Lord. They gotta let us go," the women chorused.

Cape yelled encouragement to Tolman, "Right on, brother! You're telling them like it is. The flag's gotta go! Right on, brother!"

Tolman's voice had moved into an even higher, more shrill and angrier register. "You worked us, raped us, killed us. Each time we see that damned flag, we're offended. It angers us. It tells us that in your eyes, things haven't changed very much. You still regard us as less than human. We demand that the Confederate flag, that symbol of slavery, never be raised again. We ask that our city attorney draw up the ordinance for introduction and presentation at our next regular meeting, two weeks from today. We also demand a public hearing on the ordinance that same day. We'll have lots of our brothers and sisters here to show you we mean business."

My body threatened to burst from its carefully disciplined strait jacket into which I had shoved it. I wanted for a moment to run trembling from these chambers. No, I told myself. Don't be a damn fool. You don't run from fights. Keep calm. I raised my hand for recognition by the chair.

"Yes, Mr. Bedford," Erling said.

"Mr. Chairman, fellow council members. You have heard a fiery, demagogic attack by Mr. Tolman on decent Southerners, on our revered traditions and way of life. I'm certain you recognize that it's an inflammatory attack laced with raw prejudice, hatred, reverse racism and militancy. Most of us people in the South do not fit his description. I certainly do not. I know very few people who do."

I looked slowly around the room. My heart was racing. I could feel my pulse pounding in my ears. "Mr. Tolman's words show little understanding of the history of this nation. The South did not fight the Civil War under our Confederate flag for the cause of slavery. We fought against the powerful, central government of the North to prevent the Yankees from taking away our rights as states.

"The Constitution guarantees those rights with these words, 'The powers not delegated to the United States by the Constitution, nor prohibited by it to the states, are reserved to the states respectively, or to the people.' Southerners have never revered an all-powerful central government, like so many of our citizens in other parts of the country do these days."

I glanced at Harris, then at Erling. Their smiling faces seemed to be urging me on.

"No," I said. "We did not fight for the cause of slavery. And I remind my honorable colleagues that it was the Yankees who were the slave traders. It was the Yankees who went to Africa and bargained with the tribal chieftains who then willingly sold their own people into slavery. It was the Yankee slave traders who chained the innocent, uncomprehending, frightened blacks into the holds of their ships and brought them to America."

Tolman began banging the table with his fists. He stood up, his voice sputtering like a newly started lawn mower. "Mr. Chairman! Mr. Chairman! General Bedford is out of order."

Norris Cape jumped to his feet. "What Bedford is saying is a bunch of lies. It's too painful to hear. Please stop him."

Erling banged the gavel. Gradually, the protesting voices became silent. "You may continue, Mr. Bedford."

"We asked the Yankees to let us Southerners leave the union in peace. When they wouldn't do it, we went to war to claim independent status as a separate and free nation. You see, the Yankees wanted us to knuckle under to them as lord and master."

I knew that I must not let anger seep into my words, for it would detract from my effectiveness. I sipped from my water glass, took a deep breath and continued.

"They don't know us very well. To a Southerner, that's like the matador's cape waved in front of a charging bull. We just don't like folks telling us what we can and can't do. And as I pointed out a few minutes ago, most informed citizens who have studied history know that the federal government in Washington was illegally taking away these rights reserved to the states and guaranteed under our constitution. Mr. Tolman should know this, but obviously he's allowed his racial animosity to cloud his judgment."

"I object to this personal attack on my character and intelligence," Tolman yelled.

"Yes," Cape yelled. "He's out of order."

Erling pounded the gavel. "You two are the ones who are out of order. Mr. Bedford has the same right to present his views on pulling down the Confederate flag as Mr. Tolman had when he was urging that it be banned. I heard Mr. Tolman making several attacks on all Southerners. Now, out of courtesy, let Bedford proceed."

In the dim recesses of my mind, caution signals were trying to warn me to back down, that if I didn't, I'd get hurt. Perhaps worse. But, I could not give in. It just wasn't in me. It was a matter of principle.

"History is history," I continued. "I remind my fellow council members that I do not propose to stand idly by and witness this outrageous attempt to revise our Southern history—and in the process passively endure this vilification of our revered traditions. This motion is merely another thinly veiled attack on our Southern heritage and ideals, another effort to badger, intimidate and beat down those of us who oppose such insanities.

"Banning the flying of the Confederate flag will accomplish only two things—and both of them are bad. It will further inflame the smoldering hatreds of blacks for whites, and who can deny that such hatred grows larger each day. Second, it will furnish the media more fuel to feed their constant appetite for ridicule of Southerners. They love to impute Simon Legree mentalities to those of us who stand against the raw hatreds which gave rise to Tolman's motion. They paint us as unsophisticated simpletons and bigots. Since when did taking up for the revered things we Southerners were taught to believe in become a sin?"

Victor Allen's face showed his contempt as he scribbled his notes, then slammed his note pad and pencil down onto the table and sat back in his chair with folded arms.

The snouts of the television cameras were once again shoved into my face.

"I call for the question on the motion," Harris Woolford said.

Erling moved quickly. "All in favor of calling the question signify by saying 'Aye.' "

All seven council members voted to call the question.

"All in favor of DeLong Tolman's motion to instruct the city attorney to prepare an ordinance for introduction at our next council meeting to ban the flying of the Confederate flag over the Civil War monument on the city hall lawn raise your hands," Erling directed.

"Mr. Clerk," Erling said. "Record Tolman, Cape, Dines, and Lampkins as voting 'Aye.' And voting 'Nay,' Bedford, Woolford and Erling. The 'Ayes' have it. The motion passes. I hereby instruct the city attorney to prepare such an ordinance for introduction at our next regular meeting and to advertise a public hearing for that same day."

"I move we adjourn," Tolman yelled.

Erling banged the gavel. "This meeting is adjourned."

I threw my pencil down onto the desk and stood up.

"That Baxter Lampkins," Harris said as he stood up. "He's a traitor. I'll bet he catches hell from the people for his vote. That flag is a cherished icon that arouses intense emotions in our part of the country."

"We must make certain that Mr. Lampkins does catch hell, Harris. But he's not the only Southern turncoat among us. Many of our people down here, particularly those of the younger generation, have turned against their Southern upbringing."

TV reporters and their cameramen encircled me. "I'm La Shunda Wilson," one of the women said as she held out the microphone toward me. "Can we get a statement from you Mr. Bedford for our 6 o'clock evening news?"

The media love to crowd in on office holders, since there's always the chance that, under pressure, an elected official will say the wrong thing. I smiled at her. "I said what I wanted to say a few minutes ago. Since you were recording my words, you already have me on tape for editing. I have only one thing to add. Like John Paul Jones said, 'Surrender, hell. I've just begun to fight.' "

CHAPTER 3

I was exhausted. It was good to be alone, enclosed in the quiet of my automobile, though my mind was far from being quiet. I drove toward home, slowly enough to let me review what had happened and weigh the possible consequences.

The rain had stopped. The streets were still wet and slippery as I headed for home. To the west, the lowering sun painted the ridges of the dark clouds pink. The wind was still blowing and Bedford House, the ancient family home where I grew up, would be creaking and groaning tonight.

"Something evil this way comes."

"Hmpfh," I said, talking to myself. "This something evil might have already arrived." No doubt, my impassioned pleas at today's meeting had prepared the way for its coming.

The afternoon traffic was heavy with people anxious to get home. I seemed to catch all of the stoplights, but for once I was not impatient. I needed the time to think, so I sat and waited for the light to turn green. I had let myself get angry at the meeting. It was something I always had to watch when passions flared up.

Small wonder that my mind kept running away from the raw emotions of that damned circus where some of us had been fed to the lions and spectators had cheered and yelled for blood. As I drove along, I found myself wanting to scream at the top of my voice to let it all pour out. The frustration boiling inside me was an unhealthy cauldron where cackling witches kept feeding my substance into the boiling water. "Bubble, bubble, toil and trouble . . ."

Our heated exchanges had tipped over Pandora's box of miseries in today's meeting. I grew sad. Appomattox, 1865. Lee's surrender. The South whipped. The Yankees victorious. Since that dark day, the South had never regained its freedom, for the victor in any war writes the rules for the conquered.

After Lee's surrender, the occupying armies and the greedy carpetbaggers descended upon us to rape and plunder our resources, our people and our land. Funny thing though. That was 130 years ago and the South is still an occupied country, even today. Oh, subtly, to be sure, but we still dance to the whips of prejudice that whisk through the political, philosophical and economic air and lash at our spirits and our way of life unceasingly. Our conquerors have not forgiven us yet for daring to go to war against them.

The meeting today! That evil bunch of trouble-making bastards spewing their venomous hatred onto the conduct of city business. The very idea! Wanting to ban the flying of the Confederate flag. That would be like cutting out a part of our Southern hearts.

Their announced plans were just another way to kick our Southern asses, tread on our rights, put us down, upset us, then laugh as we squirmed and turned apoplectic.

It was natural that I turn to some small amount of self-pity. The opposition had forgotten that several years ago, I had led the fight to name our main thoroughfare "Martin Luther King Boulevard"? And that I had contributed thousands of dollars to help remodel and renovate black churches?

Many of us asked ourselves, "Why not honor black heroes, support black citizens, strengthen black churches? Every group needed their heroes, their role models, the cultural beliefs which energized them in their quests for identity?"

Now I asked myself, "Shouldn't it work both ways? For whites as well as blacks?"

Finally, I steered my car off the bustling downtown streets and entered the wide expressway that ran between the fields on each side. My eyes devoured the countryside. My heart warmed once again to my love affair with this land. This land of mine! This Southland! God, how I love it. It was like a song rising from the distant tree line and lighting up the darkening skies.

I strained my eyes to summon forth the mental vision. There, in the distance. Outlined against the trees. Men in gray on galloping horses, the Confederate flag at the head of the column, streaming in the wind and smoke of battle. The sounds of war. Men in gray riding into hell and death. And victory. Men wanting only to be free to live their own lives as they desired and not dance to the tune of the ringmasters in some far distant, Northern seat of power called the Capitol.

This love of the South. It's a love that courses through our body on rich; red streams, enchants our mind and finally, with visions of lost glory, takes over our very being. There's a nobility in the very air we breathe, a strengthening of character that often colors our prayers of thanks for all of those who have come before us and struggled to make this land hallowed ground.

I passed stands of giant trees whose leaves were just beginning to turn green. A dim road ran through the trees and dense undergrowth to my left. Down that road, four miles to the east, in July of 1864, just as daylight came, a Confederate Cavalry unit had charged through the middle of a Yankee encampment. The men in blue had barely shaken themselves awake when suddenly the rebels were upon them, yelling, shooting, slashing, burning, killing and capturing some of the poor, surprised bastards.

Cavalry General Willard Bedford had led that charge that day. He died there too, shot in the back by a wounded Yankee in a last dying gasp. General Bedford had been a college professor, an intellectual, a poet. I read his diary again just last Sunday in the university library over in Athens, Georgia: "Many of us have known for years that sooner or later we'd be fighting those damn Yankees. We knew that eventually we would secede from the Union and establish our own free and independent nation—and that they'd war against us to try and force us to stay in the union where we'd always be the 'poor country cousins' and dance to their tunes.

"We Southerners are so different from Northerners in the way we live our lives—if you can call the way they live a life. They're determined not to let us be ourselves, to rule our daily lives. It's out of envy, I think, envy of our sense of personal honor, nobility and a rage to be free.

"They take offense when we don't fall prostrate before them and do things their way, like it or not. They really don't like us. In fact, their feelings for us border on arrogant prejudice. Somehow or other, they've got the idea that Southerners are ignorant, uneducated and inferior to them. They look down their noses at us and judge us unfit to govern ourselves."

Traffic had grown heavier as people pushed to escape their jobs and get home. The Honda Accord behind me honked to tell me to get out of the way. I glanced in my mirrors and moved to the right lane when it was clear. I'd become too enmeshed in the South's history and had gradually slowed my automobile without noticing.

Why were people so angry and impatient with each other these days? Had all the flowers of courtesy in our lives wilted and died in this "dog-eat-dog" world? Had our daily living lost civility, tolerance and understanding to the rot and decay of increasing stress? Well, I wasn't going to lose the stars in my eyes and my zest for living under the withering barrage of scorn heaped upon those of us trying to find deeper meanings in life.

The traffic light turned red. I braked to a stop and looked across the rolling fields to my left again, then closed my eyes. The riders and their horses reappeared.

In 1864, General Bedford had penetrated with his diary entries the mists boiling from the conflict between our two cultures—between North and South. In other passages of his diary, he had written these words: "This whole thing, secession, the going to war, the sacrifice, the killing, the dying, why it's a challenge to us Southerners, a matter of personal honor. Now, that the war has finally come, we're ready. By God, they picked this fight. We'll make them rue the day they started stomping on our rights to punish us. Most of the boys in my cavalry troop are strong, independent farm boys from Georgia, Louisiana, Mississippi and Alabama. They're not fighting to keep the Negro in slavery. Their families never owned any slaves. They're fighting for their right to be free and for the South to be a separate and independent nation.

" 'We'll get that Yankee boot off our neck, General,' they often tell me. Of course, they like a good fight, too, as do most Southerners. And these boys would tangle with the devil himself. They know no fear. They can ride and fight like wild men, yelling, spurring their horses, shooting. It's a sight to see."

The traffic light turned green. The line of cars began moving. In the inside lane, two unhappy young women stood by their wrecked cars with folded arms and grim faces. A red Firebird had rear-ended the Corvette ahead. Bumpers and shattered glass littered the pavement between the two cars. Those customary glasses of white wine when those two get home will have to wait.

The university has a large painting of General Bedford on the wall of one of the smaller rooms in the library where Civil War scholars do research. His sword, uniform, hat and saddlebags are in a glass case where there are printed paragraphs that tell his story.

The rudeness, the threats, the raw hatreds of the meeting still rankled me. I asked the questions again, the same one I'd asked myself hundreds of times. Why do black people hate us white Southerners so fiercely? Oh, some blacks and liberal whites will jump up and down and deny it with great passion, but it's true. It showed its ugly face again today. It's a cultural war.

The first shots had been fired today. There was no end in sight, yet we seem willing to go to any lengths to avoid seeing it in its cold reality.

The black culture, the white culture. The clash between them will no doubt become a fountain of blood with an endless supply of mutilated and dead bodies to feed it's terrible stream. We're rushing headlong into battle—unless we lower our voices, understand and respect each other's cultures and people as individuals. We must jettison the hate, but there seems little hope that this will happen.

I'd been re-examining my own beliefs lately, trying to reach firm ground on which to stand. I certainly don't hate blacks, because I have no reason for hating them. I suppose the answer as to why they hate whites is really quite simple. It's like my undying love of the South, my allegiance to the hallowed legends that shaped our lives, my reverence for the valor of our men in gray, and my Southern mindset. Often, I scoop up our fallen banner and charge up Cemetery Ridge. It's a thing I must do. It's in my bones.

Well, their hating white people is in their bones, too. In their coming to America, they came as slaves. Even after they were freed, they've been pushed down, relegated to second-class citizenship, spat upon, yelled at, despised. For hundreds of years, they had masked their anger in seeming humility, just to survive in the white man's world. Now, they sense that perhaps at last, they are really free. They have mounted their own charge against the enemy.

Tolman's face at the meeting, his words, his desk pounding. They were scary. The hatred blacks feel has coursed through their blood for centuries, but they were not in a position to fight back. But now that they have the power of public opinion and the federal government on their side and with the Justice Department and the civil rights attorneys to run interference for them, they're no longer afraid of the white man. Thus, they feel free to let all of their pent up fury fill the air with a constant rain of hatred's arrows. And we members of the white race are the targets.

But, make no mistake about it. It's not just the white people in the South the blacks hate. They hate white people all across the country.

Oh, I know that the liberals and the media turn away from this fact and say that this is not true. What fools. How about the riots, killings and burnings in Watts, Detroit, and Washington, D.C? Will these supposedly sophisticated white people, burdened down with self-imposed feelings of guilt, ever wake up and face reality, see what's actually happening in our beloved country? No, that's too much to hope for, I suppose.

I was nearing the neighborhood where I lived. There were strip shopping centers, suburban offices for business and professional people, schools and churches. Some of the older homes, now surrounded by encroaching commercialism, had been turned into offices for attorneys and accountants.

Today's confrontation was a glaring example of this clash between cultures. The impending war of genocide with its blinding horrors ought to launch us into action. Can we find ways to abate black hatreds for whites? And vice versa? The one thing we can't do for black people that would make the hatred disappear immediately is to make them white. A white looks into his mirror each morning and sees just a person. When blacks look into a mirror, they see their black skins and hate themselves. Isn't that sad? The Irish, the Italians, the Jews, the Chinese, the Japanese, the Vietnamese—they don't hate themselves because they're different from others.

My study of history tells me it's been that way throughout the centuries. Why, I don't know. I'll have to leave that to the philosophers. The only thing I know is that the fire of revolution is licking ever closer to me. I can feel it's heat searing my life. Dammit! It doesn't have to be that way, but it is, and it seems to be a thing that's bigger than all of us.

I stopped at the liquor store for some bourbon. Jack Daniels' Black Label. While I was looking at the wines, I heard some one chuckling behind me and turned around. It was Morris Light.

"Stoney, that was, well, to put it politely, one helluva council meeting."

"Oh, were you there?" I asked.

"Yeah. You were much too busy to see me sitting on the last row on the far left." Light was slight of build, balding and always in perpetual motion. His pencil thin mustache seemed to fit his role as a documentary filmmaker for PBS.

"I had been tipped off as to what was going to happen," Light said. "I started thinking that this battle over the flag might make a good, feature-length story for TV."

I'd known him from Little Theater days for twenty or more years. I'd played the lead in "Don Quixote" and he'd been the assistant producer. Light had always had a love affair with the theater. Those were such fun days, and I'm a ham. The reviews of the musical said I was quite good. The drama critics in the local media named me "Best Actor of the Year."

I was not impressed with his idea. "Well, Morris. The only trouble with that idea is that if you're doing it for PBS, you'd have to show only one side of it. The side that holds Southerners up to further ridicule as repressed 'Simon Legrees' wearing white sheets."

"Oh," he said. "How'd you arrive at that conclusion?"

"It's simple. That's the order of the day for all you media people. That's the only view you see when you watch PBS, NNC, Tom Brokaw, Peter Winning, and Sam Prather. They want viewers to cast the Southern white in the role of a racist bigot with his foot on the black man's neck. Then the general populace can use us as a whipping boy."

I was looking for Tanqueray gin and Martini and Rossi dry vermouth.

"It plays well with the TV audience," I said. "Or, so you think. It never occurs to people like you that there's another side to the story. The true side. But fortunately, people like Rush Limbaugh have come along to show that millions of people in America don't buy that liberal pap you try to feed us daily in news broadcasts. As Rush says, 'The majority of people in America are conservatives, but they've been afraid to admit it and stand up for their principles.' "

"Hey, man," Light said. "Ease off. Don't be so defensive. You and I are friends. We've known each other for a long time. And don't forget. I was born here in Forest, Georgia, too. Perhaps, just perhaps, I'm one windmill you don't have to tilt at the way you did in 'Don Quixote.'"

I laughed. "But, you still have to work for a living, and if you showed the true picture in a documentary, PBS would fire you. You've got to follow their philosophical slant or you're no longer useful to them."

"Hear me out, Stoney. There's something happening in America," he said. "You just alluded to it. Millions of people are not buying that crap any more. Sam Prather? Peter Winning? NNC. If people had anywhere else to turn to for their news, they'd do it in a New York minute. Like most people in my business, I was eaten up with that dumb ass, liberal shit, too."

I noticed how long his fingers were as he placed two bottles of dark chardonnay in his basket. He turned back toward me to pursue our discussion.

"But then, I started listening to Rush Limbaugh," he said. "At first, I did it for a lark. Just to see what all the noise was about and to laugh at him as a wild-eyed, extreme right-winger—like most media people do. Well, the more I listened, the more I became convinced that he was right, that the conservatives and the conservative philosophy were the only things that could save America."

"Are you putting me on?" I asked. "I'm a cynic when I hear things like that."

Morris rubbed his right hand over his mouth, shifted his weight uneasily, blinked his eyes. "I said I had a confession to make, didn't I? Hell, Stoney. I haven't been able to sleep for six months. The liberals have been leading us down the primrose path for fifty years, and I just woke up to that fact. We could be on the verge of losing our country. Unless we can reverse things. I've been going through a metamorphosis, you might say. I think a documentary film of this fight you obviously are going to wage is the least I can do to help square things with my conscience."

Could he be telling me the truth? I was still suspicious of his motives. "Wouldn't do you any good to make such a film if you had no outlets for it. If you had no way to get it to the people where they could see it."

"I've done market studies, Stoney. There's one helluva market for such a documentary. That is, if it's done right and promoted right. I can guarantee you that it will be seen. As a video alone, I figure it would sell five million individual copies."

"Who on earth would buy it?" I asked.

"The millions who have grown fearful of the militant groups who now seem to be in control of things; the thousands of Southerners who want to see some one put up a real fight to save our Southern culture and its ideals; Civil War buffs by the hundreds. Librarians, particularly in the South. You see, I've been thinking about this project, waiting for the trigger. Today's meeting was that trigger."

"It was a vulgar display of power," I said. "My stomach is still tied into knots."

"People will see today's meeting in perspective," Light said. "I'll also thread in scenes that show Southern history, footages of Gettysburg, General Lee, the carpetbaggers, and the savagery of reconstruction in the South; scenes of sad-eyed and sad-voiced Southern girls singing Civil War songs and accompanying themselves on the dulcimer. I assure you that 'the other side of the story,' as Paul Harvey says, will be told. It needs to be told and I'm going to tell it."

"The media will crucify you," I said. "The South is a whipping boy and the media's liberal zealots take savage glee in blaming us for all of the ills of black people. It gives them vicarious pleasure."

Light's passion glowed in his face. "Ten years ago, your statements would have been true, Stoney, but not today. There's a prevailing counter wind now whose currents will carry your story and your valiant attempts to defend the flying of the Confederate flag all over the world."

"Wait a minute, Morris. What do you mean, *my story*?"

"Every story has to have a hero. And there's little doubt in my mind that you are going to lead this crusade. My camera and I will live with you and the other characters in this great conflict. And, it seems certain to turn into a bloodletting."

"I don't know," I said. "I'm just a common, ordinary Southern citizen who is proud of his heritage and believes in the nobility and courage of my forebears."

"Stoney Bedford. Let's quit kidding each other. You're anything but 'common and ordinary.' And from listening to those people up there today, I think you, Woolford, Erling, and no telling how many others, could be in real danger. There's smoldering fires of hatred and savagery that will erupt. On both sides, I might add. White Southerners don't hate blacks because they're black. That's true. But you let blacks pick up arms and start smashing things the Southern white believes in fiercely, and you've moved the conflict onto a different plane."

"The idea fascinates me, Morris. And it just might be a way to tell the other side of the story on a wide enough scale, to enough people, to at least ameliorate some of the social contempt that Yankees have been taught to use when thinking and dealing with Southerners."

"I started filming the story at the meeting today. When can we get together so I can lay out my plans for you?"

I held up my hands, palms outward. "Wait a minute. You're carrying me too fast. True enough, I've got to plan my strategy. I want to win this fight to keep the Confederate flag flying, and, I want to stay alive. But the camera. I'll have to think about it. Overnight. Perhaps I'll see it more clearly tomorrow morning."

"Remember, Stoney. This is our one great opportunity to show the world the truth about many things, particularly about the real motivations of the true Southerner. And to explode the fallacies lodged in the minds of people who have been taught to hate the South. I think you'll come to the decision that you have to do it."

"I *will* think about it, but now, I've got to get home. I'm exhausted and I need a drink so I can start unwinding. Get in touch with me tomorrow, Morris."

"You can count on it, Stoney."

The traffic was thinning out even more. I'd be home in a few minutes. I thought of my beautiful, aristocratic, dead mother and her unceasing efforts to make certain we children took pride in our ancestors and lineage, about the paintings of the Confederate generals that lined the walls of the library of Bedford House, the home where I grew up.

"Study their faces, children," my mother would say as we viewed the paintings. "You are direct descendents of these noble fighters in the Civil War from both sides of the family. You should know the stories by heart, stories of our great victories, our defeats, our sufferings and sacrifices, the heroics of the Confederate fighting men—they're woven into the warp and woof of our very being and are such a part of us as to be ineradicable."

I grew angry again thinking about that damned meeting. Take down our Confederate flag? Hell no! I've been to that plain and simple, white frame house in Appomattox, Virginia where the surrender took place. I stayed there all day long, looking at the quiet, rolling hills, studying the historical documents, picturing the arrival and departure of General Lee with General Ulysses S. Grant.

I cried like a baby that day as I relived those sad moments. When Generals Lee and Grant sat down together, it was time for the war to end. Our food, supplies and ammunition were gone; the factories destroyed; our homes burned. Our men were out of food, clothing and shoes, thoroughly defeated. And hundreds of thousands of our brave men in gray had been buried in unmarked graves, thousands more pitifully wounded. Our war to be free and independent, to be a separate nation had been lost, our bright dreams turned to bitter ashes.

Abdul Karim and DeLong Tolman were shining examples of today's new breed of carpetbaggers. I know that black people read the history of those terrible days and exult with inner satisfaction and punitive glee. "They deserved it," they chorus, and I can understand the refrain of their song.

As my great-grandfather used to tell me when I was eight and nine years old, "After that day in April when Lee surrendered, our boys straggled home, most of them walking the hundreds of miles. Many hobbled on crutches, the pitiful stubs of legs blown away in battle or sawed off in those terrible field hospitals, swinging with each painful step."

The pain on the old man's face could never be erased, not even in death.

"Like the others with whom I walked over eight hundred miles," he'd say, "I was going home. To what? Sherman and his ilk had looted and burned our land, raped and killed our women and old men. Most of the time there was little if anything left when we Confederates finally did get home. I cannot describe the terror and the hardships we endured, the harsh and discouraging barriers to resuming a normal life that were thrown into our path."

The white-bearded, stately old man, then ninety years old, could never tell me about those years after the war without starting to cry.

The old and shadow-thin warrior's countless retellings of the story had burned the tragedy deep into my heart. "Almost immediately," he recalled bitterly, "the greedy, power-hungry carpetbaggers poured down from the North to 'reconstruct the defeated South.' "

Reconstruction! I hated the word. To this day, the punitive, never-ending process continues. Only now, the carpetbaggers aren't all white. Hundreds of them are black. They spring up right in our midst, spurred on daily by the goading of their own political leaders. Protected by the U.S. Justice Department, these militants push for the necessity of remolding Southerners into a more pliant people.

Reconstruction! It's enough to make a man take up arms again. Hell. Each time I see a Civil War movie on television, I find myself wishing that the South had won. I jump up from my chair, start pacing the floor and muttering to myself. My wife, Donna Elaine, laughs at me.

"How I wish we'd won that war," I say and pound my fist into my palm.

"I know how you feel, Honey," she'd say, "But we didn't."

I turned off the busy thoroughfare and drove down a wide, quiet street lined with big homes. It'd soon be dark. Two boys on bicycles waved at me. The Johnson brothers. In a few weeks, the azaleas would be blooming all over the neighborhood. And Confederate jasmine, daffodils, tulips, narcissus. The buds on the Japanese magnolias had swelled and turned red, and soon the hundreds of blossoms would burst open in a cascade of beauty.

I turned into my driveway. Donna Elaine had turned on the front lights to welcome me home. Their warm glow gave me a good feeling. The six white columns of our big house gleamed in the soft light. After a while, the moon's full face would be reflected in the lake behind our home.

And soon I'd be watching the evening news and squirming in discomfort as the film footage painted me in dark tones. And then, come tomorrow morning, Victor Allen's usually scathing outbursts in the *Ledger* would take the flavor and smell from my first cup of coffee.

CHAPTER 4

Donna Elaine met me at the door. "Oh, Stoney, I'm glad you're home. I've been so worried." She held out her arms.

I embraced the trim, petite woman and smelled the dusky scent of roses. William, my six-foot-six son, was pacing back and forth, talking on the cellular telephone, waving his right hand back and forth to punctuate the points he was trying to make. His face was red. His voice was louder than usual.

"No," he said. "You're wrong. My father is not a racist. He doesn't hate black people." He stopped to listen to the caller.

"Whoever you are, we don't see any reason to be afraid of you? You can't intimidate us Bedfords. We don't scare easily."

His big hand slammed the receiver down into its cradle. At thirty-five, he was already losing his hair. He combed the few strands still clinging to the front of his head back to hopefully mix with the thicker part of his brown hair.

"What was that all about?" I asked.

"It's distressing, Stoney," Donna Elaine said before William could answer. "The phone's been ringing off the wall. And the callers. Many of them say such ugly things." She pursed her red lips and shook her head for emphasis. The short curls of her black hair bounced with each step she took, as though on springs.

"Ugly things?" I asked. "Like what?"

"Most of the voices sounded like black people, Dad," William said. "Here's a quote from one of them." He looked at his notes. " 'We're going to get that white racist bastard. He won't be safe anywhere.' " He raised his head, a puzzled frown on his big face. "What'd you say at council meeting today to get them so riled up?"

I told the two of them about Abdul Karim and DeLong Tolman, about the passage of Tolman's motion to ban the flying of the Confederate flag. "And Baxter Lampkins voted with the three minority members. His was the deciding vote." I shook my head and sighed. "Lampkins has sold his Southern soul for power, the way many politicians in the South have done."

William whistled in amazement. "I might have guessed it. They weren't content with just one hot issue. They had to have two. The flag and the firing of Chief Crowe."

"That's hard for me to understand," Donna Elaine said. "Chief Crowe is such a fine young man."

"Dad, what is happening to our civilization? Why the hell can't people debate such things any more without anger and the threat of violence?"

"Good question, William. The Merciful Ayatollah himself, in his books, says that a state of war exists between blacks and whites and that it's merely a question of time before blood runs in the streets."

"I heard Ken Hamblin, the radio talk show host who calls himself 'The Black Avenger' telling his audience that not enough people are taking the Muslim leader seriously. Hamblin says the war is already raging throughout America. 'If you don't believe it,' he cautioned, 'you're a fool. You can see it each day in the headlines.' "

I wanted that drink to help me relax. "While I pull off my coat and tie, how about fixing me a gin martini with olives. Very dry."

"After those telephone calls, I think I'll join you," William said. He walked to the bar and flicked on the overhead light.

"We'll want to watch the six o'clock news on Channel 2," my wife said. "I know you're not ready to eat yet."

"No, Honey," I said. "I need to try and unwind first. I feel like I'm ready to explode."

I wasn't so upset that I didn't stop to admire my wife in her red dress with white piping on the edge of the long, narrow collar. Tiny waist, dark hair, long delicate fingers. And she moved with the indefinable grace of a Southern lady. She walked into the den and sat down in the blue, Queen Anne wing chair.

William could mix a good martini. I stood at the French doors to the patio and swirled the contents of the glass gently. Two men were fishing on the far banks of the lake. The sun had sunk below the horizon. It was a good time of the day to fish, especially in the spring when fish seek the shallow water to spawn. The two fishermen were skilled at spinning the bait almost on top of the spots at which they aimed. They were after the big bass that were spawning—or soon would be—at this time of the year in the shallow water near the banks.

I searched for signs of green on the tall cypress trees on the banks of the lake back of our home. Spring was slowly unfolding its magic across the land. I sipped my drink and took in a deep breath. New beginnings. New hope. The falling away of winter's darkness and dead dreams. I looked at the picture of General Lee on his horse Traveler that hung over the fire place. I lifted my glass to him in salute.

I hadn't done what I'd dreamed of doing with my life. I had dreamed big dreams in the days of my youth. I was going to change the world for the better, do great things, and do them with dash, verve, courage and compassion.

I'd been born into the Bedford family, destined to be a leader, seeded genetically to ride to glory with my great gray line of ancestors. But to come to this? Is this all I've done with the talents and heritage God gave me? I realized sadly that I'd gotten mired in the sound and fury of life's petty things that signified almost nothing. Or, as my daddy used to say, "Things that didn't amount to a hill of beans."

Oh, it wasn't as though I hadn't heard the calls to glory many times, but I hadn't answered them. I'd let the daily grind of living kill my dreaming. I'd gotten lost along the way, spun out too many years of living in comfortable ruts while others fought the battles. I saw my childhood home again, stood with my mother as we looked at the portraits of the generals on the walls of that huge library. My ancestors in those portraits were frowning down at me.

I heard the calls again. The faint sounds emanating from the myths and legends on which my life was built. Gettysburg. The bursting shells, the sounds of that fateful battle. Pickett's charge up Cemetery Ridge. Our men in gray falling by the hundreds. The withering fusillade of cannon and rifle fire. That day, for a brief moment, we'd reached the high ground, wavered, then had fallen back. God, how sad it was. If only we could have held onto the high ground, we would have defeated the North that day. We would have won the war.

The high ground! For over one hundred and thirty years, the only high ground on which we Southerners could stand has been those moments of glory, those hallowed memories we've kept in our hearts. Only through looking inward and glimpsing ourselves in the reflecting pools of our courageous fight to be an independent nation have we been able to walk tall and free, despite the fiery heat of the cynics' counter attack.

I accepted the fact that men like me were a dying breed. I was one of the dwindling number still searching for some shreds of dignity in the tattered, historical pattern of our heritage, But as long as I live, I must keep some part of me the destroyers can't reach and kill, some essence of inner nobility, some remembrance of dying men, their blood red on a field of Confederate gray, the flag planted on the high ground for one brief moment. They came again, the distant sounds of bugles, the faint roll of the drums.

The ringing of the telephone jarred me from my reveries. William answered it. "No, Mr. Bedford's not here. No, he hasn't lost his mind. Yes, he believes those great bits of philosophy he expressed at today's council meeting. No, he'll never agree to banning the Confederate flag at City Hall . . ."

I turned to my wife and held out my hand. "Let's go to the living room to escape the telephone. We've got a few minutes before the six o'clock evening news. I want to know about your day, what you've done."

She was surprised. "With all you've been through today?"

We sat down on the pale green couch. "That's exactly why I want to sit and talk to you. It'll help me forget some of these ugly things." She reached for my left hand and held it in both of her small hands.

"As usual," she said. "I was caught up in the busy whirl of activities. The Women's Missionary Union met at nine this morning at the church. We've found homes for two families who are down on their luck; furnished the houses with the essentials; bought clothes and groceries for the families; and paid for connecting the utilities."

"Our Baptist women do such decent, compassionate things," I said. "By the way, did you get the $200 we collected in my Sunday school class last Sunday?"

"Yes, we did. It was a blessing. It helped to buy a stove for one of the houses. The family we put there has three small children. At his wife's urging, one of the church's deacons hooked up the stove. When he lighted it, the mother of the three children had tears streaming down her cheeks."

Donna Elaine was rubbing my hand with the tips of her fingers. "From WMU I went to our PEO chapter meeting at eleven. Grace Singleton's home out on the lake is so beautiful. Naturally," she smiled. "There were lots of goodies for us to nibble on, too many I'm afraid." She touched the tips of her fingers to her flat stomach.

"We gave a college scholarship to PEO's Cottey College to this bright, intelligent girl from a poor family. She and her mother held on to each other and cried."

The telephone had rung three times since we'd been sitting there on the sofa. I could hear William's loud voice repeat the denials that I was racist. He hung up on some of the more vituperative callers.

"At three o'clock," Donna Elaine continued, "it was my turn to serve as one of the docents at the college's art museum."

Oh," I interrupted. "That reminds me. I must get by there to see those paintings by Gaugin on loan from the Metropolitan."

"Well, you'd better do it before Sunday. On Monday, we'll crate them up and send them back to New York."

"And I thought I'd had a full day," I said. "I'm amazed at the things you accomplish in a single day."

"From the museum, I dashed by the hospital to see Eleanor Wells."

"Fred's wife?"

"Yes. She doesn't have too many days left. The cancer . . . She's in such pain I wonder if we just shouldn't let her slip on out into eternity."

"What will poor Fred do when he's alone?" I sipped at my martini. Absent mindedly.

"I guess what any of us do when our mate dies and we're left alone. Grieve, rage, feel sorry for ourselves, then finally cope the best way we can."

William stuck his head around the doorjamb. "It's about time for the evening news."

We moved back into the den. William turned on the TV set, sat down and began cleaning and oiling the .357 Magnum pistol with its long barrel from his gun collection. When he watched television, he always cleaned one of the twenty-three guns in our collection.

"Dad," he said. "The blacks are really angry and upset about your stand." He was inspecting the inside of the pistol's long barrel. "Maybe angry enough to try something crazy."

His 6-foot, 6-inch height, plus his natural athletic ability and love of competition had earned him a spot as an All-American guard on the University of Georgia basketball team back in the '80s. Even now, five days a week, at noon, he plays pickup basketball games at the YMCA. At 5:30 each morning, he's up to jog five miles. My son prides himself on staying in shape.

"Today's top story on our six o'clock news," the woman anchor began, "is about the anger of our black citizens over the continued flying of the Confederate flag over the Civil War monument on city hall grounds." As she spoke, the screen showed file footage of the flag and the monument to General Lee in the bright afternoon sun. Then, DeLong Tolman's face came onto the screen.

"For over 350 years," Tolman sneered. "White Southerners have kept the black man here in the South in virtual enslavement. Racism is an integral part of the face the white man turns toward black people each day."

Donna Elaine gasped, "That's not true."

The reporter had obviously filmed Tolman making a separate statement after the council meeting. He continued blaming a long list of the ills of black people on whites. At no point did he refer to the responsibility blacks should assume for their own states of being.

William continued to clean and polish the .357 Magnum. Frequently, he looked down the pistol's barrel as he watched Tolman on TV.

Tolman raged on. "And that damned Confederate flag out on the lawn. They know how we blacks feel about it, but they still hoist it each day over that stupid monument to General Lee. It's a symbol of slavery."

The edited film cut to a picture of me at the meeting. "You have heard a fiery, demagogic attack by Mr. Tolman on decent Southerners, an attack full of raw prejudice, hatred and reverse racism of the ugliest sort. We did not fight the Civil War to defend slavery. We fought to claim our independence as a separate, free nation. Mr. Tolman's efforts to pull down our flag will only further inflame the already boiling hatred of black people for us whites, and give the media once again an opportunity to hold us Southerners up to ridicule."

The anchorwoman's face filled the screen. "We asked State Senator Willie Sanders, and Chamber of Commerce president Gary Wilhelm to comment on Councilman Bedford's stand."

Sanders' voice came over the telephone; his words were printed onto the screen under his photograph as he spoke. "I can't imagine someone of Stoney Bedford's stature taking the ridiculous position he did on such a serious matter. He, of all people, should know better. The war was over in 1865. The South was thoroughly defeated, its stance repudiated. Most citizens have long ago agreed that the South was wrong to fight to keep black people enslaved. Personally, I feel a great sense of guilt over what this country has done to its black citizens. The Confederate flag is a symbol of the centuries of misery we've inflicted on our black citizens."

"And these people want peace between the races?" William blurted out.

The film editor cut again to the Confederate flag, this time as it was being raised by two black workers. Then Gary Wilhelm's picture came onto the screen. He was sitting behind a large, polished mahogany desk.

"As president of the Chamber of Commerce, I am saddened over what happened today at city council meeting. Stoney Bedford's remarks were quite unwise and could lead to a greater unrest—and perhaps fiery demonstrations—in the black community. One would think that a man of Bedford's reputation would know better than to spout such outrageous things for all the world to see and hear. This is 1996. Such ideas should have been laid to rest long ago. We are one nation, under one flag. The American flag, the Stars and Stripes."

On the TV screen, an American flag fluttered in the breeze with the Lincoln monument in the background. Then the camera looked up at Abe Lincoln's statue as he sat in solemn majesty in the marble enclosure of his Washington memorial. It zoomed in on Lincoln's face.

Donna Elaine started sobbing, put her hands to her mouth and hurried from the den. William snapped the cylinder of his .357 Magnum back into place and continued polishing the gun's surfaces.

"That was a real hatchet job on you, Dad. Senator Sanders. He's just another white Southern politician who's betrayed our Southern principles and ideals."

"He's got plenty of help," I said. "It's common for politicians to trumpet such stuff."

My son was exasperated. "He didn't have to do that. But, it will make him appear as a sophisticated, intelligent person at the next cocktail party when the liberals gather around him to gush their appreciation. I wonder if he hasn't felt the new winds blowing across America from people like us who are sick and tired of politicians like him?"

I snapped off the television set. "Over the years, William, the politicians in Washington and the liberal media have brainwashed a broad segment of the population with ideas such as you just heard Sanders spout out. They've convinced millions of our own Southern people to don the cloak of guilt and lean against the wailing wall and beat their breasts in atonement."

William frowned and waved his hand toward the television set. "The excesses of the press and the militant minorities have started a back lash throughout the land. Their hypocrisy is being exposed daily by dozens of talk radio shows that lets the millions of us who hold conservative views know that we're not alone. We're stirring. We're going to take back the powers the federal government has wrongfully stolen from us."

I heard the telephone ringing insistently. Donna Elaine walked into the den and handed me the cordless telephone. "It's Roy Bester."

He's the black attorney we helped through six years of college. "Hello, Roy," I said. "I guess you just watched the evening news."

"Yes, Mr. Bedford. That Sanders and Wilhelm. What a pair! That's not the way you feel about us black people."

"No, it isn't, Roy. But they don't care what the true picture is. The media loves controversy and reporters are quite adept at stirring the pot."

The attorney's voice deepened in tone. "Mr. Bedford. I went to a meeting last night. Mostly black folks. All that happened today was planned and deliberate. You're the focal point of their political efforts. They hate you because you don't crumple with fear before their attacks. They're planning demonstrations, marches, news conferences. And, the burning of a Confederate flag."

I felt my anger boiling over. "The burning of a Confederate flag?"

"That's not all. They've enlisted the help of white liberals and the Black Muslims."

"I had an idea the Black Muslims and Tolman's followers were working closely together in this controversy."

"Karim and his crew aligned themselves with Tolman in return for Tolman and his group's agreement to help them oust Chief Dennis Crowe. Things are fixing to blow up. You're in danger, Mr. Bedford. I though I'd better warn you."

I tried to down play his concerns. "Oh, Roy. They're just 'bashing whitey' as they call it. It's great sport in the black community. They'll cause some trouble, but not enough that sensible people can't handle."

"I don't know, Mr. Bedford. This time, it's bigger than just angry words. These people are militant and determined to make a statement. They've got blood in their eyes. They're looking for some one to sacrifice. They could try to kill you."

"Kill me? Why?" That damned knot in my stomach tightened.

"Killing you would make them national heroes to many black groups," Bester said. "Remember, Abdul Karim said that the Ayatollah and the Muslims were at war with white people. Doing away with you would be a big victory for them. Hold on just a minute, Mr. Bedford."

I heard him talking to his secretary to tell the people in his office he'd be with them soon.

"Sorry for the interruption," he said. "As I was saying, Southerners like you, the Confederate flag, the South itself—you're symbols. And, they're quite certain that nationwide sentiment would be with them if they came after you. I'm just trying to warn you, Mr. Bedford. As a friend."

At eleven that night, Donna Elaine, smelling of roses, tugged me into another world, one far more beautiful that the harsh one in which I'd wallowed most of the day.

"I know what you need, Stoney," she said. "I've had my bath. I'm relaxed. I want you to be the man you've always been during the wonderful years we've had together. I know you've always been the macho man's man, but tonight you're my man."

Her lacy red nightgown dropped down around her ankles. "Well, Stoney, I've put the same thought and energy into being a woman that appeals to a man like you."

She knew I couldn't stand seeing that beautiful naked body of hers, those large, firm breasts. I got out of bed and stripped off my pajamas. In the dim light, we embraced each other, our hands dancing over each other's body. She pulled my mouth to her breasts.

"Stoney," she panted. "You're a man. A real man. Take me, the way you always have."

We fell into bed. Soon, I was lost in this woman whose magic was like the flowers of spring. The bugle calls of envisioned glory at Gettysburg were so distant I could not hear them. The Confederate flag, for the moment, had been folded into the night's oblivion.

CHAPTER 5

The telephone kept ringing and ringing. Finally, I shook myself awake. It was still dark outside. As I reached for the receiver, I glanced at the digital clock on my bedside table.

"Hello," I said, still not awake.

"Stoney, this is Harris."

"Harris?" The clock said 6:03 a.m.

"Hell yes. Harris Woolford. I know. You probably had too many martinis last night, but get your ass up out of that bed, go out front and pick up your copy of the *Ledger*. *It'll wake you up!*"

His words were a blast of cold air. "Victor Allen's story about yesterday's meeting? Is it that bad?"

"His story is bad enough, but that's not the half of it."

"There's something worse than that pudgy little egomaniac's news article?"

Donna Elaine had gotten out of bed and was putting on her robe and slippers. She looked at me, shrugged, then headed for the bathroom.

"The newspaper burned your ass in the lead editorial," Harris said. "The sorry bastards. Said you had given the blacks just cause to stage demonstrations. That as an elected official you should not have challenged their demands for removal of the flag."

"Oh, shit! Not that, Harris." My mouth felt cottony dry. I pictured the paper's editorial page, which I consistently read.

"Yes, they tore you a new one, Stoney," Harris said. "And without benefit of Vaseline."

I felt drained. I could feel my heart pounding in my ears. But, I should have expected something like this, should have known the newspaper would follow its stated policy of airing the grievances of blacks in bold, front page stories. They'd done it before. They were quite good at misdirecting the blame onto the white man's shoulders.

"I'm telling you, man," Harris said. "They made you look like the instigator, like some night rider in a white sheet. The editorial says that the blacks were right; that flying the Confederate flag on public property offends all black citizens; that the flag was a symbol of slavery that all Southerners should repudiate once and for all."

"Are you reading from the *Ledger*, Harris?"

"Got it open right here in front of me. The bastards are really encouraging the blacks to tear our asses up. They're pouring gasoline onto the fire. When it flares up around us like cannibals boiling their victims, the editors can piously say, 'We told you so.' "

Donna Elaine handed me the newspaper. She'd opened it to the *Ledger* editorial and folded it back. "I'll bring you a cup of coffee in a minute," she said.

I murmured my thanks. "My wife's just handed me the newspaper, Harris. Open to the editorial page. Damn! Why would they do something like that?"

The headlines over the editorial were printed in large, bold, black letters. They read "Bedford Fires Black Rage." "Defends Slavery's Symbol." "The Confederate Flag."

I knew they loved controversy, loved fanning the flames. They had the power over people like me. They had the ink and the newsprint. I had only the limited range of my voice. But this was going too far. The flush of anger made my hands tremble.

"Stoney, are you still there? Or have you had a heart attack?" Harris was concerned.

"Why would they do something like this?" I asked again.

"Stoney, you know that damned newspaper thinks it's their holy mission to force our society to move out of the way and let blacks claim, how do they put it, 'their rightful place in the American dream.' "

"But you and I," I said weakly. "We're not holding them back. We're trying to help."

"Man, you are dense this morning," Harris said. "Remember, we're supposed to give them anything they want. The paper's news stories and editorials preach that all conservatives are out to take food from the mouths of poor people, cut them off welfare, deny them their entitlement to federal hand-outs."

"But they've crossed the line on this attack," I said. "Stories like this damage my reputation to the point where I want to resign from the council. It just doesn't seem to be worth the struggle any longer. They destroy all the good I've tried to do."

"Not just you Stoney. They included me and Erling in the later paragraphs of both the news story and the editorial."

Rage had cut loose my tongue from its anchor of reserve. "You'd think they'd leave us some last remnant of what we were and are as Southerners; some last bit of pride in what we fought and died for by the thousands in the Civil War; some understanding of what we as a people yearned for when we waged that terrible conflict against the Yankees."

"You're too damned idealistic, Stoney. That ain't the way these people play the game."

My mind was still trying to fight back. I tried to explain myself to myself. I am what I am. It's a genetic inheritance; a cultural conditioning passed from generation to generation, a thing of the spirit. My mind flowed back in time. I was there again at Gettysburg with our men in gray, charging up Cemetery Ridge. These words in the newspaper were the bursting shells, the crack of rifles, the sun glinting on the fixed bayonets of the waiting blue coats.

I realized I was crying. Donna Elaine handed me a steaming cup of coffee and kissed me on my forehead. I noticed that tears were streaming down her cheeks, too. She walked from the room.

The editorial called my remarks "inflammatory." "Bedford has been held out to us as a leader on the council. Yesterday, he was anything but a leader. His words and actions evoked shades of demagogues standing in the flickering light of a flaming gasoline-soaked torch with blazing crosses in the background."

"Stoney," Harris asked. "You okay?"

"Yes, Harris. I'm okay. I'm angry. And heartbroken. I've struggled to build and keep my good name through years of compassionate community service and the giving of my time and money to individuals and worthy causes. This stuff in the *Ledger*. It makes me look . . ." I couldn't finish the sentence.

Harris laughed. "They don't give a damn about that shit."

"This . . . this vicious editorial is character assassination of the worst sort."

"Man, don't you know that politicians aren't supposed to have any character? We're a subhuman species walking around with our hand out, stealing everything in sight."

I ignored Harris' needling. "I feel like I did that day we invaded Salerno in Italy during the war. We took those poor bastards to the beaches in our small boats. The Germans were waiting for us. It was an ambush. They mowed us down by the hundreds the bodies were stacked in the small space like cordwood. This editorial is an ambush."

"Yeah," Harris said. "You'd think they'd value that Silver Star of yours enough to give you fair treatment. At least, better than what's in today's paper."

"As you said, Harris, what we did in the war to keep Hitler from taking over the world makes no difference to the newspaper. Nor to the radio and TV stations. To reporters, I'm still a Southern demagogue in a white sheet. The dirty, mean bastards. I fought for my country. I've earned the right to stand against anybody espousing things I don't believe in. I don't deserve this kind of whipping."

"I'm going to call the publisher and raise hell," Harris said. "I'll remind them of your record as a naval lieutenant in World War II, the battlefield decorations you earned."

"I tell you what I'm going to do, Harris."

"What's that, Stoney?"

"I'm going to write an OpEd piece for their editorial page, giving our side of the story. They'll have to run it, out of fairness."

I sipped on the coffee and tossed the *Ledger* onto the bed.

"They won't run it," the professor said. "They're the high and the mighty ones. They have the power to kick us around anytime they wish."

"But they've made me angry with this latest attack. I'll camp out in their offices until they do."

"Stoney, most people hate that damned newspaper. They hate the way they're trying to cram blacks and their culture down our throats, the way they support any enlargement of government power over its citizens."

"William said almost the same thing last night."

Harris was fuming. "I'm so sick and tired of that shit until I could vomit."

"Harris, blacks were freed by the Emancipation Proclamation during the Civil War, but now they have new slavemasters. Their own preachers and political leaders. Black leaders like Karim and Tolman have a vested interest in keeping fellow blacks poor and uneducated. And docile."

Yeah," Harris said. "That's the way the Karims and Tolmans gain and keep power over minorities. At election time they can bargain and offer their chosen candidates the blacks as a voting bloc. When the candidate they support wins, he has to deliver on his promises of more hand-outs to minority citizens."

"You'll never see these things included in the *Ledger's* news stories, Harris. In most elections, the power brokers make what they call 'street money' available to the black preachers and political leaders for the buying of the black vote."

"The media knows it goes on. They have the facts, but they look the other way. They dismiss it by saying, 'That's just politics.' Funny thing. Such skullduggery seldom occurs in the white neighborhoods."

"They're trying to fasten the albatross of guilt around our necks," I said. "They want us to hang our heads in shame and say 'We're sorry for the things we did to you black people. We're responsible for poverty and crime in the inner city. White people have kept you from living in decent housing, from getting good educations and high-paying jobs.' "

"To hell with that shit," Harris said. "Each of us is responsible for our own fates. It's about time black people accepted the responsibility for their own lives, solved their own problems."

"Thank God for conservative talk show hosts like Rush Limbaugh and Ken Hamblin," I said. "They're waking the American people up by showing them the truth about what's going on. If it weren't for people like those two—and their shows—we would have no voice at all."

"Just yesterday, I heard Hamblin say the blacks want to destroy every last vestige of white culture and reduce us all to living the way they live in 'darktown.' "

I thought about the power of the media to destroy people who didn't do their bidding. "Makes you want to run down the streets screaming, doesn't it? You wonder if there's any use of fighting back." Sometimes, I wanted to throw in the towel, surrender and skulk off to find a hiding place.

"Well, now that I've destroyed your peace and quiet," Harris laughed. "Go shave, take a shower and get dressed. I'll see you at Cranston's Restaurant at nine for the usual gathering of the 'eagles and the vultures.' "

"I'll be there, Harris. And I'll be ready to take any medicine they hand out."

"And you can count on that bunch of cynical bastards to hand out both the bitter and the sweet," Harris laughed.

William had just returned from his five miles of jogging and was standing in the kitchen when I walked in.

"Man," he said. "I feel like someone's been beating on me with a sledge hammer. I didn't sleep too well."

"I had a great night, son." I winked at Donna Elaine. She smiled.

"Well, I'd better get upstairs and get ready to go to work," William said. "Remember, I go to the monthly meeting of the Sons of the Confederate Veterans tonight. I'll be eating with them."

"I'd forgotten that this is the fourth Thursday of the month," his mother said.

William laughed. "I wouldn't miss it, not after Dad's performance at council meeting yesterday. We SCV people totally reject the propaganda that the South was wrong in fighting the Civil War."

"Here, William," I said. "Take a quick look at this newspaper editorial in the morning *Ledger*. They chop me up pretty good."

He scanned the headlines, read a few paragraphs, then slammed the newspaper down onto the counter top. "Dad, this is terrible." His face was almost as red as smoldering fire trying to burst out of its confines. "I'd better go shave and shower before I start cursing. Damn, damn, damn," he muttered as he bounded up the stairs. "Don't they ever let up?"

CHAPTER 6

As I walked into Cranston's restaurant, people at some of the tables stood up and began to applaud.

"Stoney," Damon Rogers yelled. "We're behind you one hundred percent in your stand at yesterday's council meeting."

My mouth fell open in surprise. Damon, who owned a large automobile dealership, was a political activist. People listened to what he said.

"Yeah, Stoney," Graham Kline, our former mayor, said. "You're right in what you said and in the position you took on the flag. Someone has to stand up for our Southern principles."

A stocky, middle-aged man rushed over to shake my hand. He was waving the newspaper, which was folded back to the editorial page. "This is the usual rotten liberal crap that newspapers use to try and intimidate us, Stoney. Hold your shoulders back. Smile. Know that most of the people are behind you all the way."

"Thank you," I said. "It sure helps to know that I'm not alone."

"Well," a stone-faced younger man said in a loud voice. "I ain't one of your fans." He had remained seated. "You did us all a great disservice yesterday. Fanned the anger of the blacks even higher with all that crap about that damned Confederate flag. When are we going to quit fighting the Civil War?" He glared at some of those who had stood to applaud me.

The young woman sitting at his table, smearing lipstick that was too red onto her broad bottom lip, finished the painting, rubbed her lips together, blotted them with a tissue and laughed. "Why, Dick," she said to her outspoken companion, "didn't you know that Bedford just loves to see his picture on TV and in the newspaper. That's why he spouts off so often without thinking about consequences, because he knows the media will jump on his racist remarks."

A tall, muscular young man walked toward the dissidents, stopped and slammed his fist down onto the table. The silverware jumped and clattered. "What the hell's eating you two? As you can see, you ain't exactly in the majority here. You'd probably be a lot more comfortable somewhere else."

"Yeah," I heard two or three other people say. "You two piss us off."

"Why don't you butt out, man?" the woman said to the muscular young challenger. "Or do you want me to scratch your eyeballs out?" She cupped her hands into claws and held them up toward her chin.

Her outspoken companion touched her elbow. "We were just leaving," the dissenter said. He took one last swallow of coffee, stood up, grabbed his check and hurried to the cashier's stand.

The woman was in no hurry to follow. At the check-out stand, she turned and glared at several of the diners, then said, in a loud voice that had a clipped New York accent, "You're all a bunch of ignorant bigots. But then, this *is the South.*" She laughed. For some reason she thought what she had said was funny.

The muscular challenger had not been cowed. He took a few steps toward the man and woman and said, "I oughta kick your asses. We got too many of your kind in Forest already. You might be well off to consider moving to some other place."

The dissenter picked up his change, turned, and said, "Folks like you are a dying breed. The South will be better off when you and your beliefs are buried." The two left the restaurant.

"It's a good thing that fellow left when he did," Damon Rogers said. "Or else there'd have been trouble."

"Yeah," the tall challenger said. "I was about to give them big trouble."

The "eagles and the vultures," as our morning breakfast group was affectionately known, always sat at the same table in the far corner of the restaurant. The same people gathered at Cranston's Monday through Friday, for no particular reason, except to vent our opinions on any subject we wanted to bring up. After one hour, we went our separate ways.

"Well," Harris Woolford said, a big smile on his face. "Here comes that famous man, Stoney Bedford. Or, should I say, 'infamous man.' " Others at the table laughed.

"Boy," Tom Bing said, his pale face turning red. "That editorial in this morning's *Ledger* cut you up pretty good, didn't it? But, then you weren't very smart in saying those things. Why do you have to be such a damned hot-head?" He clenched his big jaws and shook his head.

Nick Headley jumped in before I could answer. "Bing, you're the damned 'hot-head.' You're the one who's always shooting from the hip." He turned to me, "That newspaper! Most unfair attack on a decent citizen I've ever seen." Headley was a jovial, retired oilman who could be found in the center of anything political in Forest. He gave lots of campaign contributions to conservative candidates and didn't mind speaking his piece on anything that came up.

"Bing," Jim Fenner needled. "What does the *Ledger* do for you to get you to come down on their side most of the time? Give you a cut rate on your furniture store advertisements?" The ugly scar on the right side of Fenner's neck showed where surgeons had opened him to clean out his carotid arteries.

"Some times, Jim," Bing said. "You're a bigger pain in the ass at these morning meetings than you are when I'm trying to buy new golf clubs from you at your golf shop. I just might start buying from the pro at the country club."

"That'll be the day," Fenner laughed. "As tight as you are with a dollar. You buy from me because my prices are lower and I'll put up with all that horse shit you're spreading around."

Carl Chumley, a big man with a big voice, had been silent. "Knock it off, guys," the former college football coach said. "This thing is serious. The *Ledger*, the Chamber of Commerce, our great state senator—all of them are, you might say, actually urging the blacks to go on a rampage of burning and looting. Not openly, of course, but the wink and the nod are there in their words. What can we do to calm all parties down before somebody gets killed?"

"Good question," Woolford said. "I don't see that there's much that we can do. Tackling the *Ledger* would be like David going up against Goliath without even his sling short. Newspapers frighten most people."

"One thing I'm going to do," I said, "is to write an OpEd piece for the editorial page giving our side of the controversy."

"They won't print it," Tom Bing said quickly. "Why should they?"

"Oh, yes they will," Nick Headley said. "They have to run it. Out of fairness. They attacked Stoney. They hit him below the belt. They hit him hard. It was dirty pool."

"He brought it on himself," Bing retorted. "What does that damned Confederate flag mean to us whites anyway? Nothing."

"Bing, won't you shut up for just one minute," Chumley, the coach, demanded. "Hell, man. This is serious business. Things might explode and quickly get out of control."

"Yeah," Jim Fenner said. He turned to me. "An OpEd piece is a good idea, Stoney, but it'll be two or three days before the newspaper will run it. Meanwhile, Cape, Tolman, Dines, Karim will be in the headlines. They're leading a march on city hall this afternoon at three o'clock. And that turncoat, Baxter Lampkins, is marching with them."

I couldn't hide my surprise at the news of the march. "No, that'd be the wrong thing to do, especially at this time."

"Damn!" Carl Chumley said. He turned to Fenner. "How did you find out that bit of information?"

"One of Tolman's friends came into my golf shop last night after the meeting," Fenner said. "He's excited about it. Said there'd be two hundred or more people marching."

"Looks as though the blacks wanted you to know so you could spread the news," Damon Roger, the automobile dealer, said.

"I heard it on the radio on my way here," Woolford said.

The news didn't sit too well with Chumley. "After the TV cameras get through joyously filming that mob yelling, screaming and waving their placards, things will really be ready to explode. We don't need that."

"Say, Stoney," Harris said. "Why don't you phone your three black friends? The ones you helped through college. Two of them are ministers. Maybe they can talk some sense into Tolman and his crew. Before something real bad happens."

"Yeah, Stoney," Headley said. "Do that. Maybe it'll help. If anything will at this stage of the game."

"I probably ought to go and observe what happens during the march," I said.

"What?" Bing exploded. "Have you lost your mind? Stay away from that damned march, Stoney. Your being there will add more fuel to the fire."

Coach Chumley put his hand on my arm. "I'll go to the march and be your eyes, Stoney. I'll take my cellular phone, get you on the line and report every thing that happens. You stay at home and listen on the phone."

"There'll be lots of fiery speeches to rile the crowd up," Jim Fenner said. "The same old lies, half-truths and distortions we've heard a thousand times before."

"And they'll be waving signs with their insults to the whites," Headley, the outspoken activist, said. "For the benefit of the TV cameras. And the other media representatives."

"That's the big reason they're staging this march," Chumley said. "It looks as though we're plunging headlong into escalation of the conflict. Sooner or later, the two sides will come face to face and then, pfooh. The exploding fireball. Remember. Mobs have no eyes. There's no telling who the fire will burn."

Harris opened a book he had on the table. "Here's something that might throw light on what's happening. Let me read you a few paragraphs from an essay written by a conservative history professor at the University of Alabama."

"Uh oh," Bing said. "Here come words from the intellectual in the group. But maybe we need to listen."

"You mean there's such a thing as a conservative college professor?" Coach Chumley laughed, putting his hand on Bing's arm.

"I'll read it," Harris said. "Then you judge for yourself." He began reading.

"In any war, the victors write the history of the war and frame the actions of the war's peoples to reflect their own philosophy and the reasons for the conflict.

"In the War Between the States, Northern historians have used every means available to cast the war and the old South in dark terms. And who writes the history books, which our students in the South study in school? Why, Northern historians of course. To their work, they bring their prejudiced colorations of all Civil War events and other movements in Southern history.

"They wage punitive psychological warfare against the South for seceding from the union, and in so doing, broad brush Southerners as being morally and legally guilty for the war.

"Under the guise of objective academics, they impose a mental crown of thorns upon millions of gullible Southerners who know no better than to cover themselves in black robes of remorse and guilt and pray for acceptability by those who wield this power."

Harris closed the book with its beige cover and looked around the table.

"How's that for laying the truth on the line?" he asked.

"And that guy's supposed to be an objective historian?" Bing snorted. "He sounds like a lot of other prejudiced Southerners I know. Hell, we in the South are as guilty as sin. We did keep those poor black people in slavery for hundreds of years, picking cotton, waiting on those fancy

Southern belles who were too ladylike to do any of the menial work, bowing and scraping to the powdered and bewigged matriarchs. It makes me sick just to think about it."

"Bing," Chumley said. "You're as full of shit as a Christmas turkey. No one else at this table agrees with you. If you hate your own Southland so badly, why don't you move up North?"

"Hell no," Bing said. "I'm going to stay here and try to work for change from the inside out. I've got great hopes that many of the younger generation don't think like you do. I think there's hope for a better tomorrow. And people from wealthy, landed families like Bedford here, are fast disappearing. Thank the Lord." He looked around the table, glowering.

Bing enjoyed playing the devil's advocate. The sad thing about his words was that he actually believed in what he was saying and kept alive his hopes that such changes could come to pass. The man truly did feel a real sense of guilt over the plight of poor blacks.

"Bing, we'll overlook what you said, considering the source." Chumley was smiling. He knew that to show such lack of concern for Bing's words really got under the furniture store owner's skin.

Nick Headley was shaking his head. "You know, Bing, you ought to be sentenced to take Harris' course in history out at the university. Maybe at least you'd learn the truth about the South's War for Independence."

"He'd have to approach it with an open mind," Jim Fenner said. "I doubt if he could do that. Anyone who stopped to think for even a minute, knows there are two sides to everything, and the South's side in these matters is certainly not being told correctly."

"The truth is," I said. "The atmosphere of the times in which we're living, well, the voices are so shrill until no one wants to hear the South's side of the story. We've already been tried, convicted and sentenced. And that's wrong."

"But Bing," the bluff Chumley said, standing up and reaching for his check. "You're okay. Just misinformed about Southern history and ideals." He chuckled. "But, other than that you're an interesting case study. You add a lot of fire to these gatherings. The things you say sometimes raise our blood pressure, but they do make the arguments much more exciting."

As we were leaving, Chumley pulled me aside. "Go home and write that editorial piece for the *Ledger*. Get it down to the newspaper as soon as possible. It's very important. And, stay near your telephone. I'll call you at a quarter to three to give you an eyewitness account of the great protest march on city hall."

He took out his car keys and started toward his automobile. Suddenly, he stopped, turned around and said: "And for God's sake, keep looking over your shoulder. They might already be following you. And planning something crazy."

CHAPTER 7

"There it goes again," my wife said as I walked through the back door of our home and into the kitchen. "The telephone. All it's done is ring, ring, ring." She was exasperated.

"I'm sorry, Honey."

"Oh, that goes with your being a city council member, Stoney. But, after twenty-seven calls, I turned on the answering machine."

"Any more hate calls?" I asked.

"Only three," she said. "The rest were from our friends. Happily, there were several calls from complete strangers, cheering you on."

"The three nasty calls. Were they from blacks?"

"Not that I could tell in listening to accent and pronunciation of words. Two are women. One is male. All three tell you that you should be ashamed of yourself for not understanding how sensitive black people are about the Confederacy. Oh, one of the women used the phrase, 'Trying to make a case for flying that damned rebel flag. I guess he's some proud descendent of big slave holders.' The man cursed you for being one of those 'stupid conservatives who ought to be wearing a white sheet. Or a Republican party hat.' "

"Did you get their names?"

"The three who made the hate calls did not leave their names. I wrote down the names and phone numbers of the other twenty-four. Frankly, I got a lift from listening to most of the callers. They said so many nice things abut you and urged you not to back down. I don't think that most people in the country realize the depth of feeling that surrounds our fight for our Southern ideals."

"Rush Limbaugh says that the liberals who want to throw away traditional values underestimate the depth of feeling conservatives have about these things. They dismiss people like us as a bunch of right-wing kooks."

My wife resented the implication. She drew herself up to her full height and said, "I'm not a kook. And I know that you're not either." Her eyes were blazing. There were times she saw little reason for controlling her temper.

"Did a Morris Light call?"

"Yes. He said he was an independent TV producer of documentaries. What does that mean?"

"You remember him, Donna Elaine. The Little Theater production of *Don Quixote*? The one I starred in back when I still had my good singing voice. He was our producer for the musical."

"Twenty years ago?"

"That's the same Morris Light. He went on to big things in television as producer of documentaries. He wants to do one about my struggle to keep the Confederate flag flying."

"What would that mean?" she asked, her suspicion showing.

"He's done such shows for PBS for the last fifteen years. We've seen some of them. He's really quite good. He'd have to practically live with us for the next few weeks, filming and recording everything we do."

"I don't know. Would he be here at our home a lot?"

"Yes, but we've got an extra bedroom and bath. So, it wouldn't inconvenience us too much if he decided to stay overnight to pursue his filming."

"What's your reaction to Light's offer?" She was using the tips of the fingers of her right hand to scratch her short hair. That always means she's not exactly sold on something I've suggested. Or anything else that's suddenly plopped in front of her when she hasn't had time to properly digest it.

I knew better than to let any trace of combativeness show in my words. "Because we need a friendly voice so desperately, I've decided to let him do it. It's a story that could go a long way in helping to show why we Southerners are so determined to preserve what we believe in. And Light himself has, in the last few years, really seen the light." I laughed. "No pun intended."

She was still not convinced. "Will William and I be in the story?"

"Yes. It wouldn't be complete without the two of you."

I could tell she was thinking about the early mornings when she usually takes her own sweet time in the bathroom, bathing, getting dressed and putting on her make-up. Donna Elaine Bedford would not face the day—or any camera—without this precious time for herself.

"He won't make us objects of ridicule will he? More to the point, he won't turn you into a Charlie Chaplin character? Or a Ku Kluxer?"

"That was my first concern. He assured me that he would not."

"You believe him?"

"Yes, I believe him."

"Stoney, sometimes we trust people too much. We mustn't let ourselves be played for fools. Light is much younger than we are," she said. "And people his age got brain washed at our universities in the '60s and '70s. Like a lot of other things, patriotism and love of country are two examples of the bloodied casualties of that period. It became *the thing to do* to laugh at and discard cultural beliefs and moral values."

Memories of those turbulent years still tied my stomach into knots. "Those days were the worst of times for many of us. Fortunately, there's been a backlash against the terrible things those people heaped upon an unsuspecting America. Light himself has come back home, intellectually, as far as being proud of our Southern history, culture and heritage."

"There you go again, trusting too much. Leading with your heart instead of your head. You never seem to learn."

She'd put her hands on her hips to show her disbelief. "How do you know he's not setting us up? That he won't sell us out when the networks refuse to run the kind of show you believe he's going to make? Money—or the lack of it—does strange things to people some times."

"It's an intuitive feeling I got when he was trying to sell me on the idea," I said. "He doesn't have to do the documentary. It's a matter of choice for him."

"We've been taken in before by such bland assurances." Skepticism showed in her voice. "What changed his way of thinking?"

I wasn't too confident of overcoming her opposition. "Light said he's been listening to Rush Limbaugh and Kenny Hamblin on talk radio. He's seen how the liberals and the media are working together to change America and that they'll go to any lengths they have to accomplish their goals. Including lies, deception and misrepresentation."

She'd taken her hands off her hips and softened her stance. Perhaps I could convert her over to a positive attitude.

"Funny thing, Stoney. Those people think they're the saviors of the world. They see people such as the two of us as monsters lost somewhere far back in time's ancient peat bogs. Witness their current hero and heroine, Bill and Hillary Clinton. The media blithely wrap the Clintons' views into what they call 'the evening news' and many viewers don't see the untruths the president and his so-called 'first lady' pass on as fact. Of course, those two believe their own lies."

The morning was too beautiful for me to color it darkly with thoughts of those two . . . *imposters there in Washington.* I started to call them something else other than the kind of people I admired. But *I did stop while I was ahead.* Even their names filled me with a vague uneasiness.

"Honey, if we stop fighting for the things we believe in, America as we know and love it, is gone." I said." I became momentarily pensive. "We could suffer badly for my actions, you know."

She still had her doubts about the documentary. "We've got enough facing us already. Couldn't Light make it worse than it already is? Look how Connie Chung made Newt Gingrich's mother think she was saying something that would be kept 'just between us girls.' Then Chung proudly cut the poor woman up on her national BCS news show."

Donna Elaine was still scratching her head, a bad sign. "They all follow the same underhanded pattern. First, people like Chung sweet talk you into granting them an interview. They make you think they're the soul of virtue, that they're on your side. Then they edit and slant their film to support the views they want the TV audience to see. When what they've done flashes onto the TV screen, it's usually not recognizable. It tells the prejudiced story they intended to tell all along."

"I intend to have some more deep conversation with Morris Light. Then, we'll reduce our agreement into a contract that gives me the right to throw out anything I think is slanted and prejudiced against us and the South."

She laughed. "He won't go along with that. He'll probably scream to high heaven about 'artistic freedom.' "

"He won't get away with it, if he does. In most parts of the South, a gentlemen's agreement is still a gentlemen's agreement. And it is binding."

" If you'll do that, Stoney, I'll go along with it. But, I don't believe Light will agree to your restrictions."

"I'm going to telephone Light," I said. "But first, I want to talk to those two black ministers we helped send through college."

We certainly had become friends with Wash Washington and Blue Combs. We're people who respect each other and the two ministers just might help to calm down DeLong Tolman and his crowd. There were other people we'd helped through the universities also, but they lived in distant cities—or had seen fit to look upon us as 'gift horses' they no longer needed. We'd learned bitterly that some people to whom you give a helping hand turn to rend you out of envy, hatred and misunderstanding—and an effort to rid themselves of any sense of obligation.

"That's human nature," my daddy used to laugh and remind me. "Such people cover their shame and feelings of inferiority with disavowal and anger," he often said. "But, Stoney, helping poor people who deserve help is something that's expected of those of us in the South who've fared better in the world than many others."

As I turned to the telephone, she said, "I wish Reading Farnsworth and Jackson Smith still lived in Forest. They'd certainly be ready and willing to help." They were two now very prominent blacks we'd rescued from the human junk heap by serving as their mentors from their earliest years. Then, we couldn't bear not seeing them go on to complete their college education. So, we financed each of them through their medical and law degrees. Farnsworth was a physician with the National Institute of Health and Smith was an attorney in the U.S. Commerce Department.

Wash Washington's secretary seemed reluctant to put me through to him.

"I don't know whether or not he wants to talk to you, Mr. Bedford. After the ugly things you said about black people yesterday."

I insisted.

"I hope you'll go on TV and apologize to us black people," the woman said.

I did not respond.

Finally Washington came on the line. "Mr. Bedford," he said. "I've been so worried about you and Donna Elaine. So many people are angry and threatening you and your family with bodily harm."

"I don't understand their threats of violence, but that's why I'm calling, Reverend Washington. To see if you can't help to calm Tolman and the others down." He was silent for a long time.

"I'm in a bad position, Stoney. I called DeLong early this morning. I cautioned him not to whip the people in our community into a frenzy that could lead to ugly scenes."

"What did he say?" I asked.

"He cursed me. Called me 'a white man's nigger, an Uncle Tom.' Then he slammed the receiver down. Two minutes later, Cape, Dines and Karim called me. In effect, they said, 'If you cross us, we'll ruin you.' "

"That sounds unreal. How did you handle those threats, Wash?"

"Not too well, I'm afraid. There's just so far a black man can go in taking up for white folks."

"Wash," I said. "We're friends. I'd go the extra mile for you, if it were you asking for help."

"But you don't have as much to lose as I do. If I get tagged with the labels 'white man's nigger' and an 'Uncle Tom,' that finishes me and my church off. As a matter of fact, Karim threatened to do just that. 'Wait'll we picket your church,' he said, 'and hand out flyers to members of your congregation explaining how you're standing against your own people.' "

"Are you afraid to stand up for what you know to be right, Wash? You're a minister. From long experience, you know that my family and I would never harm any person. How can you harm someone when all you're doing is standing up for principles you believe in?"

"Principles don't stand for too much among folks like us who are so poverty stricken and many times, uneducated. Out here, it's a problem of survival. With me—and most of the others—it comes down to our biggest fear—the fear of white people—and the need to wrest power and control from them so we can build better lives."

"It's difficult for me to understand your refusal to help me and my family," I said. "You're my friend and a person of worth. All I'm asking you to do is to tell them that white folks have a right to believe in our culture and heritage and that the Confederate flag is very important to us. Like Martin Luther King is important to black people."

"All that is philosophy, Stoney. It's easy for you to say, but this is the real world I'm living in over here, on the other side of town from you privileged white people."

"I'm amazed. I didn't know you felt like that, Wash."

He laughed. "My skin is black. All us blacks feel that way. You're white. We don't expect you to understand. I know you don't want to put me into the horrible position of seeming to favor you over people whose skin is black like mine. Do you?"

I almost exploded in anger. Fortunately, I took a deep breath before replying. "No, Reverend Washington. I guess you've done about all you can do. Under such trying circumstances. Goodbye."

"Goodbye, Stoney. Give my love to Donna Elaine."

I don't know why I expected to fare better with Blue Combs. I probably should have known better than to call him. Nowadays, it seemed as if some people on whom you felt you could depend always failed you when it came to covering their own asses rather than making decisions based upon principle.

Combs listened while I asked his help in defusing the controversy out in the minority community.

"Mr. Bedford," Combs said. His voice was cool and very formal. "I talked to some of my deacons in our church last night, knowing you'd try to catch me up in the middle of this silly fight. They told me to stay out of this flag business. Well, they used a word other than 'business,' a most unflattering word. Of course, I'm heeding their advice."

"You're one friend I thought I could talk to, Blue."

He laughed. "I owe you and your wife a lot. But I don't owe you that much. I've got everything to lose. If you lose a fight, you still have the same world you've been living in daily. If I lose, I'm reduced to poverty and I become an object for people to spit on and despise."

I had to keep on trying to find some common ground with the minister. "Why should it be that way, Reverend Combs? When you talk about Martin Luther King and his dream for all of us, we whites don't make fun of you and your beliefs. As a matter of fact, we cheer you on, because we know black people need to dream, need to develop more self esteem. Many people like my wife and I are working to eliminate, or at least to reduce, racism."

He laughed again. I could hear him tapping his fingertips on the top of his desk. "Mr. Bedford."

When he addressed me that way, I knew he'd closed his mind on trying to help calm things down in the black community.

"Mr. Bedford, to tell you the truth, I don't like that damned Confederate flag any more than DeLong and Karim. It sends black folks a message they don't like."

His words angered me. "I thought you were my friend, Reverend Combs."

"I am, Mr. Bedford. But, if I stick my nose into this flag business, I'm finished. My deacons will throw me out of my church. I'd be finished in the community. The deacons told me so, in no uncertain terms. I can't help you. Maybe, some other time."

I went to the kitchen to mix myself a cup of Community instant coffee. The curl of steam rising from the cup reminded me of a smoking volcano. I raised the cup to my nose so I could smell the delicate aroma. There's nothing to compare with the tangy, dark smell of Community coffee.

I wondered if there were groups just waiting to take such simple things away from me as this coffee. Hell, I loved it too, and I could defend it in reasonable debate—if I had to.

Morris Light picked up the telephone on the first ring.

"Hello, Stoney," he said.

"How'd you know it was me?"

"One of those technological marvels called 'caller ID,' " he laughed. "You mean you don't have it?"

"No, but after the last couple of days, I'm going to have it installed. Maybe it'd stop some of these ugly calls."

"It won't stop such calls," Light said. "It just allows you to answer only when you want to. And you will know who's calling. The caller can't remain anonymous."

"Let's get down to business, Morris. We need to hammer out the details on this documentary you're going to make."

"Good," he said. "I've already started filming it, since I was almost dead certain you'd want me to do it."

"Already started? I don't understand."

"I visited with Cranston at his restaurant last night," Light said. "When I told him what I wanted to do, he said he was certain you'd want it done. So, I hid small cameras in three corners of his restaurant plus one over the table where your morning group gathers. I got some good stuff. That was quite a gathering. Great performances out of several characters. And, the performances were natural. They always are when people don't know they're on camera."

"I didn't see any cameras."

"Technology has enabled us to reduce the size of cameras and microphones to the point where they're easy to conceal."

"Well, I'll be damned," I said. "What if I'd said 'no'?"

"Stoney, if we Southerners don't tell our side of the story, who will? Besides, we're not going to be telling just the story about the Confederate flag. It's going to be about our way of life, our heritage, our philosophies and our willingness to stand up for the things in which we believe. The story will be told through the lives of real people, through their living, their philosophies and their day to day struggles to stand up and be counted in an age where such things often bring immediate character assassination."

"Donna Elaine is highly suspicious," I told him. "She thinks you might be pulling a Connie Chung on us, that you'd paint us as some prehistoric creatures who just crawled out of hatred's black pits."

"Chung is a beautiful woman, and, I thought, quite a competent anchorwoman. But she broke one of the cardinal rules of a good reporter. Never betray a confidence, especially if you're dealing with an older, less sophisticated person who thinks they can trust you to treat them fairly. She got exactly what she deserved."

"Nevertheless, I want us to reduce our terms of understanding to writing. I want to reserve the right to veto anything that makes me look like, well, like a night rider in sheet and hood."

"I don't think there's a problem with that. I worked through the night putting down my thoughts on paper. Why don't we get together for coffee, read over it, add your thoughts, then let your attorney put it in legal terms?"

"You're going to be easy to work with," I said.

"Yes, I am. Just don't forget, I want to see this story about our Southland told in the right way. I know how to do that, and I've proved it many times. Also, I've got a lot at stake. My reputation, my future as far as money is concerned, my personal integrity."

"You know, Morris, that we won't get a fair hearing in the court of public opinion. The media will cut us to pieces. The black community and the liberals, why, they'll yell 'Racism, Bigotry, Prejudice'—anything to discredit a documentary about the South."

"I think we're both prepared for that, Stoney. What I think you don't understand is the depth of animosity and feelings of distrust and betrayal in the hearts of millions of people all across our great land."

"With all my heart I hope that what you say about American people waking up is true."

"Believe me, my friend," Morris said. "I've traveled all across this country. It is true. You just wait and see."

I went to my word processor to work on my OpEd editorial piece for the *Ledger*. I knew that persuading the editor to run my piece would not be an easy task. But I'd screwed my courage up to the point where there was no turning back. The thoughts stored in my mind flowed out smoothly onto the screen. My fingers literally raced on the keys. I lead off with these words.

Your editorial today attacking me and my character is reprehensible, unfair and unbecoming a supposed newspaper. It represents the worst in journalism. The worst because it slanders and defames me as a Southerner who dares to stand up for the great cultural heritage that still leavens our lives; the worst because it uses half truths and innuendoes to assassinate my character as a person and as an elected official; the worst because it is deliberately written to enrage and encourage our black citizens to go on a lawless rampage against property and person; the worst because it drags the noble symbol of the Confederacy, its flag, through the mud.

It is a despicable piece. It insults the whole of our Southern population. Thousands of your readers are more angry at you than you can possibly imagine. But then, how would you know, since your wrap yourself in your determined biases and prejudices toward liberalism and the black population and retreat to your journalistic mountaintop. There you think you're unreachable, your fortress impenetrable, your position invulnerable.

Your readers have been telephoning me by the dozens. Even as I type this opinion piece for your newspaper, a man is saying to me on my telephone answering machine, 'Mr. Bedford, thank you for standing up for our Southern way of life and for the principles many of us have been taught to live by. I'm so angry at those damned liberal TV stations and that rag of a newspaper call the *Ledger*, until I could storm their offices and burn them down. Of course, I won't, because we've been taught to be civilized down South. We've also been hammered for our beliefs so often that we've become intimidated, less brave than we should be.'

Here are the opinions of others. "Why are we reviled and belittled when we stand up for our beliefs, yet others can be so revolutionary and rabid in espousing their causes and not one word is said? As an example, gays and lesbians, despite their despicable lifestyle, get sympathetic treatment in your newspaper. Yet when we dare to debate our beliefs in reasonable terms, you turn and rend us.

"Don't back off, Mr. Bedford," they say. "We applaud your courage."

Incidentally, these people boldly left their names and telephone numbers, as did all but three of the callers. Those three hid behind the cloak of anonymity, cursed and abused me, called me

74

ugly names. That's okay; they have that right. But why didn't they have the courage to leave their names?

This morning as I walked into Cranston's Restaurant, thirty or more patrons stood to cheer and applaud me. Some grabbed my hand and urged me to stand firm. In fairness, I have to say that three of those at the restaurant condemned me for my stance.

I confess that not all the callers are sympathetic. One woman yelled, "Where's your white sheet, Bedford?" Two men asked if I did not understand the terrible persecution of black people by "white slavemasters." One of them repeated the litany of problems white people are blamed for among our minority citizens. Crime, drugs, unemployment, drive by shootings, sub-standard housing, teen-age pregnancies, school dropouts, ad infinitum.

Three calls were chilling. All of them threatened me with death. One said, "Don't think you're safe living in the rich section of town with that big house. You can't hide from us. We're coming to get you."

With your influence as a newspaper in the community, I urge you to be more objective in your approach to this controversy. All we ask is to be allowed to express our views and be treated fairly. Quit prejudging us and resorting to advocacy journalism to further what you see as a necessity for imposing your views about social change on your readers.

Lorne Bostwick, editor of the *Ledger*, was surprised to see me. He threw up his hands in mock surrender. "Don't shoot, Stoney," he laughed. "I give up."

"That'd be funny Bostwick, if I didn't already have several threatening telephone calls recorded on my answering machine. Three of them said they were going to kill me."

"Oh, Stoney, that's hard to believe. People aren't that crazy." He smiled, weakly I thought, and shifted uneasily in his chair.

"I recorded the calls on my answering machine. Come go home with me and I'll let you hear their voices yourself. That editorial this morning was a gutter attack, which I didn't deserve. I resent the living hell out of it."

"What do you have on your mind?" he asked. All pretense at being friendly had disappeared. A common citizen had dared challenge the mighty press.

"I want you to run my reply to your editorial as an OpEd piece on tomorrow morning's editorial page. Here it is." I threw it on his desk in front of him.

"Well, I don't know, Stoney. That's an unusual request." His hands were shaking as he picked up the pages I'd thrown on the desk. He licked his lips.

"Out of fairness, Bostwick, the *Ledger* has to run my reply."

He was reading the two sheets I'd handed him. "No," he said. "We can't run this. Why, it'd look like we had turned tail and ran. No, we're the ones who decide the contents of this newspaper. It's out of the question."

I stayed quiet while he continued to study the words I had written. He looked up. His face was grim.

Once again, I insisted: "Out of fairness, the *Ledger* has to run my reply, Bostwick."

"Let me think about it, Stoney. I'll talk to my publisher. I'll get back in touch with you."

"Call your publisher in here right now, so we can talk about it while I'm here. I'm not leaving this office until you agree to run it in tomorrow morning's newspaper. With my picture and a bold-face headline above it."

"You're pushing too hard," Bostwick said. "Don't make me angry."

I laughed derisively. "You've known me for five years. You should have thought about my reaction when you put that dirty piece of business you call an editorial in today's *Ledger*. You know I don't run from a fight. I've got a Silver Star for valor in battle. I earned it in the invasion at Salerno, Italy in World War II. That day, ten thousand Germans were trying to kill me. I didn't run from the Germans. What makes you think I'll run from you and the *Ledger*?"

Bostwick was rubbing the back of his neck. I had hemmed him up and he couldn't find a way to get out of the jam he'd created for himself.

"I'll tell you what I'm willing to do," he said. "I'll call in a reporter and have him write this as a news story. We'll run your picture inside the story. How about us doing that?"

I laughed again. "And have your reporter twist and distort my words into something unrecognizable. Hell no, Bostwick. I want what I've written on the editorial page. I want it to appear just as I wrote it. With my picture and a bold, black headline. Or should I call my attorney?"

"We can't do that, Stoney."

"Can I use your phone, Bostwick? My attorney's waiting to see if I need him to come here to your office." I reached for his telephone.

He smacked the top of his desk with his right hand. "No. That's not necessary. I'll run it."

"Tomorrow morning?" I asked. "On the editorial page?"

He frowned and stood up. "Yes, Stoney. And we'll include your picture."

"And the bold, black headline?"

"Yes," Bostwick said. "If that's what you want." A smile lit his broad face. He shook his head. "I pity you."

"Oh? You pity me? That's a switch."

He pushed a buzzer to summon his secretary. "You can be certain that your words will be like pouring gasoline onto a fire. You're not in an enviable position. Don't say I didn't warn you."

THE LAST CONFEDERATE FLAG

CHAPTER 8

At 2:45 that afternoon, the telephone rang. It was Coach Carl Chumley. He was at the place where the protest march was forming to give me first hand reports as the marchers made their way to City Hall.

"It's exciting down here at Acorn and Main streets, Stoney. The police have traffic blocked off and a dozen uniformed officers are trying to keep order. Must be two hundred people here. I've counted eleven white people. Baxter Lampkins is here of course. And two other white men. I don't know either of them. There are eight white women circulating through the crowd, helping to get people into position for the march to City Hall."

"Where are you, Carl?"

"I'm standing across the street from where the circus is happening." He laughed. "You wouldn't like the signs they've waving, Stoney. They're crude, hand-lettered, mean and ugly."

"Signs like that play big with the media people, Carl. What's on some of them?"

"How's this for openers? 'Three of a kind. Bedford, KKK and the Flag.' "

The lie made me angry. "That's really quite clever, Carl. Crude, but clever." There was a knot in the pit of my stomach. I hated the Ku Klux Klan and had fought them and their ideas for many years.

"Say," Carl said. "I see the Reverend Wash Washington running around, smiling and patting people on their back. He's acting like a football coach trying to motivate his players to win the game. I thought he was a friend of yours, Stoney."

"I did too, but the poor guy's in a bad position, I suppose. With racial tensions at the flash point, blacks can't afford to be a friend to whites."

"Damn, that doesn't make sense, Stoney. You and your family paid his way through college because you believed in him and wanted to help. Why wouldn't he believe as much in you? Seems like a double standard to me."

"Their leaders label blacks who help whites as 'Uncle Toms' and call them the 'white man's nigger.' They become objects of hatred in the black community. Once that happens, the person is ruined."

"How the hell can things ever get better between the races if we can't be friends with each other? Uh oh! There's Pastor Blue Combs. He's waving a sign that says 'Bedford Defends Rebel Flag and Slavery.' "

"Oh, no," I moaned. "Not Blue Combs too."

"None other," Carl laughed. "One of the white women, a good-looking redhead, is holding up a sign that says, 'Bedford's Words Prove He Hates Blacks.' "

"That's a lie of course." I wanted to hang up the telephone and run to some peaceful spot, if only for a few minutes. Washington and Combs were ministers of the Gospel, but they had discarded their Christian principles to save their own hides. I knew now that they believed in the same hatreds that powered Tolman and Karim. They'd just learned to mask the beliefs under a guise of civility. What could a man count on these days, if he couldn't count on friendship?

I thought of something else my dad taught me. "Son," he'd say. "Most of us want to help black people improve their lot in life. But watch out for 'The Yassuh Boss slave shuffle.' It's something they learned hundreds of years ago to help them pry things out of the white man. When they're asking a white man for help, they usually have their hat in their hands, their eyes cast down and a pleading voice. 'Yassuh, Mr. Bedford. Thank you, Mr. Bedford. I 'preciate it, Mr. Bedford.' Most of us are suckers for this old trick. It works for them. And they know damned well what they're doing."

Well, Dad, they still know how to do the shuffle, but they've updated it. No more bowed heads; no more foot shuffling; no more plaintive pleading. Now, the shuffler stands tall and straight, his eyes bright and glowing, a smile on his face. In today's times, he wants to go to college so he can help his people "climb up to a better world." It all sounded so wonderful.

Old Stoney and Donna Elaine Bedford jumped in to help, because we wanted to and we were in a position financially to help. (In the '90s the Pell grant has largely replaced whites in helping blacks through college.) The shuffler? He still knows how to fast shuffle good old Whitey. Of course, he's learned to be more sophisticated, but he still has the same beliefs his counterpart of two hundred years ago had. Very little has changed. The white man is still his mark.

"Stoney, are you still there?" Chumley yelled into the phone.

"Oh, I'm sorry Carl. I got distracted for a moment."

"Hear that music?" the Coach asked. "Looks like part of a high school band. DeLong's leading them and acting like a band director. I see

Norris Cape and Frank Dines, your fellow council members." He laughed. "They're directing this 'love-in.'

"Now, Baxter Lampkins is moving through the crowd, shaking hands and laughing. Everyone's having a high old time, as if they're taking part in some kind of a festival."

"I'm certain the TV cameramen and newspaper photographers are having a field day," I said, wistfully hoping they wouldn't be there.

"Not only are the local TV people here. NNC, BAC, BNC, and BCS are here, too. And a reporter from the *Washington Post*. I need not tell you that the soon-to-be parade participants are vying with each other to get in front of television cameras."

I should have known that this controversy was bound to attract national media coverage. "See anything of that arrogant little piss-ant, Victor Allen?"

"Yeah, Stoney. He spied me and came across the street to ask me what I was doing. He had reporters from Chicago and Los Angeles newspapers with him."

"What'd you tell him, Carl?"

"I said I was talking to my office and watching what was going on. It seemed to satisfy him. Fortunately, he doesn't know who I am. At least, not to my knowledge."

"You see other TV people there, people you can't identify?" I was thinking of Morris Light.

"As a matter of fact, a fellow by the name of Light was standing next to me a few minutes ago, his TV camera whirring away. Said he was making a documentary of this controversy. There were two other people working with him."

"By the way, Carl. My OpEd piece runs in tomorrow morning's *Ledger*. Lorne Bostwick wasn't too keen on doing it. We argued and I won. Fortunately."

"That'll help our cause, Stoney. Damn! This is terrible."

"What's terrible, Carl? What's happening? Are they after you?" My emotions had leaped to form the worst possible picture.

"No, I'm okay," Carl assured me. "But you aren't going to like what I'm seeing. Two young men have a large Confederate flag on a pole, upside down, and they're running through the crowd, dragging the flag through the dirt."

"Oh, no!" A great sadness came over me. I thought of Gettysburg and Pickett's charge. My pulse started pounding in my ears. These people were dishonoring the Confederate soldiers who'd died that day for the things they believed in and revered. For one brief moment, they'd gained the high ground and planted our flag, then had wavered and fallen back. The battle was lost. Thousands of them died during those terrible hours. And now, this . . .

"Now, the two are inviting the people to spit on it," Carl said.

"Is that what all the cheering's about?" I had the urge to run to my car and drive down there to stop them. Our flag . . . our flag . . . our flag.

"Yes, they're cheering and going wild. Some of them are stomping the flag. Now, they're beating the drums vigorously to incite the mob to even more vigorous stomping."

A long groan escaped my throat. I couldn't help it. Why were they doing such despicable things? Why, it was as though they were stomping me, spitting on me, defying me—or any Southern white person—to do anything about their desecration of the Confederate flag. It was uncontrolled rage being spewed out. They were striking back at white people whom they believed to be the source of their frustrations, their low self-esteem, their feelings of inferiority, their hopelessness. When will they take responsibility for their own fates, as other minorities who've come to America have done?

Instead of accepting their blackness and making their separateness an admirable thing, they angrily demand to be admitted into a white society where basically most people don't want them. I've concluded that Negroes hate themselves because they are black. Can you imagine a Vietnamese hating himself because he's different from the white race? No, they cling to their customs and beliefs, see the opportunity in America, grab hold of it, and rise, rise, rise. You have to admire them in the way they overcome almost insurmountable odds. They work inside of America's traditional economic system and succeed wildly, yet they've been in America less than twenty-five years. It works because they believe that being in America is a great privilege. They don't hate whites. What a difference.

Carl started talking faster. "Things are really heating up now, Stoney. They're starting the march to city hall. DeLong Tolman and Abdul Karim are out front, leading them. The sign that Karim is carrying reads, uh oh, 'Crowe Must Go. He Hates Blacks.' The band's playing marching music. The participants are falling in behind the band. Police cars are in front and back of the group, their lights flashing. Uniformed cops are walking along on each side of the demonstrators.

"Well, what do you know? Lampkins is waving a sign that says, 'That Damned Flag Must Come Down.' One of the white women, a pretty little brunette, is having a ball. Her sign reads, 'The Confederate Flag Stands For Slavery.' "

I could hear the marching music. Often, the police sirens whooped.

"Damn, it's getting wild," Carl said. "Some of the marchers are shattering store and office windows on each side of the street. The cops are continuing to walk and look straight ahead. It's as though they didn't see this lawlessness."

"The police aren't trying to stop them?" I could scarcely believe what Carl was saying. My mouth was suddenly dry. Outside my windows, the grass in the backyard running down to the lake was turning green as the spring sun warmed the earth. Carl's description of the march had long ago warmed me, for I had grown more and more angry. I remembered the TV pictures of happy looters after the Rodney King verdict, the smiles on their faces, their explanations for looting, stealing and burning.

"This is awful, Stoney. The police officers are not trying to stop these damned criminals. The officers are still looking straight ahead, as though they don't see what's happening. Two young men are ripping the dress from a store mannequin. Each of them have pulled an arm off the mannequin. Her body is being passed from hand to hand over the top of the crowd. The television cameras are whirring away."

I could hear Carl breathing hard. "Don't hang up, Stoney. I've got to find another location. I'm too close to the action and I might make a fool of myself."

I could hear the band playing "Stars and Stripes Forever." The crowd noise was almost deafening. The police cars were whooping steadily now. Perhaps the police were at last trying to establish some semblance of order.

"Okay, Stoney. Are you there?"

"I'm here, Carl."

"About a dozen of the marchers practically cleaned out a small men's store. Jackets, men's suits, shirts, ties. Some of them have several ties around their neck. If the coat of the suit doesn't fit, they pass it over their heads back through the crowds until someone claims it. When the storeowner protested, they dragged him out of his store onto the sidewalk and beat him senseless. When he fell to the concrete, they began kicking him. The crowd is cheering them on."

Shades of Los Angeles the night the blacks took to the streets to protest the Rodney King verdict. That night, the police had also stood by—or disappeared entirely—and watched the looting and beatings take place. I remembered the television footage of that poor truck driver on his knees in the street and the casual way he was almost stoned to death.

I wondered how the big city media witnessing this happening would report the news. Of course, they'd drop a paper curtain around today's events and somehow or other explain it away as the acts of an angry people protesting white rule. And this controversy over the flying of the Confederate flag. They'd give such slanted and biased reports that no reader would be able to see the truth of what was happening. In the media's world, the telling of the truth and objective reporting have long since been replaced by advocacy journalism. Reporters slant their news stories by choosing only the facts—and interpreting those facts—to support the things they're advocating.

They'd show us as zealous bigots and Simon Legrees in coats and ties and beautiful homes. Television coverage would be certain to include clips of me and DeLong Tolman speaking at the council meeting; then they'd cut to views of the Confederate flag flying over General Lee's monument. Reporters would then start talking about oppression in the South while showing the signs being carried by the protesting marchers. The looting and beatings would be excused as 'the venting of repressed rage by a downtrodden people.'

"Now, we've arrived at city hall, Stoney." Carl was breathing hard. "Let me catch my breath," he said. "I climbed the steps to the second floor plaza. From here, I can see and hear most things. DeLong Tolman's standing in front of a microphone. He's leading the crowd in a chant. Listen, can you hear it?"

"Pull the flag down! Pull the flag down! Pull the flag down!" I could hear the chanted words clearly.

"DeLong's waving his arms to quiet the crowd," Carl said. "They've laid the mannequin's body at DeLong's feet. They're throwing the tattered Confederate flag over the mannequin's naked body. The crowd is quiet now. I'll let you hear Tolman's words."

DeLong had started. "Look at that hated symbol of slavery, the Confederate flag, flying in the breeze over General Lee's statue. You know why it's there? That's simple. Both the monument and the flag were put there at a time in the past when black citizens had no power to protest. Even though times have changed, Bedford and his crowd continue to run that despicable banner up the flagpole daily. It doesn't matter to white people that it offends black people because it reminds us of the most shameful period in all of history. The hundreds of years that black people were slaves in the South!"

The chanting started again: "Pull the flag down! Pull the flag down!"

Acid bitterness coated his words. "Councilman Stoney Bedford said, 'You can't make us take down the Confederate flag.' It's part of our heritage, part of Southern history. You can't wipe out the tragic struggle of the Civil War. You can't rewrite history.' "

"Pull the flag down! Pull the flag down!"

"Well, Mr. Stoney Bedford. And all of you other Southern bigots. We blacks have a heritage too. Oh, ours is not the heritage of mansions, magnolias, drawing rooms and slaves as servants. Ours is the terrible heritage of the brutality of slavery. History? We blacks have that too. Ours is a dark and tragic history of abuse by whites in America and our fight for Civil Rights against the George Wallaces and the Bull Connors with their attack dogs at the bridge in Selma, Alabama. Or, have you forgotten so conveniently?"

"Pull the flag down! Pull the flag down!"

"You white bigots murdered our race's greatest hero, Dr. Martin Luther King, for no reason other than he dared to tell the world about repression of black people by the white Southerner. What a terrible night. The hotel balcony in Memphis. The crack of a rifle. Dr. King falling mortally wounded. I was a young boy then, eleven years old. I asked my mother, 'Why would anyone want to shoot Dr. King, momma?' She was crying, too. 'Because white folks rule our land and rule us black people,' she answered."

I could hear low, plaintive moaning rising from the crowd. I could imagine their having linked their arms, closed their eyes and starting to sway as they moaned. "Killed our leader! Killed our leader!"

"Yes, they killed Dr. King, but I say to the white racist Southerner, 'You can't kill all the black people. There are too many of us. And now we have the kind of power you've never had to deal with before. Political power, the power of rage and the power of fear. Yes, at last you're afraid of us and we no longer are afraid of you. That damnable flag will come down.' "

"Pull the flag down! Pull the flag down!"

"We'll try using the law first in our efforts to get the flag down, of course, Mr. Stoney Bedford is leading the white efforts to keep it flying, and, I must say, he is powerful and fearless. And his heart is in this fight. But, if

Bedford stands too fearlessly in our way, if he won't step aside gracefully, he will rue the day. We have harsher methods to remove those who won't yield to us. Like most white bigots, Bedford thinks we blacks are an inferior race. In wars like this one, even the mighty fall."

I read between the lines. The plans for violence seemed perfectly obvious to me. I'd be wise to step aside . . . if I didn't I'd rue the day . . . if they had to, they'd use harsher methods to remove those who won't yield to the demands . . . even the mighty fall.   I felt a coldness down my spine!

A different chant broke out. "Bedford Hates Blacks! Bedford Hates Blacks!"

"Are you listening, Stoney Bedford?" Tolman asked. "Are you listening?"

"And now, brothers and sisters, I want you to listen to another fearless black leader, Abdul Karim. He'll tell you why Police Chief Dennis Crowe must resign. Or face the consequences."

Carl Chumley started talking. "Heard enough Stoney?"

"Too much I'm afraid. What they're saying is scary."

"Yeah, Stoney. It's plain that these people mean business. They're in no mood to compromise."

"I'm not either, Carl."

"There are many of us you can count on, Stoney. We'll stand with you. But you are the focal point, I think they somehow know that they've got to get rid of you."

"Getting rid of me. That came across loud and clear," I said.

"I'm worried about your safety," Carl said. "And about William and that gracious lady, Donna Elaine."

"I am, too, Carl. Tonight, William and I are sitting down together tonight to plan our strategy. We're not foolish enough to think that this flag controversy is going to blow away. We plan to stay alive, and, we're tough enough to do that."

I walked into the kitchen to prepare a cup of coffee. While the water was heating, I gulped down a large glass of water. Sometimes, the water helped me to relax.

Ten years ago, New York Senator Daniel Patrick Moynihan, our greatest public philosopher, and certainly no racist, said it best. "The central conservative truth is that it is (a people's) culture that determines the success of a society. The central liberal truth," he goes on to say, "is that politics can change a culture and save it from itself." (Or so the liberals ardently believe.)

I poured hot water into my cup, then added instant coffee as I tried to sort through things.

Conversely, Senator Moynihan, when the political process pliantly surrenders and goes along with efforts by one culture to destroy a society, as we are currently witnessing, that society is a willing accomplice to its own destruction. It's so tragic to see hundreds of thousands of our citizens falling prostrate at the altar of self-imposed guilt.

The opposing forces in the cultural war between white and black people had sent out their patrols to probe each other's lines here in tiny Forest, Georgia. What happens here is a portent in microcosm of things to come.

Cannot someone sound the alarm, as did Paul Revere? I had decided that only a few citizens were listening and that fewer still understood. Most whites have been intimidated into hiding behind thin fences of rationalization. The lanterns we tried to hang in freedom's belfry were crashed to earth by howling mobs. Those of us who rode through the countryside to sound the alarm and tell of the enemy's coming were pulled from our mounts, called racists, and stoned.

CHAPTER 9

Morris Light and his assistant had moved into the spare bedroom upstairs after the rally on city hall lawn. "Try not to notice our being here," he told us. "While the cameras are rolling, we never want you to be conscious of it. We'll be as inconspicuous as possible. Just go about your routines. And be natural. We're not looking for actors and actresses."

"As far as we're concerned," Donna Elaine told him, "you're members of the family. We want you to act as though you're at home. Have your meals with us. Help yourself to anything in the refrigerator. If there's something you need that you can't find, just ask for it."

Before William and I got home, the documentary maker and his camera had accompanied Donna Elaine to church, then followed after her as she checked on two of the new families our church's Women's Missionary Union were helping through some difficult times.

"You Bedfords are just good people through and through, what I call 'real,' " Light said to me later. "My camera is going to tell that side of the story as well as the uglier details of what is happening. And what is likely to happen. Blacks also have their side of the story, which must be told through their words and actions. It will reveal just how they feel about whites, the flag and why they feel that way."

His words emphasized the darker hues that might be smeared onto the unfolding canvas of our lives before this conflict was resolved. I was caught up in one of those "lost causes" for which Southerners had always been willing to fight, sacrifice and sometimes die. It was the way I was made up. I had not been able to find a way out.

Light was methodical as well as inventive. "I've also located some wonderful Civil War footage in old movies about Gettysburg and Pickett's charge up Cemetery Ridge, the opening shot of the great conflict with the shelling of Fort Sumter, General Lee's surrender to General Grant at Appomattox and other footage to help flesh out the story," he said. "I've charted out the entire story as I see it now. But this thing is running off in directions I'd only imagined. There's no telling what lies ahead. But, it's exciting."

"There's no telling what lies ahead . . ."

I would have laughed if I hadn't been so tied up in knots, both mentally and physically. I wasn't my usual, easy going self, not by any means. That evening, William and I relaxed over our martinis and watched the evening news. What we saw did not contribute to our sense of well-being. *BAC's* reporter in Forest sneered as he showed DeLong Tolman and the marchers, then cut to Abdul Karim and his coldly efficient reasoning for combining both the removal of the Confederate flag with the firing of Police Chief Dennis Crowe.

There was not too much levity over dinner. None of us seemed hungry. I found myself staring into space, reviewing the details of what had brought us to this point and wondering if my family and I were really standing in harm's way.

After dinner, William, Donna Elaine and I retreated to the library to size up the situation and try to get a handle on what we had to do to get through this controversy and stay alive.

"Dad," William said. "I've got an uneasy feeling over this whole thing. People are angrier than I've ever seen them. Feelings are running high. We may not be as safe as we think, here in this house, in this secluded neighborhood."

I watched my son unfold his tall frame from the deep wing back chair and walk to the tall, floor-length windows to watch the rapidly falling darkness. William was creative director of the town's biggest advertising agency. He could sketch in quick broad strokes the illustrations of his ideas, write the advertising copy and do the voice-overs for television commercials. But his most highly paid skill was his ability as account executive for the agency's three largest advertising clients.

"That son of yours can charm a bird out of a tree," William's partner in the agency, Brad Huie, was fond of telling me and William's mother. "He's as smooth as silk. I've never seen a person he couldn't get along with. When people leave William's company, they always seem lifted up."

"William," Donna Elaine said. "I'm worried too. You need to hear this story. Six of us women from the church went to lunch today at the Hilltop Restaurant, and, well, it was exciting. But I wouldn't say it was a pleasant, relaxed occasion. At least, not the kind I prefer."

"Let me guess," William said. "To most people, Dad is a hero, but they're worried that someone might try to kill him."

My wife winced. Somehow, William's words seemed out of place in our quite large library whose walls were lined with books and paintings. The two soft couches, several deep chairs and the fireplace made it the most comfortable room in the house.

Donna Elaine was not exactly relaxed and happy. "How did you know that that's the same thing several people told me today in the supermarket and at the church. It made me so nervous and tense. I came home and went for a long walk. And, I walked fast. It helped some, but not enough."

"Could we be over reacting?" I asked. "I mean, we're caught up in an emotional issue and are being whirled around in a web that won't let us go. That's hardly a position from which we can be objective."

"Dad," my son said. "We know each other too well to be playing games. Just look at your face. It's drawn and tense. That bright smile you usually wear is not there any more. While we were watching the news on TV, I drew this quick caricature of you. Here. Take a look."

The exaggerated sketch showed my broad, freckled face with a pinched look as though I'd been eating green persimmons. My flared nostrils seemed to be venting flames. The black hair was streaked with gray. There was a hint of a hollow under each of my high cheek bones. My blue eyes were narrowed to thin slits with dark circles under them. My wide mouth curled down at the corners. The face he had drawn even hinted at the freckles I detested. The caricature suggested the steel spring tension coiled inside me. He had caught the way I felt. Exactly.

"That BAC news report was just awful, Stoney." My wife's jaws were clenched, her face drawn. "They cast you into a role of intolerant bigot and that's not the way you are at all. And the other networks did about the same thing."

"What you've been saying doesn't make you a bigot in most eyes," William said. "Your voice may have been fiery when you were debating the issue, but yours was an impassioned, reasoned defense. But no Southerner ever gets a break in the national news media; unless he's taking a stand against everything we believe in. Then, they play him or her up to be a hero or heroine, one who speaks only the truth."

I walked to the windows to look out onto the front yard. A southeast wind rippled through the leaves of the ancient live oaks. A blue jay darted at a squirrel who had dared invade his territory. And he was doing it with raucous cries. The media were the squirrels who had encamped in my territory and there seemed to be no way of rooting them out.

91

"The local media," I said, breathing deeply. "They do the same thing, and, if possible, they're even worse than the national news media. They've inflamed the blacks deliberately, why, I don't know. Well, I don't know exactly, but I have my opinions."

Donna Elaine's words were clipped. "Stoney, you and I are leaving Forest at eight tomorrow morning to drive to Ames to see my mother. Both of us need to get away from the telephone, the newspapers, television. And from other people."

"I'd like that," I told her. "I do need to get away from this rat race for a few hours."

"We'll spend the night and come home the next day," she said.

"Let's get back to some serious thoughts," William said. "Mom, both you and Dad know me well enough to know that I'm not paranoid, but common sense tells me we've got to plan our strategy to cope with whatever might happen in this war."

"You used the right words, William. It is war. A war between two cultures," I said. "The strategy. What'd you have in mind?"

"While you two talk," Donna Elaine said, "I'll call Mother to tell her we're coming. Then, I'm going to run over and check on Polly Edgell. She's just home from the hospital after angioplasty. Some of us cooked meals and carried them by earlier, but her poor husband, Gerald, looked absolutely helpless."

She opened the door, then turned back to us. "Morris Light and his assistant want to come in and film. Is it okay?"

"Sure," I said.

She disappeared into our bedroom.

"That's Mother for you," William said. "Always doing something for the less fortunate."

I remembered my conversations with the two preachers earlier in the day and shook my head sadly. "I asked for help today, but I didn't get it. I called Wash Washington and Blue Combs to see if they'd help us calm things down in the black community. Each of them crawfished out."

William stood up and pounded his right fist into the palm of his left hand. "After all the money and encouragement you and Mother gave those two. What about Roy Bester?"

"I fared much better with him. Bester told me he feared for my life. 'Karim and the others,' he said. 'They might kill you.' "

"He said that?"

"Yes, and Bester doesn't exaggerate things."

My wife walked back into the room. "I'm going now. I'll be home in about an hour. After I check on Polly Edgell, I want to run by and see if the Youngers got their electricity turned on. And if they've got food in the house. They're another one of the families down on their luck we're trying to help. Mr. Younger's been disabled and out of work for seven months."

"Be careful, Honey," I said. "Watch for anything out of the ordinary. Strange cars that might follow you too closely and for too long. Keep your car doors locked. Look around you before you re-enter the car. The usual things we've talked about."

A puzzled look flitted across her face. "Now that you mention it, I've noticed a car parked down the street for the last hour. About fifty yards away. It doesn't belong to any of our neighbors. I didn't think anything about it. That is, until you used the words 'strange cars.' "

William stood up quickly. "I'll go upstairs and use the night vision binoculars to check it out."

"Don't worry too much about me," Donna Elaine said. "I've got my .38 chief's special right here in my handbag." She patted her purse. "I can take care of myself. And I'll use my pistol if I have to."

"Good girl," I said and kissed her.

William came hurrying down the stairs. "There's a man in the car, Dad. He's using binoculars to watch our house."

"Well, I'll be damned," I said. "They may just be trying to intimidate us. Roy Bester may have known more than he told me when he said things were serious. This means we had better get on with our plans to take care of ourselves in any situation that arises during this controversy. The responsibility is ours, and ours alone."

"I want to run upstairs again," William said. "To make certain that the person in that car didn't follow Mother. While I'm checking it out again, why don't you call Chief Dennis Crowe. Explain the situation to him and ask for police protection. Or, whatever's needed."

I knew Chief Crowe's unlisted telephone number. "Dennis, this is Stoney Bedford. How are you?"

"Okay, Stoney. What can I do for you?"

"There's a fellow in a strange car parked down the street from my house watching our movements through field glasses. Probably the star light kind that can help you see at night."

"How do you know that?" Crowe bristled. I couldn't understand his attitude.

"My son William is upstairs now, watching the guy though a special pair of binoculars called night vision glasses. I want one of your officers to check out the man in the parked car."

"Gee Stoney," Crowe said. "I'd rather not get involved in this silly dispute over the flag, if there's a way it can be avoided. You know how touchy my situation is at present with Karim and the other Muslims."

"Dennis," I said. "A strange man in a parked car down the street has his field glasses trained on my house. Man, that's something that the police need to look into."

"Is he bothering you?" Crowe asked. "Has he threatened you?"

"Dennis, you know damn well he hasn't, but it just makes good sense to look into such a thing before something does happen. Now, how about doing your job, Chief Crowe?"

"Stoney, please understand my situation. If one of my officers checked this car out and its occupant was a black, Karim and his crew would have another charge against me. Hassling a black man just because he happens to be in your tony, exclusive neighborhood, sitting in a car, parked on a public street. There's no law against that."

William came back into the library.

"Hold on just a minute, Chief."

"The occupant of the car is a black man, Dad. He's still watching our house through his field glasses. He has a gun on the seat beside him. I watched him pick it up and look at it. He checked to make sure there was a bullet in the gun's chamber."

"Chief, the man has a gun on the seat next to him."

"Stoney, there's no law in Georgia that makes it a crime for a person to have a gun in plain sight on the front seat of his car. Call me back in an hour if he's still there." Crowe hung up the phone.

"Well," I said to William. "The chief refuses to have one of his officers check the man out. How about that kind of an action out of a fellow whose hide I tried to save at council meeting the other day?"

"Looks as though Chief Crowe has been brow-beaten and intimidated by Karim and his crowd. When it comes to saving their jobs, some people will do anything, including compromising away their principles."

"He's afraid of losing his job, William."

"Dad, isn't it time we got rid of the roses and grasped the thorns in this situation we're in? I'm afraid, too. Afraid that some of the Bedford family might lose more than a job. Our lives, for instance."

The way the controversy was escalating frightened me too, but I knew that now the situation was out of my control. Still, I wanted to go as slowly as possible. "Maybe we're blowing this thing way out of proportion, William. Making a mountain out of a mole hill."

"Dad, you know that's wishful thinking. No member of this family has a character trait like that. Above all, we're realists. Now let's talk about what we must do to take care of ourselves, whatever happens. I went shopping today. I bought another pair of night vision binoculars for you. I've got the field glasses and some other things I bought in the trunk of my car. I'll bring them in."

I poured myself a glass of orange juice and gulped it down to give me some quick energy. The nervous excitement was robbing me of the zip I needed to assess our situation.

William returned with several packages. "Here's your set of binoculars, Dad. And I bought each of us a bulletproof vest, including one for Mother."

"You did?" I was startled. "Bulletproof vests. Damn! That's scary, son."

"Lots of things are happening that scare me, Dad." He handed me one of the vests. "For a while until some of this tension eases, I think each of us should wear them from the time we leave the house until we go to bed at night. And as long as we have strangers watching our every move with night vision glasses, we'd probably better wear them while we're in the house during the evening."

The idea of sitting down to relax with my evening martini, wearing a bulletproof vest, seemed incongruous. "Wear them even at night when we're sitting around?" I asked. I was rubbing my hand over the vest. The steel under the fabric felt comforting to the emotions stirring far back in my mind. Some of my friends wouldn't have died in the war if they'd had one of these vests on when the snipers deadly bullets found them.

William was frowning at my reactions. "Especially in the house, Dad. If they come, they'll come at night and attack our house under cover of darkness."

"But William. We don't need to wear these things. All we have to do is to dial 911."

"Dad, when and if they come, the first thing they'll do is to cut our telephone lines and those of our neighbors. These people are mean, tough and smart. And they're used to fighting with guns—and winning."

"I never thought of the phone lines being cut."

"Dad, I have the opportunity to know some of the radical black activists up close. I should. There are three of them who work in our advertising agency. When you're kind to one of them, they consider it a weakness. They're suspicious, always wondering 'now, why did he do that?' "

"I try not to believe that, William," I said. "For if all of us think that way, there's no hope of bridging any of the racial gaps."

William was shaking his head, sadly, I thought. "People my age, and younger, have learned to live in the world as it is, not as we wish it could or would be," he said. "We accept the fact that younger blacks have been taught to hate whites, because supposedly, we cause all of their problems. They consider themselves in a state of undeclared war against people like me and you. Their one reaction to anything that doesn't please them is to yell 'racism' and try to reverse the action. Whatever it takes—words, influence, power, arguing, guns—they use what weapons they need and plunge into actions without thinking."

My son had been thinking about this controversy on a detailed scale. "I had starlight scopes mounted today on our two 30.06 rifles and my .357 Magnum and laser sights for our Glock automatics and your long-barreled .38 pistol. Tomorrow, I'm picking up a Glock automatic pistol with a laser sight for you and one for Mother. If they attack, we'll need to see and kill them and we'll need lots of firepower. You can bet they'll have automatic weapons of all kinds the latest. I also bought 500 rounds of ammunition for each of the guns."

The enormity of the situation had suddenly hit me with the force of a wrecking ball and I was fighting my sense of inadequacy and regret. All I wanted was peace, but the challenge that would lead to violence was real. William was trying to make me see that it had come down to "them" or "us" and that the choice was obvious. A Southerner views everything that happens to him or family members in terms of personal challenge.

It was now a matter of honor. I heard the faint sounds of the drums and the bugles at Gettysburg, the bursting of shells, the crack of rifle fire and knew that William and I had to take the high ground and hold it at any cost.

I had been reluctant to accept the challenge, but the gauntlet had been thrown down at my feet. At that moment I knew I had to pick it up.

I became conscious of the bright lights Morris and his assistant were using as they filmed and recorded our actions and words. "Is our story coming together, Morris?" I asked

"I'm excited," the filmmaker said. "It has everything in it. I couldn't write a better script than the natural one that's unfolding before us. I appreciate the way you've let us blend into this controversy and scarcely noticing that we're here with our cameras."

I turned to my son. "William, you'd better fix us each a drink while I absorb all of this . . . this . . . this new equipment you've bought for us. Night vision binoculars, bulletproof vests, laser sights, starlight scopes, Glock automatics. Are things really that bad?"

Immediately, I regretted asking such a foolish question.

"Dad," he said. "While I fix us two bourbons and water, you go upstairs and use these glasses on that man in the parked car a few yards away. Ask yourself why he's there; why he's got his binoculars trained on our house; why that pistol is on the seat beside him? Then, come back and tell me what you think."

The unknown man was still there in his parked car, the gun still on the seat beside him, the binoculars glued to his eyes as he constantly scanned the front of our house, the downstairs, the upstairs, the back yard, the shrubbery. Then it hit me. I turned the glasses in the other direction and scanned the street. Damn. There's a car parked on the street to my right, a few yards away. No, it's not one of our neighbor's cars. Our neighbors don't park on the street and sit in their cars after they've parked them. I zoomed in on the car with the glasses. The man was sitting on the front seat, field glasses trained on our home. I could see the sawed-off shotgun on the seat beside him. He was black.

When I got back downstairs, William handed me a tall, frosted glass. Bourbon and water. "Convinced, Dad?"

"I'm convinced, William. Guess what? There's another car up the street in the opposite direction. Its lone occupant is a man with field glasses trained on our house. And, the gun on the seat beside him is a sawed-off shotgun."

William whistled. "Son-of-a-bitch! This makes the cheese more binding. That's a murderous weapon. It'll really blow a person away."

"In TV programs, when they fire such a weapon, it looks like an artillery blast."

"That's why we have to make extraordinary efforts to stay alive. Okay. Mom, you and I, the three of us, each have permits to carry a concealed weapon. Each time when you and I leave the house, we'll wear our bulletproof vests. Mother, she'll have her pistol, but no vest. They're not likely to kill a woman in broad daylight."

"Your mother is a brave and courageous gal, William. And she's a fighter when that's the only way out."

"But I'm really worried about her safety, if and when they open fire on our house."

"I hate to think of it." My voice broke. I struggled to regain my composure. "I'm going to try every option that might be available to us for solutions with honor; things that might calm all parties in this controversy down to a level where we can discuss things on a rational basis."

"The only thing they'll listen to is a complete and unconditional surrender," William said. "I don't know about you, but I've reached the point where that's no longer an option for me."

My stomach tightened into knots; my muscles tensed like piano strings. Suddenly, I felt tired. Very tired. Our backs were to the cliffs. We couldn't retreat anymore. If you surrender too many of your principles, life becomes a dull, gray, meaningless fog that shuts out joy and happiness. There are times when death is preferable to the gray fog of surrender and retreat.

I dipped even deeper into my reserves of strength and forced my mind back onto our battle plans. "When they come, they'll attack from both the front and the rear of the house."

William was not afraid. His face was animated, his words swift and certain. "One of us must stay upstairs and serve as lookout all through the night. When the attack comes, the three of us will want to get upstairs immediately. Hopefully, with a warning from the lookout that the attack is coming, we can each be at our battle stations with our guns and ammunition."

"Wouldn't it be smarter for the three of us to start sleeping upstairs until this is over?" I asked.

"Yes, it would." He raised his arms to flex his muscles. He was so tall until he could easily touch the ceiling.

I thought of those men in gray at Gettysburg, attacking up the ridge in broad daylight, marching abreast in columns. All the Yankees had to do was aim their guns down the slope of the hill, fire, and watch the rebels fall.

They couldn't miss. God, how awful. Mowed down like toy soldiers. By the thousands. The death. The destruction. They couldn't take the high ground that day, and that was their only chance of victory. I wanted to cry. The distant sounds of the bugles, the muffled roll of the drums. But, when the attack came on the Bedford house, it'd be William, Donna Elaine and me holding the high ground. We'd not wither and fall away. By God, if they want a fight, let them come.

"When the attackers first come," William said, "I'll take a position in one of the dormers at the front of the house. If they reach the back yard, I'll run to the rear of the house and fire through our upstairs back windows. I'll have several openings through which to fight them off. I'll duck from one window to the other. You'll have to cover the three dormer windows on the front of our house. We'll have fully loaded guns at each station."

"I'm just not reconciled to the idea of Donna Elaine being exposed to dying when they attack." Fear's dark shadow was beckoning me into a dance. He was always out there, just beyond the circle of light. The fiendish bastard.

"Perhaps we ought to send Mother out of the city for a few weeks." He was rubbing the upper part of his left arm with his right hand, a frown on his face.

"Ah, Lord," I shook my head. "Your mother won't buy it. Family and staying together mean everything to her."

"She can hide in the inside closet, the one in the middle bedroom. We'll show her how to lie down on the floor in order to minimize the chances of gunfire hitting her."

I sipped thoughtfully at my drink, turning the battle plans over and over in my mind, picturing the battle stations. "William, we'd better have a Glock automatic at each battle station. And a rifle and a shotgun. Each of them should be fully loaded and ready to fire. And we need more ammo."

"I'll buy it tomorrow."

"Suppose they burst through either a door or window on the front or back of the house?" I asked.

"We'll install chains across the front and rear doors and all the windows across the entire front of the house. That's as much as we can do. We'll depend upon our firepower and our marksmanship to keep them at a distance. But, if they do burst through . . ." He was weighing the price we might pay. "I'll lie on the floor at the top of the stairs with one of the twelve-gauge shotguns loaded with buckshot. They'll never get up the stairs."

"What if they kill either you or me? Or both of us?" It was a painful question to ask.

He breathed deeply and paced back and forth for a few seconds. "Dad, I've talked this over with my fiancée, Julie. It's been difficult, because we both know they might just kill all of us. That's why they'll assault our house in the dead of night, hoping to catch us all together and asleep."

He was rubbing his arm again and looking off into space. "I'm not going to buy the idea that they'll win and exult over our dead bodies." His jaws were clenched, his chin jutted out. He swallowed and his Adam's apple bobbed up and down.

"Both Julie and I are planning for me to be alive for our wedding in July. She's buying her trousseau. The invitations are going out. The bridesmaids' dresses are being made. We've chosen the songs to be played and sung at the wedding and made our reservations for our honeymoon. We've had some good times talking and planning for the day we'll be married."

I placed my left hand on his shoulder and stayed silent.

"I've read enough to know that if you go into battle thinking you might die, then, chances are you'll be killed," he said. "Dad, you know that's true. From your own war experiences."

"I remember the devils of fear before the battle started, William. But once it starts, you become a fighting machine. You do what's necessary to kill the enemy."

"When they attack . . ." He looked at me. "You notice, I'm no longer saying 'if' they attack . . .' " He was pacing the floor again. "Each of us will be wearing our bullet proof vests. Both you and I are skilled marksmen. And fear has never been a part of my personality, Dad, thanks to the way you and Mother raised me. And I know damn well, you're not afraid."

"Let me play the devil's advocate, William. What if they break through and get upstairs?"

"It'll never happen, Dad. Never." He was rubbing his left arm again. "Our twelve-gauge automatics and Glocks are deadly weapons in close-range fighting. When the red dot of that laser sight is on a person, about all you have to do is pull the trigger and 'Bang.' The attacker's gone."

He paused to moisten his lips. "If they kill me at the back, it'll be up to you to keep them from getting upstairs. I figure, at the most, they'll have only seven minutes before the police get here. Perhaps only five."

"Seven minutes? But you said the phone lines would be cut. How would the police know?"

My tall son smiled. "I bought something else for us today. Three cellular telephones, one for each of us. You can't cut a cellular phone line."

My confidence was returning. "William, that's brilliant. You have any more surprises?"

"Yes, a big one. Tomorrow, I'm having something special delivered to our home here. These nights when I couldn't sleep, I mapped out our plans to stay alive to the last detail. At least, I hope I've done my homework."

"The surprise, William."

"I have a friend who owns a welding shop, Dad. He's taking three long steel tanks and cutting them apart with a blowtorch, dividing each of them into two halves. They make natural armor for each battle station."

"Like an army pill box?"

"Yes. We'll place one for each of us at the dormer windows in front, one at the back windows, one for mother as she hides in the closet and one at the head of the stairs." He laughed. "I don't think they'll have enough fire power to penetrate our steel shells. The only part of us that won't be protected is our backs, and we have to depend on each other to keep them away from our flanks."

I turned to Morris Light and his assistant a few feet away in the darkness behind their bright lights. "What do you think, Morris?"

"Makes me very proud of both of you," he said. "It also tempts me to jump into the middle of this thing and fight alongside you. You are brave people."

"Insane, maybe?" I laughed.

"As you pointed out the other day, Stoney," Light said. "Too many people have forgotten the principles that have always been more important to Southerners than almost anything else. In the cultural war in which we're engaged, and make no mistake about it, we are fighting a cultural war, the easiest course for any of us is to cover our intimidation and cowardice under a veneer of rationalization and sophistication."

"I know my stance makes me an object of ridicule in many places," I said.

"When your detractors talk about people like you," Light said, "they explain you so conveniently by saying, 'Oh, he's living in another century, fighting a war that's been over for more than a hundred years. It's sad, but you have to overlook people like him."

"Then, they laugh and refill their cocktail glasses. You and I—and William—we're not 'sophisticated' in the way the word is used to denigrate us. That's why liberals and the media hammer at us each day. And, sadly, that's why so many of our young people here in the South no longer care about what happened between the North and the South in the 1860s."

"What will you be doing when all the shooting starts?" I asked. "You certainly don't need to be here with us." Standing next to William, Light seemed even smaller than he was.

"I'll mount surveillance cameras and microphones all over the inside and outside of the house," he said. "And on the trees in your front and back yards. That way, I'll have all the action on film. Along with most of the voices and other sounds."

I turned to William. "I'm glad we're on the same side in this fight, son. I'd just never have thought of all of these things." I started smiling and nodding my head. "Of course, if the media knew we were preparing to defend ourselves, they'd yell that we were inciting violence. They'd have our heads on a platter."

"What does it matter, Dad? Those people don't like you and they want to see you eliminated, although they'd never come out and say it. I can hear them now, intoning in their solemn voices, 'Those who live by the sword. . .'Your friend Bester told you he thought they were planning to kill you."

"That's right. And I've never found Roy Bester to be an alarmist," I said.

"As for me," William said. "I like to be prepared to win any game I play. I learned that while playing basketball for the University of Georgia Bulldogs. Besides, I'm not planning to die in all of this. Julie Peel and I have planned our wedding on July 12th. I certainly want to be here for my own wedding."

"That makes two of us, William. I tell you what let's do. Since Chief Crowe is afraid to have his officers investigate these men in those parked cars, let's pull an end run on him."

"And just how do we do that?"

"I'll phone my friend Allen Hart who lives a few houses away. One of the cars is parked in front of his house. I'll tell him to phone 911 and report these two cars. Chief Crowe won't know it's happening, so he can't instruct the officers to ignore the call. They'll investigate Allen's complaint about those strange cars and their occupants."

"Do it, Dad. It'll be fun to watch what happens."

We trained the night vision glasses on the suspicious cars. Within five minutes after I called Allen Hart, police cars, each with two officers, their lights flashing, came from opposite ends of the street and converged on the two vehicles. As the two officers approached the car parked to the north of us, gunfire broke out. One of the officers fired both barrels of a sawed off shotgun. You could hear the windshield shattering. There were no more shots.

I looked to the south to see what was happening at the other mysterious car. The man who'd been inside had gotten out of his car and was standing with his hands on the side of the vehicle as the officers searched him.

In the distance, ambulance sirens wailed. "Let's go down there and see what happened, William."

The anonymous watcher who'd been in the first car and had opened fire on the two officers was dead. Most of his face was missing. The ambulance attendants put him onto the stretcher, covered him completely with a white sheet and loaded him into the vehicle. They drove off.

I put my hand on William's shoulder. "Let's get back to our home, William," I said in a low voice. "I see the TV cameras coming. I'd better not be here."

We scurried home.

Fifteen minutes after the neighbors had dispersed and left the scene, Donna Elaine drove into the garage. I could hear her talking to someone. Soon, the door opened. She walked into the house, accompanied by two small girls.

"Stoney. William. I want you to meet these two pretty little girls. This is Janet Younger. And this one is Phyllis Younger. They're going to spend the night with us."

"I love pretty girls," I said. "Can I have some hugs?" They flew into my outstretched arms. "I'm glad you've come to visit us. Would you like a coke?"

"And some cookies?" Donna Elaine asked.

"Oh yes," Janet said. "We're hungry. We've had nothing to eat all day. But, we'd rather have a sandwich and some milk."

"Well, young ladies," William said. "We can certainly accommodate that request. But, I bet you'd rather have pizza wouldn't you?"

"Oh, could we?" Phyllis said. "Could we?" She was six years old.

"Why, I'd like to carry two pretty girls like you to Pizza Hut," William said. "Let's go get into my car."

Their eyes were glowing. Both of them skipped out of the house, following William.

"That sweet boy," Donna Elaine said. "He's got a heart of gold." She turned to me, her voice sad. "The Younger family is in bad shape, Stoney. Financially, emotionally, any way you look at it. It makes me want to cry."

"Sometimes, we don't know how lucky we are, do we?" I put my arms around her and hugged her fiercely.

CHAPTER 10

Early the next morning, my wife and I drove away, heading for Ames, Georgia, eighty miles southeast of Forest. William had promised to drive Janet and Phyllis, the two Younger daughters who had spent the night with us, to school at seven thirty.

"Dad," William said before I walked out the door. "Your vest?"

I rubbed my chest and smiled. As we drove along, Donna Elaine read my OpEd piece that was on the *Ledger* editorial page. Bostwick had done what he'd promised to do and I felt good about it. I knew the words would cause a big stir throughout the city and that the telephone would ring all day. The television and radio people would want to talk to me, but I'd not be there. Secretly, I was pleased to be out from under pressure from the media, if only for a few hours. I needed relief from the tension and anxiety. I hadn't slept too well last night, but the skies were blue and the sun was shining brightly. At 8:15, the dew in the grass and undergrowth glistened in the sunlight.

My wife let the newspaper fall to her lap and looked up. "That's a great piece of writing, Stoney. It's clear, concise and powerful. People will be cheering for you again, and some will detest you and your philosophies even more."

She pushed the buttons to start an Andrew Kostelante tape of soft, romantic melodies. The violins began to work their hypnotic spell. "But today," she said, "we're going to forget the flag and all those angry people. We need to be alone, just the two of us. We need some time to ourselves; time to regain perspective; time to remember what's important in our lives; time to hold hands and fall in love again."

She reached for my right hand. If I had said anything at that moment, my voice would have broken and I would have cried. I glanced at her and thanked God for a wife so genuine, so lovely, so graceful. After a while, she pointed to the newspaper. "I see where that man in one of the cars parked down the street from our house was shot and killed by the police last night. That frightens me. And our poor neighbors . . ."

"You didn't need to know. You came home with those two little girls . . ."

For a while, she said nothing. She was biting her bottom lip. "I know it must have been bad. Tell me about it."

I told her how I'd asked Allen Hart to call 911 and what happened when the police showed up.

"The dead man had on an expensive double breasted suit, a white shirt and a red bow tie. That's the uniform of the Black Muslims."

She sighed and looked out the window at the countryside flowing by. "I love the coming of spring to this wonderful land." She waved her right hand in a big half circle. "There's a special magic about this time of year that makes a person feel as though they were waking up from a long winter's nap."

She grew wistful. "It was springtime when I met you, Stoney. Forty-six years ago. At the University of Georgia."

"How I remember that night, pretty girl. The Kappa Kappa Gamma sorority house. I almost didn't come to your sorority's spring formal, but something kept telling me to go. I shudder when I think that I almost missed meeting you."

"But you were such a big football hero, Stoney. All the girls were after you. I don't know why you chose me." She was being coy in her wide-eyed manner.

I laughed. "The moment I saw you, I knew I was going to marry you. Without thinking, I started walking across the room toward you."

"My date was a little miffed until I explained to him that you were a stranger to me. But when you and I danced together—ah-h-h. It just felt right."

"The guy didn't like my dancing with you as many times as I did."

"He let me know about it in no uncertain terms. As a matter of fact, he got real unpleasant as he walked me back to the dormitory. I think perhaps he was a little jealous."

"You finally gave me your telephone number," I said. "But it was three weeks before you'd date me? Why?"

"Frankly, Stoney. You scared me to death. You were older. Then I found out you were a returned veteran of World War II. You'd been overseas in Africa and Europe. And in Chicago and New York, and I'd never been anywhere like that. You were what my mother called 'wise to the ways of the world.' I didn't think I was sophisticated enough to handle such things when we first dated."

"But you did handle things, and beautifully. I was shocked when you wouldn't kiss me on our first date. But, I was intrigued. Few, if any girls, had ever held me off like that."

"I didn't want you to think that I was that kind of a girl."

I chuckled. "When our son William hears us tell that story, it cracks him up. He can't believe it."

"Well," she said. "Things were different with our generation. Our innocence, our closely circumscribed codes of conduct. Much more different than William and his age group can imagine. Girls just held boys at bay. We were taught and trained that was the way a lady acted."

"Sometimes, I'm amazed at how different things are these days between William and others in his age group. The girls call him all the time. Not once did you ever telephone me. I had to do the calling."

She climbed onto her soapbox and I had to smile. She felt strongly about what she viewed as a sad state of affairs in modern day courtships.

"Tell you what I think, Stoney. Girls, even today, would be far better off if they let the guys do the telephoning, if they were far less aggressive. The 'Rules of the Game' protected both the boy and the girl as they explored the possibilities of establishing a relationship. But, that's not the way it is nowadays. William and his generation have new rules by which they relate to each other."

We drove along in silence for a short time. I was remembering those wonderful early days of our courtship and the struggles of our first few years of marriage. "I always felt bad about taking you out of college before you were graduated," I said. "I'm so glad I kept urging you to go back and get your degree. That mind of yours was too bright not to be put to better use than sitting around the house and letting it rust away. You needed challenges."

She laughed. "It really helped when we started our convenience stores. It gave me the self-confidence I needed to face some of the problems I had to solve. You were busy in other directions and you needed someone looking after our money who wouldn't steal us blind. We had to make every penny count in those early days."

"You were a Godsend, gal. There were many times during those early years that I didn't know whether or not we could meet payrolls and keep the business open. Marrying you and having you by my side, those were two of the smartest things this old boy ever did. The way you dealt with our bankers always amazed me. You had those loan officers eating out of your hand."

She was smiling. "We hung on for dear life those first four years. But then, things started falling into place. The business started growing. 'The harder we worked, the luckier we got.' Isn't that how the old saying goes? It wasn't easy. We earned everything we have. Sixteen hour days. Pinching every penny. Reinvesting in new stores."

"I count our blessings each day and thank the good Lord for watching over us. We've got enough money to give us that secure feeling. We can have the things we want. Yes sir. Life's been good to us. And my chief blessing is you."

She squeezed my hand. "Yes, sweetheart, I thank God daily for the blessings he's poured out on us. I thank him for you, for William, for our home, for our church, for our friends, for our good health."

I looked at my watch. "It's about time for coffee. Let's stop at Leslie's. We always see some of our friends there."

Leslie greeted us warmly. He hugged my wife, then turned to me. "Stoney, I hope you noticed that flag pole out front and the Confederate flag. It flies there each day."

"It's the thing I look for when I turn off the expressway and drive into your parking lot."

Two wizened little ladies in hats, obviously 'old Georgia matriarchs,' approached our table. I stood up to greet them. "Mr. Bedford, we are members of the United Daughters of the Confederacy and we just want to tell you that we need more Southern men of principle like you. We're praying for you."

"Thank you ladies," I said. "You do me great honor."

"We hope those angry people don't try to hurt you," one of the UDC ladies said. "But, when I see them on TV, study their faces and hear the tone of their voices, I'm afraid they just might try to do you in."

"We'll try and see that doesn't happen," I told them.

Mary Margaret was standing at the front door as we drove into her driveway. "Well," she said. "I thought you'd never get here." It was the same phrase she always used to greet our arrival.

After the older woman hugged her daughter, she turned to greet me. I patted the brown bag I held in my left hand. "I brought you something, Miss Mary Margaret."

"I hope it's what I think it is," she said.

I pulled out the Jack Daniel bourbon whiskey and rubbed the bottle's black label.

"It is!" Mary Margaret squealed. "It's my favorite. Let's fix ourselves a drink. And fix one for my friend, Notie, too."

I sniffed the odor of food coming from the kitchen. "Do I smell collard greens and ham hock cooking?"

"You do," the sassy woman with the deeply wrinkled face said. "And black-eyed peas and hot water corn bread. Notie knows what real Southerners like."

"What about me?" Donna Elaine pouted.

"You haven't been left out, young lady," her mother said. "Wait till you see that bowl of banana pudding Notie has fixed for you."

When I handed Mary Margaret's cook and companion a tall glass of bourbon and water, her black face gleamed. "Aw, Mr. Stoney. You know I ought not to drink that old whiskey."

"Notie, a lot of us do things we ought not to do, but somehow or other, I believe we'll make it to heaven."

"You sho nuff got that right," Notie said. She started toward the electric stove, moving her two hundred and eighty pounds with slow grace. "Come smell what Notie's cooking for you and Miss Donna Elaine."

She lifted the lid off the deep, black iron pot. The steam rose in a cloud. I moved close enough to smell the collard greens and ham hock. My mouth began to water. "Notie, it's a little bit of heaven. And are these the black-eyed peas?" I used a potholder and lifted the lid off a smaller pot.

"It sho nuff is" she answered.

Two large green bowls of banana pudding sat on the counter top. "I'm beating the egg whites right now so's the meringue will be high on those two bowls. Then, I'll slip them into a hot oven for just a minute in order that the ridges on the meringue will turn a deep brown."

I lifted my glass of bourbon and water. "A toast to Notie, one of the finest friends I have."

She lifted her glass and clicked it to mine. "Thank you, Mr. Stoney. You's my friend, too. For many, many years."

"Where's my Jack Daniel and water?" Mary Margaret yelled from the living room. "I've been waiting."

I hurried into the parlor and handed the tall glass to her. Her silver white hair and rouged cheeks reminded me of still life paintings of Southern matriarchs come to life and stepping from the frames.

"To good friends, good times, long life and the South," she toasted.

"I'll drink to that." We clicked glasses. "Notie's bringing you a cup of hot tea," I said to my wife.

"Stoney and I thought we'd take you out to eat," Donna Elaine said to her mother, knowing that it was a futile gesture.

"What? You think we're going to some restaurant and leave that good food Notie has cooked especially for the two of you?"

I smiled. That woman had the grace and charm of bygone days, days where life seemed to move more slowly and more gently than today's frenetic pace of living.

"Besides," Mary Margaret said. "I don't want to leave my drink and my soaps. At 12:30 each day, Notie and I sit down and watch the soaps on TV. They're exciting. They make us laugh or cry. And sometimes, we get mad as hell at them wicked women and mean men. All time slipping around on their wives or husbands, shacking up with somebody they shouldn't be rolling around with. And there's one fellow that's been beating his wife. We keep yelling at her to get a shotgun and blow his head off."

We ate until I was so full I was about to pop. It was the company, the food, the drink. By two o'clock in the afternoon, all four of us were asleep in the big deep chairs in the parlor.

"Mother," Donna Elaine said as we shook ourselves awake, "I believe you snored the loudest." She laughed.

"Hmpfh," her mother said. "I offer no apology. When I'm happy and relaxed, especially after a couple glasses of bourbon, I really sleep good."

"Come the evening," I said, "and the television network news, we'll have some more of that good bourbon, Mary Margaret. And you too, Notie. We're here to visit and have a good time with people we love."

That night, Donna Elaine and I slept in the feather bed she'd slept in as a girl. As I waited for her to cleanse the make up off her face, I studied the framed pictures hanging on the wall and those sitting on the dresser and chest of drawers. One of them, I especially loved. It was Donna Elaine when she was a pudgy little girl of three in her bathing suit and Mary Jane shoes. Her hair was short and bleached white from the sun. Under her left arm was a Raggedy Ann doll.

In the center of a grouping of pictures on the bedroom walls was the wedding picture of Donna Elaine and me. It had been taken in a flower garden. I couldn't help saying out loud the words, "What a beautiful woman." In my tuxedo, I stood at least fourteen inches taller than the petite woman standing beside me. November 30th, 1948. She was nineteen. I was twenty-three. The years since then had been such wonderful years.

I tried to peer through anxiety's curtain as I wondered about the days that lay ahead for us.

CHAPTER 11

We should have stayed in Ames with Donna Elaine's mother and Notie. The world there had been a far more peaceful one than that to which we came home.

It was detailed in the *Ledger*. The anger of the black people in Forest was bubbling like a cauldron of witches' brew and the media seemed to delight in stoking the fire and stirring the pot. Searching through the darkness of ancient hatreds for rhyme or reason was like looking for four leaf clovers in the fast growing clumps that spring brings. The wall that prevented communications between blacks and whites seemed to have grown even more impenetrable in the last two days.

"Police kill Black Man on White Neighborhood Street," trumpeted the headlines. The stories hinted strongly that the man had been killed only because he had the temerity to be sitting in a parked car on a street in an exclusive white neighborhood.

The *Ledger* quoted Abdul Karim. "If the truth be known, our brother was brutally murdered on orders from Police Chief Dennis Crowe. The murder took place only a hundred yards from Stoney Bedford's palatial home. Crowe was probably returning a favor he owed Bedford for sticking up for him at the recent city council meeting. It is well known from his public statements that Bedford hates blacks. And in Forest, white people don't want blacks in their exclusive white neighborhoods at any time of the day or night, regardless of the reason. And this is supposed to be a free country. That's laughable. The sad fact of the matter is that only white people can walk the streets safely these days."

When a reporter leaves out certain elements of a news story, it gives readers an entirely different slant to what actually happened. The article did not say that two cars had been parked on the street for days and that the occupants had night vision field glasses and weapons. It did point out that an Alan Hart had phoned 911 and had asked that the strange cars with their male occupant be investigated.

"All citizens are entitled to police protection," Hart was quoted as saying. "The unidentified man in the car fired on the two policemen first. I saw it happen; I heard the sound of the shot.

"There was no deliberate plot for the shooting of a black man, other than possibly by those in the group to which he belonged who exercised authority over the unknown men in the two cars that were parked on our quiet street. Perhaps their leaders knew the possibilities were high that something like this would happen. I certainly did not know why the two automobiles were there. I did not know the men in the automobiles were watching my neighbor's house through night vision glasses and that they were armed. When I did become aware of them, I wanted police to investigate. It was their duty to investigate. It was only right that they did."

"A plain citizen called 911," Chief Crowe told the *Ledger* and the TV and radio stations. "I had no knowledge of the call. I was at my home watching TV when the duty officer phoned me and related what happened. Any citizen has the right to ask our police to investigate suspicious things on the streets of their neighborhood."

Karim and DeLong Tolman saw it differently of course. Karim was further quoted as saying: "That these things happen to black people in neighborhoods like the one in which Bedford lives has come to be expected. It springs from their love of the Confederate flag and the prerogatives with which they think their Southern history endows them. Damn their culture and their vaunted heritage. Damn them for finding in their cast of mind reasons to abuse and even kill black people."

I read the stories in the *Ledger* and shook my head sadly. Don't reporters and editors see that black leaders such as Karim and Tolman have a hidden agenda. What these two said was a smoke screen that attempts to hide their real motives. Black leaders select only those things that will strengthen their cases and give them more power in the political arena. Then, they twist and distort those selected half-truths into verbal battering rams to use against opponents. They see nothing wrong in doing such things. To them, it's just a game, albeit a deadly serious game. Much like "king of the mountain" which each of us had played when we were kids.

I dreaded it, but it was necessary that I listen to the calls on my telephone answering machine. The number of telephone calls from people who wanted me out of the way had grown considerably. Some accused me of killing "a soul brother because you didn't want him in your neighborhood and certainly not parked close to that big home of yours."

There were four death threats. One in particular made my blood run cold. The voice was flat and rustled like a rattlesnake shaking his warning rattles before striking. "Your days are numbered, Bedford. We're coming for you, your wife and your son. The police can't stop us. There's no place for you to hide. The time? We'd never tell you exactly. We want the fear of not knowing to choke you."

After listening to that call at least three times, I had to fix myself a cup of fresh coffee to get the kick of caffeine to lift my mood. You damn right such calls scare me. My wife? My son? They were innocent. That didn't make any difference in this frenzied whirlwind *that had now taken on a life of its own.*

Noblesse Oblige. All the good things we Bedfords had tried to do to help the less fortunate. Those things didn't matter. Hatred and thirst for power make people blind to anything decent a perceived enemy has done. The Forest Rescue Mission that I chair, ministers to the sick, the hungry, the homeless and those down on their luck, be they red, white, yellow or black. Or just dark-skinned. We provide meals, beds for the night, clothes, shoes. We find them jobs and care for them until they can get back onto their feet. We secure medical treatment for them and furnish volunteer attorneys to help them out of legal jams.

I was feeling sorry for myself again.

I know that in the United States, and all over the world for that matter, it's no fun being a black person. But I console myself with how far we as a country have traveled, how whites honestly try to help minorities enter life's mainstream. Americans are a generous people, but good deeds don't make exciting news stories. It takes controversy. I paced the floor, angry at myself for letting my feathers be ruffled with such thoughts.

I was a man whose back was against the wall. *"Something evil this way comes."* The feeling wouldn't go away. Above all, I was a realist and used to facing and solving difficult problems.

Liberals preached that the money and help Southerners so generously give to the downtrodden, are shams, a cover up, a disguise to cloak our guilt for the black-hearted deeds of our forefathers. It was the white man's way of apologizing to blacks without saying the words.

Of course, it's a lie. I'll be damned if I was going to go willingly *into that dark night.* The thought shook me momentarily like a blast of wintry winds through a door that had suddenly blown open.

I turned on my radio to listen to Rush Limbaugh's radio talk show. He was saying, "You conservatives out there ought to know that you're not alone when you take a stand for traditional morals and the values that have made America great, despite what the liberal media repeat; day after day.

We're a free, capitalistic society, which rewards men in proportion to their willingness to work, save and invest—and live a decent life. There are millions of us and we're not going to go away."

Boy, those words helped me to feel a helluva lot better. "The liberals, the greedy freeloaders with their hands out, the media, they hate this show," Limbaugh pronounced." They'd do anything to discredit the conservative truths I reveal to my 20,000,000 listeners, but they can only rail, rant and write more bilge to try and brainwash America into socialism with its all-powerful central government."

I knew I was reaching deeply into the hidden depths of my soul, trying to shore up the door against fear, a door that was splintering by the hour as the assaults continued. I sighed and continued to try and rally my spirits. *It is difficult to contemplate one's own death.* The grim reaper in his black hood now lurked constantly out there, in the edge of darkness.

Thank you, Rush Limbaugh. As a free American, I am entitled to walk through this world with grace and dignity—and without fear. I am not going to run from this fight. In the far reaches of my mind, I heard the faint calls to glory, the distant roll of the drums, the notes of the bugle, the sounds of war. I was now holding the high ground. No enemy was going to dislodge me.

I was feeling low. I needed to talk to a friend, so I telephoned Harris Woolford at the college.

"Where you been man?" he asked. "I've called you several times. Things are getting even hotter. I think both of us ought to head for the hills and find a cave in which we can hide." He laughed sarcastically.

"That damned Victor Allen and the *Ledger*," I said. "Quoting the lies and distortions of Karim and Tolman. I don't mind telling you, Harris. I'm finding it increasingly difficult to maintain enough objectivity to keep my feet on the ground. They're rubbing salt into my wounds."

"Stoney, don't do anything irrational. We don't need any words or actions the other side can use against us. Don't forget that Able and I are in the boat with you."

"I'm dreading Tuesday's meeting."

"Who knows? Maybe we'll get enough votes to beat them," Woolford said.

"Can we change Lampkins' vote?"

Woolford laughed. "Able Erling and I have been pulling some powerful strings on Mr. Lampkins."

A faint wisp of hope floated through my mind. "What have you done?"

"Together, we visited the three biggest customers of Lampkins' office supply firm. They're even more rabid in their devotion to the Confederate flag than we are. Hell, they jumped to their feet and started cursing Lampkins for his vote the other day."

"What'd they do, Harris?"

"If you can contain yourself long enough, I'll tell you. While we were sitting there in their offices, they telephoned old Baxter. Claude DuPont yelled into the phone. 'Lampkins. You some kind of a damned traitor? Voting to introduce that damned resolution to ban the flying of our flag?' The other two customers were just as vehement. One told old Baxter, 'Cancel that $23,000 order I gave you the other day until you come to your senses.' Then he hung up the phone on Baxter."

I could tell Harris was enjoying this story.

He laughed. "I can guarantee you that Baxter Lampkins ain't gonna vote to pull down our Confederate flag, Stoney." He had said the words slowly and with great emphasis.

"Harris, I'm holding the phone and dancing around like a wild man," I told the professor. "That's the best news I've had since our last meeting."

"Able and I went to his house and drank a half bottle of good Scotch."

I grew fearful again. "You're sure that Lampkins *will* vote with us?"

"Phone Able. He'll verify it. Hell, you ought to know I wouldn't make up a story like this. As important as this issue is."

"Damn. You two guys deserve a medal."

"I've been lining up people who hold our same views to speak at Tuesday's meeting against that damned resolution," Harris said. "Your son, William, has three fireballs coming to represent the local chapter of the 'Sons of Confederate Veterans.' "

"William isn't coming, is he?"

"No, Stoney. That wouldn't be wise. But the three guys he's sending are all highly intelligent college graduates. And each of them is in business for himself. I've visited with them about what might be best to say. I think you'll approve."

"The TV people and Allen have been calling me for statements," I said. "I'm avoiding them. I'm not going to do it and I told them why I would not. They're not exactly happy with me."

"They've never been happy with you, Stoney. Call Able Erling and buck him up. He needs to hear from you. He's also been taking a real beating over the phone."

"Able? Stoney here. How you doing?"

"Okay, I guess. At least I don't have men in parked cars on my street watching me and my family through night vision field glasses. Damn. That shooting business was bad stuff."

"It didn't play too well with the people in this neighborhood, Able. They're angry at everyone. Even me and my family. They hold us responsible for what happened."

"Did Harris tell you what the two of us accomplished?"

"I'm still dancing in jubilation, Able. You think Lampkins will stay put? That he'll really vote with us?"

"He will if he wants to stay in the office supply business," Able said. "It's hard ball tactics, but it's something we had to do. He actually called me last night to tell me that he's going to vote with us."

"Can DeLong and his buddies come up with a way to buy him off?" I asked.

"They're trying," Able said. "I got a call this morning from my sources in the governor's office. Tolman called Governor Sackett to see if he couldn't get state office supply business for Lampkins. But, we've got that headed off. I had our Republican state representative phone Sackett and threaten to deprive the Governor of the votes he needed on vital issues in the legislature. Bill Tompkins told me that the governor was out of it."

Able was a consummate politician. "Able, that was a smart move. We owe you and Harris a vote of thanks. I needn't tell you that I've been down in the dumps. These death threats I've been getting over the phone do not exactly contribute to peace of mind."

"I don't mean to add to your troubles, Stoney. They may not be idle threats. You better take as many precautions as you can."

CHAPTER 12

I was in a party mood as I sipped my very dry martini with olives.

"Donna Elaine," I said. "You look so pretty tonight until I don't think I can stand it."

She laughed and squeezed my hand. We were sitting in our living room waiting for William to return. He'd gone to pick up his fiancée, Julie Peel. The four of us were going out for dinner.

"Now, Stoney," she said. "You must behave your bad self. But I thank you for the compliment. In this blue dress, I feel pretty. Of course, spending the afternoon at the beauty shop getting my hair done is always good medicine. It builds a woman's morale. Boosts her ego." She touched the right side of her short, dark hair.

"I'm glad that the two of us like to dress up when we're going out for dinner, Honey. I know we're swimming against this horrid casual tide that has swept the country, but I'm not going to surrender to it. Hell, a suit and tie makes me feel dressed up, like we're going out on a date." I sipped at my dry martini.

She looked at me and smiled. "I admire you for having the discipline to stay slim and trim all these years, Stoney. I know how you pride yourself on not having one of those beer guts ballooning out over your belt. Argh-h-h! They can make a man look, well, the kindest word I can come up with is 'grotesque.' "

"Such stomachs are fashionable nowadays, especially with young men. And if the man is a junior executive, it seems almost a necessity, a badge of his living good. A badge of status." I grimaced. "To me, they're a sign of self indulgence and lack of discipline." I reached for a salty pretzel.

"I wish we were going dancing, Stoney." A dreamy look came over her face. She closed her eyes and began swaying. "The cha cha; the rhumba; the swing. Oh, I love dancing with you. I just fade into another world." She laughed. "Not bragging, but, we *are* good dancers. Perez Prado. I hear his music. 'PATRICIA.' Ah-h-h! Don't wake me up. I'm dancing the cha cha. Now, I'm doing the chase. I love it!"

Donna Elaine was in a party mood, too.

I think the two of us started falling in love on the dance floor while we were college students. Her face told me she was still dancing. The familiar look of soulful disdain was there. She'd done that so many times at our college dances when the band was playing Latin tunes. It had captivated me. I remembered that special flair as she turned easily and moved her feet with intricate grace. It oftentimes drew applause from other dancers who'd stopped to gather around us on the dance floor.

"This chardonnay tastes so good," she said. "It's one of the rare privileges I allow myself when we're going out to dinner."

The lights in the room were soft. The paintings of elegant ladies in long gowns descending from a carriage in the soft glow of a street corner gaslight fascinated me. A painting of my childhood home with its two stories and white Doric columns hung on another wall. Memories of long ago added to the festive atmosphere.

"Remember the nights at college when I'd call for you at the Kappa Kappa Gamma sorority house and we'd walk across campus to the fraternity dance?" I asked.

"Weren't those great days," she said. "You in your tuxedo; me in my long evening gown. We danced till midnight and loved every minute of it."

"How does that song go? 'Those were the days my friend . . .' Our romance . . . The thrill of falling in love with you: . . It was an age of innocence. Most of us were too naive to be anything other that what we'd been raised to be, people bound by the decent, moral principles of our day."

She laughed and wagged her index finger at me. "Innocence? There were always a few scoundrels around, Stoney Bedford. And if a girl let down the barriers for one minute, well . . ."

"Yes, I knew two or three of those kind," I said. "Late at night, in our dormitories, they'd regale us with their imagined tales of sexual triumph. Even though we knew they were making up the stories, we hung on their every word."

We heard William letting himself and Julie in through the front door. Julie was radiant, a tall, slender girl with long black hair and brown eyes that showed her joy in living. She wore a simple black dress with a straight skirt. A gold leaf pin was fastened to her left shoulder.

"Julie," Donna Elaine said, hurrying to embrace her. "We're so glad to see you. You look stunning."

"And so do you, Mrs. Bedford." Her voice was golden honey, like a remembered passage from "The Sound of Music."

She turned to me. "And you, Mr. Bedford. You look, well, like you and Donna Elaine were ready for a Junior League fundraising dance."

Humming "Moonlight Serenade," I caught her around her slender waist and danced her around the room. She had the grace of a wild gazelle. She threw her head back and closed her eyes as we danced.

William applauded. "I can tell that this is going to be a fun evening," he said. "I feel good enough to go out in the back yard and howl at the moon."

It was always a shock to see how tall William really was.

"Dad, help me mix our drinks." He motioned with his head toward the bar in the den.

I knew he wanted to tell me something. He dropped ice cubes into the two glasses, poured in Tanqueray gin, dry vermouth and began to swirl both glasses gently. The low light glistened on the ice cubes.

"There are the olives and toothpicks," I said. "Over there with the cocktail napkins."

"My car was followed, Dad," he said, spearing olives with the ivory toothpicks. "To Julie's house, then back here. A long black car with dark windows. When we got back here, he parked down the street in about the same place as the dead man parked the night the police came."

I fought against the rising anxiety. My party mood fled. "I've got on my bullet proof vest," I said. "And I'm carrying my .38. What about you?"

He rubbed his hand across his chest. "And I'm wearing my '38."

"William, we can't let them frighten us into being scared rabbits. Your welder friend delivered the steel shields today. I had the men carry them upstairs and place them in the locations on which we'd decided."

"Have you outlined our plans to Mother?"

"Yes," I said. She listened calmly, asked several questions and said only that she hoped things wouldn't come to that."

"Did you tell her it'd be safer for her if she went to Grandmother Mary Margaret's in Ames for several days?" He placed the napkins around the bottom of each glass.

"She won't hear of it, William. She's adamant about staying right here. She reminded me that we'd been through many bad times together and that we'd go through this one together."

"Frankly, I was hoping she'd go," William said. "Things are escalating. I can feel them in the air." He shrugged his shoulders. "We could all be killed."

We walked back into the living room.

"I thought you two had forgotten us," Julie laughed.

"How are the July wedding plans going?" I asked Julie.

"The church has been reserved. I've ordered my wedding gown and have chosen the fabric and styles for my attendants' gowns. Mother and I decided on the invitations today and the printer will have them finished by Friday week." She turned to my wife. "Have you finished your list of those to invite to the wedding?"

"I have about six more addresses to look up," Donna Elaine said, "and our list will be finished. How many attendants will you have?"

I have decided on five of my dearest friends," Julie said. "Of course, I want my KKG roommate, Molly Heald, to be my matron of honor."

"And you, William?" I asked.

"I'll have three of the guys I played college basketball with and my partner in the ad agency, Blakely Furman, as four of those in my wedding party."

"Four?" my wife asked. "Who'll serve as your best man?"

"I want my dad as best man," William said.

I blushed and choked up.

"I hope you two don't mind," William said to his mother and me. One of the groomsmen from my basketball days is black."

"I certainly don't mind," I said. "A friend is a friend." I thought of Wash Washington and Blue Combs and sipped on my martini to hide my disappointment in those two.

"You know that neither of us will mind, William," his mother said.

I glanced to my left through one of the floor length windows that opened onto the narrow veranda. My eyes swept past the white columns, and I found myself straining to see beyond the edge of the darkness. It was a gentle spring night. Inside this room there were gentle people—and happiness. Out there, down the street, waiting in the darkness . . .?

"Let's mix another drink," I said to William. "Donna Elaine? Another glass of chardonnay?"

"No, Stoney. I haven't quite finished this one yet."

Once we were at the bar in the den, I turned to William. "Go upstairs and use the night glasses on the two cars," I said in a low voice. "I'll mix the martinis."

He eased up the stairs.

I noticed the musical tinkle of the ice cubes falling into the three glasses, wondered why bottles of Tanqueray gin were always green, read the label on the dry vermouth called Martini and Rossi, speared two olives on toothpicks for each of the three drinks *and waited.*

My son came back down the stairs, shaking his head. "I don't understand all I've seen dad. There are four women in each car."

"Women? That's odd."

"And I'd swear that two of the four in each car are white and the other two black."

'What do you think it means?" I asked.

"Two things," he said. "One, they're still trying to scare us, intimidate us or kill us. Two, they know the police won't shoot women. That is, not as readily as they'd shoot men."

I swirled the contents of my glass. "A funny thought just fleeted through my mind, William. Suppose the four people in each of those cars aren't women at all, but men dressed as women?"

His face paled. He sighed and said, "I suppose we'd better rejoin the women."

"What restaurant are we going to for dinner?" Donna Elaine asked.

"Well," William said. "I know we all like Italian food, so I made reservations at La Roma over in Marton."

"That's twenty miles away," Julie said.

"I think we'll have more privacy there," William said. "Dad's been on TV so much. Perhaps there, he won't be as readily recognizable and there won't be too many friends—or enemies—stopping by the table."

"Shall we finish our drinks and go?" I said. "I'm getting hungry. William, do you have your new cellular phone in your car?"

"Cellular phone?" Donna Elaine asked.

"Yes, Honey," I said. "We bought four of them yesterday. One for each of our cars, and one to keep here inside our home."

"Why would we need one inside our home?" my wife asked.

I tried to be casual. "Oh, just on the chance that our phone lines might go dead on us."

"Oh," my wife said. "I guess that makes sense, what with all of this ruckus that Karim and DeLong have stirred up."

"I want to make a phone call before we leave," I said. I went into my study and dialed my long time friend, Bob Rawls, the chief of police in Marton. I guessed he'd be at home this time of day.

123

"Bob, this is Stoney Bedford."

"Stoney. How you doing, fella? I've been reading about you and the Confederate flag. Don't back off, Stoney. Don't let them scare you."

"You can count on me sticking by my guns, Bob. Right now, I need a little help."

"What can I do for you?"

"William and his fiancée, Julie Peel, and Donna Elaine and I are going to drive to La Roma for dinner. There'll be four people in a long black car with dark windows following us. They might try using shotguns on the four of us on the highway."

"You mean they'd try killing you?" Rawls asked.

"That's what I mean, Bob. And I'm not being paranoid about this thing."

"I guess you're right, Stoney. I read about the man the police killed near your house the other night. That incident and what you're telling me tonight, sounds like you're dealing with people out to kill you all right."

"Bob, can you help me?"

"Hell yes, Stoney. What color and kind of car will you be driving?"

"A new black Cadillac DeVille. Four doors."

"One of my deputies and I will be waiting at the Marton city limits. You got a cellular phone?"

"You bet."

"Here's my car phone number, Stoney," Rawls said. "Telephone me from your car and greet me as an old friend. Just say you're on your way to La Roma for dinner. Let's see. It's 6:45 now. You ought to be at our city limits by say, 7:30 p.m.?"

"The timing sounds about right, Bob. What will you do?"

"We'll turn on our police car lights and stop them for—oh—exceeding the speed limit. I'll make them follow me to the jail to post bond to guarantee their court appearances."

"You'd better be careful, Bob. I'm certain they have automatic weapons and that they'll not hesitate to use them."

"We'll have two cars then. I'll use a bullhorn and make them exit their car. Before we approach them, I'll make them lean against the sides of their vehicle." Bob Rawls was a seasoned veteran of law enforcement.

"That should take care of the situation, Bob."

"What if they pull alongside you," Rawls asked, "and start blasting away before your car is close enough for us to spot you?"

"William and I both have pistols and I'll have a 12-guage automatic shotgun loaded with buckshot on the back floorboard. If they start pulling alongside, I'll run my window down and blast them with the shotgun."

"Seems to me you've got things pretty well figured out, Stoney. Does your wife know about this?"

"Yes, she knows. And we'll have to tell William's finance, Julie Peel."

"Will the women be armed also?" Rawls asked.

"Yes, Chief. One other thing. The four people in the car will be dressed like women, but we don't believe they're really women. We think they're men dressed as women to fool the police. Don't be fooled by their clothes when you do stop them."

"You can bet on that. I'll have our toughest woman cop in one of the cars. She takes no shit from anybody, man or women."

Five blocks from our house, William said, "We've got company, Dad."

I telephoned Chief Bob Rawls in Marton. "We're on our way, Bob. And they're right behind us."

"Okay, Stoney. I'll handle my end. For God sakes, please be careful. I don't want to attend your funerals."

"And I don't want to be the guest of honor at such an occasion," I said.

It would do little good for us to turn back for home. "Just drive normally, William, unless they pull alongside. If they do, we shoot first.

"Will someone tell me what's going on?" Julie said.

William told her.

"We're just trying to stay alive," I said, and I'm sorry you're caught up in this. However, all of our precautions might come to naught, so let's keep trying to have a happy evening together. Donna Elaine, you have the cellular telephone ready to go. If they start pulling alongside, dial 911 immediately." Most of the happy memories my wife and I had experienced earlier in the evening had long since fled.

"The long, black car's still back there," Donna Elaine said. "Long black car," she laughed. "Doesn't that sound ominous?"

Julie was not the least bit phased. "I'm enjoying this. It's exciting. I've got my small automatic in my bag. And I've been trained to shoot and shoot straight. Count me in when trouble starts." She removed the gun from her purse and pumped a shell into the chamber, then clicked on the gun's safety.

"Julie, I'm glad to know you carry a gun," my wife said." I do, too I've got my .38 right here. And, I'm ready to use it. If I have to."

"This is a tough old world we live in," Julie said. "People have to take care of themselves. Don't you two men worry about us?" She patted Donna Elaine on the shoulder.

"We could all be killed," William said. "They're still following us."

"Don't worry, sweetheart," Julie said. "You and I have already talked about this thing. I knew we were being followed when you picked me up and we started for your home. Then, when we drove away, I checked again in my side mirror. Those people back there are not out on the town just to have fun."

"Somehow or other," I said. "We men just don't like to think about women being exposed to danger. About their being killed. I guess it's old fashioned, but the way I was raised, men were supposed to protect women."

"William," Julie said. "If you are killed, most of my reason for living would disappear. So, we're in this thing together."

William checked the car behind us again. "They're maintaining the same rate of speed as we are, Dad. So far. If they try to speed up, I'll floor-board it. All we have to do is to get to the Marton city limits where Chief Rawls and his people are waiting."

I checked my watch. It was 7:25. Soon, the Marton city limit sign would be coming up.

"Uh oh!" William said. "They're speeding up. Fasten your seat belts." He showered down on the accelerator. "They weren't expecting that. They've fallen back. Temporarily. Now, they're beginning to gain on us."

We passed the Marton city limit sign. Bob Rawls and his two patrol cars were waiting. Their lights starred flashing, their sirens started wailing.

"Thank the Lord for a friend like Bob Rawls," I said. "For a while, we can relax."

"Unless the other car was following way back," William said.

We were having wine at La Roma and waiting for our entrees when Police Chief Bob Rawls sat down at our table.

"Stoney, those four in that car that followed you were bad customers. And all four of them were men, as you suspected. Each of them had automatic weapons. They're in jail and there'll be no bail until Monday when the judge gets back from his fishing trip. And they'll not be allowed to make telephone calls. We had to rough two of them up. Pretty good. They didn't want to obey the orders we gave them. Our gal cop enjoyed bashing their heads in."

"Thanks, old friend," I said to Chief Rawls. "You probably saved our lives."

"Stoney, did you say there were two automobiles of the same kind?"

"Yes. Why?"

"That second car was a half mile behind the first one. See those four at the table ahead of you and slightly to your left?"

"Yes. I see four women seated at the table under the La Roma poster."

"Watch this," Chief Rawls said as he stood up.

He walked to the cashier' stand, motioned to two men and a woman. Slowly and casually, Chief Rawls, joined by his three deputies, walked toward the table under the La Roma poster. Two of the officers walked past the table. Suddenly, Rawls and his three deputies placed pistols behind the heads of each of the four women seated at the table.

"Hands on the table, ladies," Chief Rawls said. "Please do as I say or we'll blow your heads off."

"What the hell are you doing?" one of the white-faced ones shouted.

"Shut up and keep your hands on the table," the chief shouted. The restaurant had grown deathly quiet.

Chief Rawls turned toward the customers seated at the tables. "These four are drug traffickers," he explained. "I hope you'll forgive the excitement and finish your meals. Go ahead. Eat and enjoy. The manager here has told me that waiters will be coming to each of your tables to serve red or white wine, compliments of the house."

The police officers disarmed each of the imposters. "How strange," Rawls said to the restaurant patrons. "Women with Glock automatics hidden inside their bras. But then, there was room enough for them, since these people are men and not women. By dressing as women, they knew the police would be less likely to stop them."

He turned to the imposters. "Each of you will have a gun to the back of your head as we walk out of the restaurant. It will be very nasty if you make any quick moves or try to get away." He turned to his three deputies. "Kill them if they make one false move."

The procession filed out. The four of us had survived another night filled with the prospect of dying and perhaps, dying quickly.

CHAPTER 13

Oh, the joy of that first taste of freshly brewed morning coffee. The aroma as the water drips through the dark brown grains awakes one of those associations buried deeply in the mind that activates a feeling of pleasure and anticipation. I confess. I'm hooked on coffee. I drink far too much of it, and vow to cut down. But then morning comes. Thoughts of that first cup drag me from bed early to satisfy the craving. Yesterday's resolve for greater discipline melts away.

All through the day, you can find me walking around with a partially filled coffee mug in my hands, and, to Donna Elaine's dismay, sloshing coffee onto the kitchen tile floor. I talk and wave my coffee mug at the same time, and after a while the spatters of brown liquid dot the floor. You'd think that sooner or latter, I'd learn better, but over the years, I still keep to this ritual.

It was not yet daylight. I could hear ducks calling to each other down on the lake behind our home. Through the years, some of them had stayed behind when the flocks returned north for the summer and had become almost domesticated.

Earlier, I had tucked my pistol into the pocket of my robe and walked down the driveway to pick up the morning newspaper. The events of the last few days had made me fearful enough to take such precautionary measures.

In the semi-darkness, I could feel the stirring of the southeast wind against my cheeks. The ghosts in the ancient, moss-draped live oaks whispered their legends to me. They would soon flee the coming of day. The birds were awake and singing loudly. They were as happy that spring was on the way as most of us humans were.

Before I ventured out the back door, I had stood in the darkness of our living room at the floor length windows with the night vision glasses glued to my eyes and searched the streets. There were no parked cars, no early morning walkers that I didn't recognize. The answer to the absence of strange cars parked on the street had to be that Karim and Tolman did not yet know about what had happened last night, though I found that difficult to believe.

William came down the stairs. "I need some of that coffee, Dad."

"Help yourself. It's there on the stove. You might need to heat it up a bit."

I scanned the first three pages of the *Ledger* quickly. No news stories about the Confederate flag, Karim, Tolman—or me. There was a letter to the editor about me and the flag. It called me "racist, prejudiced, uninformed, and ignorant."

"It took me a while to drop off to sleep last night," William said as he slid onto the bench by the table and sat his coffee mug down on a coaster. "Last night. That was quite an evening."

"What did Julie think about it?"

"Dad, Julie's always ready to fight anyone who tries to crowd her. Being an IBM computer salesperson has made her as tough as a marine drill sergeant when she's being challenged."

"Yet, she's still a lady."

"Her performance in computer sales never ceases to amaze me. It's a stark contrast to her background, especially when you know the fine old family from which she's descended—and her parents, brothers and sisters. Her mother embodies all the legends of evening shadows, moonlight and magnolias used to describe a Southern lady."

"I like that girl, William. You know the moment you meet her that all the breeding and training are there, just beneath the surface, as well as the steel in her spine. You can sense it."

I thought of John Updike's *Run Rabbit Run* and how starkly he portrayed Rabbit's almost immoral adaptation to the changing world. Julie Peel was a far cry from that furious, almost pathetic creature. "She has one foot in the old, gentle world, the other squarely in today's different world," I said.

"I'd agree," my son said. "Nowadays, women have a new role to play in the fast moving business world. She's just adapting the protective covering all of us need to defend ourselves against the daily, uncivilized assaults that have become standard in our society."

"You have to have a central grounding in character and stability to do that and still remain essentially the person you've been reared to be," I said, holding my coffee mug in both hands against the morning chill.

"This flag controversy that we're caught up in can't be happening. I keep telling myself that it's not real, but I know it is." He was obviously trying to penetrate to the central meaning of what was happening to us. He wasn't having an easy time. "Yet, those who are not close to what's happening to us, like last night, dismiss it as a bunch of silly children fighting on the school grounds."

"People often assume a stance of moral superiority and bay such empty phrases to any who will listen. They like to make such pompous judgments."

"A dozen times people have told me that if we'd just shrug our shoulders, turn our backs and keep quiet, let Karim and Tolman have their way, supposedly it'd all blow over."

"You don't believe that for one second, do you?"

He grinned at me. "No, Dad. If it wasn't this flag thing, they'd be crowding us on other things." He picked up the *Ledger* and glanced at the front page. "Nothing worth reading in this damned 'yellow dog journal.' " He put the newspaper back onto the table and picked up his coffee mug.

"You know the real reason whites and blacks are arrayed against each other, don't you?" I asked.

"Cultural warfare?"

"The conflict is deep, the division between us inerasable. The beliefs and feelings on both sides will not diminish. The rancor and bitterness they breed will grow and grow and grow until the resultant conflict involves the whole of the United States in revolutionary fighting between the races."

"The apocalypse perhaps?" He was scowling.

"Our way of life could vanish," I said.

William nodded his head in agreement. "Voices of reason are drowned out in hidden agendas. The deeper reasons for conflict are far bigger than anything you see on the surface. This thing about the Confederate flag is just a cover, a smoke screen for something far deeper."

The telephone rang. William jumped to answer it quickly, since his mother was still sleeping. He listened for a few seconds. "Who is this?" he demanded angrily. "You're gonna get us Bedfords? What the hell do you mean?"

I suspected the caller didn't give him a direct answer, but accused us of another bad action. "No, you're wrong. We didn't shoot the black man in his car. The police did." He slammed the receiver down and returned to the table.

He sat down again. "One of your 'fans' calling, Dad. Wouldn't give his name."

"Yeah. The threats are coming daily now," I said. "I try to be philosophical about it, but it's difficult." Philosophical? I was kidding myself. Worry and anger brought weird dreams each night.

My son pounded the table and stood up. "That Confederate flag is part of our history. Why can't Southerners revere it without hordes of people becoming militant and accusing us of all kinds of prejudice and bigotry? Everyone's yelling. No one is listening."

"Blanket condemnations of one's enemies is a new political technique," I said.

"Yeah. Make straw men out of those who oppose you, then run them through daily with verbal thrusts."

"But I can't see any way of quieting things down, short of running up the white flag of surrender. And damned if I'm going to do that."

William straightened his back and stood tall. "White Southerners must quit retreating. Sooner or later, we're going to have to dig in and fight back against these kinds of assaults."

He turned to look through the big bay window onto our back yard. "That tree out there," he said, motioning to the back yard. "The winds of winter stripped away its leaves, leaving it bare."

He was now an ad copywriter, creating pictures in his mind.

"I've been reading a book about General Sherman's 'March through Georgia' during the Civil War," he continued. "Like the winter winds, the book strips away the lies and bares the real reasons we fought the Yankees so long and with such fierceness."

He was rubbing the whiskers on his face. "Long before the war started in 1861, the Yankees wanted to impose their wills on the South. Today, in 1996, the blacks want to impose their demands on us, despite what we might want. Sherman was a mean, ruthless bastard. Many of his men raped our women, burned our homes, smashed furniture, looted stores, barns, smoke houses, drove our farm animals off to feed the Union soldiers. You name it, they did it."

"Sherman knew his business. The South was already mortally wounded, but he showed no mercy."

"If we ever have to go to war with the blacks, they'll do the same things to us that Sherman did on his march to the sea. Their pent-up rage will be let loose. They'll loot, burn, kill, and no telling what else."

"Yes, and it scares hell out of me." I paused to sip at my coffee. "That book must have been written by a Southern historian," I said. "And it would have to have been written many years ago."

"The author is John Lingallen. He was a professor of history at a major Southern university during the 1920s. Sherman was a monster. The book shows the terror of what armies will do when their efforts are fueled by rage and they have unchecked power over others."

"His march through Georgia was designed to break the South's will to keep up the fight," I said. "I guess it accomplished that. He understood and practiced the 'scorched earth' theory of warfare."

"Lingallen points out in his book that Sherman's excesses were largely political. Lincoln needed some big victories if he was to be reelected president in 1864. Grant had not been able to defeat Lee at Petersburg. The people in the North were sick and tired of the war."

"Did he tell of the anti-war riots, the Yankee rebellion over continuing the fight against the Rebels?"

"Many Yankees wanted to sue for peace," William said. "But Lincoln and his generals knew they had to crush the last traces of Southern resistance—or we'd come roaring back at them."

My ears picked up the sound of a car door being slammed, a motor being revved up for high-speed take-off. It seemed very close, but my conscious mind was occupied with "Sherman's sacking of Atlanta." "His victory over women, children and men too old to fight," I said, "made the necessary headlines in the Northern press and turned the sentiment toward Lincoln's re-election."

I could see that William wanted to tell me something else, so I sat and listened.

"The Sons of Confederate Veterans teach the true account of how things were, Dad. Northern historians' views of the Civil War are the only one reflected in today's school textbooks. These books teach that the South went to war to keep the institution of slavery in place."

"Well, think about it, William. For a hundred years, one generation after another of our Southern people have received no information to the contrary, no truths to counter these railings against the South as a bastion of evil. Now, our enemies trumpet the charges of a conspiracy to deprive blacks of their rights."

"Don't they ever stop to think about how such unfairness makes us Southerners feel?"

"They need a whipping boy, and we're it, William."

I held up my hand to interrupt our discussion. "William, I think I'll check the front door of our house. That car door slamming; the motor whining for a fast start. That shouldn't be happening on our street this early in the morning."

"I heard that, too," he said. "But remember we mustn't ever let our guard down. First, let's use the binoculars to check the lawn and the street for any suspicious signs."

I picked up the glasses from the dining room table and eased to the windows. I searched our lawn and the streets for several seconds. In the half-light of the approaching dawn, I found nothing. "It seems to be clear," I said.

"You stay there with the glasses, Dad, while I slip out the back door and ease around to check the front. Someone might have left something dangerous at our door. There's no telling what."

I continued my searching through the glasses until I saw William walking cautiously past the front windows and down our sidewalk toward the front entrance.

He stopped and froze. "There's something sitting by the door. On the threshold." he yelled. "In some kind of plastic sack." He eased closer toward the door. "And there are great big globs of something sticking to the front door."

"Careful, William," I yelled. "It might be a bomb."

I watched him move closer to the front door, straining to see more clearly. He stopped again and seemed to be sniffing the air.

"My God," he moaned.

"What is it, William. What's wrong?"

"They've thrown human feces all over our door," he yelled. "And left a plastic bag full of shit. The smell is terrible."

"I'll open the door," I said.

"No, Dad. Don't. There may be something else in the sack other than shit. Don't open the door until I hook up the hose and wash as much of it off the door as I can."

The sudden flooding of anger made me sick to my stomach. I heated the coffee, filled my cup and sat down at the table again. My legs were trembling. I could hear William hooking up the hose, turning on the outside faucet, shooting powerful streams of water at the front door. I reached for my Bible. I knew I had to use God's holy words to at least, partially, take away my anger. After a while, William came through the back door.

"Was there anything else in the sack?" I asked.

"No," he said. "Fortunately."

The telephone was ringing again. He picked up the receiver and listened. "Who is this?" he demanded. When the caller didn't identify himself, my son slammed the receiver down into its cradle.

"Was that the culprit?" I asked.

"The caller said that we were wallowing in shit and he wanted to help us feel at home."

The smell was seeping into the house. I wanted to vomit. For a while neither of us felt like speaking.

Daylight had come. William was gazing into our back yard. "Oh, look dad. There, in the crabapple tree. It's a red bird. The scarlet against winter's still lingering coat of dull gray. Red against gray. That picture might be a creative stroke to use in one of our advertising campaigns."

"I always feel a special excitement with the coming of spring. It's as if everything has been asleep and is now waking up. It's a new hope that things will be better."

He had forgotten the cardinal in the crab apple tree. "New hope?" His voice had turned bitter. "When we've just had our house splattered with shit?"

"I'd rather think about spring, William. About the red bird in the crab apple tree. About the strength that still exists in our Southern people."

My words seemed to quell his anger.

"Yes," he said. "We're not defeated yet." He took a deep breath. "I do have tonight to look forward to. The hunting camp is one of my favorite places. We've had so many good times there during the years I was growing up." He laughed. "And so did the dozens of uncles, cousins, nephews and friends who were always around."

"I'm glad, William. My father took me there often while I was growing up. I love the place; I love the woods, guns and hunting. And right now, I could use the solitude a person can find there in the woods. Sometimes, I have the feeling that God is near and that perhaps he, too, is there in the woods, hiding out for a little while from the world's ills."

"Where's Mom going to spend the night while we're gone?" my son asked.

"About the safest place I know, William. At our preacher's home. I don't believe anyone would be foolish enough to bother her when she's staying with the Horns. Besides, no one but the preacher and his wife know she'll be there."

"I hope no one knows we're going there to practice shooting with those new night vision and laser sights. Just in case we have to use them soon."

"Look at my hands, William. Just thinking about having to shoot somebody gives me the shakes. But, I'm a realist. We have to be ready, if and when an attack comes."

"It'll be good to see Bedford House again," William said. "To walk through those beautiful, quiet rooms and be reminded of some of our family history."

"I phoned Lettie, the housekeeper, and her husband, Archie, yesterday. Those two people are the salt of the earth."

"I'm hungry," William said. "I'll run upstairs and take a quick shave and shower, then prepare us some eggs, bacon and English muffins."

"I'll do the bacon while you're gone, William." I placed eight strips of bacon between two paper towels and put them into the microwave. That's the only way to cook bacon these days.

After we finished breakfast, I shaved, showered and dressed. When I came downstairs, Donna Elaine was putting the finishing touches on her make-up. She never ate breakfast. It was one of the reasons she stayed so trim and wore clothes so beautifully.

"After you and William load the car, you can follow me to Dr. Horn's house," she said. "By the way, I found out the other day that his wife and I are sorority sisters."

"Don't tell me," I teased. "Dear old KKG. You two will have a lot to talk about. I'm glad."

"She's just a good person, Stoney. You ought to know her. She puts in sixteen hours a week at the rescue mission. She works with the children of those poor families."

"The next time I see her, I'll express my appreciation for the good work. Sometimes, the problems we handle out there, the needs and plights of the unfortunates who come to our mission, are so sad until they'll get you down if you're not careful."

The young black man pumping gas into our automobile busied himself with checking the fluid levels, cleaning our windshield and checking the tire pressure. I noticed the happiness on his face and mentally contrasted it with the sullen anger that nested perpetually on Karim's and Tolman's faces.

"You go to the university?" I asked.

"Yes sir. I'm finishing my sophomore year. In communications."

I noticed the tone of openness and friendship in his voice. "What do you hope to do when you finish college?"

He rubbed hard to clean the streaks from my car's windshield. "I'm going into television news," he said. "We get a lot of practice in the university's TV lab. We watch ourselves on the monitor. It's great feedback. Helps us correct our voices, expressions, enunciation and presence."

He finished checking the tires. "By the way, Mr. Bedford. I know Roy Bester. He tells me you put up $20,000 to help him get through law school. That's a wonderful thing you did."

"Roy Bester is one of our city's most precious resources. My family has been doing the same kind of thing to help blacks for sixty-five years," I said. "We're proud of the young men we've encouraged."

"A white professor at the university is doing the same thing to help me."

"Mind if I ask who?"

"Dr. Harris Woolford. He's a friend of yours."

My face must have registered my surprise. "Woolford. That sly fox. As good a friend as he is, he never told me."

The smile left his face. "If it's any comfort, Mr. Bedford. Many of us black people think what Karim and Tolman are doing is wrong. They ought to be trying to help other black people instead of attacking whites for their beliefs. Common sense tells many of us black people that white people are not responsible for most of our problems. We blacks ought to assume the responsibility for solving our own problems because it's ours."

His training was showing through. He sounded like he was doing a TV newscast.

He handed the credit card sales slip for signature. "Some of your efforts are misguided though."

"Oh. How's that?" His words took me by surprise.

"Out of compassion and fairness, whites have voted for greater and greater welfare payments on the assumption that it would help us black people climb from poverty. It's made things worse, not better. Welfare traps so many people into destructive living patterns through helping to destroy self-esteem, killing initiative, and creating life long dependency."

I wondered if the shock of what he was saying showed on my face. "I'm surprised to hear you say that," I said. "Aren't you afraid of the consequences?"

"I do have to be careful," he said, "or I'll be labeled a traitor and treated as an outcast."

"If what you say is true, why is it that when Congress tries to revamp welfare approaches to correct some of these ills that people like Tolman scream bloody murder?"

"Ignorance, Mr. Bedford. They won't admit it, but many of us blacks fear that we can't make it on our own in our economic system. And Tolman's fights with white people gives him political power in the black community. You notice that Tolman isn't poor; he doesn't live in cheap, rundown, subsidized housing. He drives a Cadillac and wears thousand-dollar suits, and socially, his friends are not the ordinary black person. They're people who are wealthy just like him."

William had been listening quietly. "You wouldn't be trying a snow job on us, would you?"

"I wondered when you would let your suspicions come out," the young attendant said. He chuckled; a big grin lighted up his face.

"Well," William said. "I've got sophisticated young blacks working in my advertising agency, and they sure in hell don't say the things you've been saying."

"I'm not doing the new version of the old time black shuffle," the young man replied. "I don't need to. I'm going to make it on my own, in the American economic system. The same way you or anybody else does."

"What's your name?" I asked.

"Thomas Arlen."

"Thomas," I said, shaking hands with him, "talking with you has brightened my day. Such fights as the one in which I'm now engaged catches a person up in a fury that can lead to a lot of self doubt."

"Then you don't believe I'm snowing you?" he asked.

"No, Mr. Arlen. I think you're shooting straight with us." I sighed and shook my head. "It's all so insane. Pray for me, Mr. Arlen. Pray for all of us that the fires of hatred don't consume us."

"I will, Mr. Bedford. If the fires do blaze up, they'll burn us all. Blacks as well as whites."

I couldn't help myself. Three miles outside the city, I began to cry. My heart had been troubled for days and finally the dam broke. I'd been praying to the Lord for guidance and comfort. My cries to heaven were filled with the pain and anguish I felt.

William didn't speak for a long time. Finally, he asked, "Can I help, Dad?"

"No son. I guess I'm not handling things too well. These last few days have been bad days for all of us. We're prisoners in our own home."

"And I don't like it worth a damn."

"Look out there." I motioned to the pastures and rolling hills. "This is the South. This is our land. Our love of the South is just a genetic part of us, you might say. We have a right to freedom from fear; freedom from harassment, freedom from social contempt."

"Take off your rose-colored glasses, Dad. We have those rights, but we aren't allowed to use them too openly."

"And that's a strange thing. We're intimidated by those who use us as their whipping boys. If one stands up against the persecutors too fiercely, well, you can get into a lot of trouble. Look at what's happening to us Bedfords. It's a pretty good bet right now that there are killers stalking you, me and Donna Elaine."

My son had gotten worked up again. "I'm like you, Dad. Boiling inside because we've been pushed into a corner. I'd like to strike back hard. But, the mobs would really come after us then. People who want to kill us are closing in. But, what can we do?"

Different scenarios flashed through my mind. "I've asked myself that a hundred times. Those cars that are again parked down the street from our home. Then, last night. Those long cars with darkened windows that followed us to the restaurant. The men inside them, dressed like women, carrying automatic weapons. The four of us with weapons. You and I wearing bullet proof vests and carrying pistols. Starlight scopes and laser sights. Steel shields at home to hide behind when the attack comes. What's to become of us? Why can't we just live and let live?"

My anguished sobs must have lasted for several minutes. I fought to regain my composure and reassert self-control. Occasionally, William patted my left shoulder. The tension must have been unbearable for him, too.

"You know, son. Our forebears at Gettysburg, when they charged up Cemetery Ridge, must have been praying and crying, too." My sobs became louder for a few seconds. "And the Confederates died there that day by the thousands. I can hear their moans, the bursting shells, the roll of the drums. They gave their all because they believed in a great cause."

I looked across the fields to the tree line and remembered General Bedford's courageous death. The gentle scholar, poet and professor. "Pull down our flag?" I said out loud. "I will not dishonor them by turning coward in this fight."

"Let's remember that the blacks feel just as strongly about the flag and the Civil War as we do, but in a different way," William said.

"That's the trouble. I don't suspect that they'll back off either. Catch 22?"

Two Harleys with helmeted riders dressed in black roared around our car. They were obviously enjoying the sounds and the power of their motorcycles.

I looked at my son. He was so young and vibrant, so full of life. His whole future lay ahead of him. He and Julie would be married in July. Great pangs of conscience swept through me. Had I selfishly involved him in this seeming madness? Or was he too acting this way because it was the way any proud Southerner would act when faced with the same things?

"We're not hurting any one," William said.

"That's not the way Karim and Tolman see it."

"It's so damned unfair. Our family has never hated black people," William said. "We've never sneered at them, never abused them. On the contrary, we've tried to help them. Yet, no one stops to think about that. The automatic assumptions that we're bigoted, prejudiced, and contemptuous of minorities is what pushes those who want to crush us down again. Like we were in 1865. Because we're white, we've become the enemy."

"Reconstruction has never ended," I said. "The South has not become compliant enough to suit others."

"You know," my son said. "It's not equality the blacks want. They want our positions switched. They want to be where we are and for us to be where they are. Blacks want our homes, our lands, our money, but they want us to give them all of these things without a whimper. They'd like to see us living in the ghettos of the inner cities, on welfare and drugs, killing each other the way they are now killing each other. They want to ascend to the positions of power and control and lord it over us."

"Sh-h-h-h-h, William. Don't say that where others will hear you."

For a moment, he was taken aback." Why not? It's true, isn't it?"

"That's not the point. It's so unpleasant until most people quickly deny it. It's easier to look the other way; to skirt the issue; to hide our heads in the sand."

"This reversing of positions between blacks and whites. It'll never happen," I said, tapping my knuckles on the dashboard. "Look at Somalia and Rwanda. It's a holocaust. In three years, the native tribesmen have killed each other to the tune of well over a million. I find it difficult to imagine killing on such a scale."

"Dad, you're hiding from the awful truth again."

"I keep hoping there's a way out. I have to keep on hoping."

"Did you ever stop to think that if minorities gained the power and control they want, that they might turn to killing whites on the same kind of scale as is happening now in Africa?" he asked.

He pounded his fist against the leather-covered steering wheel. "They cry 'Give us jobs; give us self esteem; give us respect.' The secret is that one can't give a person these things. You have to earn them the same way any of us earn them. By the way we live and work and love our country; by who we are in the process of becoming in our efforts to earn our bread and honor God and others."

The darkness of waning hope came again. "It's easier to take the things you want—by force—than it is to earn them. Not as honorable, but easier."

CHAPTER 14

Bedford House was still a great, columned house, an outstanding example of Georgian architecture. Two stories. Twenty rooms. After my mother and father died, I couldn't bear to let it pass out of Bedford hands. It'd been built by my father and mother ninety years ago. My brothers and sisters and I had grown up there and now I was the sole survivor of our immediate family.

I knew that the expense of keeping up a place as large as Bedford House didn't make good economic sense. Why do I do it? It's part of my family heritage and I couldn't allow the house and it's memories to blow away in the dust of history.

The giant live oak trees that lined the quarter mile-curving driveway were majestic. They'd been there since the early 1900s. Long tendrils of moss hung from their limbs and swayed in the gentle breeze. It was like a page from a book of ancient Southern homes, the kind you see pictured in those volumes often found on living room coffee tables.

"Hush, hush, Sweet Charlotte." At times I expected to see Bette Davis and Olivia deHaviland standing on the house's balcony as we drove up the driveway as they did in the movie.

But it wasn't those two we saw. Instead, it was Lettie Jones, the housekeeper, who stood on the balcony and waved to us. As we got out of the Bronco, she opened the house's great door and walked out onto the flag stone veranda to greet us.

"Mr. Bedford," she beamed and held out her hands. "I'm glad to see you're still alive and well. After those awful things I've been seeing about you on television." She turned to my son. "And how are you, William?"

"Fine," he said. "Bedford House looks so good, thanks to you and Mr. Jones."

"It's a lot of work," she said. "But we enjoy living here. I often wonder why you Bedfords don't move back to this place and live like your mother and father used to live."

"My fiancée and I," William said. "After we're married in July, we just might move out here to Bedford house. Both Julie and I love the house."

"Oh, that would be wonderful," the stocky, gray-haired woman said. "Me and my husband would love keeping house for you."

Archie Jones, dressed in khaki pants and shirt, and wearing a sweat stained, felt hat, came around the corner of the house. He had pruning shears in his hand and was carrying a spade over his right shoulder.

"I've been working the flower beds out back," he said.

"Does it look good for the rose this year?" I asked.

"Out of pride, I'd have to say so," Archie said. "Roses are my favorites. They get special care."

"You and Mrs. Jones have the place looking wonderful" I said to the tanned and wrinkled man with work calluses on his hands.

"I've got lunch prepared for the two of you," Mrs. Jones said. "Will you be sleeping here tonight?"

"No," I said. "After lunch, William and I will drive his Bronco down through the woods to the hunting camp. We'll sleep and eat there. We're going to enjoy the peace and quiet of the woods. These last few days have been rough on all of us."

Before we sat down for lunch, William and I walked into the library. It was a ritual for me each time I came to this place filled with so many memories. I could feel the presence of my mother, Betty Jane Bolling Bedford, that imperial Southern lady who had ruled Bedford House like a queen. I could almost hear her lecturing to us children about our proud family history. I felt strangely comforted.

I pulled back the velvet draperies that covered the room's floor length windows. Sunlight flooded into the room. We paused to look at the full-length painting of Confederate General P.A.T. Bedford, my father's grandfather. He exuded bold recklessness. His gold epaulets, the sash, his sword, his black boots, the gray hat with its rolled brim, which he held in his hand. His bearded face showed his strength.

He had died that day at Gettysburg. They said they had found his body at the top of Cemetery Ridge, still clutching in his left hand the Confederate flag he'd snatched up from a fallen comrade as they charged into the withering fire of cannons and rifles. His empty pistol was in his right hand. He'd been one of the ones that had made it to the high ground for a few short minutes. If only we could have held the high ground that day. If only . . .

My mother always cried when she told us the story and read us General Lee's letter that had been written to my great-grandmother. The letter itself was in a gilt-edged frame on the wall next to the painting.

"And this is my great, great uncle, Stuart Bedford," William said.

I moved to stand beside him. "Yes. He fell in the Wilderness campaign. Shot from his horse. Neither he nor General P.A.T. Bedford ever came home. They were buried with their fallen comrades."

A painting of my mother's father, General A.P. Bolling, hung on another wall. He survived the war and came home to Forest to find that his wife had been raped and killed by looters. The young Bolling sisters, including my mother, were living in the burned out plantation house and grubbing for food. All the slaves had long since moved into the city where they and the carpetbaggers smoked cigars, confiscated any houses they desired, lolled in drunken revelry on the streets and laughed in derision at General Bolling when he came into town to search for the essential things needed to rebuild their lives.

Neither of us spoke much. When you're steeped in memories, the mind takes over and paints silent pictures that somehow or other don't seem to need words. There were six more paintings of Confederate colonels, captains and lieutenants from both sides of our family. After a while, we saluted them and closed the draperies again, then walked into the sun lit garden room to eat lunch.

To reach the hunting camp, we drove the Bronco over dim roads and through places where no roads seemed to exist. Deer ran across our path. Rabbits scurried along in front of us until they could dart into the dense undergrowth to escape the two of us who had disturbed them in their domain.

Lettie and Archie Jones had recently scoured the hunting camp from top to bottom. It was clean and spartan. The plumbing worked. The butane stove lighted easily. So did the four Coleman lanterns that furnished light when darkness fell.

William and I sat on campstools we had moved onto the cabin's porch and inspected the pistols, rifles and shotguns with their recently mounted laser sights and their starlight scopes for night shooting.

"I don't know about you, Dad," William said, "but I need some practice with each of these weapons. I figure we ought to do some target shooting before dark. Just to sharpen our skills."

"Did you bring those targets?"

"I'll go get them. They're lying on top of my bunk."

For an hour we practiced. William was an accomplished marksman. I'd taught him well. I was happy I hadn't lost my touch. Afterwards, we sat on the campstools and enjoyed the peace and quiet. "After it gets dark," I said, "we'll go into the woods and practice with the scopes and laser sights. I figure we'll see plenty of raccoons, possums and rabbits.".

"Dad, what do you think? I figure it might be helpful if we ran from tree to tree and practiced snapshooting. The way we might have to do if they do attack us at home."

I laughed. "William, if other people knew what we were doing out here, and the reasons we're doing it, they'd say we had turned into raving lunatics."

William wasn't laughing. "Only those who have not been pressured the way we have would say such a thing. Dad, believe me. We're not paranoid. Those people are out to kill us. I want to stay alive so Julie and I can get married and have a family."

I didn't speak for a long time. I was hearing the faint sounds of bugles at Gettysburg. "William, I've had this terrible feeling I can't get rid of. It's clawing at me night and day."

"I think I know, Dad. I've also had this premonition that we all might wind up dead."

I picked up one of the 30.06 rifles and fired into the trunk of a red oak tree fifty yards away. Once, twice, three times. Pieces of bark jumped into the air as the smoke from the rifle's barrel drifted upwards. I guessed I was trying to lash out at the hooded wraith hovering in the dark, outer edges of my conscious mind.

"I didn't want to tell you, but I've been having nightmares. In them, I see us dead. You, me and Donna Elaine. Strangely, there's no one weeping. Black people are dancing joyously around our dead bodies. There are also many white people in that crowd, looking, pointing, gesturing triumphantly. They're congratulating four black men, shaking their hands, slapping them on the back. It's so real until I wake up yelling, 'no, no, no.'"

William's voice broke. "The pressure is almost unbearable," he said. "I don't want to die. I don't want you and mother to die. I just want to live and marry Julie, raise a family, and be reasonably happy." He was crying softly.

I watched him go inside the cabin and heard him blowing his nose. After he came outside again, we walked into the woods and practiced running, ducking behind trees, shooting at the targets we'd tacked to trees, then running to another tree and firing again.

"Damn, William. I'm impressed. You move fast. And you haven't wasted a single shot."

I didn't move as fast as William, but my shots hit their targets as accurately as had his.

We came back and sat on the campstools again. I looked at my watch. "It's five o'clock, William. Let's have a martini before we eat."

"I'll mix them," he said.

About six o'clock, we heated some beef stew and corn bread that Mrs. Jones had prepared for us and spooned it into plastic bowls we had brought with us. We sat down at the table with its rough pine boards and began eating. The sucking of the lighted Coleman lanterns as the flame burned the gas was a familiar sound. We could hear the owls hooting deep in the woods. The insect chorus rose and fell as though some conductor was waving a baton before them.

My son was beginning to relax a little. He breathed deeply and exhaled loudly as though sighing. "Ah-h-h. Listen to that night symphony. If you close your eyes and listen closely, you can imagine they're voices of ghosts, especially with the sucking noise of the lanterns. It's eerie, but I'm fascinated."

Night was squeezing out the daylight. At seven o'clock, we walked into the woods, carrying two rifles, two pistols and the shotgun. William also had his long-barreled .357 Magnum. He stopped and raised it to a position in front of his right eye and searched the woods through the star light scope mounted on the gun. "There's a big fat possum out there about thirty or forty yards away. I can see him plainly." He held the fearsome weapon in both his hands, extended them, aimed and squeezed the trigger.

"Come on," he said. "Let's go see if I killed the possum." He led the way, stopped and pointed to the base of a sweet gum tree. "There he is, dead as a door nail. Your turn, Dad."

We walked deeper into the woods. A few yards further on, I lifted the 30.06 rifle to my shoulder and sighted through the scope. It reminded me of earlier days as a boy when I hunted with a carbide light fastened to a cap. The lighted gas flame in the center of the reflector shone a bright beam far into the woods. I remembered how I could see a thousand insect eyes that were not visible to the naked eye. Through the scope, I searched the woods ahead by moving the sight until I saw a coon next to the bank of a small creek fishing for food. Slowly, I squeezed the trigger. Through the scope I could see the animal's body fly into the creek. We walked the fifty yards until we verified the kill.

"Good shooting, Dad," William said. "Now try this pistol."

The Glock felt good in my two hands. Fifty feet away, through the scope, I saw a rabbit. The bullet went through the rabbit's body cleanly.

"Now, the laser sight," I said. "Wherever that dot is on the target, that's where the bullet will go."

"Right," William said. "That's why the laser is so good as a weapon to prevent attacks. Most of those who stalk their prey on the city's streets know that when the dot's on them, they'd better back off. One of my friends had to use his recently. He said the two would-be attackers started begging him not to shoot and backed off with their hands up."

I liked the laser immediately. There was no need in sighting through the gun's sight. You just aim the dot at the target and pull the trigger.

After an hour and a half, we were satisfied with our ability to handle the starlight scopes and the lasers. We walked out of the woods and settled down on the campstools we'd left on the front porch of the camp. Deliberately, I let myself meld into the night's symphony of woodland sounds and drift away from current troubles.

My father and I used to sit on stools like these, tired from the day's hunting and absorbed in the good times and the joys of life. My dad was a big, bluff man with a hearty voice. "Stonewall," he'd say. "You're one damn fine hunter, the kind a man can hunt with and not be afraid he's going to fire off a crazy shot that can kill him. I like the kind of man you're becoming."

In his University of Georgia yearbook, the editor had written about my father: "Stonewall Bedford. All American end for two years on the Bulldog football team. He could do it all. Block, catch passes and keep opposing backs from turning his corner."

I remembered studying his strong, handsome face as he lay in his casket. I was eighteen when he died. To me, he seemed to be smiling the way he'd been in life. I could hear him saying, "Stonewall, I'm proud of you."

My dad and I were very close. He was a true friend who taught me ten thousand things. I loved him. To this day, I still miss him.

My mother, Betty Jane, the queen, after Daddy's death, ran Bedford house as her private domain. The annual trips to Washington, D.C., and New York for museums, plays and the opera continued until we went off to the

University of Georgia. When she died at age eighty-six, she looked as imperious in death as she had in life. I could hear her saying, "You children have a great heritage to live up to. A Southern heritage. Unequalled. Never, never, never dishonor your family's proud history. Walk tall and hold your head high. You have a right to do that. Your forebears died to guarantee that right."

I heard again the distant sounds of the bugle's call to glory. My great-grandfather had reached the high ground at Gettysburg, carrying the Confederate flag and holding his pistol in his right hand. He'd emptied the pistol before he died there.

I had not yet reached the high ground. When the call to glory comes, I wondered if I'd meet the challenge with courage and honor.

CHAPTER 15

Late Sunday afternoon, after William and I returned from the hunting camp, I sat relaxed in my red leather chair in the den, watching the professional golf tournament in Florida. William had gone to Julie's home and Donna Elaine was back in the library studying a large picture book of Louisiana plantation homes.

One of the golfers sharing the tournament lead at eleven under par stepped onto the tee box at the par three hole. The green was an island completely surrounded by water, except for the narrow walkway that stretched from the tee, across the water, to the green. He swung his eight iron, hooked his ball and watched it fall into the water to the left of the island green. He dropped his club, sank to his knees and clasped his hands together. The camera closed in to show him moving his lips. There were tears streaming down his cheeks.

"His share of the lead in the tournament just vanished," the announcer said in a low, controlled voice. "It looks as though he's fallen to his knees in prayer. I don't believe I've ever seen this kind of emotional display in a championship tournament before."

I answered the telephone. "Stoney, this is Allen Hart. Did you know there are ten black people marching back and forth along the sidewalk in front of your house? They're carrying crudely lettered signs with ugly messages."

"You're not kidding, are you?" I asked hopefully.

"I wish to hell I was," Allen said. "I wish you'd do something about it. It's disturbing all of us up and down the street."

He hung up the phone before I could reply.

Cursing, I walked to the tall windows in the living room and looked out. Damn. Allen was right. There were six men and four women walking slowly back and forth on the sidewalk, carrying signs. Why would they be doing such a thing? I asked myself. The globs of shit thrown onto our front door had been bad enough, but this. Hell, I didn't deserve anything like this. And certainly my neighbors who lived in this quiet, respectable, upper class neighborhood didn't deserve it.

The phone started ringing again. I picked up the receiver. "Hello."

151

"Stoney, can't you do something to make those black people stop walking in front of your house. Make them go away?" It was the widow Alice who lived across the street.

"I don't know what I can do, Alice," I said.

"Why don't you and your wife leave town until this flag controversy blows over?" she asked. "You're creating trouble in the neighborhood which we don't need."

"Alice, this is our home. Those black people have no right to be doing what they're doing. Not even our disagreements about the Confederate flag is reason enough for this."

"Stoney, these are our homes, too. And we have a right to live here without having to endure the things that have been happening here recently." She slammed the receiver down. The dial tone hummed.

Chief Dennis Crowe, I thought. He can stop this. It's got to be stopped. Who the hell did these people think they were? My neighbors and I have rights that have to be protected too.

"Hello," Crowe said.

"Dennis, this is Stoney Bedford."

"Oh," he said. "What's your problem now?" The tone of his voice told me he wasn't too happy hearing from me.

"Ten blacks are walking back and forth on the sidewalk in front of my house carrying signs. I want you to stop them. Make them go away."

There was silence on his end of the line.

"Dennis, did you hear what I said?"

"Yes, Stoney. I heard what you said. I knew they were going to start picketing your house. Knew it yesterday."

"You knew? And you didn't do anything to stop them? Didn't telephone to warn me?" I was incredulous.

Yes, I knew. And I can't do anything to stop them." His words came slowly and evenly, devoid of emotion.

"You can't do anything to stop them? Why the hell can't you?" I could feel the flushing in my face.

"They're not breaking any law. The sidewalk is public property. They have a right to walk back and forth on a public sidewalk."

"Crowe, you're pissing me off. I stuck my neck way out for you, yet you don't seem to be the least bit interested in helping us. These people are disturbing the entire neighborhood. All my neighbors are calling, and they're angry. It's making me and my wife nervous wrecks. Don't we have rights, too?"

"All I know to tell you to do is to stay inside your house with your draperies closed. That way, you don't have to look at them." The chief was ducking behind legal camouflage.

"But the neighbors are calling me and they're frantic."

"I can't help you, Stoney. Or them." He hung up the phone.

My wife walked into the den. "Who were the people calling on the phone?"

"Neighbors. Go look out the front window. You'll see why they're telephoning."

"Oh, my God," I heard her cry out. "Stoney. This is terrible. What'll we do?"

"I wish I knew what we could do, Honey."

"But something's got to be done," she said. "They can't do that. The people up and down our street are decent people. We have rights, too, and this is private property."

"I called Chief Crowe. He said the sidewalks are public property and that there was no law to prevent the pickets from doing what they're doing."

The glint of battle flashed in her eyes. "I'm going right out there and give those people a piece of my mind!" She started toward the door.

"No, Donna Elaine." I caught her arm. "Don't go out there. I'll go."

I started walking down my driveway, not knowing what I would say or do. I felt about as insignificant as one who is hopelessly lost in the woods. Several of the neighbors were standing in their front yards. When the widow Alice saw me, she ran across the street and up the driveway.

"I've never been so embarrassed in all my life, Stoney. Look. The television cameras are coming. Both channels. Their trucks are down the street and they're equipped for live broadcasts direct from the scene."

"It's awful, Alice."

"For God's sake, Stoney. Do something! You're a city council member. You're supposed to be able to handle things such as this. Our neighborhood needs to be protected from such scum."

Allen Hart walked up. "Stoney, I'll help you. Tell me what to do. We've got to get these sons-of-bitches out of our neighborhood. Nothing like this has ever happened around here before."

"There ain't nothing you can do, Whitey." The woman was short and dumpy, at least seventy-five pounds overweight. Her braided hair flipped as she chewed her gum vigorously. "We ain't gonna go away. We've got scores to settle with old Bedford here, and they've done festered up, ready to pop."

I looked at some of the signs and cursed. "Bedford Hates Blacks"; "Bedford Defends Confederate Flag and Slavery"; "The Flag Must Come Down." My stomach had turned into a churn and someone was moving the dasher with searing strength. I'm not guilty of any of the charges on those signs, except loving the principles for which the Confederate flag stands. Wasn't I free to express my views as a citizen? Obviously not. The great double standard shut me up in a cage but left my enemies free to stomp on my rights.

"Those TV cameras are shooting pictures," Alice cried. The cameras were turned from the marching pickets toward me, Allen and the bleating Alice. "Oh, my God," Alice cried. "I don't want to be on television with those . . . those . . . people."

Like a wounded gazelle, Alice started running back across the street. Her spindly legs were too old and tired for running. She stumbled and fell. The cameras closed in on the fallen Alice and kept grinding.

"Help me, Stoney," she cried. "My right arm. I think it's broken. Oh, God. Help me."

Allen and I ran to her and bent down. I saw that her arm was broken between the elbow and the shoulder. The bone had punched through the muscle and the skin. Her pain must have been unbearable.

"Oh, God, help me," she prayed. "This pain." She tried to cover her face with her left hand. "Those TV cameras, Stoney. Make those people point them away from me." With her left hand she tried to smooth her clothes. "Is my dress pulled down?"

A woman television reporter stuck a microphone in my face. "Mr. Bedford. What's your reaction to those pickets marching in front of your house?"

I did not answer. "Allen, please tell Donna Elaine to call 911 for an ambulance." He ran up my driveway.

"Alice," I said, smoothing her bluish, white hair. "I'm so sorry. Just lie still. We'll have an ambulance here soon."

"Stoney," she cried. "I'm seventy years old. My arm may never heal. Oh, God. What did we do to deserve this?"

"Look at that old racist white woman," one of the male pickets laughed, shifting his cigar in his mouth. "She fell and busted her ass. Ain't that too sad?" The others laughed.

The woman reporter was insistent. "Mr. Bedford. What's your reaction to all of this?" She waved her hand toward the pickets and my house. Her face seemed to glow with excitement and happiness.

I stood up. "Look at what has happened here. Don't you have an ounce of compassion in your body? Look at this poor women. Look at her arm. At her age, this is a critical injury."

The reporter from the other TV channel rushed up to us waving a microphone. "We've already filmed her fall, her broken arm and you two men standing over her," he said. "Now, I need your comments. What are you going to do about those pickets?"

He smiled and shoved the microphone into my face again. The volcano of rage inside me erupted. I grabbed the microphone from his hand and smashed it into his nose. He screamed and put his hands to his face. I hit him again across one of his upraised hands. His nose was spurting bright red blood. My sense of helplessness fled. I felt surges of joy.

The man's cameraman rushed up to us and swung his fist at me. I caught it in mid air and twisted it sharply to his right as I smashed the microphone into his face. I grabbed the camera from his shoulder and threw it onto the concrete as hard as I could. It shattered and the parts skidded in several directions.

Two of the pickets ran toward us to aid their wounded television allies. They knelt down to them and dropped their signs onto the street. I grabbed up both the signs and charged like a crazed bull at the other eight marchers who stood frozen with their mouths open. I began flailing at them with the signs on their stout poles. The group of pickets broke and scattered. Three of the neighbors rushed up. Malcolm Rufert grabbed up another fallen sign from the surface of the sidewalk and chased after three of the bolting marchers, beating them across their backs and shoulders.

Two more neighbors joined the fray. They ran toward the other TV reporter and her cameraman. Bob Cowley tackled the cameraman at the knees and rolled on top of him. Ted Smith pinned the woman reporter's arms to her side. His wife ran up and grabbed handfuls of the woman's hair and began savagely jerking her head from side to side.

"Help me," the woman reporter screamed. "This old woman's gone crazy. Don't let her hurt me."

"You weren't interested in helping poor Alice Hoffman," Delores Smith yelled and spat into the woman's face. "Now, we're giving you some of your own medicine." She yanked savagely on the handfuls of the woman reporter's hair. Some of it finally came out. Delores dropped it onto the street, then began viciously slapping the woman's face. Blood appeared at the corners of the reporter's mouth.

A police patrol car and an ambulance arrived at the same time. An older policeman jumped out of the patrol car and ran forward. "What's going on here?" he yelled.

"Officer," I said. "This seventy-year-old woman's arm is badly broken. The bone has punched through the muscles. These heartless bastards," I waved my arm at the television people, "they're responsible. Alice fell as she ran away from the cameras."

"Yes," the officer said, surveying the scene. "I can see that this woman is hurt." He pointed to Alice, still writhing on the surface of the street. Then, he looked at the male TV reporter and his cameraman. Their noses were still spurting blood. "Those two are also hurt."

"Help me," the woman reporter screamed. "These people are trying to kill me."

Ted Smith let go of the woman's arms. She dropped to the pavement on her knees.

"My hair," she cried. "Help me. This crazy old woman pulled out some of my hair. I know she did. Help me find it and put it back." She was moaning and crawling around on the street, still searching for the elusive, drifting tufts of hair she imagined were there.

The male reporter with the broken nose was thrashing around on the concrete and groaning. His cameraman sat up and kept screaming. "This man broke my nose and busted out my teeth. Look." He opened his mouth. Three teeth dangled across his lips. Pointing at me, he said, "He busted up my camera, too. What will I tell my producer?"

"You callous bastards," I yelled. "You caused this seventy-year-old woman to break her arm. She's in serious condition. You were too busy recording everything with your precious camera to offer her aid or show any mercy. To you, poor Alice Hoffman running away from your camera and falling was just a good story. Good footage for TV audiences. I hope you rot in hell."

"Officer, do something," the wounded cameraman pleaded. "These crazy people, this man here." He pointed toward me again. "He attacked me. That's against the law, isn't it?"

The cameraman tackled by Bob Cowley stood up. He rushed at Cowley with flailing fists. This time, Ted Smith tackled him from behind, while Cowley smashed his fists into the man's kidneys. Cowley had been a Marine raider. He knew that a person's kidneys was a great place to attack without leaving visible scars.

The patrolman stepped back as the EMT attendant ministered to Alice Hoffman. "I'd better call another ambulance for that man over there with the busted nose," the officer said. He walked over to where we were standing.

"All I saw were some decent people fighting off attackers," the policeman said. "You had a right to defend yourselves."

He entered his patrol car, used his telephone to summon another ambulance, then drove away.

Another ambulance arrived. The EMT technicians placed the reporter with the smashed nose into the vehicle and drove off.

The woman reporter was still crawling around, yelling obscenities and feeling for the hair she'd thought had been pulled out. "You heartless bitch," Delores said. "Get up onto your feet and get out of here. While you still have some hair left." Delores pulled the slender woman to her feet and shoved her toward the station's vehicle. "Now leave here! While you are still able to walk."

Cowley and Roberts finished smashing the second camera into pieces and turned to the remaining cameraman who had struggled to his feet.

"No," the man pleaded. "Don't hit me anymore. I'm leaving. Please. I'm leaving." He continued backing away toward the TV news truck.

Smith grabbed the man before he got to his station's TV truck. "If any of you tell lies on television about any of us here on this street," Smith said, "we know where you are. Decent people have had enough of you arrogant, lying television people and newspaper reporters. From this day forward, we're taking matters into our own hands. You'll not abuse us anymore."

Cowley punched the man in the pit of his stomach twice. "Oh, that feels good," Cowley said. "Get the message, mister? No more poking and prying into the lives of innocent people just to get a story. No more laughing at seventy-year-old women whom you made to fall and break her arm. She'll have such pain that she may not heal. He punched the pleading, crying man two more times in the stomach. "Now git, mister."

After the TV news trucks drove off, Ted Smith said, "Stoney, let's go inside your house. I want to make some urgent telephone calls." He turned to his wife. "Delores, you and Bob come with me."

We walked up the driveway. My legs were weak, my arms were shaking. Once inside the house, Smith dialed the phone number for Channel Four.

My wife Donna Elaine came into the room. She was crying. "I saw what happened. I was afraid."

I hugged her. "It's all right, honey. We've got things under control now. Let's listen to Ted."

"Who is your manager?" Smith yelled into the phone. "Vane Murphy? Get him on the line." Obviously, the person who answered the telephone protested.

"Listen, woman," Smith snarled. "What I have to tell Murphy is going to cost your station about forty million dollars and the yanking of your station license by the FCC. You'd better get Murphy on the line."

In a matter of seconds, the station manager was on the phone. "Murphy, this is Ted Smith. I live on Bayou Drive three houses from Stoney Bedford. Your reporter and cameraman pursued a seventy-year-old woman right in front of our eyes and frightened her so much that she fell onto the street. Her arm was horribly broken. The bone was sticking out through the muscles. She cried for help. Your people happily ran up to her yelling questions and poking the microphone into her face. Did they help her? No. All Alice Hoffman represented to them was a good story. She's now in the hospital. Her attorney will be filing suits against your station next week for twenty five million dollars and against your two employees for five million dollars each. And your station is responsible, because they were working when they made Hoffman fall.

"Don't interrupt me, Murphy," Robert barked into the phone. "I haven't finished yet. When several of our neighbors tried to get them to leave poor Alice Hoffman alone so we could tend to her, your two people attacked four of us. We had to defend ourselves. Each of us is suing your station and each of your two employees for five million each." Murphy obviously tried to interrupt again. "Wait a minute, Murphy. There's more. Our attorneys will file charges of inhumane treatment of people against you with the Federal Communications Commission."

"What" Smith exploded. "You'll ask your people if I'm telling the whole story? Of course, they'll lie to cover their asses. But we've got a dozen witnesses to corroborate our story. Oh, and one more thing. If you run one damned word about today's happenings on Bayou Drive, the suits filed against you will multiply, both in number and amounts."

Smith listened for a few seconds, then exploded again. "I don't give a damn about your lies, Murphy. Don't you understand what happened in the November 8, 1994, elections? The people of America said to the media, "We've lost faith in you. We've had enough of your lying, twisted, distorted news reporting. We've had enough of affirmative action, welfare, crime, violence and government interference in the lives of its citizens. Your days are numbered, Murphy. You and your kind no longer frighten us ordinary citizens. We're mad as hell and we'll fight back.

"By tomorrow afternoon, our Republican senator in Washington will have told our story of abuse by your two employees to the FCC. We're going to fight to take your station's license away come renewal time. We think we can do it, after what happened on our street today."

Smith listened, hooted and listened some more. "You've certainly changed your tune since this conversation started, Murphy. And, incidentally, Stoney Bedford was one of the people abused by those two ruffians who work for your TV station. He'll be filing suit against you also."

Smith hung up the phone and turned to us. "Now, I'm calling Channel Seven's manager to give him the same message. I need a drink, Stoney. Would you mix me one?"

Ted finished his conversation with W.A. Zang at the other TV station and came into the den. "I'd say," he laughed, "that the people's revolution against liberals and their lap dogs, the media, has started in Forest, Georgia. We're not going to take it anymore."

"Amen, brother," I said. "Thanks to the courage you four displayed—and that of our other neighbors—we may have slowed down these arrogant bastards. I salute you." We clicked our upraised glasses together.

The telephone rang. It was the *Ledger's* Victor Allen. "No, Allen. I'm not going to talk to you. As far as we people on Bayou Drive are concerned, nothing happened today. No, Allen. I've said all I'm going to say." I hung the phone up.

Ted turned to his wife Delores. "Honey, would you and Donna Elaine telephone all our other neighbors and tell them to refuse to talk to Victor Allen?"

The two women walked away with their arms around each other's waist.

The next morning at eight o'clock, the pickets were back, all ten of them, waving their crude signs, shuffling along the sidewalk and chanting, "The flag's gotta ago. The flag's gotta go. The flag's gotta go."

Fifty feet away, two policemen leaned against the patrol car's front fender and watched for any signs of trouble. I guessed that Chief Crowe was doing what he thought he had to do. He was struggling with the lines that Karim and Tolman had drawn in the dust.

I hadn't told Crowe about Roy Bester's warning. He'd not accept it on its face value anyhow, but it had filled me with fear and foreboding. I couldn't shake the anxiety and apprehension.

CHAPTER 16

Hospital waiting rooms are grim and silent places, curtained off from the outside world, where each person waits in his own private world with anxiety and dread. The several of us from Bayou Drive sat there and said little to each other. The light always seems to be so dim in places like this until, that in itself, heightens the morbid fears of those who wait and keep watch.

The day had seemed unreal. It was eight twenty on a Sunday night and cold and dark outside.

Our neighbor, Alice Hoffman, was in the operating room, and had been for two interminably long hours. I remembered bending down to help her and seeing how the bone stuck out through the upper part of her broken left arm. How strange it was to see the bone protruding through the layers of flesh. And not a drop of blood.

"You know," I said to Delores Smith. "It's strange, but Alice's arm didn't bleed."

"I wondered about that, too," she said.

"Alice is seventy," I said. "A break that severe is very dangerous to older people. Quite often, they can't stand the trauma."

"I guess all we can do is to pray for the surgeons," Delores said, twisting a white handkerchief in her hands.

"Poor woman," Bob Cowley said. "There she was, screaming with pain and all those two heartless television reporter could think of was getting some good footage of an old woman lying in the street. The fact that it was in front of Stoney Bedford's house made it even more exciting to them."

"Filthy damned bastards," Allen Hart said. "I'd bet that if their mother was dying, all they'd think about is getting a close up of her gasping for her last breath."

Pudgy Malcolm Rufert held up a white foam coffee cup, grimaced and looked at the others. "Damn, if I drink any more of this stuff, I'll have indigestion so bad they'll have to admit me here as a patient."

Ted Smith didn't seem ready to put his cup of coffee down. "Folks, let's quit complaining. It's our neighbor, Alice, who's in the operating room. She's the one who's suffering, not us." With his left hand, he gently swirled the contents of the foam cup. I noticed his long, bony fingers and the big LSU class ring he still wore after fifty years.

I leaned back in the deep chair covered with ivory naugahide, closed my eyes and started praying for Alice. If it hadn't been for those blacks picketing my home and the eager television news people, she wouldn't have been running across the street where she fell. I felt sad and guilty.

"Oh, Lord," I prayed silently. "You have said, 'Take no thought for anything, but in everything, through prayer and supplication, with thanksgiving, make your requests known to God. And the peace of God which passeth all understanding shall keep your hearts and your minds.' I pray for Alice and lift her up to you and ask for your healing. I believe, I believe, I believe. Thank you for healing Alice, for bringing her safely through surgery. We know that you are guiding the hands of the surgeons at this very moment. Thy will be done, oh Lord, not mine."

"Here comes the surgeon," I heard Delores Smith say.

Some hidden respect for doctors pulled each of us to our feet. While Dr. Ellis Hardfin was still twenty feet away, I could see from the set of his jaw and the solemnity on his face that the news about Alice was not good.

"Are each of you friends of Alice Hoffman?" he asked.

"Yes," Allen Hart said. "How's Alice doing, Dr. Hardfin?"

"The news, I'm sorry to say, is not good," Hardfin said. "Alice died on the operating table. The trauma; the complicated surgical procedures. She lapsed into a coma and stopped breathing. The code blue team could not revive her."

"Oh, no," Bob Cowley said. "Alice? Dead? Why, that's not possible. Just yesterday at our breakfast room table. . ." His voice trailed off.

"I'm sorry," Dr. Hardfin said again. "Things like this happen often to older people."

"Alice has no next of kin," Malcolm Rufert said. "She was alone in the world. She had nobody. Nobody."

"Donna Elaine and I will look after funeral preparations," I said. "I'll sign the necessary papers and pay for everything."

"You'll need to go to the business office," Hardfin said to me. "The coroner has been notified. I've attested to the cause of death. Well," he said. "I must go now. There's another patient waiting for me in the operating room."

Not many people showed up for Alice's funeral services in the funeral home chapel. Most of those who did come were Alice's neighbors from up and down Bayou Drive.

Donna Elaine and I sat down front. The casket was closed, the organ music sad and hypnotic. This is the way it is when you get old and die I told myself. Especially if you're not from a large family and you've outlived most of your friends.

I don't understand all I know about death and dying. Funerals always scared hell out of me. Dark, foreboding, unanswerable questions flooded through my mind and made me pensive. As Oscar Wilde said, "It is impossible for a man to contemplate his own death."

How true. I had tried to imagine my lying cold and stiff in a casket, then the coffin's lid being closed, the impenetrable darkness, the thudding of the dirt on top of me after they'd lowered my casket into the grave. My mind reared away from such thoughts like a wild-eyed horse fighting to keep the bit from being pushed between his jaws.

Death. No more being with Donna Elaine and William and sharing with them. No more sitting on the banks of the lake behind my house and watching the gentle falling of darkness onto the calm surface. No more sudden dawning of life's great truths as I read and meditated. God's holy words floated in from a vast distance. No more striving to attain and hold onto life's high ground as I heard the distant calls of the bugle, the muffled roll of the drums urging men on to the attack.

The minister prayed, read brief passages from the Bible, said a few perfunctory words of kindness about Alice Hoffman, then pronounced the benediction. Eleven minutes. That's all it had taken to signal the end of a human life. Eleven minutes.

Those at the cemetery were even fewer in number. Fourteen, I counted, including the six of us neighbors who served as pallbearers. The graveside prayer was less than fifty words. Then the handful of dirt. "From dust to dust . . ." the minister droned as he crumbled the dirt and let it fall onto the ground.

As we walked away from Alice's grave in the bright sunshine, I saw the funeral director pushing the button on the metal frame that allowed the straps to lower the casket into the pine box in the bottom of the grave.

I looked back as I entered my car and saw the broad top of the pine boards that were nailed together to fasten them to the strips of one by two.

It slid down into the grave to fit over the coffin and inside the frame of the pine box.

Donna Elaine clasped my hand. "How sad," she said. "And for what? Nothing. She was running from a TV camera. . ." Tears glistened on her delicate cheeks. "You, William, and I. We're caught up in the same crazy patterns that ended Alice's life. I'm afraid, Stoney. Afraid of what's going to happen to us."

Fifty yards away from Alice's grave, partially hidden by the trunk of a huge live oak, a worker started the motor of the grave digging machine and headed toward the dead woman's grave. The driver maneuvered the machine expertly into place and began using its blade to push the red clay onto the top of Alice.

I almost ran to my car to flee the sadness of the burial and the loneliness of the cemetery

"From dust to dust. . ." I shuddered and began to cry. The pent-up emotions of the last few days gushed from me in deep, convulsive sobs. My wife gathered me into her arms and held my head.

CHAPTER 17

"Conflict resolution?" I asked. The caller was Gary Wilhelm, the thirty-eight-year-old president of the Chamber of Commerce. "And just how does the chamber propose to resolve this controversy about the flag between Karim, Tolman, and myself?"

"Something has to be done," Wilhelm said. "Wouldn't you agree?"

"I keep praying that the matter can be resolved peacefully," I said. "You don't know just how bad things have become."

"This picketing of your home," Wilhelm said. "The police murder of the black man just because he was sitting in a parked car on a street in an exclusive neighborhood. This whole matter is just, well, it's just so childish."

"What's your experience in, what did you call it, 'conflict resolution'?"

"At Harvard, we studied the techniques for an entire semester," the rich man's son said. "Once a week, for three hours, we broke up into groups and practiced a lot. I've also asked Tolman, Karim, and Senator Willie Sanders to meet with us here in the chamber offices at 10 o'clock tomorrow morning. I'll have our chamber attorney on hand to finalize any agreement we reach."

His words sounded so ridiculous until I almost burst out laughing. "Let me get this straight, Wilhelm. You studied conflict resolution for a whole semester at Harvard and practiced in the classroom? I'll bet that was exciting."

He didn't realize I was belittling him. "Yes, Mr. Bedford. It really proved what intelligent, reasonable people can do by getting together and talking out a problem. Especially, if we can get participants to lay aside old, outmoded ideas and come together with a real desire to resolve the conflict."

"Outmoded ideas?"

"Yes," Wilhelm warmed to the subject. "Here in the South we were taught many such things that no longer can stand the light of day. At Harvard, I learned to card through all these Southern myths, legends and propaganda and become a far more intelligent, objective, sophisticated person."

"I'll just bet you did, Mr. Wilhelm," I said. "Sure, I'll attend your meeting, but I'll bring my own attorney with me."

"Your own attorney? Really, Mr. Bedford, there's no need for your doing that. This is not a trial. It's just an attempt to get us together around a conference table and talk these matters out on an intelligent basis."

"Listen, Wilhelm. I remember what you said on the television news the other night. How did you put it? 'Stoney Bedford's remarks about flying the Confederate flag were quite unwise. Such outrageous ideas should have been laid to rest long ago. After all, this is the '90s.' Those words tell me that you certainly won't be bringing an open mind to this meeting. You've already proven that. That's why I'm bringing Carl Krippendorf with me."

"Krippendorf? Why, he's over seventy. And crippled to boot. At least bring someone younger and better informed than that old fossil Krippendorf."

"You sniveling little pipsqueak," I yelled into the phone. "If I were where you are right now, I'd jerk a knot in you for saying such a mean thing."

"Really, Mr. Bedford. There's no need to lose your temper."

"There's very good reason, Wilhelm. Do you know how Krippendorf got crippled? No, I know you don't. It was at the invasion of Salerno, Italy in World War II. He and I were small boat officers in the amphibious forces. Our boats were loaded with American infantry soldiers. We were taking those poor sons-of-bitches to the beach when a German .88 artillery shell hit his boat and blew his left leg off. I dove into the water among the dead bodies of our American boys and pulled Krippendorf aboard my boat. He lived. That limp you refer to is from the artificial leg they fitted him with."

"That's a sad story, Mr. Bedford. But really. It was so long ago. People these days are not very interested in war stories. There are so many other things that occupy our daily lives. And war stories are, well frankly, quite boring."

I made my words come out slowly, the only way I knew to cap the boiling cauldron of anger bubbling inside me. "Mr. Krippendorf and I will be there at ten tomorrow morning. Oh, Wilhelm. I'd advise you four objective, rational, sophisticated, modern day human beings—and I'm referring to you, Tolman, Karim and Sanders—not to try to frighten and overwhelm Carl and me. It won't work. Better men than you four have tried that. We're also quite skilled in conflict resolution. We've been resolving knotty problems for over fifty years. Good day to you, sir."

THE LAST CONFEDERATE FLAG

At three-thirty that afternoon, Manley Dexter phoned me. After we came home from the war in 1946, Manley started a drug manufacturing and distribution firm in Forest. His corporation's annual report showed 1994 sales of $450 million and profits of $38 million. Almost three thousand people worked at the plant.

"Stoney," he said. "I had lunch today at the Executive Club with Gary Wilhelm. He told me about the meeting and his phone conversation with you. He inferred that you were some ancient monster awakened from the swamps. Your philosophy about the Confederate flag—he just doesn't understand your reasoning."

I laughed. "That certainly came across very clearly, Manley. That little snob is so intellectual and sophisticated until he made a brilliant discovery while he was at Harvard. In his long hours of research and study, he concluded, as he said, that the principles I still believed in, held up to the light of reason, were outmoded and should be replaced by more progressive principles."

"That's why I called you, Stoney. After I chewed on his sophisticated ass for an hour, he just might have reinvestigated some of our Southern ideals and beliefs and found a great deal of truth and knowledge in them."

"You actually think there's hope?"

"Yes, I do. I told him the only reason he had a job as marketing vice president at Forest Machinery was that his daddy owned the company."

I laughed. "Manley, you might have hurt that sophisticated young man's feelings."

"He pissed me off, too, Stoney. I asked him how he'd like to see his daddy's business lose eighteen million a year in sales. I thought that brilliant, sophisticated fop would faint. His face turned white. He began to sweat."

"Surely not, Manley. Why, people like you, me and Carl Krippendorf are relics of another age. Wilhelm? He's one of those new creatures for today's modern age."

"Stoney, that boy probably messed up his pants when I told him that the members of the drug manufacturing association I head up as president could easily buy their machinery from companies other than Forest Machinery."

"I'll bet he wasn't expecting that."

There was a sneer in Manley's voice. "I told him about a company other than his over in Atlanta who wants this business badly—and that they flew the Confederate flag daily in front of their plant, on a flag pole right beside the American flag; that the people who control the company are quite proud to be Southerners who believe in our great heritage."

"I'm getting a real kick out of this story, Manley. What was the great Wilhelm's reaction to that?"

"He excused himself for a few minutes to go to the men's room. Leon, the headwaiter, came and whispered to me that Wilhelm was in the toilet vomiting. When he came back to the table, he looked as though he'd seen ghosts. I think, Stoney, you'll see a chamber president tomorrow morning with far less arrogance and sophistication. I wouldn't be surprised if his attitudes didn't closely reflect the attitudes of us real Southerners."

"I owe you one, Manley."

"No you don't, Stoney. You owe me nothing. You're a good and decent man that the liberals and the media are trying to kick around unfairly. Many of us are pissed off, including Wilhelm's own father. I called him to discuss his son's attitudes and he exploded."

" 'I don't know what I'm going to do with that boy,' the older Wilhelm told me. 'He's just been brainwashed up there at Harvard. I see few signs of any common sense. He's far more interested in seeking approval from his peer group out at the tennis club. When he gets back to the plant, I'll stomp his ass into the middle of next week. Hell, we fly the Confederate flag each day in front of our plant. Next to the Stars and Stripes.' "

"It's a different world we live in, Manley," I told my friend. "Sometimes, it gets mighty rough."

"Yes, Stoney," Manley said. "It's a different world, and, may I say, one to which I refuse to bow down to. Hell, members of the current generation haven't discovered the Holy Grail. Not that I know of. If it weren't for people like you and me preparing the way for them, I'm not so certain they'd get by too well."

You could tell by looking at Wilhelm's face the next morning that his arrogance and high expectations for conflict resolution at this meeting had diminished to low voltage. He made a great show of welcoming Carl and me to the chamber boardroom. State Senator Willie Sanders was already there.

The politician jumped to his feet with effusive greetings. Carl looked at me, raised his eyebrows and smirked. Long ago, my friend had learned to recognize phoniness when he saw it.

"Good to see you guys," Sanders said. "We needed this meeting to defuse the tensions in the black community. Flying the rebel flag upsets the blacks. Anything we can do to keep the situation from exploding will show leadership."

"Oh, Senator," I said. "You think we can prevent further looting of businesses such as that which we saw on TV the other day. You know, during that march by the blacks to city hall? Wonder if their actions might have upset the whites?"

Sanders laughed and shook his head. "Oh, Mr. Bedford. Those folks who did that were just showing their anger at a system like ours that deprives them of the nice things in life. Things they don't have and which the four of us take for granted. Being poor is tough, you know."

"Do you know how stupid those words sound, Senator? They don't play well with thinking people," Carl said.

His choice of words, his measured emphasis, his tone of voice. Carl sounded as though he were summing up a case for a jury. "Yet I hear many of you liberal do-gooders offering that same rationalization to excuse such criminal conduct. If a thing is wrong, it's wrong. If a person engages in criminal actions, he should be punished. Nothing excuses looting, burning and stealing. Many of us were poor when we grew up, but we had a code of ethical conduct that taught us not to do such things. We learned that if we worked hard, we could someday earn those things."

Sanders laughed again, this time even louder. "Mr. Krippendorf, everything is relative. There are no absolutes. Deciding whether or not a thing is right or wrong, depends on the position you occupy in our society when you're looking at the action. If people have denied you the things you want, the things people like you and me have, you see this so-called 'looting' in a different light."

"Oh," I said. "Your rationalizations sound like Fletcher's situation ethics. Moral relativism. No absolutes. Whether or not a thing is right or wrong depends on the situation at that moment?"

"You got it, man," Senator Sanders said.

Abdul Karim, tall and ramrod straight, and DeLong Tolman with his huge belly and heavy jowls, walked in. They nodded to Sanders, but neither of them spoke to Carl and me. Wilhelm touched a buzzer. "Tell our attorney we're ready to start the meeting."

A slightly built young man with brown hair walked in. His brief case seemed too heavy for him. "This is George Frederick," Wilhelm said. "He was just graduated from Harvard Law School at the end of last semester. He's a native of California and made straight A's in law school."

Wilhelm looked pleased to reveal this information about Frederick. He was a small man with buckteeth. He smiled and nodded to us, then sat down at the long oval table with its highly polished surface. He looked at the reflection of his hands before resting them on the table.

Wilhelm cleared his throat. "Each of you know why I called this meeting. As president of the Forest Chamber of Commerce, I say to you that we must resolve this conflict over the flying of the Confederate flag in front of City hall. Confrontation and loud voices are not good for our city, not good for business. All of the bad publicity we've been getting in the national media makes us look like backwoods simpletons. The media is having a field day at our expense."

"That's not the only thing on the table in this meeting today," Karim interrupted. "We're also going to talk about the firing of Police Chief Dennis Crowe for failure to divert enough resources from white neighborhoods to adequately police our inner city neighborhoods. It's racial discrimination, pure and simple. Black people will no longer tolerate such injustice."

"That damned flag is part of the same problem," Tolman said, hammering the table. Each time his fist hit the table, his fat face jiggled. "It offends black citizens in Forest. Stoney Bedford has sparked racial tensions to the point of explosion by refusing to vote to take down this symbol of racial oppression."

"Your hatred of blacks," Karim said. "Your failure to give us good jobs and decent housing has robbed the majority of black people of hope."

"Wait a minute," Carl interrupted. "I thought we were here to lower our voices and seek solutions."

"Wrong," Tolman said. "Karim and I are here to press our demands."

I thought of the way movies portrayed Hitler's conduct of meetings. With shouts, he outlined his demands and then waited for others to obediently comply. The only thing wrong with that scenario was that Karim and Tolman weren't dictators and Carl and I certainly were not compliant robots programmed to do their bidding.

Wilhelm rapped a gavel. "Gentlemen. Gentlemen. Please. This is a big problem. Let's approach it in a calm, reasoned manner like the intelligent people we are. It does appear that the old reasons for flying the flag are no longer valid in today's complex world. This is the '90s. Hopefully, most of us native Southerners have long since shouldered the guilt we should feel over enslaving black people and the fighting of a bloody war to keep them in bondage."

Krippendorf began to laugh and pound the table. "I can't believe what I'm hearing. Guilt? Enslavement of black people? We didn't fight that terrible war over slavery. It was the South's War for Independence, our rebellion at the Yankees' efforts to tell us what to do. You should know that a real Southerner won't stand for anybody sneering at him and trying to tell him what to do. He'll fight you at the drop of a hat, anytime you challenge him."

"That's one of the main reasons the Nation of Islam has declared war on all white people," Karim said in a loud voice. "You lie about the reasons for the Civil War. You keep us black people pressed down—and you still treat us as inferiors even though we've been emancipated."

"Right on, brother," Tolman exclaimed. "That's telling him."

Karim was encouraged. "It's whites who won't listen to reason. We've tried so long and been rebuffed so often, until all hope is gone. It will be your grave mistake not to take our declaration of war seriously. As a matter of fact, we hope you don't. It'll make it all the easier for us to win."

"We've heard those outrageous lies before," Carl said. "Many times."

Karim began sputtering. "Just who the hell do you think you are, old man? You can't talk to me that way.

"Karim, you're so full of prejudice and hatred until you're like a robot that's been programmed to speak."

"For a moment, it looked as though Karim would attack Carl.

I held up my hand to get an opportunity to say something.

"Yes, Mr. Bedford," Wilhelm said. He was eager to grasp any opportunity to calm the heated rhetoric.

"If we're to make any progress in this meeting, we must start by being honest with ourselves. Mr. Karim is dead wrong in his assumptions. In America, it's not up to white people to give the blacks jobs, housing and welfare checks. If you really wanted to solve the problems of black poverty and crime, you'd start rebuilding family and moral structures and teaching the work ethic to blacks."

"Wait a minute," Karim objected. "You're a god-damned liar."

"Please, Mr. Karim," Wilhelm said. "Let him finish. He didn't interrupt you."

"Most people in America," I said, "are sick of such phony excuses for inner city deterioration. You'd do far better in helping blacks if you discarded your agenda of hatred for whites and substituted plans designed to reshape the way blacks think about getting ahead in the free enterprise system."

"We're hearing the same old mumbo-jumbo," Tolman yelled. "What a crock of shit."

Krippendorf jumped back into the discussion. "Your two demands, one for the firing of Crowe and the other for pulling down the Confederate flag over General Lee's monument are not the real reasons for the controversy that's been created."

"The great war hero is enlightening us now," Tolman sneered.

Carl let the insult slide by. "Your stated reasons are cover ups for the exercise of power." He looked at Karim, then at Tolman. He turned to Wilhelm. "Those two are using these emotional issues as smoke screens to hide their real reasons for escalating tension between blacks and whites. By stirring up less informed black people to riot and demonstrate, it increases their power."

"What you're really afraid of is that we got you white bastards running scared now," Tolman rasped. His words seemed to hang up in the fat throat. "We know that you're afraid of us—and for good reason."

"If you think that," Carl said, "you're even dumber than I thought."

It looked as though Tolman's entire body had inflated and would burst into small pieces at any minute.

Wilhelm struggled to regain control of the meeting. "Please gentlemen. This kind of soapbox harangue solves nothing. Let me hear one constructive idea on how to resolve this conflict, how to defuse this explosive situation. We don't want people getting killed, yet if we don't calm people down, this could happen."

"Take down that damned Confederate flag," Tolman yelled. "That'll solve the problem."

"No, Mr. Tolman," I said. "That will solve nothing. Within a week, you'd have other outrageous demands to make on the city council. But, if you will listen, I do have a compromise that will defuse the anger and quiet things down."

"Let's hear it," Wilhelm urged, banging the gavel.

I pulled a check from my pocket. "This is a check for $5,000 payable to the Martin Luther King Memorial Fund. Let's build a memorial to this great black statesman on the lawn of city hall, one hundred feet west of the Confederate memorial to General Lee. I'll serve as one of the three co-chairmen of the fund raising drive, along with Karim and Tolman. We'll raise $300,000 to build such a monument. I have nineteen other business leaders who have pledged to each give $5,000 to the fund drive. With a monument to a great black leader and a revered white Confederate leader side by side, we can let both blacks and whites cling to the ideals and principles in which they believe."

I had dropped an unexpected bomb into the middle of our discussion. The silence became deafening. Sanders was smiling and nodding his head. Karim and Tolman were not pleased. Like scorpions, their stingers had been plucked from them. They didn't know how to react.

"I must say, Mr. Bedford," Wilhelm said. "You are very generous. That's a solution with real merit. An honorable one that should please both black and white people. I think I can get the Forest Chamber of Commerce to pledge $50,000. And we'll furnish the architect to design such a memorial to Dr. King."

"That idea will work, Mr. Bedford," Sanders said. "I'm just speechless. I congratulate you."

"It's a textbook case," Frederick, the young attorney recently of Harvard, said. "Each side gives, each side receives something in return."

"You're full of shit, Harvard man," Karim sneered. "You're not dry behind the ears yet. You've got a lot of growing up to do."

A sickly look settled onto the young man's face.

Tolman had recovered his offensive thrusting. "Wait just a cotton-picking minute before you get carried away with such a crazy idea. Once again, you whites have managed to out maneuver us blacks. That damned plan won't solve nothing. You whites will still be lording it over us black people, smiling, slapping each other on the back at your private clubs—and chortling over your slick deals. We blacks would still have to see that fucking symbol of slavery flying each day over that damned saint, General Lee. No. The only solution is to pull that damned flag down. Forever."

Tolman's true feelings about General Lee had slipped out without his knowing it. Or without his caring if it showed.

Karim banged the table and launched into another fiery tirade. "It's hypocritical. You're trying to snow us, divert our attention. We want the flag down and Crowe fired. We'll not be taken in by that statue shit. We don't want no statue. Martin Luther King is dead, and we can't solve our problems by weeping at his feet. We want what you white people have denied us for so long. We want what you have. And we'll get it one way or another, even if we have to kill every last one of you."

"You want. You want. You're very skilled on making your demands, Karim," Carl said. "But you're not intimidating us. It's been tried before and didn't work. It won't work now. You see, we're not afraid of you and your kind."

"Wait a minute, gentlemen," Wilhelm said, gesturing toward the two black leaders. "I don't see this compromise that's being offered in that light. It's reasonable. It's fair. It will work. Mr. Bedford has certainly moved forward and extended an olive branch that seems highly acceptable to me."

"Mr. Karim. Mr. Tolman," Senator Sanders said, still smiling. "Let's think about this generous offer of Stoney Bedford's and the Chamber of Commerce. I'm certain I know enough lobbyists who will give substantial money toward such a memorial monument to Dr. King. As a matter of fact, I'll guarantee to raise $50,000 toward the project."

DeLong Tolman stood up. "C'mon, Abdul. I knew that attending this meeting was a bad idea to begin with. We've just heard another way that the white man has figured out to fuck the black people."

The two left the meeting.

Wilhelm shook his head. "That's sad isn't it? I don't believe those two want anything except an escalation of the tension."

"I certainly agree with Mr. Wilhelm," Frederick said. "I'm taken aback at the lack of desire on the part of those two to reach an acceptable compromise."

Karim stuck his head back in the door to deliver a demagogic ultimatum. "Unless Crowe is removed and the flag comes down, you white people will live to regret it. We will not be pushed around any more. You will listen to us black people, or you'll pay a terrible price for it." He clenched his fist and raised it above his head, then slammed the door.

"Now there's a reasonable, rational man," Krippendorf said, throwing his pencil onto the polished surface of the table. "Those two don't want to settle this controversy. I don't think they care who or how many people might get killed."

"I'm afraid you're right, Carl," I said. "It's sad that they wouldn't even listen. I spent half a day getting these nineteen pledges to go with my own. Those who pledged their support applauded the idea. But, I guess it comes to naught."

174

"I've gotten a different view of you, Mr. Bedford," Frederick said. "You're not the prejudiced, horned devil I'd imagined."

"We wear well, Mr. Frederick," I said. "If a person can lay aside their prejudices long enough to get to know us. I thought erecting a memorial to Dr. King would please them, but I was wrong."

"The media people have been waiting in the press room down the hall," Wilhelm said. "Do you mind if I have them come in so you can explain your ideas to them, Mr. Bedford?"

"No," I answered. "Not at all. I think they'll be disappointed though. They'll pay scant attention to the compromise that was offered. Karim and Tolman will get the headlines for walking out of the meeting."

"Surely not," Wilhelm said. "It's such a marvelous idea." He buzzed the receptionist and told her to have the press come in.

We waited. The buzzer on Wilhelm's telephone sounded. He picked up the receiver. I could see his face turning crimson. "What? They're out in the lobby interviewing Karim and Tolman? I can't believe what I'm hearing." He listened a few seconds longer, then hung up the receiver.

Carl Krippendorf and I stood up and began to gather up our papers.

"Victor Allen told the receptionist that the press conference was out in the lobby," Wilhelm said. "And if you and Mr. Krippendorf wanted to come out and join in, you could. They see no need to come back here. He said that Karim and Tolman had already told them about your phony offer, but you'd be welcome to give them your side of the story."

"No," Carl said. "It'd do no good. We know what slant they'll give the story. The media thrives on controversy. They don't care whether or not they get the facts right, just so they have, as they call it 'a hot story.' "

"We prepared a statement outlining our proposed compromise," I said. "Mr. Wilhelm, would you please give it to the media people for us?" I handed Wilhelm ten copies of our statement.

Carl and I left the chamber offices through the side door.

CHAPTER 18

It had been a long two weeks since the storms of controversy flared up, but the day for *the* city council meeting came at last. Today, we'd make the decision on whether or not to continue flying the flag. It was another one of those grey, dreary spring days when a slow rain dripped through the new leaves on the trees and encouraged people to stay in bed. I'd been awake since four a.m., tossing, turning, visualizing different scenes that might happen during the next twelve hours.

At 5:30 it was not yet daylight. I dragged myself out of bed and made strong coffee. Today, I used the kind that was heavily flavored with chicory. I wanted the dark, bitter flavor that burrowed deep into my taste buds. The aroma as the hot water dripped through the small dripolater pot to which I still doggedly clung wafted up in tiny clouds of steam and announced to my reluctant spirit that a new day had been granted me by the Lord. I was grateful.

For an hour, I immersed myself in reading the Bible. I needed to feel the spirit of Jesus the way the multitudes must have felt as the Savior preached the Sermon on the Mount. Thank God for Matthew who so meticulously recorded it. Now and then, I'd pause to reflect on the meaning of certain verses. I closed my eyes and prayed, "Oh, God, help me to walk tall—with humility—through this day as I try to practice the great truths in these verses. Help me always to remember that you are closer than hands and feet; closer than breathing. I know that all things are possible through Christ who strengthens me."

William walked down the stairs in robe and pajamas. "I didn't sleep too well last night, Dad."

"I didn't either, son. Get yourself a cup of that coffee on the stove. It's good and strong. It'll snap you awake. Then come in here and sit down so we can talk."

"The way the media treated your offer of compromise to Karim and Tolman was so unfair," William said. "But, as you said, 'It's what we knew they'd do.' "

"They did have a lot of fun making light of it, didn't they?" I said. "Those headlines on the *Ledger's* front page this morning are virtually the same thing we saw on TV last night. The newspaper went television one better though. It has an editorial that sneers at the proposed Martin Luther King memorial and urges me to give in to pulling down the flag."

He was scanning the front page. "They say that your surrender is the only thing that will lessen the tension between the races." He shook his head and let the newspaper fall onto the coffee table. "That's the only thing they want to see. Stoney Bedford running up the white flag of surrender."

"It'll never happen, William."

"And today's the day of decision." He sniffed the aroma of his coffee, then lifted the cup to his lips. "There's no telling what will happen at the meeting."

"Happily, I don't think anyone else knows that we have Baxter Lampkins' vote, so we know we've got enough votes to vote the ordinance down. But people are so stirred up. On both sides of the issue. There'll probably be some big trouble out of Tolman and Karim's folks."

"Five members of our Sons of Confederate Veterans chapter will be there to speak against taking the flag down. We decided it'd be best if I did not go to the meeting."

"That's probably a wise decision, William."

"And, the United Daughters of the Confederacy will be there in force," my son said. "Those ladies are hopping mad. And when they're riled up, watch out."

"I'd hate to have them angry at me," I said.

"We know so many of them personally. UDC ladies epitomize everything that's good about the South. They're the kind of people that pass on our history and legends to the younger generations. Through them, the South endures."

I was rubbing my stomach, which was broadcasting its tenseness. "My stomach is tied in knots, William."

"Is there something more than just today's meeting?"

"The *New York Times* and the *Washington Post* want to interview me at ten this morning. Then BCS, BAC, BNC, NNC, FOX and PBS are scheduled at 11:30."

"I understand that the media people are really interested in that compromise solution you worked out, Dad. The news about your offer has spread like wildfire. Everybody's talking about it."

"Frankly, I'm not surprised, William. The reactions of people have actually restored some hope in many hearts that the controversy can be amicably settled. I've been hoping, too."

William was more cynical than I was, perhaps wisely. "But Tolman and Karim have thumbed their noses at the idea of a memorial to their civil rights leader next to the Southerner's own Civil War memorial to General Lee and the Confederate flag."

"To them," I said, "it only works one way. They're not content with letting us have our dreams and our pride while they content themselves in being just as proud of their dreams as expressed by Dr. King."

"Not to change the subject, but today's also a big day in our advertising agency," William said. "We start planning and laying out the advertising campaign for the biggest account we've ever landed, Atlanta Surgical Equipment."

"That's big news. When did you land that account?"

"We got the okay late yesterday afternoon." He laughed. "It only took me two years, but it was worth it. Five million a year in billings."

"And a bonus for William Bedford?" I asked, smiling.

"Yes, and a hefty one, I'm proud to say. It'll come in handy for me and Julie when we're married." He turned to go upstairs to get ready for work. At the foot of the stairs, he stopped and looked back at me. "You think all this trouble we've been having will be over after today's vote?"

I had to be honest with him. "I wish I could answer 'Yes' and mean it, William, but I don't believe Tolman and Karim will call off their dogs until they run me to earth. One way or the other."

"You do remember to wear your bullet proof vest, don't you?" he asked.

"I don't leave the house without it. I notice those strange automobiles are back again, parked in their same spots. This time, there are two men in each car. With night vision glasses and pistols on the seat beside them."

"Yes," he said. "I saw them last night. By the way, I now wear my vest every day, too."

The police and fire marshal were standing at the elevator doors on the fourth floor at one p.m., turning people away. "We have no more room," they told people. "Too many showed up for the meeting."

Several disappointed people were arguing and registering very loud protests. The meeting room holds only one hundred and fifty people. The fire marshal had agreed to allow another fifty people to stand in the hall outside the doors to the council chamber. The mayor had made arrangements on the second floor for closed circuit television in two large courtrooms with combined seating of two hundred.

"Oh, Mr. Bedford," Police Captain Ben Shell said on seeing me coming off the elevator. "Come on through the crowd."

Several people stuck protest signs in front of my face as I pushed through the mass of people in the hall. "Here comes that old Southern demagogue," an expensively dressed young white woman said in a loud voice. "He's living back in the 1800s. He's to be pitied. And despised."

A fat, gleaming-faced black woman appeared in front of me. "You old white racist bastard," she snarled. "You better vote to take down that damned flag."

"And if I don't?" I smiled at her, a quizzical expression on my face.

"You'll be sorry. Bad things will happen to you. Real bad things. Do I have to draw you a picture?" She clenched her teeth and tossed her head defiantly.

"Oh, worse than those things that have already happened to me?" I asked. I was surrounded by angry people, people who moved in short, quick steps to keep me surrounded. They wagged clenched fists like coiled snakes preparing to strike their victims, hoping for a target on which to vent their frustration.

The fat woman sneered. "A thousand times worse. Maybe even . . ." She drew her finger in knife fashion across the rolls of fat beneath her chin.

One of Karim's Muslims, a tall, handsome, immaculately dressed black man, grabbed her arm and guided her away. Some friendly supporters wedged themselves between me and the muttering militants and cleared the way for me to get into the meeting room. I pushed through the double doors and stopped to catch my breath.

I counted five council members already in their seats. Able Erling, Harris Woolford, Norris Cape, Frank Dines, and Baxter Lampkins. Six in all, including myself.

"DeLong?" I asked our council president.

"Oh, he's huddled in one of the back offices with Karim and some of the other militants," Able said. "They're planning to cause us as much trouble as they can. I'm certain of that."

Without thinking, I caught my right hand seeking the reassurance the bulletproof vest gave me. I walked to the seating area in the back of the chamber where spectators were seated to shake hands with several friends. The five members of the Sons of Confederate Veterans gathered around me.

"We've rehearsed what we're going to say, Mr. Bedford," Mike Chapman said. "You'll be proud of us."

I guessed he was about forty years old. I clasped his hand and said, "I know I will, Mike. William has told me you and some of the others would be here."

"We've disavowed the Ku Klux Klan, Mr. Bedford," Claude Follin said. "At our national convention six years ago. But, the media keeps painting us with that black KKK brush. It's unfair."

"Yes, Claude. My son William showed me the resolution you adopted in convention. Those bigots in the KKK dishonor our Confederate flag. I wish we could stop them from using it in any way, but we can't. They believe in what they're doing, just as the NAACP believes in their philosophies. This is still a free country and that freedom cannot be restricted just to certain groups we favor."

Morris Light and his assistant were in the back of the room taking footage for their documentary. My family and I had grown so used to having him everywhere we went until we scarcely found it necessary to acknowledge his presence. I looked his way and smiled. He nodded slightly.

I talked with Carl Krippendorf for a few moments. "There's lots of favorable reaction to the compromise solution you offered in yesterday's meeting," Carl said. "It's been on the national television news networks. I also saw it in two major national newspapers."

"But did you also read where the NAACP and the Merciful Ayatollah have denounced it, Carl? The only thing that will ever satisfy them, they say is. . ." I shrugged in resignation.

"Yeah, I know," Carl said. "Pull the flag down and fire Chief Crowe. And push so hard on whites until eventually the power roles will be reversed."

Some people next to Carl had been listening in on our conversation. "Those reporters," a stern-faced, older man said. "And those militant blacks. All those lousy bastards want is to cause us trouble. Well, that works both ways, Mr. Bedford." His words were ominous. The tone of his voice was flat and deadly. His eyes had narrowed to small slits. He wore the clean, rough clothing of a man used to working hard with his hands.

"They're not going to take over my world," his stocky, balding friend said. "We've had enough. We're not going to take much more of this crap."

"Let's play it real smart," I said, and patted him on the shoulder. "Let's don't let them push us into doing anything foolish."

"What we do won't be foolish, Mr. Bedford," the older man sneered and clenched his jaws shut. The light in his steel grey eyes was hard and unyielding.

I looked toward the media's raised platform in the back of the meeting room. It was crowded with reporters, photographers and television cameras. The *Ledger's* Victor Allen motioned for me to come over. In confidential tones, he told me, "I owe you and apology, Stoney. For my conduct at yesterday's press conference at the Chamber's offices."

He's up to something, I thought. Playing me for an even bigger fool than I am. I'd play along and see what happened. "Victor, I can't believe what I'm hearing. You? Apologizing to me? Will miracles never cease?"

"I know," Allen said. "I deserve a kick in the ass. My bosses at the paper chewed me out and told me to grow up and 'try being a real reporter instead of an advocate.' Your offer to help build a memorial to Dr. King was very generous. It surprised the hell out of us at the LEDGER. We don't understand why Karim and Tolman didn't jump on it."

The guy's still being too clever. I decided to burst his little balloon. "Yet, this morning's *Ledger*," I said. "The news stories. That editorial. It didn't appear that you were impressed. You made it plain that you'd chosen to side with Karim and DeLong."

"You're right, but something happened this morning you need to know about. Frankly, several of our big advertisers converged on our owners and editors this morning in a real blood-letting," Allen said.

"Don't tell me they came down hard on you bastards?"

"Did they ever. It wasn't a nice meeting at all. Matter of fact, it was mean and to the point. The business leaders hammered us for encouraging racial trouble instead of trying to defuse the situation."

"They ought to starve your newspaper out of business by withholding their advertising."

"They laid the law down to us and told us to make our coverage objective, or else. The major stockholders in the *Ledger* corporation were there in the meeting, too. When they saw what the paper had been doing, they came down on us hard."

I couldn't believe it. A reporter was actually telling me the truth. "If my mouth is hanging open, Victor," I said. "It's not because my jaw is paralyzed or that I've had a stroke. I'm just dumbfounded at your words. You mean, some few individuals among that arrogant group of would-be Gods over at your newspaper have finally figured out what Karim's and Tolman's hidden agenda really is?"

"Go ahead," Victor said. "Kick us hard."

"How will you 're-educate' yourself, so to speak." I guessed Victor had been thinking about that 180-degree turn he had to make.

"It hasn't been easy to step back and look at things objectively," Victor said. "It's easier—and a lot more fun—to tear people's asses up. But I think we've gotten the message. We've been discussing the possibility that what those two are doing is a smoke screen, as you've pointed out. A cover for their real motives."

He looked around the room and shrugged his shoulders. The perpetual arrogance seemed missing. "I guess the ordinance to pull the Confederate flag down will pass today," he said. "The vote's still 4 to 3, isn't it?"

"Who knows? Maybe Tolman will change his mind and vote with us. Miracles do happen, you know."

"Fat chance of that happening," Victor laughed. "You know, Stoney, one of the things that gets you into trouble is that you are a man of principle. It'd be easier to figure you out if you really did hate blacks."

"What bothers you, Victor, is that I have the courage to defend my principles, despite who and what is standing in my path."

I checked my watch. The time was 1:58 p.m. Two minutes to get to my seat. Half way up the aisle, someone with a protest sign nailed to a stick hit me behind my head. "Ouch," I said, grabbing the back of my head. "That hurts. Part of a nail or a tack went into my scalp." I turned around. Three black women with protest signs nailed to sticks were laughing.

"Oh, excus-e-e-e-e me, Mr. Bedford," one of them said. "I must have dropped my sign."

"Yeah, that's what she did. Dropped her sign," one of her companions said. "It just happened to hit you in the head as it fell." The three were waving their signs back and forth, slowly, like a panther moves his tail before he pounces on his victims. They laughed again.

"You had no reason to do that," I said.

They were still slowly waving their signs. "Accidents do happen, you know," the youngest one of the trio said. "I bet you're in a lot of accidents these days. Somehow, accidents happen all the time to racist white folks."

I hurried to my seat. The president rapped the gavel as I eased down into my chair.

"I want to call this regular meeting of the Forest City Council to order," Able Erling said. "Roll call, Mr. Clerk."

Tony Angell called the roll. All members of the council answered except DeLong Tolman. "DeLong Tolman," Angell said again.

"Present," Tolman yelled as he pushed through the doors to the meeting room. Being late for roll call was a deliberate technique of Tolman's to attract attention. He stopped just inside the doors and looked around the room. He smiled, nodded to several people in the audience, then walked with measured slowness to his seat. He liked his 'big moments.'

"Mr. President, you have all seven members present," Angell said.

Immediately, chants broke out in the spectator's section. "Pull down the flag! Fire Chief Crowe. Pull down the flag. Fire Chief Crowe. Pull down the flag. . ."

Erling banged his gavel. "Order," he shouted into his microphone. "Order. If there are any more outbursts like that, I'll have the officers clear the gallery."

Abdul Karim jumped to his feet. "I wouldn't try that, Erling. You'll have more trouble than you can handle." He turned to at least twenty, well-dressed young black men who were seated next to each other. Their white shirts, red ties and black suits gave an aura of power and discipline. "Stand up men, so the council members can see what they'll have to deal with unless they meet our demands."

They stood up and raised their right fists into the air in a black power salute.

"Right on, brothers," a woman yelled. Applause broke out.

"We'll fight any one that touches us," Karim said, "police or not. Now go on with your meeting, Erling."

Able called on Harris Woolford to deliver the invocation. I had to agree that Woolford prayed the most intelligent prayers I'd ever heard. His thoughts came out in eloquent phrases; they sounded almost like poetry. Inwardly, I chuckled. What a pity to waste such thoughts on this gang of council members.

"Stonewall Bedford will lead us in the pledge of allegiance," Erling said.

"Better put the Rebel flag up there for him," one of the Muslims shouted. "That's his flag." Laughter ran through the spectators.

I noticed that Karim and the other Muslims refused to stand and pledge allegiance to the United States flag. This disrespect for our country's flag angered several of those in the crowd, who turned to glare at the composed, stone-faced Muslims.

Erling requested a motion to adopt the minutes of the last meeting as mailed. The vote was unanimous.

"There's really only one important piece of business on the council agenda today," Erling said. "And that's the debate and vote on the ordinance concerning the display of the Confederate flag over the Civil War monument on the city hall lawn."

The chanting started again. "Pull down the flag! Fire Chief Crowe. Pull down the flag. . ." Several of those in the spectator's gallery leaped to their feet and waved protest signs. They began marching around the room, chanting as they went and bobbing the upper part of their bodies up and down in rhythmic timing to their chants.

Erling looked at me and shrugged. He waited patiently for the chanting to stop and the protestors to take their seats. It took five minutes for the marchers to realize that no one was trying to stop them. Once this fact dawned on them, they quickly took their seats again.

Karim's voice boomed out again. "We serve notice that the matter of firing Crowe will be the main item on the agenda, not for today's meeting, but for the next regular council session."

My suspicions had been confirmed that banning the flying of the Confederate flag would be the main thrust by Karim and Tolman today. I glanced at DeLong. He was smiling broadly.

"I call upon our Council clerk to read the ordinance to be debated and voted on," Erling said.

Tony Angell read the simple ordinance that would ban the flying of the Confederate flag anywhere on city hall grounds.

"Just yesterday," President Erling said, "Council member Stoney Bedford came forward with a very generous offer of compromise that could defuse the racial tension that is building to the flash point over this matter of the flag. He has received pledges from twenty prominent citizens—make that twenty-three citizens now—to donate $5,000 each to erect a monument to Dr. Martin Luther King on City hall grounds one hundred feet to the west of the present Civil War monument. The Chamber of Commerce thought so much of the idea that their president pledged $50,000 on the chamber's behalf. As did State Senator Willie Sanders. Bedford has further offered to co-chair a fund-raising committee, along with Abdul Karim and DeLong Tolman, to raise the balance of the $300,000 needed to pay for the monument."

Able paused to sip from his glass of water. "But," he lowered his voice to a tone of resignation, "the black community has refused to accept this offer. At least, that's what their leaders tell us. Could it be that, no matter how hard we try; the opponents really do not want to get along with the white community? Could it be that they have another agenda which has not been unveiled? We do not understand."

"Bedford is a racist! Bedford is a racist! Bedford is a racist!" The chanters were marching again. The waving signs reminded of breaking surf on Florida beaches.

"Pull the flag down! Pull the flag down! Pull the flag down!"

There was a rhythm to their chanting that had the hypnotic spell cast by a charismatic preacher in a tent revival.

I watched Abdul Karim walk to the podium. Once he got there, he turned his back to council members—as he had done at our last meeting—and punched his right fist into the air to punctuate the chanting which was still going on. After five minutes, he motioned to the protesters to sit down. Then he turned to face us council members.

"Give your name and address for the record," Erling said to him.

"My name is Abdul Karim, as if you didn't know. I live at 114 Iota Street. Long ago," he began, "each of us black people erected a monument to Martin Luther King. We built it in our hearts and in our memories. We do not need a concrete and stone monument to Dr. King erected on city grounds."

Applause broke out. There were cries from the spectators of "You said it, Brother. You said it."

"This so-called generous offer of compromise by Stoney Bedford," Karim continued. "This white Southern racist has made a slick maneuver that we will not accept. The black people of Forest are united behind our two demands, and we will not be bought off with such foolish appeals to our battered egos as having a monument erected to Dr. King. Long ago, some of us blacks moved past being impressed by such grandiose schemes."

Demonstrators took to the floor again, chanting. Able's face showed his vast patience. After quiet settled in again, Able began talking. "At council meetings, we encourage citizen input, but we do have rules to help us maintain some semblance of decorum. We respect the rights of each individual in this room. In turn, we ask each of you to show the same respect to his fellow citizens. The chanting and the marching will not sway the opinions of council members one-way or the other. It does not intimidate us. Your threatening remarks only serve to sadden most of us and lead us to ask ourselves why this woeful lack of understanding and respect for the democratic process."

Booing and groans rose up from the audience. Erling continued his remarks.

"I'd like to remind Mr. Karim that I will not allow him to control this meeting. My patience does have its limits. I allowed your earlier remarks that were definitely out of order to go unchallenged so that you and those who support you could see that you would be allowed to speak your mind on the issues at hand.

Able Erling, as council chairman, was fair and impartial in his conduct of the meetings.

"Under our rules, those on both sides of an issue, the pros and the cons, are allowed thirty minutes to make their views known," the chairman pointed out. "That time can be divided among the speakers any way the leaders of each side deem best. I know that by now, each of you have been assured that your views will be heard and that you will be treated with fairness and respect. Now, let us proceed to discuss the ordinance before us that would ban flying the Confederate flag anywhere on City Hall grounds. Those who are for adoption of the ordinance will be heard first. Mr. Karim, since you appear to be their leader, you may begin."

The imposing Karim stood silently at the podium. Anyone would have to agree that his very presence demanded respect. He did not immediately begin to speak. His face was impassive; his jaw jutted forward in defiance. In mock solemnity, he bowed to Erling. "We black people thank our white lords and masters for their grave concern about the rights of people."

A derisive murmur ran through the spectators.

"Yes, we are mightily impressed," Karim intoned, the centuries old soft shoe shuffle of blacks as they dealt with the white man showing in his voice. He was doing it by design.

"The great television series *Roots* showed how greatly concerned the white slave traders were when they captured and beat black Africans and forced them aboard the slave ships. Those pathetic captives were shackled in irons and brought to America against their will. You whites allowed us such great dignity as individuals, especially as we stood on the auction blocks in the slave markets while the white man bid for us, as if we were a bale of cotton instead of a human being."

The Muslim leader knew he had things going his way and that what he was saying was being broadcast all over the world.

"Our black women felt the spirit of equality granted black people when the white man's semen spurted into their vaginas. These women felt especially flattered that their bodies were attractive enough to induce their white masters to slip off at night to the slave quarters to have their fun."

Several of the black women had risen to their feet, linked arms, closed their eyes and swayed and moaned. "Oh, Lord! They tore at our bodies. Oh, Lord! They feasted on our bodies. Oh, Lord! They spurted their baby seeds into us. We had no power to protest. We could only endure and hate."

The effect was eerie. If you closed your eyes, you could hear the voices of Stephen King's characters as they realize they could not hide from evil's dark spell.

Karim had bowed his head until the women sat down. "The metal tipped ends of the overseers' whips biting into our bodies imparted a special reminder of how greatly white people valued us as individuals. And the more flesh the whips tore from our backs, the greater the bonds of freedom that bound us together as Americans. How glorious it was to breathe this air of freedom accorded us by whites."

Hoots and jeers rent the air. People shifted nervously in their seats.

Karim's bitter sarcasms were acid poured onto my soul. He'd seen such virulent presentations in the movies, read such twisted lies in the works of Erskine Caldwell and Tennessee Williams, learned such half truths at school in the vicious slanting of our history books by the Yankee victors. His sneering words were the red capes waved in front of his hate-filled brethren who even now were being reminded again of how fiercely they should hate white Southerners.

He was a virtuoso coaxing the discordant notes of volcanic eruption ever closer to the surface from the assembled players.

The TV cameramen had walked toward the front of the room with their cameras on their shoulders and turned toward Karim in order to zero in on his handsome, magnificent presence. There was nothing we could do to stop the raining of Karim's words into the minds of Americans across the country who would see the story unfolding on television. It was such popular coin so easily spent in the media's hypnotic bazaars, for simply, it furnished the kind of lurid details that fired the emotions of the unthinking.

The drama being played out in council chambers today in Forest, Georgia would give television commentators and newspaper columnists limitless opportunity to spear Southerners again and again with their prejudiced barbs tipped in charges of racism's poison. The tube's anchor-people loved to pontificate from their lofty heights of assumed moral superiority as they made us their convenient scapegoats. I could hear again their eager, sneering voices, reading their denigrating headlines.

Karim continued. "White Southerners loved black people so much that they went to war in 1860 to keep us in slavery's loving embrace. Blacks were property and the rebel soldiers fought bravely and fiercely for the things in which they believed. And, you have to admit that the men in gray almost won that terrible conflict. Never question a Southerner's bravery. They simply outfought and out maneuvered the Union armies for over three years."

He looked directly at me. "I tip my hat to you, General Bedford."

The hoots and jeers came again. Karim turned back toward the audience. He held up his hand to command their attention. "No, I'm sincere. Lee and his armies invaded the North and whipped the Union forces in almost every confrontation. Any thinking man should have been frightened at what almost happened."

He turned back to us council members, lifted a glass to sip water, and continued. "Fortunately, God saw fit to break their spirits and destroy their will to fight on that July day at Cemetery Ridge in 1863. I've watched the video of that great movie *Gettysburg* a hundred times. I cheered each time the blue coats mowed down those poor bastards in gray uniform who kept on coming. The Confederate general Pickett urged those brave and foolish lads onward and upward in their insane charge up Cemetery Ridge toward the heights occupied by the Yankees."

Woolford had his chin propped onto his hand. He was listening intently. I looked across at Baxter Lampkins. His face was drawn and grim, like that of a man sentenced to death who was waiting for the warden and the priest to escort him on his last march to the execution chamber.

"President Lincoln freed the slaves in 1863," Karim said, "We were free at last. Free at last. We had the Emancipation Proclamation to prove it. Or so we thought, but once again, the black man took it in the neck. You see, we weren't really free. Not free until a hundred years later when black people charged the Confederates and broke their backs again, the same way the Union forces broke their backs at Gettysburg.

"This time, the field of battle was Selma, Alabama. The opposing armies were a determined brigade of black people charging up the ridges of the South's prejudice and racism to hurl themselves against the defiant enemy, the armies of white, Southern segregationists.

"Noble black soldiers—and hundreds of white people who'd joined our fight for freedom—mounted a different kind of charge that day, a charge to be free of the yoke of oppression. Waiting for us at the end of the bridge was Confederate General Bull Connor with his electric-powered megaphone and his massed troops of Southerners determined not to yield to Supreme Court edicts and bent on keeping 'those uppity niggers in their place.' Their weapons were powerful fire hoses, shields, batons and vicious attack dogs.

"Oh, yes. The Confederate flag was held high that day by many in General Connor's army. The *valiant actions* of Southerners that day at the battle of the bridge in Selma especially endeared the rebels to the hearts of us black people. The Confederates used their weapons very effectively and left many of our ragged forces bloodied and wounded. The whole world waited and watched and could not believe such actions against a people yearning only to be free."

"Right on, brother! Amen! That's telling it like it is!" Karim was, for the moment, their preacher in the pulpit and they were his mesmerized congregation.

Harris Woolford passed me a note. "Can you believe this shit that's being dumped onto us? Karim's parading all the tired old cliches of prejudice before the media again and they're eating it up! Just look at them."

I looked toward the back of the room where the reporters, photographers and television cameras were busy recording the show. Harris was right. They were enjoying the slashing attack on the South. (Morris Light and his assistant were among them, but those two were recording these scenes with a different purpose in mind. A documentary to tell the true story of the flag and the way Southerners feel about our land and our heritage.)

Karim's impassioned sermon continued. "You'd have thought that the loss of the Civil War would have led white people of the Confederacy to see the sheer hypocrisy of their comforting rationalizations for slavery and the reasons they fought the war. It didn't, for Southerners are the greatest guerilla fighters the world has ever known. After Appomattox, they didn't stop fighting. They simply took their war underground and fought silently by day as they hid behind their masks of social ostracism for the freed slaves and anonymously by night, usually from horseback and with flaming torches and white sheets in campaigns to strike terror into the hearts of blacks. Their weapons? Fear, unity of purpose, determination and elaborate bulwarks of social customs.

"Before too many years had passed and reconstruction had lost its steam, Southerners once again controlled the political, economic and social processes with an unseen, iron hand. They hid behind their smiles of beneficence and courtesy and masqueraded behind high blown moral pretensions of helping us black people 'find our way to individual freedom.'

"They erected memorials to that terrible war all over the South, ran up the symbol of slavery, the Confederate flag, and sang a song called *Dixie* in their schools, their parades, their sporting events. They lost the Civil War, but they won their battle to keep black people in inferior societal roles. They denied black people their freedoms and dignity in a thousand different ways."

Karim showed a terrible ignorance of Civil War history—or he was deliberately ignoring the basic facts. Doesn't he know, I asked myself, that ninety percent of those who fought for the Confederate cause were small farmers, shopkeepers and tradesmen who never owned a slave?

The South had a right to break away from the union and form their own separate nation. Southerners value individual freedom to decide their own futures above anything else. It's in our heritage and we'll fight any government who threatens to encroach upon our freedoms, even as we fight today's central government efforts to force us into rigid molds. Hell, those brave men in gray who died in that terrible conflict that left 600,000 dead weren't fighting for slavery. That wasn't important to them. They charged up that ridge in Gettysburg as a matter of individual honor. Oh, if only we could have held onto the high ground. We had the opportunity at Little and Big Round Top to seize and hold the high ground, two days before Cemetery Ridge, but we let it slip through our fingers. If only . . .

"Not only," Karim said. "Not only do we want that hated symbol of slavery pulled down and banished forever from the grounds of City hall. Now hear me closely. We also want that *damned monument to Lee pulled down.*"

The audience exploded with whoops and shouted phrases. "Break Lee's head off. Pull him down. Break Lee's head off. Pull him down . . ."

As if on signal, the marchers clogged the aisles as they stomped loudly in protest. One of them banged his sign down onto Mike Chapman's head and opened a cut that started bleeding. Chapman slugged the man and yelled for help. Blacks and whites started trading blows. Karim's twenty soldiers, at his command, rushed in to separate the combatants and restore order.

Woolford scribbled another note and passed it to me. "Decapitate Robert E. Lee? How about the busts of U.S. Grant and General Sherman? These people want to stomp our asses into the dust. They're not interested in fairness and equality. They want total domination of whites."

"Black people have been carefully taught to hate whites," I wrote back. "A tragedy of immense proportions. Not much hope for building bridges across this chasm. A war of genocide could easily break out."

Karim signaled for quiet again. "I have a surprise enlistee in our ranks as we battle you white racist Southerners," he said. "He's one of your own, spawned from your own cultural ranks, but blessedly, he's a man who has pierced through the fogs of your distorted beliefs and prejudices, your venomous racist views. He's a senior at Harvard University. I did not know him until he telephoned me three days ago.

" 'I want to help your cause,' he said. 'I'm flying South today to join you in your efforts to banish the flying of that hated flag.'

" 'What's your name?' I asked him."

" 'Thomas Farris,' he said. 'I was born and reared in Forest. My daddy is a rich doctor there.' "

Laughter broke out. A few groans of disbelief escaped the throats of some of the whites in the audience. Farris, as Karim knew, was a surprise lancer on a black horse ready to thrust his words through our defenses.

Farris was tall and thin. Acne scars covered his ridged, red face. His brown hair was already wisping away. His stooped shoulders betrayed the social disdain his peers had probably accorded him as he was growing up. I knew his daddy, a bull of a man who operated on patients twelve hours a day, non-stop. His beautiful, imperious mother was one of Forest's ruling social matriarchs who reminded me of my own mother, Queen Betty Jane Bolling.

Young Farris' voice was strong. He spoke without a trace of the Southern accent. His first words into the microphone made it obvious that he had disavowed his Southern upbringing.

"I was ashamed of being a Southerner," the acne-scarred young man said. "I am ashamed of that Confederate flag you so arrogantly fly on City hall grounds. Any thoughtful person knows that flag is a silent fist waving in the air as a warning to black people. It makes statements. It says, 'my parents taught me black people are inferior to white people. Black people must stay in their place on their own side of town.' It's a symbol of hatred and oppression of black people.

"Robert E. Lee? Cloaked in his mythical nobility and military genius. Enshrined in bronze and concrete in hundreds of places throughout this poor bedraggled land I once called home. 'Marse Robert' as his men used to call him with the reverence usually reserved for gods. What a pity that Lee's men did not kill him as did General Stonewall Jackson's men."

"You dirty bastard," someone in the audience blurted out.

Farris smiled and continued. "It was only after I arrived at Harvard as a student that the hypocrisy of my Southern upbringing, of the beliefs so carefully instilled in me by my cultural milieu, became clearly evident. For months, I was in a state of shock. I could hear my mother's oft repeated warnings. 'We don't mistreat black people,' she'd say. 'But we don't mix and intermingle with them socially. Never, never, never. We stay in our places and let them stay in theirs.' "

Groans from some of the spectators were laced with hostility. The chanting started, this time, the words were: "Bedford hates blacks." "Bedford Hates Blacks." "Bedford Hates Blacks." I could feel the anger rising inside me and ran my fingers around the inside of my shirt collar. I caught sight of the *New York Times* and the *Washington Post* reporters furiously scribbling down Farris' words on their long yellow legal pads.

Farris asked: "And just what is this place that my mother warned me that was allocated to blacks, the 'place in which they should stay'? When I was growing up, we called their places 'Nigger Quarters.' Now, it's euphemistically called 'The Inner City.' "

I could say one thing for Farris. He wasn't afraid. You could see the disdain for things Southern blazing on his face, hear it wrapped around his carefully chosen words. He was enjoying this release of his pent-up hostilities. A turncoat fouling the nest in which he had been nurtured.

Farris was hacking his own people with blunt, verbal axes. He's a perfect example, I thought, of the way deconstructionists attack true history. "The herd mentality," as John Steinbeck called it. It's easier to seek solace in being like everyone else than it is to be an individual who stands for principle. I wanted to shrink away from such impudent vulgarity.

"You know what Harvard and the Yankees have taught me?" Farris paused for dramatic effect. "The so-called nobility of the Southerner's beliefs and principles are a fraud, an illusion to which they cling to avoid feeling guilty about the way they've mistreated blacks. Through rationalization and renowned civility and courtesy, they've imputed noble reasons to why they fought the Civil War and have tried religiously to inculcate these false reasons into the minds and hearts of each succeeding generation.

Yes, Farris. Many of us strive to perpetuate our Southern heritage through the cultural transmission belt, but you are a perfect example of how we've failed.

"Well, thank God, I learned the truth at last. As Jesus said, 'Ye shall know the truth and the truth shall set you free.' I crossed those carefully constructed barriers of separation of the races that had been instilled into me. I found that blacks were real people too."

A big smile lit up his face. "I'll be married upon my being graduated in June to a beautiful, lively, intelligent black girl. She's also a senior at Harvard. It gives me such a good feeling inside my heart." He touched his fist to his heart and squared his shoulders in bold defiance as martyrs throughout . history have done before they were burned at the stake.

"Oh, no!" someone in the audience shouted. "Marrying a Negro? Not another one of those!"

"You traitorous son-of-a-bitch," another white moaned. "The poor children will not know whether they're black or white."

Farris grew bolder. "Fortunately, my wife and I will live in the North where we won't be scorned. Both of us will teach at a university in Vermont where hopefully, we can show others the error of their beliefs about Southern ideals and supposed nobility of soul.

"I'm here in Forest to help pull the Confederate flag down and topple the noble General Lee into the dust where he belongs."

Cheering and groans broke out; the chanting started as if on cue; the marchers charged up and down the aisles once more with renewed fury. "Bedford Hates Blacks! Bedford Hates Blacks!" A new chant broke out. "Topple Bedford Too! Topple Bedford Too! Topple Bedford Too! Behead General Lee! Behead General Lee! Behead General Lee!"

The words held an ominous meaning for me. The dread dark strokes of fear brushed my thoughts again. "Topple Bedford Too!" What did they mean by that? My left hand rubbed the front of my throat.

Baxter Lampkins' face showed no trace of emotion, but then, Baxter was an opportunist, and as long as he had chosen the way that would best benefit him, there was no need to show any concern. This handsome, dark-haired man enjoyed his world with a free-spirited abandon. He loved playing golf at the country club and afterwards, joining his playing companions on the "nineteenth hole" and drinking vodka and tonic. This gave him ample opportunity to hob nob with the very rich around the polished mahogany tables hidden deep inside the interior of the men's clubhouse and not readily discernible to the uninformed, casual observer. The feeling of exclusivity was important to Baxter.

What did principle matter to Baxter? Almost nothing. He would change his vote on the flag ordinance because he was a pragmatist and if he lost his three largest customers and the seventy percent of his income that came from commissions on supplies and equipment they purchased from him, the life style he loved would be lost, too. Without enough money, the country club and the invitations to the brilliant social parties he and his wife loved would disappear. And Baxter couldn't stand being a nobody.

I became aware that a hush had fallen onto the meeting. Farris had finished his brutal hacking of us. A look of pride and evil satisfaction settled onto his face. He had humiliated Southerners one more time. In his mind, he had showed the world the hypocrisy of Southern ideals and principles, the "shameful" world of grand illusions in which we wallowed. By his words and examples, he had lent credibility to the hauling down of the Confederate flag on Forest City Hall grounds— and the destruction of Lee's monument. The young man's smug assurance told me that he felt that he delivered the final blow that had routed us "unreconstructed rebels" into acceptance of the inevitable.

I wanted to strike back against the torturers. I searched for and found the faces of Wash Washington and Blue Combs in the gallery. I fastened my gaze onto them until I caught their eyes. They each grinned sheepishly and turned to whisper to each other. How could these two ministers square themselves with their consciences? Donna Elaine and I had sent the two through college with love and generous amounts of money. Now, their bitter coin of repayment was their icy disdain. They felt perfectly justified with their abandonment of me and their rationalizations for it.

I found a friendly black face. Roy Bester's solemn visage gleamed in the low light. It showed pain over what was happening to me. He tipped his head to me ever so slightly and smiled.

Able Erling rapped his gavel. "Now," he said. "We'll hear from those who oppose the ordinance that would ban flying the Confederate flag. Let's see. I understand that Mr. Carl Krippendorf is their spokesman. Mr.

Krippendorf, will you come to the podium and state your name and address for the record."

Carl's painfully slow limp toward the microphone on his steel leg brought a deadening silence to the meeting chamber.

"My name is Carl Krippendorf, attorney. My office is on the second floor of the Oglethorpe Building, corner of Bedford and Jackson avenues. I'm a Southerner and proud of it. I will never turn traitor to the South and disavow my heritage. As did this poor, misguided wretch named Farris, now a man without a country."

Applause and rebel yells rent the air. Several people stood as they cheered and whistled. At last, one of their own was speaking out for the things in which they believed with every ounce of their being.

"The United Daughters of the Confederacy," Krippendorf said. "I'd like for these lovely ladies to stand and be recognized."

Eleven older women stood up with regal bearing and smiled at the applause. I recognized four of them, especially Eloise Robb. She served as a docent with Donna Elaine at the museum. Another, Helen Wills, had a right arm so crippled with arthritis until she had to lift it with her left hand. The face of Doris Blackmore glowed with determination and hope. Sonia Etcheman had both fists clenched. Her feisty manner told of her dedication.

"Now," Krippendorf said. "I want the representatives from the Forest chapter of the Sons of the Confederate Veterans to stand and be recognized. I'm so proud that these men are fighting against great odds to preserve some small part of the heritage and ideals that enrich the true Southerner's life and living."

He waited for the rebel yells to die down. "Mike Chapman. Will you please come forward and speak to the city council?"

"Your name and address for the record, please," Erling said.

"I'm Mike Chapman, 907 Jonesboro Road, Forest, Georgia. I'm an X-ray technician. Since I'm not an accomplished speaker like Tom Farris from Harvard—and lately of Forest, Georgia—I'll read you a statement by Judge Ben Smith, Jr., of Waycross, Georgia, as printed in *The Confederate Veteran.*

He started reading.

All over the Southland we are plagued with an epidemic of do-gooder educators and mindless politicians hell-bent on obliterating all reminders of the Southern Confederacy. It is said that they do not wish to offend minority groups and members of the new enlightenment. Ancient symbols and time-honored traditions will be swept away as worthless encumbrances to the new breed of Southerner. Our children are taught to despise these totems of a once proud people. The new-style censorship is considered to be a splendid and humanitarian thing, a giant step on the way to the true brotherhood of man.

"No, no, no," some of the whites in the audience cried out. "We have a right to believe in these things."

Chapman continued to read from the judge's statement.

What arrant nonsense. It never occurs to these manipulators that catering to any kind of pressure to invoke the banning of symbols and displays of regional heritage is itself a contemptible form of intolerance. It cannot be a greater sin to offend other citizens who want to enjoy the privilege of free expression under the First Amendment of our Constitution.

Cheering broke out among the white spectators. "Listen to that, Mr. Karim. And DeLong Tolman. It works both ways," one of them yelled.

No, the American way is to tolerate the viewpoint of all, to play *Dixie*, *We Shall Overcome* and *The Battle Hymn of the Republic* at the same public gathering and let those cheer who want to cheer whenever their song is played. Fair play always, but censorship never.

An older generation of Southerners loved and revered the Confederate Flag, the flag which was peculiarly their own. It was the thrilling symbol of the courage and staunchness of their forefathers. If it was ever a symbol of oppression, it was the symbol of their own oppression under the military occupation (by the Yankee victors). How can anyone ban its display in public and remain within the framework of the Constitution? The suppression of ideas and regional culture by any group is not to be tolerated by Southern Americans or any American. The idea that some self-anointed arbiters of taste can decide what is best for us and what might be offensive to some group or other should never take root in this Republic less we become a rabble unworthy of freedom.

Now it was the whites who broke into cheering, leaped to their feet and began marching around the meeting room. A deep voice boomed out, "You blacks are the intolerant ones. Quit pushing us. You keep your heritage; we intend to keep ours."

The shouted words came from the older man who had intimated to me before the meeting started that black militants and liberals were pressing Southerners too hard.

Chapman waited for the tumult to die down, then continued.

The political avant-garde of today are the most intolerant breed to appear in modern America. These mischievous people are after votes and care little for constitutional principles. They are the worthy successors of the radical Republicans of another time (those who swarmed Southward during the reconstruction period to plunder, steal and occupy the seats of power). They have done more to polarize the races in the South than they have done to establish the good feeling that ought to exist between them.

If I am offended by someone who is expressing his ideas and not disobeying the law, that is just too bad, for both black and white, yellow and red, have every right to celebrate their heritage. The point is citizens who express their ideas and personal philosophy in song, poetry, symbols and rhetoric, so long as those enterprises are within the law, must not be prevented from doing so. It is irrelevant that someone is offended by this lawful behavior. This is the Land of the Free and the Home of the Brave—or so it used to be.

There were tears in Chapman's eyes as he finished. He bowed his head as many of the whites in the audience stood to applaud. Joyful whoops and rebel yells broke out.

Three immaculately dressed young white women had not stood with the other whites to join in their jubilation. The cool composure of the three had fled as Judge Ben Smith's words punctured their outward sophistication. They fidgeted in their seats and pulled at their suit jackets and skirts. I was convinced that they would have hurried from the room had they been able to do so without drawing notice to their actions.

The two preachers, Wash Washington and Blue Combs, had lowered their heads but they were certainly not praying.

Thomas Farris had a silly, embarrassed grin on his gaunt acne-scarred face. He sat next to Abdul Karim who was whispering to one of the large, double-chinned black women who held a sign with hand lettering that said, "Pull Down The Flag."

DeLong Tolman started shouting and waving his right hand frantically. "Mr. Chairman. Mr. Chairman. How much longer do we have to listen to this sentimental drivel that only further distorts Southern myths and legends?"

Able Erling answered Tolman. "I'd like to remind Councilman Tolman that Mr. Krippendorf and the opposing side still have a large bloc of their thirty minutes remaining." Able turned to face the audience again. "Mr. Krippendorf, you may continue."

Krippendorf hobbled back to the podium. "Forgive me for walking so slowly," he said and tapped on his artificial leg with his hickory walking stick. "Hear that sound? Those of you who don't know me closely, will not guess that it's the sound my walking stick makes when I thump it against the metal of my artificial leg. I lost the leg when the Americans hit the beach at Salerno, Italy in World War II. We were fighting a diabolical, fiendish German oppressor of nations and people called Adolph Hitler. He was out to enslave the whole world. Nation after nation fell to his ruthless armies.

"Hitler had a whipping boy, too, a symbol he used to divert people's attention from their real problems. 'All of Germany's problems were caused by Jews.' He taught German people to hate the Jews fiercely enough to execute millions of them. I ask you. Is this a portent for America? Aren't blacks being taught that we white Southerners are the source of all of their problems? Think of what this hatred visited upon an innocent people.

"He seemed unstoppable—until America sent millions of us to fight against him and eventually win."

I wanted Carl to tell the story of how he lost his leg, the saga of his courage and bravery, of his slow and painful recovery from the wounds he received in fighting a maniacal dictator whose amoral, unreasoning hatred led to the oppression and annihilation of millions of innocent people.

"The fragments of a German .88 shell tore off this leg," Carl said. "I was blown from the landing craft into the water in a state of shock and would have drowned except for that man sitting up there named Stoney Bedford. He dove into the water and pulled me aboard his landing craft and somehow was able to get me back to the mother ship where God and the doctors saved my life."

"We don't need to hear your war stories," Tolman yelled. "You and Bedford ain't heroes to us!"

"Thank you, Mr. Tolman," Carl said. "For your great concern for my well being."

Harris jumped into the fray. He pointed toward the media. "I want the whole world to see Mr. Tolman's lack of regard for other human beings. His actions are vulgar."

"What'd you expect from him?" The yell came from the defiant, older man who had earlier voiced his ominous threats. "He doesn't know what courtesy and tolerance are."

Erling rapped his gavel for order. "Please continue, Mr. Krippendorf."

"Back in 1861, the South went to war against the North to fight off the oppression they were attempting to force onto us. The Yankees couldn't tolerate our resisting their efforts to tell us how to live our lives. Had I been alive, I'd have willingly charged up that hill at Gettysburg—and died if necessary. Southerners are born to fight off the yokes of oppression."

"I wish you'd have been there," Tolman laughed. "If you had, you'd be dead and we wouldn't have to hear your horror stories."

Carl forged on. "Let's contrast the reasons the men in gray fought the war for independence from the North to why the blue coats went into battle. Here's a journal entry from a nineteen-year-old Confederate soldier who volunteered, as did all of the men in gray.

Them Yankees ain't gonna tell us Southerners how to live and what to do, We'll fight them and whip them. They challenged us and by God they're going to get what they deserve.

But those poor boys in blue? Thousands of them were in the Yankee army because they didn't have the money, $300 I believe it was, to pay another man to fight in their place. They weren't fighting to free the slaves. It was two years after we fired on Fort. Sumter before Lincoln issued the emancipation proclamation. Nor were the soldiers in blue fighting to force the South back into the union.

Oh no. It was the northern politicians urging on the war as a means of punishing the South. Most of you don't know about the anti-war riots that occurred in dozens of Northern cities. In New York alone, one riot took the lives of over one thousand people. And guess what? The newspapers of that day detail how the rioters searched for and found hundreds of black people whom they promptly hanged.

"They were fighting to free us black people," one of the Muslim women yelled.

"You really think so?" Carl asked. "Lady, you're dead wrong. The newspapers of that period tell the true story. This was in the North, not the South. Why do you choose to ignore history's reality? The newspapers of the North ran story after story about how sick and tired the populace had become when victory did not come quickly; when the war went on far too long to suit those grieving mothers and fathers back home who received word their sons and husbands had died on the battlefield. The South was whipping hell out of the Yankees."

Krippendorf sipped from a glass of water and wearily shifted his weight. It was obvious that he was in pain. "The Southern fighting man," he said, "is known throughout the history books for his uncommon courage and valor. When the war was over, he came home to an occupied land where carpetbaggers ruled and swaggered up and down our streets. Thousands of the returning men in gray were sick, injured and without resources, yet they rebuilt our homeland."

DeLong Tolman's face showed his disgust at what was occurring. He threw down his pencil and began reading some papers he had before him. The faces of many in the spectator's gallery were happy and smiling. The faces of others were impassive and unmoving. The dozens of media people on the raised platform at the back of the room were lost in intense concentration on Carl's words.

"But the victors in any war always write the rules by which the defeated people live," Carl said. "There was no charity exhibited in the hated Reconstruction Act, nor in the occupying forces that streamed South to rape and plunder our people and our resources. The North almost destroyed Southerners with their hatred and oppression. Why, we treated our World War II enemies, the Italians, the Germans and the Japanese, with a far more gentle hand than the North treated the people of the South.

"At the end of World War II we did not plunder the lands of the conquered nations nor their people. With the Marshall Act we rebuilt their countries and made them prosperous. Yet, even to this very hour, the North oppresses the South with the Civil Rights Act and the Voting Rights Act and Justice Department supervision over drawing the lines of voting districts. We in the South are not free. We still have those in place who would be our masters if we did not resist fiercely.

"Our land and its people are still undergoing reconstruction. We're still an occupied land, but we will never surrender."

The whooping, the applause and the rebel yells burst forth again, this time even louder. People throughout the auditorium were standing. My emotions compelled me to jump to my feet and applaud. Harris Woolford stood and began to emit piercing whistles with his fingers between his lips.

Carl had bowed his head. I watched him feeling in his coat pocket for a handkerchief. He lifted his glasses and wiped the corners of his eyes. When the spectators quieted, he began again.

"I'd like to disabuse many of you of the idea that black people are more loved and readily accepted in the North and that there is no prejudice directed toward them. If you have such beliefs, you are living in an unreal world. The *Wall Street Journal* writes in-depth articles on the frustrations of blacks who are named to mid-level executive positions in large Northern corporations. They frequently quote these black executives as they tell of their social isolation and lack of acceptance. Black students at college all over the land, excluded from the fellowship of white students, have resegregated themselves in order to enjoy the social acceptability of other blacks."

"You can't force people to associate with or love other people," the older man with the ominous voice yelled. "We got a right to choose our friends and you're trying to pass laws to take it away from us. It won't work."

"Mr. Chairman," Tolman yelled. "That old white racist bastard is out of order."

"No more than you have been, Mr. Tolman," Erling smiled. "Please continue, Mr. Krippendorf.

"And this pitiable young man, Thomas Farris. The fellow who had disavowed his heritage out of the weaknesses in his own self-esteem. People like him hate themselves so intensely until they struggle daily to prove that they are not worthy. I'd say that Farris is a living, breathing example of this self-hatred. Wait until he and his black bride begin to feel the scorn and prejudice heaped upon couples in an interracial marriage. And their children? God pity the innocent ones who cannot exercise a choice. They are scarcely accepted anywhere in our country, not even by other black people.

"Now, this striking figure of a man, Abdul Karim. He says he watched the movie of Gettysburg and cheered when the Confederates died by the thousands as they charged up Cemetery Ridge. Mr. Karim, did you cheer as the black people in Somalia, Burundi, Zaire and Rwanda slaughtered over one million of their own innocent black brothers? And for what reasons? Hatred. Tribal hatreds. It is a holocaust I see often on television as they show the thousands of bodies of black children, women and men who have been slaughtered in these god-forsaken lands."

Several of the whites in the audience gasped. One yelled, "That's what the blacks will do to us if they ever get enough power." It was the balding, older man I'd spoken to earlier.

Carl raised his voice. "Where is your outcry over this, Mr. Karim? Where are the anguished cries of other people across this nation? These are the same people who so readily criticize and condemn Southerners, yet their voices are strangely silent. Why have we allowed ourselves to become so desensitized to the death of millions of black people in Africa that we shrug our shoulders and quickly turn the pages of the magazines or change TV channels to escape the pictures that show their lifeless, hacked and bleeding bodies. Is there a double standard?"

"There's none so blind as those who will not see," Mike Chapman yelled.

"How right you are, Mr. Chapman. At least at Gettysburg, we were fighting the oppressors who would thrust down upon our heads a crown of thorns that they yet struggle to make us wear, even today. We fought for our lofty longings to be free of the Northern boot, for nobility of purpose and ideals, the same nobility that motivated Stoney Bedford to risk his life at Salerno to save my life; the same nobility that led him to make his magnanimous offer to help build a memorial to Dr. Martin Luther King on the grounds of City Hall, only 100 feet west of the Confederate Memorial."

"Oh," Tolman groaned. "Here comes more of that 'how noble we are' business."

"Why not, Mr. Tolman," Carl asked. "It is plainly evident that black leaders in Forest have an agenda that is far removed from being noble. It is an agenda of warring, as Karim says, against the whites in America. Sadly, many of us are convinced that the only thing that will satisfy black people is for their skins to become white. It is the hatred of their own black skins that creates among themselves and in their communities such crime and lawlessness as to make living conditions almost unbearable. Do they take responsibility for cleaning up their own house? No, they prefer to blame everything on white people. 'You've got to give us this, you've got to give us that, you've got to. . . And on and on it goes."

Carl jutted his chin out and spoke slowly to emphasize his closing words. "We will not let you remove the Confederate flag nor tear down the monument. It is hatred and thirst for revenge, the grasping for political power regardless of the price to be paid, that energize your efforts. That flag, that monument is a symbol of our Southern way of life. We will never surrender. Never, never, never."

Bedlam broke out among the white sympathizers in the audience. Whooping, cheering, rebel yells, applause, the stomping of feet, ear piercing whistles. It was almost ten minutes before quiet settled over those in the audience.

"Let's vote," Tolman shouted. "Let's vote, let's vote, let's vote." He was banging his fist on the top of the counter that ran in front of the entire council membership and linked us together in a horseshoe. "I move the adoption of ordinance number 2911 of 1996."

"Second the motion," Frank Dines yelled.

"We'll vote by machine," Able Erling said. "A 'Yes' vote means the flag comes down. A 'No' vote means it continues to fly above the monument."

He turned on the voting machines that sat in front of each council member. Once members cast their votes and he illuminated the board behind him, people could immediately tell who had voted "yes" and who voted "no."

"All those in favor of adopting Ordinance 2911 vote 'Yes.' All those opposed to adopting the ordinance vote 'No.' "

Council members began pushing the buttons in front of them that recorded their decision.

"All right," Able said. "Before I press the master button to flash our votes onto the board behind me, make certain you've voted the way you wished to vote. This vote is final and I'll adjourn the meeting immediately after your votes are shown on the board. There will be no changing of your vote once the board is illuminated. Has everyone voted? All right."

He pushed the master control button. Three red checks for "Yes" showed on the tally board. The four red checks for "No" brought a stunned silence.

"The ordinance is defeated 4–3," Erling announced. "The Confederate flag will still fly on City Hall grounds. This meeting is adjourned."

"Baxter," Tolman yelled. "You voted against us. You lousy bastard. Just remember. What goes around, comes around."

Lampkins smiled and shrugged his shoulders. "I reconsidered my position on the issue and changed my mind," he said. "Your reasons for pulling the flag down are a subterfuge. They hide your secret agenda, as Carl Krippendorf said."

An ominous hush had fallen onto the crowd, as though some unseen force had squeezed the elation of victory and the gloom of defeat from them and left them unable to speak. From the resigned slump in their bodies, I could tell that several of the losers had not taken their defeat with grace.

Others had not caved in and surrendered in their battle. I watched as Abdul Karim and his twenty ramrod-straight Muslim converts walked swiftly from the room.

"I can understand their disappointment," I said to Harris.

"Piss on those prejudiced bastards," Harris laughed. "They don't understand anything about the way we feel. It's just a political power game to them. Why should you be disappointed for them? To hell with them. No love for us has been lost in their hearts. It never was there in the first place."

The spectators and the media people surged forward and converged upon Baxter Lampkins. As the opportunist walked from the meeting room, he was surrounded by a forest of cameras and photographers and reporters.

I sought out Carl Krippendorf and Mike Chapman to express my thanks and to exult with them and several others for a few moments over our victory. Our voices were subdued as though a blanket had been thrown over us to muffle expressions of our triumph. I thought it odd but said nothing.

Able, Harris and I caught the elevators to go to the first floor. Outside, the sun had pierced through the dark clouds and lifted some of the dreary somberness that had depressed me before the start of the meeting. In the parking lot, the three of us rejoiced for a few minutes.

"This thing isn't over," Able said. "Not by a long shot."

"You can bet that the Ayatollah's soldiers haven't given up," Harris said.

"I find little comfort in today's vote," I said. "I've got this feeling that something's waiting out there in the dark for me. And it ain't good. I wish it'd go away."

Donna Elaine handed me the telephone the moment I walked into the house. "It's Harris Woolford," she said.

The professor was yelling. "Damn, I can't believe it! I just saw a news flash on television. Baxter Lampkins is dead. Murdered by a carjacker as he stopped at the traffic light at the Elm and Burton street intersection one block from City Hall. Eyewitnesses say that two black men shot him in the head. Twice. Then dumped his body on the street in the middle of the intersection. They were laughing as they drove away with Lampkins' car."

My heart began racing like a trip hammer. "Lampkins murdered? It can't be true," I said. My cynical mind jerked into overdrive. Carjackers? That's a lot of bullshit. I kept muttering, "Terrible. Terrible. Terrible."

"Stoney," Harris yelled. "What the hell are you saying? I can't hear you. Don't you understand? Lampkins has been murdered."

"Harris, I'm numb. I don't know what to say. Carjackers? Hell, you know as well as I do that Karim and Tolman ordered Lampkins killed. That's why Tolman, Karim and their group exited the council chambers in such a hurry."

"Yeah," Harris said. "Poor old Lampkins. Dead. I can't believe it. Just a few minutes ago, he was alive and smiling. You don't think it was carjackers?"

"Hell no, Harris. That gang we were fighting up there today had him killed. To pay him back for not voting with them."

Harris had partially calmed down. "That makes sense. Those folks are meaner than snakes. You don't cross that bunch and live. Lampkins is proof of that. I guess."

The evil, unseen presence weighed heavily on my chest and restricted my breathing. "I've crossed them, Harris. Does that mean I'm marked for killing?"

"Oh, shit, Stoney. All that trouble they've been giving you. I'm sorry, but for a moment, I had forgotten." Harris knew he'd stumbled into the mental quagmire where I was struggling to right myself and survive. "I didn't mean to imply they'd kill you."

"Remember, Harris? Those telephone death threats? And Roy Bester's warning that they'd kill me if they thought it necessary. I had this nightmare last night. I was running from a howling mob. Running for my life. Frankly, I'm scared."

CHAPTER 19

About eight o'clock that evening, Donna Elaine and I drove to the Lampkins' home. We dreaded the ordeal, for we knew the knifing trauma that had cut through the hearts of his wife and children. The number of parked automobiles told me that many others had also hurried to the Baxter place to empathize with his family. My feet and legs were reluctant as we walked slowly up the sidewalk.

Two uniformed police officers stood at the entrance. They nodded to us.

"Evening, Mr. Bedford," sergeant Paul Wilson said.

"How's Mrs. Lampkins?" I asked.

"Stunned, as all of us are. She's in a near state of hysteria. The doctor was just here to give her a shot to calm her down. He said she'd be better in about ten minutes."

"Baxter? Where'd they carry his body?"

"To Bagdorf Funeral home," the sergeant said.

"It's a tragic thing."

Donna Elaine took my arm. "Let's go see Mrs. Lampkins, Stoney."

The sergeant opened the door for us. Women were already at the dining room table spreading the food that neighbors had started bringing to the home as a way of expressing love and sympathy.

A tall boy and a younger girl stood in the hallway near the door. "Good evening, Mr. Bedford," he said. "Baxter Lampkins is our father. I'm Bart and this is my sister Elisa."

"Oh, son," I said. "I'm so sorry about Baxter. It's such a terrible thing that should not have happened. It's brutal and senseless."

Elisa started crying. Donna Elaine gathered the dark-haired young girl into her arms. "There, there honey," my wife said. "You go right ahead and cry."

"I've about cried myself out," Elisa sobbed.

"Any of the other council members here?" I asked.

"No," the boy said. "I'm worried about my mother. She's in a state of hysteria. She can't seem to regain control of herself."

More people were coming in through the nearby front entrance. Donna Elaine and I walked on down the hall toward the den where I could see several people with sad faces standing around and talking.

Baxter's wife was screaming, "Why, why, why? They killed my husband. For no reason. Oh, what will I do? How can I stand it?" Her pitiful words became even louder. "Oh, God, help me. Help me. Help me."

She looked up and saw the two of us. "Stoney Bedford! You and that horrible old Confederate flag. Today, he voted with you to keep it flying. That's why Baxter is dead. I just know it is. It wasn't a carjacking. It was cold-blooded murder."

"I can't tell you how sorry we are, Gertrude," I said. "We're shocked, too. Donna Elaine and I came to express our sympathy. We don't understand his death either."

"Oh, God, help me," the distraught woman moaned. "Please, help me." She began screaming again. "Why? Why? Why?"

Donna Elaine put her arms around the bereaved woman and began to pat her shoulder.

Suddenly, Gertrude pushed my wife away. "Right now, Donna Elaine, I don't feel kindly at all toward you and Stoney. Baxter's death is somehow connected with your husband's stand on keeping the flag flying. I don't know why Baxter changed his mind and voted the way he did today. I suspect your husband had something to do with persuading him to do it. Perhaps it would be best if you two left us alone with our sorrow."

My flushed face reflected my embarrassment and anger. My pulse began racing. "Gertrude, how can you say such a thing? I didn't shoot Baxter and steal his car. The news bulletin said it was two young black men. I understand your emotional upset, your sorrow. We'll leave, but you have offended us both greatly."

Gertrude rushed at me and began beating her fists into my chest. Her son, Bart, pulled her away. "No, mother. You're hysterical. Mr. Bedford is not responsible for Daddy's death. Several people have told me that they're certain Abdul Karim and DeLong Tolman had Dad killed for changing his vote."

We had started walking toward the door. "Bart," I said. "I've reached that conclusion, too. But, we can't prove it. My wife and I are leaving now. We're truly sorry about Baxter's death. Truly sorry."

"Thank you both for coming," Bart said. "Hopefully, mother will quiet down and come to her senses. I apologize for her behavior."

As we left, we heard Gertrude screaming, "Stoney Bedford's responsible for my husband's murder. I just know he is. Some how and in some way. My Baxter never really felt comfortable around the high and mighty Bedfords."

The *Ledger's* Victor Allen telephoned me at 9:30 that night.

"I guess you're in a state of shock like all the rest of us," he said. "I mean. Baxter's death."

Automatically, my guard went up when I was talking to the little arrogant bastard. I chose my words carefully. "I still don't know how to react, Victor. It's been such a long day. I'm drained. And now, this senseless killing of Lampkins."

"Somehow or other, there's a connection between his murder and today's voting," Allen said. "I can't quite figure it out. Nor can Chief Crowe."

"The killers are too clever. It's perfect for them. Two unknowns doing someone else's bidding. It'll be almost impossible to tie today's killing to Baxter's vote and the anger of the power players. But, I think you're right."

The tone of his voice changed abruptly. "However, that's not the real reason I called," Allen said. "I just got a fax from Thomas Farris, the Harvard man. I know you'll be interested in what he proposes."

"A fax? What's it all about?"

"You won't like what he says, Stoney."

I deliberately waited for a minute. Victor would tell me after he'd played his cat and mouse game long enough to fulfill his sense of importance.

"Farris is putting on a really big show tomorrow at 4 p.m near the Confederate memorial on City hall grounds."

"The fax? Please read it to me, Victor."

"These are his words. 'Come to our one-hour festival tomorrow afternoon at four o'clock on City Hall grounds. We'll have a high old time. There'll be a huge rebel flag there for you to spit on, stomp on, piss on, or what have you. Then, I'll soak the symbol of slavery with gasoline and burn it while the band plays "Dixie." Expect lots of cheering, whistling and foot stomping. Then, we'll have four, four-wheel drive Jeeps with chains to pull down the statue and jerk the head off Robert E. Lee. We're going to have fun, fun, fun. National television and newspaper coverage. No speeches. Just fun.' "

On top of all we'd been through today? The sudden anger made my hands tremble. "Allen, you're not making up this shit just to taunt me, are you?"

He chuckled. "No, I read you the actual fax. What's your reaction?"

"Allen," I said. "They've really taken advantage of this insipid, weak-kneed, cowardly traitor to everything Southern. The instigators have really loaded Farris' wagon down. His feelings of self-worth have been reduced to almost zero. His sense of guilt about having been born a Southerner is pushing him to do this in order to prove what a sorry bastard he really is. A case of self-flagellation if I've ever seen one. In doing this, he's striking back at his poor parents, lashing out at anything Southern."

"Can I quote you on that?" Allen asked.

"Yes. You can also quote me as saying he needs to be seeing a psychiatrist. He's mentally unbalanced. Tomorrow, he'll be playing with fire. Many, many people will not take kindly if he does what he says he's going to do. I wouldn't want to be in his shoes."

Victor whistled. "Those are pretty strong condemnations. Aren't your words bordering on libel?" Allen asked.

"After Farris' performance at City Council meeting today? You've got to be kidding. He entered the public arena voluntarily. We've got his inflammatory remarks on tape and on television footage. And now, this flag burning and the decapitation of General Lee tomorrow. No jury in Georgia would ever award Farris a penny if he sued me for libel."

"That's an angle I hadn't considered. Will you be at Farris' festival tomorrow?"

"Hell no, Allen. If I showed my face there, I'd be asking for trouble. No, thank you. I'll watch it on television."

"So will millions of others," Allen said. "All the major television networks told me they'd be covering it from beginning to end. Gotta go, now. Thank you for talking to me."

"Victor, wait a minute. The *Ledger's* new efforts at objectivity you told me about yesterday. Are they still in effect?"

"Boy, you are a cynic, Stoney. To answer your question, 'yes.' We'd all like to keep our jobs down at the newspaper. The story will be reported in detail but not slanted to show favoritism."

Able Erling, Harris Woolford, and I sat in my den watching television coverage of Farris' so-called festival. There was a crowd of at least 4,000. I spotted Morris Light and his assistant as the TV cameras panned the media section. I pointed him out to Erling and Woolford.

"I'll say this," Harris said. "You and your family are, as they said to Gunga Din in the movie, 'braver than I am.' How can you stand those two dogging your every foot step? And with a TV camera to boot?"

"Once I convinced myself that he'd tell this story honestly," I said, "we made the necessary adjustments. And, he's smart enough not to try and film us when we first struggle awake in the morning. Or in our bedrooms."

"You think he's setting you up as the chief chump in all this?" Erling asked.

"You don't think I'd be that damn dumb, do you?" I still had lingering doubts about Light's documentary.

"If it's done in the right way, I think it's great. It's a story that needs to be told," Harris said. "You, Donna Elaine, and William are not just a bunch of prejudiced nuts running around in white sheets with whips and blazing torches. You're decent people fighting for principles, the same as Able and I with our votes on the council. It's strange to me; they've picked you out as the villain. Why not me? Or Able?"

"Yeah," Able said. "I haven't even come close to getting the virulent reactions you have. A few nasty calls on the telephone. No death threats. Why are they picking on you?"

I laughed. "I was unwise enough to stick my neck out too early. And too far," I said. "And the Bollings and the Bedfords make good targets, because our families are old South. To our opponents, we are the Civil War and slavery. If they can get rid of the flag, they'll have won an important victory. In their eyes."

"Let's just hope Morris Light can get wide distribution of the story he's filming," Harris said. "When it's over."

"Yes," I said. "When it's over—if it ever is. When this controversy is settled, one way or the other, we three Bedfords might be corpses. Like poor old Baxter Lampkins."

"Most folks would say you're over-reacting," Harris said. "Are you?"

"Hell no," I said. "What'll it take to convince you that some of us could be killed?"

"Let's concentrate on what is happening," Able said. "It's is a great show. Free hot dogs and soda pop. Dad said old Gene Talmadge used such a technique to draw crowds for his political rallies. And he was a powerful man in Georgia politics for many, many years."

"It's more like a circus than a festival," Harris said. "They're a bunch of clowns without make up."

"Look at those four-wheel drive vehicles," the announcer said. "There are four of them parked around the Confederate monument. Will they decapitate the famous Civil War general? As they have boasted. Uh oh! Here comes young Thomas Farris himself. And, he's dragging a huge Confederate flag through the crowd. We've asked him to wear a microphone so we can pick up his words."

"Hey folks," Farris yelled. He was a college cheerleader encouraging spectators to throw themselves into urging their team on to victory. "Spit on this hated symbol of slavery. And imagine it's old Bedford himself. C'mon. Don't be bashful. It's your show. Stomp on it. Piss on it. Here, I'll be the first one to wet it down."

Blessedly, the cameras changed their angles as Farris unzipped his fly and began urinating on the flag. The crowd loved it. Many of them joined the bold, young man. People were having a great time. Like the gargoyles of Rome's fountains, their streams of urine flowed onto the flag they hated. It lay crumpled on the ground.

Then, they began to hark and spit visible white gobs of sputum toward the same spot where the human fountains flowed.

Farris kept waving to others in the crowd to come forward and show their contempt. "What's the matter?" the slender young man yelled. "Are you afraid to show the world what you think about Bedford's great, what does he call it, 'Southern heritage'? Let's keep Bedford and his kind on the run. We've got them afraid of us now. C'mon. Are you cowards?"

Dozens more, yelling their defiance, jumped onto the flag and stomped. Some women squatted and joined the pissing brigade, although most of them kept their dresses in a position that hid their genitals from the camera's prying eyes.

"Now's your chance," Farris yelled. "Show your anger at the Confederate flag that flies over property owned by taxpayers. Taxpayers! That's folks like you."

He was reaching out and grabbing people by their arms to urge them into frenzied participation in the spectacle. He'd run a few paces dragging the

214

flag, then stop while the people in the crowd spat on it, stomped on it and pissed on it. The jeering, yelling and arm waving was increasing in intensity.

"Look at that traitorous bastard." Able said. He stood up, pounding his fist. "I can't imagine a son-of-a-bitch who'd stoop so low as to tell people how ashamed he is of being a Southerner."

Harris was worked up, too. He jutted his chin out and rubbed his right hand across it in frustration. "I wonder if that character ever thinks about the shame and agony he's causing his mother and father," he said. "And, they're decent people. I know them both."

It didn't appear that the tall, young man with the acne-scarred face was thinking about anything but enjoying himself. He'd thrown himself into his role with enthusiasm and malevolence. His smiles, his energies, his cajoling of the crowd—he was blending them all into whirlwind action.

His microphone picked up a new ingredient to stir into the boiling pot of violence he was so cleverly mixing. "We've got a special treat for you this afternoon. See that stuffed dummy over there hanging on that tree? That's an effigy of old Stoney Bedford, white racist bastard. The great defender of the Confederate flag. Descendant of a long line of Confederate generals and fighting men on both sides of his family."

He paused and waved his arm around at the crowd. "Now, I know that most of you young men are carrying switch blade knives," he said.

Dozens of young black men answered him. "Hey, Bro! Lookit this!" Hands holding open switch blades shot into the air.

The pitch was reaching levels of insanity "Good," Farris yelled. "Now, let's have some more fun. I want each of you to stab old Bedford hard. And as you're stabbing that dummy, imagine you can feel your knife ripping through human flesh. Stoney Bedford's."

"Yo, Bro," was the acclamation that rent the air. Dozens of the festival participants ran toward the effigy, yelling, plunging knives into the straw filled dummy. Their motions were violent and fierce. Several were not content with one ripping of the effigy. Some continued their assault until pushed away by others who had not taken their turns.

I jumped to my feet. "Look at those mad dogs," I said. "That's the way they'll do me if they get the chance. Farris should be arrested and charged with 'inciting to riot.' "

Able and Harris had stood also. "Damn," Able said. "I can't stand too much more of this. Reminds me of what I saw on the evening news last night over in Somalia and Rwanda. The Huttos and the Tutsus are savaging each other just like that."

"Shit," Harris said. "And the whole damned world is seeing this. Those blacks ought to be plunging their knives into that emaciated bastard, Farris. He's making them look like ignorant Zulu warriors charging the Boers in South Africa."

The television announcer and his camera crews described the knife attacks on the effigy of me in vivid language. "Several of the attackers seem lost in trances," the male voice said. "I'd say they actually feel as though their knives are being plunged into Stoney Bedford's body."

When the tumult partially died down, Farris began waving his arms for quiet. "Now, clear the area," he said. "Move back at least fifty feet. We're going to pour gasoline onto the flag of shame and strike a match. The fire will run down the thin stream I've poured as I back away. Then, pfoof! When it does, I expect you to show your pent up hatred of this damned symbol of America's darkest days."

People started moving back. Farris' back was to the street twenty feet away. The dismal, decrepit buildings on the other side of the street were old and crumbling, vacant, two- and three-story structures.

"That's it," Farris urged. "Back up another ten feet or so. That's good. Now, if Councilman DeLong Tolman will bring me the gallon can of gasoline he's been holding in safekeeping for me." He motioned toward a row of chairs a hundred feet away where Tolman, Karim, and others were seated.

Harris was groaning. "Look at that shit-head, DeLong. He's playing to the crowd and the cameras. Waving, smiling, bowing."

"Now," Farris said into the chest microphone that was attached to his shirtfront. "I'm soaking the flag with gas. I'll use the entire gallon, because we want a real, good fire."

"I'll say one thing," I laughed. "Farris is a showman. He's making certain that he doesn't miss a single spot on the flag."

Farris evidently knew about the explosive qualities of gasoline and its fumes. Before he relinquished the container to Tolman to carry away, he had poured a thin trail of the liquid as he backed up to where he now stood, some fifteen feet or so from the flag.

He was wringing all possible drama out of the situation. These were his moments of glory, his solo theatrical performance in the circle of light. He was in no hurry. "Now, here's a box of common kitchen matches," he said, holding up the box to television cameras. "This is the main attraction of our festival and I want loud cheering, lots of applause and the waving of your signs when the flag goes 'pfoof.' " He snapped his fingers to illustrate the flash when the trail of fire exploded on reaching the gasoline soaked flag.

He bent down, struck a match and lighted the tiny trail of gasoline that led to the flag. He straightened up, smiling, his hands in the air as though he was an official declaring the scoring of a touchdown on the football field.

The vapor trail ignited, ran toward the flag and exploded into flames once it reached its goal. The fire leaped into the air. The cheering was deafening. The spectators were jumping up and down. Some were waving signs. Their faces were masks of joy.

"Wait a minute. Something's wrong with Farris," the announcer yelled into his microphone. "The look on his face. He's stumbling forward toward the burning flag. My God. He's fallen into the fire, onto the burning flag. This is incredible! His clothes are now on fire. It's unbelievable, something out of a special effects movie scene. Has Farris planned this all along? Surely not. No, something unexpected has happened."

The camera zoomed in for a close up of Farris, screaming and wallowing piteously in the searing flames. Something protruded from his back. It was an arrow! It had gone all the way through his chest. Its protruding tip could be seen beneath his chin. He'd been shot by a deadly, silent archer using a crossbow from some unknown hiding place across the street in one of the old buildings. Dying, he'd stumbled forward and fallen into the flames. Even his hair was now blazing up.

DeLong Tolman rushed forward, circled the flaming flag, grabbed Farris' heels and dragged him backwards until his body was free of the flames. "Somebody help me put out the flames!" he shouted. He peeled off his coat and began beating at the flames. Others rushed to join him. Some held their noses against the scent of burning human flesh.

The network TV announcer broke in. "We've just been told that Farris is dead. The arrow from the deadly crossbow that entered his back went cleanly through his heart and the point is sticking from his chest. As if that wasn't enough, he stumbled forward as he died and fell into the flames where his clothes and hair were set ablaze."

The announcer's voice fell into a lower register. His words slowed as he said, "Farris' good-time festival has ended abruptly in grisly tragedy.

"Where did the arrow come from? We've been told that it was fired by an expert marksman using a crossbow, probably from the third-story window of one of those deserted, crumbling buildings across the street.

"Ten minutes have elapsed since Farris was shot in the back and only now are the police running across the street to those dilapidated old building. Any reasonable person would assume that the assassin has safely fled by now.

"In my twelve years of reporting television news for this network, I have never seen anything like this. It was awful! Incredible! Completely unexpected!

"We had hoped to interview DeLong Tolman, but no doubt, seeing Farris assassinated and fearing for his own life, he has hurried away to safety. We'll have more details for you on the evening news."

I remembered the old man and his balding companion who had listened to my conversation with Mike Chapman at yesterday's Council meeting. The stern-faced spectator's ominous words haunted me. He had predicted that those who were adamantly set on pulling down the Confederate flag had gone too far and that they would be made to pay for their stomping on the rights of Southerners who loved the flag.

I was sick to my stomach. And, I wasn't feeling too secure myself. "Yesterday, Baxter Lampkins was shot to death. Today," I said. Farris' death makes four so far. I'm scared. What the hell's going on?"

"Maybe," Able said, "the war of genocide between blacks and whites has gotten underway with a vengeance and this is our Fort Sumter. Karim declared the existence of the war the other day in no uncertain terms, knowing that few whites would believe such a thing."

"Stoney," Harris said. "I'm scared, too. If it's any comfort to you."

"Who will be next?" I asked.

Chapter 20

I had almost reached the breaking point. I needed help from the outside, which could only come from God—if I could find Him. I searched desperately for the Almighty, but in the scorching winds of anger and violence in which I'd been caught up, it was proving more and more difficult to let go and let God's spirit blossom again in my soul.

I was a man of peace. I'd had my fill of war, of death and dying on the beaches of North Africa, Sicily, Italy and France during World War II. I did not want to be a retreaded warrior who still lived only when he once again entered the killing darkness. After discharge, I came home to an atmosphere of peace and goodwill. Like thousands of other returning veterans, my whole being had been aimed toward the future. My thoughts, my plans, my actions—they had combined to propel me forward, ever forward. The years had been happy, productive years. Foolishly, I thought they'd last forever. The realization that peace in my life had disappeared was bitter gall.

Now, my heart and mind were weighted down with the endless parade of the damned who marched through the nightmares of my sleepless nights. The morning newspaper lay on the table beside my chair. It had taken two cups of strong coffee for me to force myself through its tales of horror, through the pictures of Thomas Farris lying on a burning Confederate flag, an arrow through his back, his hair and clothes in flames. The police had no clue and very little on which to go as they started their search for the assassin.

I walked to the French doors that opened onto my patio. In the clear, morning sunlight, the surface of the lake was a mirror that reflected trees and tufted clouds in the skies. An enormous blue heron stood in his favorite place at the edge of the bank on the far side. All of the wild ducks had not flown north yet. Four of them flew by just above the water's surface at a speed that must have been close to sixty miles an hour. Four tame geese swam by slowly, calling noisily to each other.

For the hundredth time, I asked myself, what has happened to my life? Hell, I'm a healthy, mature individual in love with life and living during these golden years. I have money, prestige, friends, a wonderful wife and son, and honor. These are supposed to be my good years. I don't need to be a captive of this madness that has fallen over me like a gladiator's net. I haven't hurt or abused anyone; I haven't stolen from anyone; I haven't stormed the traditional, acceptable barriers to any man's home to break in and destroy. I am not crashing through the world spilling vengeance onto groups of people. Live and let live has always been one of my life's guiding principles. Where did all of this anger come from? What were its causes that had proved to be so virulent as to have resulted in the deaths of four people? Four people. Even one would have been too many. But four? It's unreal. And they died for reasons that didn't make sense.

Across the lake, on the opposite bank, two dogs were lapping their tongues into the water. What were the forces in today's society that had set loose packs of mad dogs to tear the flesh from people's bodies. That straw-filled dummy hanging from a tree at Farris' flag burning festival had represented me. And those savage people with their slashing knives, yelling, laughing, thrusting clenched fists into the air. It would have been the same if the dummy had been the real me.

I tried to still the disturbing thoughts cresting on wave after wave of emotion. The morning was so quiet and peaceful. I tried to melt into the faint breezes pushing gently against my cheeks. I couldn't imagine anything such as the last few days being a part of the American scene. We're supposed to be a government of law, not of men. But like many other traditional values, this one seems to have also flown away.

A mourning dove was cooing in the distance. I cocked my head to hear his lonely call. This neighborhood, this quiet street. It was not a place for killing, yet there had been killing here a few days ago. The black stranger who died from a shotgun blast through the window of his parked car. Alice, my neighbor across the street. Poor Alice. If it hadn't been for me, she'd still be alive.

I eased from the back door and walked to a small boat dock built on the edge of the lake. Over the years, I had made it a habit to rise early and come to this spot, for here, I came the closest to communing with the Creator. I saw my reflection in the still water and stood there quietly. Searching.

Why me, God? I looked to the heavens and opened my palms. Stop this hurtling train, please. Let me off before it plows headlong into immovable objects. I don't want to die. We have such a good life, God. Donna Elaine, William, me. And soon, Julie Peel will be joining our family as William's bride.

I can only be what I am, God. A Southerner, born and bred, a product of a proud Southerner's ideals, principles, moral values and sense of nobility and honor. Nothing more. Nothing less. They are the winds on which I fly to heaven's peace and quietness.

I kept shaking my head. The mental burdens and pressures clutched at me like an iron maiden. An effigy of me. The thrusting, gleeful stabbing. Laughter on gleaming faces, holding hot dogs in one hand a bottle of soda pop in the other. The band's throbbing, martial music.

Why am I being made the scapegoat? My daddy used to say, "Stonewall, if you take strong stands in this world, you'll attract strong enemies. The only way not to rock the boat is to be a self-effacing, non-entity. Even then, people will kick you around, because the human being automatically detests weakness in another.

"It brings out the savagery buried in each of us," Daddy would say. "It's like the weak animal that falls behind in a herd of antelope. The wolves follow closely, sense that the straggler is weak. They close in and wrestle the animal to earth to tear off its flesh. People are that way, too, Stonewall. It's better to be a strong man with unbending principles than a fawning weakling trying to please everybody and garnering nothing but kicks in the ass."

Yes, Daddy. You were right. People are exactly the way you described them. I tilted my head back and looked upwards. Lord, I asked. Is there no peace left for me in this world? Is there no place I can hide from life's storms, especially when the eye of the storm contains death? When I was a young Boy Scout sitting with other Scouts at night around a campfire, we used to sing a song with great gusto. Let's see. How did it go? "Oh, there's no hiding place down here; no hiding place down here. I went to the rock to hide my face, the rock cried out no hiding place. . ."

It struck me forcefully that my family and I were under siege and that I had become the lightning rod on which Karim and Tolman could focus all of their anger and the rage of their followers. That was a fact I had to accept. Last night, I had again begged Donna Elaine to go and stay with her mother in Ames until all this trouble had blown over.

"I will not leave you nor my home," she said with a firm set of her chin. "Stoney, you and I have never lived our lives in fear and we're not about to start slinking away from problems at this stage of our lives."

"But what if they come to kill us, Honey? There's no sense in your being exposed to such terror. Southern men are raised to protect their ladies."

She had grown defiant. "Stoney Bedford. You, William, and I can face the storms and survive. We've proven it a dozen times by facing some hard times together and winning. We can take care of ourselves. We're prepared. We've got the quarter-inch steel shields, our bullet-proof vests, our cellular phones, the night vision glasses, the laser and starlight scopes—and our tough desire to defend ourselves, to stand for principle."

"But there'll be so many of them, Donna Elaine. They may overwhelm us with sheer numbers and break through. If they do, we could all die."

"Stoney, look at it another way. Maybe, just maybe, it will be all of them who die. Our guns can kill, too, and we certainly know how to direct them at the necessary targets for killing—if that's the way they want it. I've been praying about things, too, just like I know you have. We have to trust the Lord—and keep our powder dry."

"There's no calming things down," I told her. "I've tried all the things I know how to try. There is no rational discussion; no reduction in the levels of flaming hatreds and it's companion anger. And we can't depend on any protection from the police until something happens. And you know as well as I do that it will be too late then."

Her tiny fists were doubled up and lying on top of her lap. "Thus, there's nothing for us to do but to stand and fight. If I were not here, and you died in an attack, I'd never forgive myself anyhow. Now that that's settled, let's move on to other things."

The morning sun was climbing higher. It was time for another cup of that Cajun dark roast Community coffee with the slightly bitter taste of chicory. It needed warming first. I filled my mug and put it into the microwave. Let's see. Forty seconds should do it. I pushed the button and listened to the peculiar noise the oven fan makes, then heard the "bong, bong, bong, bong, bong" that signaled that the oven's work was done.

I set the coffee down on a white, wrought iron table on the patio and opened my Bible. I turned to Romans, Chapter eight, in the New Testament. Often, I found comfort and strength in Paul's words. I closed my eyes. "Oh, Lord, give me wisdom to understand these Holy Scriptures and the comfort that comes from knowing thee as my Savior.

"For as many as are led by the spirit of God, they are the sons of God." I prayed some more. We are the sons of God, fashioned in his image and after his sight. We are brothers and sisters to Jesus Christ. I believe,

Lord. I believe. Thy spirit is leading me through this dark valley where the shadow of death hovers.

"The Spirit itself beareth witness with our spirit that we are the children of God." Yes, Lord. Even Karim and Tolman are your children. Melt away our hatreds and prejudices. Help us to love each other.

"Likewise, the spirit also helps our infirmities for we know not what we should pray for as we ought, but the spirit itself maketh intercession for us with groanings which cannot be uttered." Lord, I feel your Holy Spirit groaning for me as it struggles to lift these crosses from us. Give us peace.

"And we know that all things work together for good to them that love God, to them who are called according to his purpose." Yea, Lord. Even these last few days have their meaning in all of our lives. Help me to see the divine purpose in what is happening.

"What shall we then say to these things? If God be for us, who can be against us?" Oh, God, you have always been my loving father. I know you will shield and protect me and my wife and son.

"For I am persuaded that neither death, nor life, nor angels, nor principalities, nor powers, nor things present, nor things to come, nor height, nor depth, nor any other creature shall separate us from the love of God, which is in Jesus Christ our Lord." Yea, Lord. I feel united with you again. I belong to you. "I can do all things through Christ who strengthens me."

I lifted my arms to the heavens and cried out: "Oh, Lord, bless my enemies. Bless Karim and Tolman. Let thy wondrous spirit flood their hearts and souls and give them peace, health and happiness. We are all of us the children of God. Reach thy hands down and steady us on our journeys through life. Thank you God for your many blessings. I believe, I believe, I believe. Amen."

"Dad," William said as he sliced a banana onto his bowl of corn flakes and poured in skim milk. "While you were on the patio meditating, I watched the network TV news. The killing of Farris and the burning of the flag were the top stories."

"That poor, stupid young man. It took some unexpected turns, didn't it?"

It took some time for William to answer. "It was tragic. The rawness of human emotions. Farris' face as he died. The expressions of joy on the faces of those young blacks as they plunged their switch blades into 'Stoney Bedford.' "

I shuddered from the remembered pictures. " Some of them actually had to be pushed away so that others behind them might have their fun."

"That one who imagined he was stabbing you in the testicles," William said. "He screamed as he thrust his knife low between the dummy's legs and cut upwards."

"That arrow in Farris' back. The person who did that had to be a great marksman."

"Not necessarily, Dad. With the crossbows you can buy now for hunting, and the sights on them, anyone with even the slightest experience can hit the target. They're as accurate from fifty to seventy-five yards as a rifle. I know. Some of my friends hunt deer with the crossbow and do quite well."

"One day, let's go to Griff's Sporting Goods so you can show me more about how they work.

On the last spoonful of corn flakes, I saw that some of the milk had run down his chin. He dabbed at it with the paper napkin, took a deep breath and exhaled. "I'm trying to shake off this funny feeling I've had for the last couple of days. It's a dark feeling, as if something was out there waiting to grab at me. It wakes me up at night in a cold sweat. I keep seeing Julie in her white wedding gown waiting at the altar and I can't get to her."

I looked at my son and felt like crying. I nodded my head and studied the bright shafts of sunlight falling across the floor. "Is everything in place? In case they come?"

"Yes. I just checked again before I came downstairs."

After lunch, I went to pay my respects to Baxter Lampkins. The owners of the funeral home had converted a beautiful old columned, two-story house into a quiet place for the final exit of the dead from today's turbulent world. It sat far back from the street. Five ancient live oaks with long, drooping limbs shaded the wide, front lawn. Mockingbirds flitted from tree to tree and chirped their bright songs. The sun was high in the sky.

In the parking lot I rubbed the back of my neck. Visiting the dead at funeral homes somehow brought a reluctance and awe that made my legs hesitate to take the steps toward the front door. Try as I might, I had never understood death. That last fearful step into God knows where. It's a step I think most of us don't really want to accept. I know I'd turn aside and follow another path if I had the choice.

The room where Baxter lay in state was banked with flowers. In the low light, the handles on the massive bronze casket gleamed. I sniffed that peculiar smell I'd trained my nose to detect in funeral homes down through the years. I'd labeled it "the smell of death" for nowhere else do you find this smell except in a funeral home.

Bart, Baxter's son, a young man suddenly thrust into the role as head of the family, was the only other person in the room. He stood up as I walked toward him. His gray suit, white shirt and red tie made him look older than sixteen. He stuck out his hand.

"Thank you, Mr. Bedford, for coming to see Dad," He said.

"It's something I had to do, Bart. How's your mother today?"

"The doctor has her under heavy sedation," the boy replied. "I don't think she really understands what's going on. She's moving around, talking to mourners, nodding at their words of sympathy, but her face. It's blank. It registers nothing."

I sighed. "That's understandable, Bart. She's in a state of trauma." I shook my head from side to side. Why didn't the carjackers just let Baxter get out of his car without killing him?"

"That's not the way carjacking works, Mr. Bedford. The killing is part of it." He glanced toward the cold, immobile face of his father a few feet away. "By the way, the police found his car this morning in Fogleman Park. It hadn't been stripped the way such automobiles usually are stripped. Nothing was missing."

Somehow or other, I'd expected that if the car was found, the stripping would have left only the shell. "Damn. Not stripped. That's really something, Bart. It probably tells us that the reasons for his murder were much deeper than a carjacking."

"The police said the same thing." He took a deep breath and you could see his shoulders falling back into resignation's unhappy slump." You want to see Dad?"

"Of course," I said. We walked to the casket. The morticians had used wax and makeup to hide the gunshot wounds in his head. The shock of brown hair still hung down onto his forehead.

Dead bodies. My mind staged its usual protest against death with thoughts that glanced off its impenetrable shield. Why do Americans go through such elaborate rituals for the dead? Why do they spend such vulgar sums of money to "put him (or her) away nicely?" The poor dead bastard lying there in that expensive casket didn't feel anything. He couldn't hear the moans of grief nor the small talk people engage in as they stand there looking down into the face of the corpse. At such times, the chatter is inane, simply because people don't know what else to say or do. The dead person can't see or smell the beautiful flowers. He can't sit up and say, "Hi, Stoney. How are things going?"

"He doesn't look like Daddy," the son said. "I remember him always laughing and teasing us. Swinging his golf club out in the back yard once he got home from work, 'to relieve the tension' as he'd say. Mixing drinks for people before he and mother went out to dinner with the couples."

"Baxter was a superb salesman. That office supply firm will find it difficult to replace him."

"This morning when the family viewed the body," he said, "I thought to myself, that's not my daddy. It's just an object. A cold dead object. Lifeless. Unmoving. But mother seemed to be pleased and that was good enough for us."

I stepped back from the casket a couple of paces, bowed slightly, saluted and said, "Baxter, you were a damned good man and I'm going to miss you. So long, old friend."

Bart was crying as I left.

Roy Bester's office was in an ancient, red brick building that stood on the edge of the decaying inner city.

"Mr. Bedford," his secretary said. "It's good to see you." Maggie Garden was middle-aged, graying, and quite efficient. When she smiled, it lit up the room.

"Hello, Maggie. I took a chance that Roy would be here. Is he?"

"Yes he is. Let me tell him you're here. I know he'll be glad to see you."

The furnishings in Roy's office were spartan, his law library markedly old. The bindings on the backs of several of the volumes were splitting apart and hanging open, revealing the threads laced together with the original glue.

"Stoney," he said, his huge hands enveloping mine. "I was trying to think of what to say when I telephoned you."

I've never known Roy Bester to be at a loss for words.

"Words," he said, shrugging as if in apology. "These words will come hard, Stoney. One of my sources called me this morning and said,

'Something big's gonna happen tonight to your friend Bedford. He's going down. It's Karim and his boys.' "

I could feel my heart racing into high gear. I could hear it pounding in my ears. "The information, Roy? Is it reliable?"

"From this particular source? Yes. He's never been wrong."

"When?"

"It'll take place at two o'clock tomorrow morning. They'll use three black cars, four men to a car. Automatic assault weapons. AK 47s and Glocks. They plan to get in, do the job and get out in five minutes."

"There's always 911," I said. I could feel the steel wrecking ball swinging toward me and I was powerless to escape its path.

"Karim has a sympathizer in the switching department of the telephone company. It's simple to fix the computers. If you know how. All the phones in your neighborhood will go dead at 1:55 a.m. for twenty minutes."

Unconsciously, my hands were rubbing my stomach. Damned anxiety. Balling into knots down there. Creating painful gas pressure pushing upward from the bottom of my chest. Firing up the pressure headache in the back of my head. Pounding in my ears like war drums each time my heart beats.

Roy continued. "At that time of morning, they figure they can surround your house, disable your alarm system, break in through the French doors and kill all three of you in three minutes. Karim has reserved you for himself. The whole operation is charted with military precision. They are an army, you know."

"But we're smart enough to have cellular phones," I told Roy. "We'll dial 911 and the police will be there in five minutes."

"Karim has thought of that, also. At 1:45, fifteen minutes before he and his crew of killers get to your house, two hundred black people will start dialing 911. Your call will not get through and, even if you did happen to get lucky, all available police cars will be busy roaring through the city on false alarms. No cars will be available to come to your rescue.

I was clasping and unclasping my hands. "Their plans are thorough and efficient. But why Donna Elaine and William? They're really after me. I'm the only one that matters to them. The one they really want eliminated."

"They say all three of you must die." Bester's pain was showing on his broad face. "Remember, to them, it's a holy war against whites. The things you and I use to reach decisions and govern our actions are missing in their framework of reasoning."

"There's one good thing, Roy. They won't know that we know they're coming. Thanks to you."

"I don't know that that's much comfort."

"The three of us, Donna Elaine, William and I, don't intend to be like sheep led to the slaughter, Roy. Wash Washington and Blue Combs? Do they know about the plans?"

Bester hesitated. The pain showed in his grimace. He shrugged his shoulders and took a deep breath. "They were present at the meeting when Karim outlined the plans. They both prayed for Karim and his men. For the success of their mission."

CHAPTER 21

We gathered for a council of war, Donna Elaine, William and I. It was a grim twenty minutes. They listened with passive faces as I told them about the information Bester had given me. I didn't mince words.

"Can't we get the police to stand guard?" my wife asked.

"No. Chief Crowe is really not taking this thing seriously," I said, shaking my head slowly. When I looked at her, my heart ached with both love and fear. 'Things like that don't happen in Forest,' Crowe told me. 'Karim and Tolman are too smart to openly do such an outrageous thing. And I can't assign my officers to guard your house just on the basis of some wild rumor. The blacks are already making the charges that I divert too many of the department's resources to whites and their neighborhoods.' "

"We've known for days that the Chief's not on our side," William said. "But then, he's not by himself. Not many people have taken the 'declaration of war' seriously. It's dismissed as mere rhetoric. As political bombast."

"That's the tragedy of this whole thing," I said. "Such talk disturbs people too much; interferes with their daily routines; complicates their struggle to cope with their own problems; derails their groping to find a level of comfort that helps them face their tomorrows. So, they avoid the implications of racial war talk with easy rationalizations."

I had to stop briefly. My voice had broken. Donna Elaine put her arm around my waist and squeezed.

I took a deep breath and said the words plainly and slowly. "Crowe won't take preventive action. He said his men can only act after a crime has occurred—or while one is actually happening. Anyhow, Karim and his crowd have Crowe intimidated. He's fighting to hold onto his job."

My eyes had filled with tears. There was a catch in my throat as I looked at my beautiful and determined wife. She stopped me before I could urge her again to leave.

"I know what you are going to tell me, Stoney," Donna Elaine said, her jaw set in firm lines. "It's no use. I'm going to be with you and our son when the trouble comes. So, save your breath."

"But, Mother," William protested. "This is serious business. These people are coming to kill us. Southern men don't expose their women to this kind of thing. If they can help it."

She touched her son's cheek. "Bless you, William for being Southern to the core, but you must remember that our families have always stood together and fought together throughout our history. My great grandmother, when her husband was in Virginia fighting with General Lee, stood against the Union deserters who came to our plantation to plunder, kill and rape. She killed two of the drunken looters bent on raping her and the two daughters. Buried them in the garden under the rows of corn and peas."

The soft and radiant beauty that usually lighted her face had given way to grim determination. Her chin was raised. Her eyes had taken on a grayish hue. "I'm not some fragile something that's going to blow away when the fierce winds spring up. Anyhow, if you and William are gone, my world would be smashed to pieces. So, let's get back to the original plans we made in hopes of staying alive when and if something like this did happen."

"Well then, I suppose the die is cast," I said. "We'll start rotating watch duty at ten tonight. Roy said they'll come at two a.m., but they just may switch their attack time in case of leaks. It'd just make sense."

"I'm scared," Donna Elaine said, reaching for my hand. "None of us want to die. But then, cowardice is worse than dying."

I squeezed my wife's hand. "I'm so frightened my knees are trembling."

"I feel as though what I ate for supper has lodged in my throat instead of my stomach," William said. "But we're prepared. We know how to fight and shoot. The attackers won't know we're ready and waiting. They won't be expecting us to fight back. Let's decide right now that we're going to survive this thing."

Morris Light and his assistant were filming our actions and listening to the decisions we were making. "You people amaze me with your tenacity and conviction," he said. "People won't believe it until they see our film."

"You and your assistant can't be here when they come," I said.

"I know," Light said. "At midnight, I'll switch on my surveillance cameras. Put them on automatic. Then, my assistant and I will drive away. I had hoped against hope that the documentary would not take this kind of turn. But, if something does happen to the three of you, at least, I'll be alive to complete your story."

"That would be the wise thing to do, Morris. We must get this story completed and viewed by thousands of people throughout the country. It will show them that we're not living in a tight little world of prejudice and hate, that we're not lost back there somewhere in history."

"It could be a wake-up call," Light said. "When the nation sees the results of this cultural conflict that has been deliberately planned and launched against ordinary citizens, perhaps then, our leaders will step in, seize control of the warring factions and chart a course that protects us all."

We went upstairs once more to check our positions, the night vision binoculars, the guns with their laser sights and night vision scopes, the ammunition, the four, quarter inch, five and a half feet tall steel shields. We moved one of the shields into position at the top of the stairs and carefully placed the shotgun with two boxes of shells within easy reach. The shells were loaded with buckshot.

Tension hung in the air. Our voices and actions were slow and measured, as if we were sleepwalking. We were soldiers preparing for an enemy attack. I remembered the hours just before we launched our invasions against the Germans in the Mediterranean. It had been this same way then, each deep in his own private world, yet very much a part of the worlds of those who would be fighting shoulder to shoulder with him.

"When they come," William said, "and if they break through and get into the house, I'll slide this shield around to give me protection as they start up the stairs."

He picked up the shotgun. "A shotgun, at short range, is a murderous weapon. They'll not make it past the top three steps." He was matter-of-fact, very much a man you could count on when the fighting was fiercest.

There was no turning back now. The war was in progress. We could only run away or stand and fight, and we damned sure weren't going to run. Southerners don't run from a fight when they're convinced their cause is just. This was our home. We had a right and a duty to defend it, whatever the cost.

Without speaking, we checked the other three steel shields. The one I would use was in the middle dormer in front of the window that looked out onto the large, front lawn and the street. William's shield was in front of the windows in the middle bedroom that faced the back of the house and the lake at the foot of the gentle slope. The fourth shield was in the large inside closet that opened into the middle bedroom. It was the one designed to protect Donna Elaine.

"Let's check our guns again," I said.

I picked up my shotgun and placed it next to my shield, along with my 30.06 rifle with its starlight scope, my Glock automatic pistol with laser sight, the night vision binoculars and plenty of ammunition. I was wearing my bulletproof vest.

"I've already checked my station, Dad. The loaded guns, the ammunition, the night glasses. And my vest." He rubbed his rib cage for reassurance.

"At ten, I'll put on my vest," Donna Elaine said. "My .38 pistol and plenty of shells are in the closet beside my shield. But, I'm not going to hide in a closet when they attack. I'm going to take one of the windows, too. I can handle a rifle. My daddy made certain of that when I was growing up."

"No," I said. "I'll have to draw the line on that, Donna Elaine. I know you have great courage. What you really ought to do is leave now and drive to your mother's in Ames, but since you won't, you'll be safer in the closet behind the shield. It'll give William and me less to worry about when the firing begins. But, if the two of us are no longer shooting back at the invaders, have your pistol ready and extended over the top of the shield and aimed at the door. Shoot anyone who opens the door, because William and I will be either dead or wounded to the point where we can't shoot anymore."

An involuntary sob shook her tiny body. She shrugged and said, "It's impossible for a person to contemplate their own death. God will watch over us and we'll do our part. What is to be will be."

"Do you have your cellular phone, mother?" William asked.

"Yes. Right next to my pistol on the floor of the closet. When we see the three cars pull up and stop in front of our house, I'll dial 911."

He turned to me. "You have your phone, Dad?"

"Yes. It's in the middle dormer on the floor, next to the guns and ammo."

"It's time for a cup of hot tea," my wife said. "Anything to ease this tension of waiting, of not knowing."

I rubbed the back of my neck. It had been such a long time since I'd remembered having this acute pricking sensation down my neck and back and along the top part of my arms. This was the way I felt before each of the four invasions we made in the Mediterranean in World War II. Each of my senses had became sharper. Butterflies danced in my stomach. The muscles in my legs, arms and shoulders tightened and coiled like springs. My whole being rose to another plane where actions were automatic. Each of us had reached that plane now.

William smiled and touched my shoulder. "It's the old 'fight or flight' syndrome we studied it in college psychology classes. Energy levels zoom as the adrenaline surges."

"Well," my wife said. "We're not going to run. We're going to fight." She rubbed the back of her small hand across her forehead. "I'm so nervous my legs are trembling. I need something in my stomach to give me some quick energy." She clasped my hand again.

It was a good night for attack forces. Dark and moonless. A breeze whipped the still naked tree limbs into wild, erratic dancing. In the stillness, I could hear the grandmother's clock downstairs ticking. None of us could sleep. The windows in front of each of our battle stations had been raised to allow us to fire through them without first breaking out the glass.

William and I crouched near the front windows using the night vision field glasses to continuously sweep the street in front of our home. Around two a.m. we saw three long, black cars without lights moving slowly up the street toward our home.

"This is it," William said loudly.

"If they get out of their cars with weapons," I said, "let's fire first. They won't be expecting that. They think we're sleeping. If we work quickly, we can take out four of them before they can react."

I nudged my wife. "Sweetheart, go to your station and dial 911." She walked away toward the bedroom closet.

"Shoot them through the head," William said. More than likely, they're wearing bullet proof vests, too."

"Let's do it," I said

He ran to the dormer window on the left front of the house. The three long, black Cadillacs with darkened windows stopped quietly in front of the house. I sighted through the rifle's starlight scope and waited. I could see as if it were almost daylight. The two right side doors on each of the three vehicles opened quietly. Four tall men with their AK 47s eased out of the doors and stood still, waiting for the others to exit. I squeezed off a quick round, quickly moved the cross hairs to another man's head and fired again. I could see his head explode. Both of them fell against the car and slid to the ground.

"I got one of them also," William yelled. His laugh was high pitched.

Several of the attackers started running up the driveway. Others ran across the front lawn. William and I sprayed bullets at them with our Glocks.

I fired at the legs of the sprinting figures. Two of them went down on the grass of the front lawn.

Some of the killers started firing their AK 47s from behind the parked automobiles. It was a deadly curtain of automatic fire that ripped through the walls of the house and splattered against the shields. William ran behind me and into the back bedroom where another shield faced the lake. I heard him open up through the back windows and knew that the attackers had reached the backyard and were returning our fire.

The attackers out front were now hidden behind the automobiles. It was time to return to selective targets. I eased my rifle over the top of the shield and sighted through my scope. One of the killers was leaning across the hood of the second automobile and firing his AK 47. The red streaks from his rifle barrel marked his position. I found him through my scope and centered the cross hairs on the spot. I squeezed the trigger. The bullet splintered the stock of his rifle. I saw him straighten up and grab his face. I fired again. He fell backwards.

Their streams of rifle fire from the front pierced the walls and splattered harmlessly against my steel shield. William left the back bedroom and ran down the hall behind me to take up his position at the head of the stairs. Another shadowy figure tried to run across the front lawn but stopped and ran back to the safety of the automobiles when I opened fire with my Glock.

The glass shattered in the French doors downstairs that led to our back patio. I knew they had broken through. William fired the shotgun twice. I heard screams of pain. He was cursing and yelling, "Come on, you sons-of-bitches. We'll give you more than you bargained for."

His Glock was chattering.

I knew I had to keep those out front pinned down if we were to stay alive. I raked the automobiles on the street with my Glock. One of the attackers darted from behind the third automobile and sprinted up the driveway. There were two men lying on the front lawn. I found their heads in the rifle sight and fired.

I counted five of them down. Three by their cars and two on the front lawn. I couldn't see the man I'd shot on the other side of one of the cars. William had blasted another of the attackers who broke through the French doors. I counted two more behind the automobiles from the red streaks of their AK 47's. That left three of them still attacking from the rear of the house.

William was firing his Glock now. I fired my 30.06 rifle at one of those standing back of the first car's hood. He moved slightly to the left. The bullet missed him. He had ducked his head so that I couldn't find him again. Nor could I find any of the others in the scope.

There was a momentary lull in the firing; then I heard glass breaking in the back of the house to my right and to my left. Damn, the one thing we hadn't counted on. They'd used a stepladder in the back of our house to climb to the roof of the first floor. There they could gain access to the second floor by breaking through the windows.

"Oh, Lord. No" I shouted. Donna Elaine was in that middle bedroom closet hiding behind her steel shield.

They must not find her. I grabbed up my shotgun and sprinted down the hall to my left. As I rounded the door facing and dove toward the floor, I saw the attacker jump through the window and run to his right through the bathroom toward the middle bedroom.

God help me. They must not reach my wife. They must not. Oh, God. Help me.

"William," I yelled. "The bedroom window to your right. Watch out!"

An automatic pistol sputtered. William screamed.

I jumped to my feet. The bedroom closet. God, please. Don't let him open the closet door. I heard a single pistol shot. The man screamed. His automatic chattered. Donna Elaine cried out. "Stoney. Stoney. Help me!"

I vaulted into the room, swung my shotgun to the left just as Abdul Karim appeared in the door from the hall where moments ago I'd been firing from behind my shield. I jerked the shotgun's trigger. Karim's chest exploded.

A dead man's body was jamming the door to the closet where my wife had been hiding. There was a hole in his forehead. I yanked his limp legs and jerked him out of the way. I switched on the closet light.

Donna Elaine was dead. Her face had been riddled by the killer's pistol fire. Oh, God. No. She's the most precious thing in my life. Don't let it be so. Please help me.

William! At the head of the stairs. He had screamed. I ran down the hall and saw his body sprawled in scarecrow fashion across the top of the shield that faced down the stairs. Karim had shot my son in the back of his head.

No time to stop. I was still fighting a war. The other attackers. I ran back to my original site in the middle dormer that faced the street. The three Cadillacs were speeding away. That's strange, I thought. There are only two bodies on the sidewalk; none on the lawn. They must have picked up the bodies of the others and thrown them into the three cars.

I heard the sirens of police cars and guessed they were still several blocks away. My mind was a jumble of thoughts and emotions. My son collapsed across the stairway shield. Dead. Donna Elaine. Get to your wife. I kicked Karim's body aside and knelt on the floor of the closet, gathering my wife of forty-six years in my arms. I began to rock and cry.

"Mr. Bedford! Mr. Bedford!" A man was shouting. "Where are you?"

"Up here," I yelled. "Help me. Please help me."

They were prying my arms open. "There, there, Mr. Bedford. Let us have her. We'll take over." Then I blacked out.

"Mr. Bedford, it's Julie Peel." I heard a woman's voice as though from a far distance. Someone was shaking me gently. "Mr. Bedford. Wake up. Please. It's Julie Peel."

I opened my eyes. Julie was leaning over the hospital bed, bathing my face with a cold cloth. Her face was close to mine. She was crying.

"Thank God, you're awake," she said. "I'll buzz the nurse's station."

"Julie. Where am I?"

"In Green Mountain hospital," she answered. "You're going to be all right. Two bullets went through your left side below the belt. You lost a lot of blood. You were in surgery for seven hours."

I closed my eyes for a long while. I felt the searing pain in my left side and reached my right hand down to feel the bandages. Then, I remembered. Donna Elaine. William. My body began to shake. I began struggling to lift myself from the bed.

"My wife? My son? Where are they?"

Julie was pushing me back onto the bed. "I'll give you all the details in a few minutes," she said. "I'm looking after them. I love them too."

A doctor and a nurse rushed into the room. "I'm Doctor Jarold Rawls," the tall, broad-shouldered man said. He reached for my hand and searched for my pulse. "You've had a rough time, Mr. Bedford, but you're going to make it."

I saw the plastic tubes leading from clear plastic bags that hung from a metal bar on top of a tall steel rod with arms like a stick man. My left hand was strapped to the bed. Needles in my hand and arm were freeways for feeding the liquids from the plastic bags into my body.

"Oh, God," I groaned. "I've got to get out of here. I've got to get to Donna Elaine and William." I turned to look at Julie. "Where are they?"

"They're at the funeral home, Mr. Bedford. I've made all the arrangements."

I must have blacked out again.

When I regained consciousness, Julie was caressing my cheek gently. She held a wad of tissues in her left hand and dabbed at her sad eyes.

I can't recall the following two days with much clarity. The haze of pain and grief were like dark, billowing fogs that wisped around me. I faded in and out of merciful darkness.

I remember attendants in white uniforms helping me from bed and easing me into a wheel chair. The plastic tubes and the steel bar stick man from which the bags of liquids hung were rolled alongside my chair.

At the funeral home two men, one holding the plastic bags and tubes and the other pushing my wheelchair, rolled me up next to the caskets so I could touch the face of my dead wife and son. I called their names over and over in hoarse cries.

The light in the stateroom at the funeral home was dim. Much too dim, as the light in staterooms always is. I sniffed. There it was. That peculiar funeral home smell. It was coming from the solid rows of flowers that were banked along every available wall. The room where they had Baxter Lampkins had smelled that same way.

At the cemetery, the sun was bright and there were hundreds of people standing everywhere. The reporters and television cameramen at least maintained a respectful distance as they recorded the services. Julie stood by my wheel chair, holding my hand. The attendants protected the tubes through which the liquids dripped. Dr. Rawls and a nurse stood behind me.

I touched each casket over and over and called out loud for God to help me. He did. The merciful darkness enveloped me again.

Chapter 22

The day I limped from the hospital, leaning on Carl Krippendorf and Julie Peel, city police officers arrested me. They put my hands behind my back and snapped on handcuffs. The media people knew it was another big story. Photographers snapped dozens of pictures for newspapers and the wire services. The red eyes on the television cameras signaled that the evening news would carry all the details about the arrest of Stoney Bedford and the filing of murder charges against me. The grand jury had indicted me two weeks ago while I still lay in a hospital bed more dead than alive.

Other than Julie and Carl Krippendorf, only two visitors were allowed to see me, Harris Woolford and Able Erling. Nightmares of pain and sedation enveloped me often.

Harris tried to interest me in media coverage of what had happened. "The story is the major headline in the newspapers and on television and radio. They don't quite know how to play it, whether or not to sympathize with you or to cheer the tragic things that happened in the attack."

"I've lost everything," I mumbled. "I've lost my reasons for living."

"Millions of people around the world are pulling for you," Able said. "The mail. The telephone calls. The faxes. You wouldn't believe the enormous volume."

"The attack has brewed up storms of protest the militants weren't counting on," Harris said."

"But my wife. My son. They're out there in the graveyard."

"Yeah," Able said. "No one can feel the depths of your sorrow. We just wanted you to know that we haven't forgotten."

Despite the sometimes profane protests of Carl Krippendorf, the arresting officers insisted that I ride in the patrol car to the courthouse to be charged before a judge.

"Why don't you bastards back off?" Carl yelled. "What you are doing is not necessary. This man is not resisting. He's in such a weakened condition he can't stand rough treatment. Why do you insist on treating him this way?"

"It's orders," the police captain said. "The D.A. says Bedford is a high-profile case. We have to make certain the people see that he's not treated any differently than others just because he is who he is."

"But you're going to the extremes," Krippendorf yelled. "At least, take off those handcuffs and let him ride with Miss Peel and me. We'll follow you to the court house."

"Unless you get out of our way old man," the young assistant D.A. accompanying the two officers said to Carl, "we'll charge you with obstructing justice. Now, why don't you just back off, fellow. This is a new age. Time has moved on and left you far behind." It was the all too familiar face of arrogance of the young against the old. "We made our plans weeks ago to make an example out of this old Southern blueblood."

I touched Carl's arm. "It's all right," I told him. "Just meet us at the court house."

I was too weak to fight any harder. All the fire in me seemed to have turned to dead embers. The handcuffs on my wrists held a strange fascination for me. The whole scene seemed like a replay from Franz Kafka's *The Trial*. At least I knew what I was being charged with. The television news I'd watched in my hospital room had kept me informed as to the bizarre happenings.

The U.S. Justice Department had wedged itself "into the Stoney Bedford case to teach Southern racists that they can no longer murder innocent citizens at will and violate the civil rights of black citizens." Such inflammatory political pandering was like pouring gasoline on an open flame.

The indictment for murder by the state of Georgia took precedence over the federal charges of civil rights violation. It would take a federal grand jury to hear these charges. After the trial for murder, the bloodhounds from Washington would be stepping into the fray to run me to earth—unless I'd been put away from society to suit their whims. This was politics and the outcome of my trial was far too important to be ignored by the federal government. Minorities were an important voting bloc and their militancy was always exploding onto the political scene.

Knowing this, I should have expected what happened when I arrived at the courthouse for my arraignment. As we entered the courtroom, the Justice Department attorneys were there talking animatedly to the Forest County District Attorney. Tighe Boring ran the D.A.'s office like a personal fiefdom. Getting reelected and building a power structure were far more important to Boring than seeing that justice was meted out even handedly. I had tangled with him several times before when I led the city council's assaults on his bloated budget and succeeded in getting huge cuts voted through. He had no love for me, for I had even backed the Republican who ran against him in the last elections.

In the courtroom, three handsome, well-dressed black Muslims were seated on benches. As soon as they saw me, one of the three, a lithe young black woman in long black caftan, jumped to her feet, pointed at me and yelled, "There's the white racist who murdered seven of our people in cold blood!"

One of the other Muslims gently pulled her back down into her seat.

A bailiff intoned the usual words. We rose to our feet. The somber, black-robed judge entered from a door in back of his bench, mounted the steps to his leather chair and sat down.

Morris Light was there in the courtroom, sitting quietly on one of the hard benches. I saw his assistant on the other side of the room. I knew that they were using hidden cameras to film the proceedings and tiny microphones to pick up our voices.

For the first time in weeks, a smile creased my face. They were both there—Harris Woolford and Able Erling, fellow council members. When I caught their eyes, both of them waved at me. Harris clasped his hands together and raised them over his head. His even white teeth were a sharp contrast to his dark complexion.

The judge peered over his glasses and asked, "Is counsel for the accused here?"

"Not yet, your Honor," Boring laughed. "Carl Krippendorf is old and might have lost his way." He winked at the three Justice Department attorneys who snickered. "Oh, here he comes now!"

Carl and Julie Peel entered through the side door. My attorney moved slowly with the aid of his cane. The pinched look on his face told me that the artificial leg was hurting the stump to which it was fitted. "It's the phantom limb pain that almost runs me insane at times," he often told me. "You'd think that after all these years, it would be gone. But, it's not."

"Mr. Boring," the judge asked. "What are the charges being brought against this defendant?" He nodded at me.

"Murder, your Honor," Boring said. His voice had the thrust of a knife through the heart. "First-degree murder."

"Let the record reflect the state's charges," the judge said. He turned to look at me. "And how does the defendant plead?" he asked.

I was living a Kafkaesque nightmare, an obvious farce, based on trumped up charges that completely ignored what had really happened that night. Those men attacked the home of a decent, law-abiding citizen in the dead of night. They killed my son and my wife. The killers had destroyed my reasons to keep on living. And they would have killed me except for the merciful intervention of the good Lord.

Yet here I was. Stoney Bedford. A decent American citizen. Charged with murder. How could that be?

Long before the attackers assaulted our home, we tried to alert the police about Karim's plans, begged them for help. The authorities laughed at us, said we were exaggerating things, that intelligent black people would never do a thing like that. The sad truth of the matter was, the authorities had ample reasons to know what was happening. The police had killed the black man in his car as he watched me and our home through night vision glasses with a gun on the car seat beside him. The endless parade of the pickets in front of my home. The death of poor, sad Alice in the operating room as doctors tried to repair her broken arm after she fell on the street running from television cameras. Reasonable people could have seen these events as a warning of impending disaster.

But the law closed its eyes, winked, looked the other way, as so often happens nowadays when fanatical blacks push too hard against the white power structure. Under such unrelenting pressure, whites find it easier to bend, sway, give in and give up precious freedoms bit by bit than to stand up for what's right. If the heart of our cowardly police chief had been in the right place, if he hadn't been intimidated and fearful of losing his job, the flag controversy would not have bloomed into such a deadly flower of death.

All we three Bedfords did was to shoot back when they stormed our home, our fortress. And in America, a man's home is his castle. We killed several of those who were coming to kill us. My wife. My son. We stood together, and now they were dead. Me? Charged with murder? Not just plain murder but first-degree murder? It would have been funny, only these people in the D.A.'s office were serious.

I should never have taken a public stand for the flying of the Confederate flag. It was just not sophisticated in today's present political climate. My reasons for defending the flag and the South were anchored in the darkness of a bygone age—or so some of the modern pariahs argued. I thought of the hundreds of people like Farris who had disowned their homeland. Poor Farris. He had died as he tried to absolve his ingrained sense

242

of guilt by groveling before those who had obliquely imposed the death sentence upon the tortured, acne-scarred young man—through goading him on.

There was a stir in the courtroom. The bailiff was whispering something into the judge's ear.

Johnson rapped his gavel, raised his shoulders to assume a more majestic pose and said sharply, "The media outside these chambers are clamoring to be admitted with their television cameras. I have once again denied their request. Their attorneys have vowed to seek a federal court order to try and force me to admit them. It will not be done."

My tired, wounded mind kept offering up reasons why this nightmare was unreal.

Surely any jury in America, any group of twelve citizens, would laugh at such a ridiculous charge. The grand jury should never have indicted me. They should have indicted those who murdered my wife and son. But justice no longer seemed to be of laws as had been envisioned in the Constitution. Now it was of men and was oftentimes despotic, oftentimes crushing innocent citizens.

The Justice Department had brought their formidable political power to bear on this case. They had persuaded Boring and the state government to make an example of me. Using the Civil Rights legislation to support their intervention, they had stepped in and argued persuasively and long for the grand jury to bring in the indictment for murder.

Caught up in fighting for the principles in which I believed mightily, I had refused to recognize that the political climate had been created in which this could happen to ordinary citizens like me. The death of faith in our system of justice was a heart-rending process. Small wonder that this death was occurring in the hearts of thousands of other Americans across the country.

The President of the country, the Attorney General. Both of them were Democrats and lived only for the consolidation of their power. And the black vote was very important to them and their political party. National elections were coming soon and bloc voting was a real consideration for the president's reelection—and the chief determinant of many of their party's attempts at legislation and law enforcement.

"And how does the defendant plead?" the judge asked again. He was an anteater peering over his glasses and searching for juicy morsels to suck up into quick oblivion.

Carl took his time as he hobbled forward. "Your honor," he said. "These charges are untrue and outrageous. This court should apologize to Mr. Bedford for even condescending to hear them proffered against a decent, American citizen."

The judge rapped his gavel. "Mr. Krippendorf," he said sternly. "Any further remarks of such character will force me to fine you for contempt."

"It is the court that should hold itself in contempt for this proceeding lifted directly from the pages of a Franz Kafka novel."

The judge rapped his gavel again. "This court finds Mr. Krippendorf in contempt of due process of the law and the violation of the dignity of this court. I fine you $1,000!"

"I assure you, Judge," Carl said, his voice cold and filled with disdain, "that I will appeal the contempt charge all the way to the Supreme Court if necessary. And furthermore, I will institute proceedings against you based on your abuse of judicial powers. I will strive mightily to topple you from your lofty position."

"That is your privilege, Mr. Krippendorf. Now, I ask again, how does the defendant plead?"

"I plead 'not guilty,' your honor." I spoke loudly. The anger showed through my tone of voice and was reflected on the grimness of my face. My hands were trembling and shaking.

"Your honor," Carl said. "May I inquire as to why these Justice Department attorneys are accorded the honor and privilege of being seated inside the railing?"

"Yes, you may, Mr. Krippendorf," the Judge answered. "I granted them this special privilege as representatives of the United States government. As attorneys, they are automatically officers of the court. You know that it is well within my power to make such decisions don't you?"

"It is not within your powers to grant them the right to intervene in this so-called trial for murder." Carl tapped his cane on the oiled surface of the hardwood floors. And I wish to lodge objections to such for the records we will use if an appeal is necessary."

"Granted, Mr. Krippendorf. That is your privilege."

Tighe Boring, the District Attorney, rose to his feet from the table to our right where he and an assistant were seated. "Your Honor, we're asking that Bedford be held without bail until the trial starts."

The anteater peered over the top of his glasses at Boring. Momentarily, his probing for prey was suspended. "Isn't that an unusual request, Mr.

Boring? Mr. Bedford is not your common criminal. He has just been released from the hospital. He's certainly not dangerous."

"Judge," Boring said. "The entire world, especially this nation's black citizens, is watching these proceedings to see if justice is dispensed fairly and impartially, regardless of a person's stature in life. Or the color of his skin."

"Humpfh," The judge snorted. He leaned back in his high-back leather chair that squeaked loudly in seeming protest. He began stroking his chin with his right hand.

Boring was pressing his point. "In a matter as serious as this one, Judge," he said, "we'd treat people of lesser status in the same manner. Stoney Bedford is rich and able to flee the country and live in splendor anywhere in the world he chooses. He should not be granted special privileges just because he is who he is."

Carl Krippendorf rose to his feet, his face distorted with rage. "Judge Johnson," he exploded. "This is America, not Nazi Germany. In the United States, people have a well-known right to defend their person and their property against unlawful assault. These cold-blooded killers came in the dead of night to storm the Bedford's home in efforts to kill him and his family who were hiding in their own home. Bedford's pleas to the police chief for help went unheeded."

Carl tapped the floor again with his cane. "It was the assassins who attacked and killed my client's wife and son. And they wounded him, almost to the point of death. It is the assailants who should be standing before this bench today, not Stoney Bedford. This man has already gone through hell. He doesn't deserve such treatment. Any red-blooded American would have done what Stoney Bedford did."

My old friend lifted his cane and pointed it at me. "My client is still so terribly weak that it is doubtful whether or not he should have been brought here today for arraignment. He is not a well man. He still has a long way to go to recover completely. A reasonable bail should be set so that Miss Julie Peel and I can take him home and nurse him back to some semblance of health."

"Judge Johnson," Boring interrupted. "The U.S. Justice Department is quite concerned that justice and equality prevail here today in this courtroom. Bedford has violated the civil rights of black people who were merely walking along a public sidewalk in front of his home. He did worse than violate their civil rights. He murdered several of them."

Carl's loud voice interrupted Boring. "Objection, your honor. The District Attorney says my client murdered someone. I thought that this was what the trial is to prove or disprove. I believe Boring deserves a reprimand."

The judge rapped his gavel sternly. "You do have a point, Mr. Krippendorf, but I must remind you that the process of objecting to the points being made by the prosecution has little, if any place, in determining the question at hand."

The anteater's proboscis was probing and sniffing again. The judge lowered his head to peer over his drugstore reading glasses. "You may continue with your point, Mr. Boring."

"It is clear from our point of view," Boring said, "that racism, hatred of blacks and violence have been used by Bedford as a rationalization to kill black people who just happened to park on a public city street in front of a rich man's house and get out of their automobiles to stand on a public sidewalk to discuss their concerns with each other about a symbol of hatred and oppression which Bedford was championing. These are some of the reasons we are asking that Bedford be held without bail until the date of his trial."

"Thank you, Mr. Boring," the judge answered. "This is an unusual case. The violation of a citizen's civil rights may or may not be involved, but the shooting down of black citizens certainly is at the heart of this matter. And, I can understand the concerns of black people."

Krippendorf asked simply, "What about the concerns and rights of white citizens, your Honor? Most fair-minded Americans see this matter before us here today from an entirely different perspective than that of Boring and Hindsmith, the lead Justice Department attorney. White citizens too, are waiting and watching what happens in this matter. Already, there are outcries of rage from many groups across the nation over Stoney Bedford's treatment. These kinds of actions make citizens ask if they can any longer trust their government to do the right thing.

"Political correctness has become more important than justice and fairness. Hundreds of our citizens have written to protest the high-handed methods of Boring and Hindsmith. And of our weak-kneed police chief. Who failed to protect citizens from these killers. Isn't it true that all citizens, not just black citizens, deserve the same fair and impartial treatment in any court in our land?"

"Yes," Judge Uranus Johnson said, interlacing his fingers and feigning solemnity. "However, because of the volatile nature of this high profile political case, I direct that Stoney Bedford be held in jail without benefit of bond."

Johnson rapped his gavel, rose to his feet, looked around the courtroom with scathing eyes, adjusted his robes with a motion that conveyed his disdain for what was happening then exited slowly through the door that opened onto the judge's chamber behind the bench.

Julie Peel was sobbing quietly. "It's just not fair, Mr. Bedford."

I tried to console her. Carl was ramming papers into his worn, brown brief case with unnecessary vigor. "Stoney, I'll appeal Johnson's ruling this afternoon to a higher court. This isn't justice. It's a damned kangaroo court, the kind Franz Kafka wrote about in *The Trial*. And this action here today is mute testimony to the truth of George Orwell predicted. For our country under the age of 'Big Brother.' That age has arrived."

Boring and the three Justice Department lawyers were slapping each other on the back and voicing their happiness. "We won, today," Boring exulted. "We won."

"Man, we won in a big way," Hindsmith said. "At least this county will be a safer place for black people with Bedford locked up, away from his guns and that damned flag."

"You bastards," Carl snarled and pointed his cane at the four of them. "You'll not get away with your high-handed methods. Somewhere in this country, at least in a few places, a white man can still get justice when he's bold enough to fight against black militancy. Mr. Bedford and I happen to believe that one of these places is here, in Forest, Georgia.

"If you haven't learned yet, that millions of Americans are outraged about such machinations as yours, you soon will." Carl's jaws were clenched together. He nodded his head up and down. "Yes. I predict you soon will learn how people who have been wronged feel about fears that they can no longer receive a fair trial by our government. And it might be nasty." If I were you four, I'd be afraid to be out on the streets at night, after what you've been able to pull off here today."

Hindsmith bristled. "You are threatening us, old man. You sound just like that radical on the radio, Rush Limbaugh."

"You have paid me a great honor, Hindsmith, and I thank you for it." He bowed slightly to his accuser. "Rush Limbaugh is almost solely responsible for waking up the decent, conservative people in America and urging us to fight for our principles. And we are doing that. We'll see you in court."

Carl changed his mind and turned to face Hindsmith. "And if you make any further reference to my age during this trial, I will lodge charges against you and enjoy the courtroom proceedings immensely. I'll further guarantee that you will never have another peaceful day in your life. You'll discover quickly that you are not as high and mighty as you apparently believe yourself to be."

The solemn Hindsmith did not reply.

They led me out, still handcuffed, through a different door than the one through which I had entered. At the door, I paused and looked back. The District Attorney was so happy until you'd think he'd been named to a Federal judgeship. Hindsmith was still pumping Boring's hand and touching him on the shoulder.

Jubilation! They'd hacked away at my rights and had pulled off a political coup of the first order. Now, they were celebrating. They had not even considered the costs to me. I could still hear the bedroom windows breaking as Karim and his thugs busted through from the roof. The screams of William and Donna Elaine pierced my tired mind again. Then I heard the shotgun blast that blew Karim's face away; saw William's twisted body sprawled on the stairs, then returned to the closet to clutch Donna Elaine's body to mine. I held her in my arms as her life ebbed rapidly away.

The three Muslims were hugging each other and doing a strange jig I had never seen before. It reminded me of the game we played as children. "Put your left foot in, take your right foot out, do the hokey pokey and shake it all about. . ." I believe that's how the words went. They had always sounded so silly to me. Doing the hokey pokey. I almost burst out singing the words as their strange jig continued.

They put me into a cell with two black men and a younger white guy. I guessed that two of the three were going through withdrawal from drugs or alcohol since they were hugging themselves and shaking uncontrollably like bowls of gelatin.

"Help me," they kept begging. "Help me. Give me something. Please. Help me." Occasionally they vomited all over themselves and their bunks. One of them sank down onto his back and wallowed in his own puke. In his agony, he didn't know or care.

"What you in for, Whitey?" the stocky muscular black man who wasn't shaking asked. "You erase somebody?"

I didn't reply, for my mind was going through an upheaval similar to the projectile explosions from the mouths of those writhing souls begging for help. In college, Dante's *Inferno* had fascinated me. Now, I found myself in a hell similar to the one he painted so forcefully. Even the hellish inferno's tongues of fire had been ignited in my weary, heartsick mind that was rebelling at the stench and recoiling from the fear that had enveloped me.

The pain in my left side was like a thousand acupuncture needles that had carelessly been inserted too deeply. I searched for a place to sit down in the cell, but there was no place—except for one of the lower bunks reeking from vomit and urine.

"You got any money, Whitey?" The powerful man was now standing in front of me and grasping my arm.

"I don't think so. I've just been released from the hospital." He could see there was no fight in me, no resistance. Dark swirls of horror continued to boil in my mind. This couldn't be happening to me? I was Stoney Bedford, the prisoner in Kafka's *The Trial*, but unlike Kafka's character, I had been charged with a monstrous political crime. I was a political prisoner, only because I had dared to fight against those who had come to kill me and my family.

The strong man clasped my arm so tightly until the pain was shooting through my arm and shoulder. "Ain't I seen you somewhere before, man?"

"I don't think so," I answered. "If I have met you, I don't remember. I've been sick and in the hospital for weeks."

His fingers on my right forearm were like the steel tongs of a giant crane grabbing at the tumbled down ruins of a burned out building. "Say, man. Don't you jive old Dave York. I'm in here because I killed a man with my bare hands. Choked him to death."

He loosed his grip on my arm and turned my face toward his. His gaze was a blazing beam of hate. "Ah-h-h. You ain't nobody. You's old and sick. I don't need to get worked up 'bout nobody like you."

The darkness of fear lessened. I looked at the bunks and guessed that one of the top ones was to be mine. In my condition, I knew I'd never be able to climb up and get into it. I put my back against the cell bars and slowly slid down into a sitting position. I closed my eyes and thought about my patio at home and the peaceful surface of the lake's slowly moving water. I felt myself fading into the merciful darkness again.

When I regained consciousness, I was in a small room with white ceilings and walls, lying on my back in the single bed, the only one in the room. Dr. Rawls, the physician who had treated me while I was in the hospital, and Carl Krippendorf sat nearby in steel chairs welded to the floor. Dr. Rawls stood up and walked to the bed and took my hand to search for my pulse.

"Mr. Bedford," the doctor said. "Somehow or other, we're going to get you out of this hell hole. We've scheduled a press conference at two p.m. to present the facts about your health and to demand your release."

"You are a political prisoner, Stoney," Carl said. "Pure and simple. In the wildest stretch of my imagination, I could never have conceived of this happening in America." He pounded his fist into his hand. "What is happening to our country? A man kills those who are trying to kill him, yet he's charged with murder. I can't comprehend it. I simply cannot believe it."

"Oh, God, Carl," I said. "Please. You and Dr. Rawls get me out of here, or I shall surely die."

"I know," Dr. Rawls said. "You have a high fever now. In your weakened condition, your body cannot stand this kind of punishment. When we found you, you were lying on that concrete floor, unconscious. And one of the prisoners had vomited on you."

"We had to seek a judge's order," Carl said. "Habeas corpus. We were almost refused. If it hadn't been for the persuasive arguments of Dr. Rawls, Tighe Boring and the Justice Department lawyers might have prevailed. Those three from Washington! They're the most fiendish people I've ever come in contact with. Their burning motivation is hatred of whites and a gleeful desire to punish you."

Carl had been squeezing my hand. I noticed that his cheeks were wet with tears.

"I want to go to Bedford House," I said. "The place where I grew up. It's far out in the country, away from the frantic confusion of this city life. I can perhaps find some peace there. For a while at least."

"Stoney," Carl said. "This case has attracted nationwide attention. You wouldn't believe the number of people pouring into Forest. They come from all parts of the country, many of them in camouflage and clutching their rifles. Of course, the kooks have been attracted to the party because it gives them something to protest. But most are just plain citizens who are riled up that such a thing is happening to a decent, innocent man.

"The media is here, many from Europe, Asia, and the South and Central American nations, the media powerful from all parts of the country, clamoring to interview us. And Archibald Xerxes, the famous defense attorney from Atlanta, is driving to Forest to help us. He should arrive soon."

"I've watched Xerxes on TV many times," I said. "But we can't afford to hire such a high-powered individual such as Xerxes for our defense. His fees are far more than we could afford and have it make economic sense. Besides, you're the only attorney I need."

"Xerxes has volunteered to help us at no charge, Stoney." I could actually see some enthusiasm on Carl's weathered face. "And the telephone calls have become such a flood tide that I've hired three extra women in my office to help talk to the people who are calling to offer money, help, advice and comfort."

"I didn't know that many people would care about what happens to me," I said.

"Care?" Carl asked. "Stoney, people are aroused to fever pitch. They're sending money. Quite a lot of it. Demonstrations are already being staged in some of the bigger cities over the treatment of you and the handling of your case. It could get out of hand at any moment.

Carl straightened his back and tried to stand tall. I was glad to see him do it, since it took a lot to pierce his cynicism and resignation. "Newspaper editorials are questioning these actions. Talk radio has taken up your cause. I think our politically ambitious D.A. has bitten off more than he can chew, though Hindsmith and the Justice Department intervention in the case bothers me a great deal. They're difficult to handle."

"What are the blacks doing?" I asked as Dr. Rawls pumped the blood pressure monitor's bulb once again to measure my pressure. Obviously the first two readings did not measure up

Carl's voice turned angry. "Oh, they're raising hell, marching, demonstrating, chanting for the death penalty for you. Tomorrow at noon, they've vowed to march around the jail until, as they put it, justice is done."

The face of the older gray-haired man and his pudgy, balding companion at the city council meeting that day swam through my thoughts. I heard again his matter-of-fact announcement to me: "They needn't think they can trample on us whites and get away with it. We've had enough. More than enough."

Tom Farris had learned that truth the hard way, as he died with an arrow through his back and fell face forward into the flames of the gasoline-soaked Confederate flag he himself had set on fire.

Dr. Rawls glanced at his wristwatch. "It's ten till two," he said. "I'll ring the bell so they can bring a wheel chair for you, Mr. Bedford. You can't walk, but with a wheelchair, we can get to the courtroom on time for the press conference. It's the only place in the courthouse that's big enough to hold the expected crowd."

This time I sat in the judge's high-backed leather chair with Dr. Rawls on one side and Carl Krippendorf on the other. The dapper Archibald Xerxes made quite a stir as he hurried into the room carrying a brief case in each hand. In person, he was taller than he seemed when I saw him on television. He was still the handsome, graying, slightly arrogant defender of people and causes. His presence exuded power and poise, qualities that had helped him to earn millions in fees and a reputation for aggressive intellect and a stiletto use of the English language.

Xerxes walked to the front of the chamber where the three of us were seated. Carl grabbed his hand enthusiastically. "Xerxes, how glad I am that you are here to help us. From the way things have been going, the additional power and emphasis you can add can help us reverse things."

"I'm mad as hell, Carl. As are millions of other Americans throughout the country." His distinctive voice and the way he pronounced his words would make almost anyone turn and give him a second look.

"When I open the press conference," Carl said, "can I turn it over to you so you can make a statement about Stoney Bedford's being held as a political prisoner?"

"I will indeed," the tall man said. "I came prepared to do just that, among other things. Mr. Bedford," he turned to me and offered his hand. "I've come to help free you from the government and your other tormentors."

"Thank you, Mr. Xerxes," I said. "I believe you were graduated from the University of Georgia, too."

"That's right," he exclaimed. "Are you a Georgia Bulldog, too?"

"Yes, I played football for the 'Dogs.' "

"No wonder I like you," Xerxes said.

Carl interrupted. "I'll make a brief statement to open the press conference. Then, Dr. Rawls here, Stoney's personal physician, will tell them about his patient's physical condition. After that, it's your turn to spellbind this bunch of cynical bastards out there." He motioned to the fifty or more media representatives. "Most of them would like to see Bedford hanged by the neck until he is dead."

"You're not going to have Mr. Bedford make a statement, are you?" Xerxes asked.

"No," Carl said. "I don't think it would be wise. If Stoney spoke, it might jeopardize our case."

"I think you're right, Carl," the dapper Xerxes said. He turned to me. "You're not well, are you?"

Even the short journey to the courtroom in the wheelchair had drained me of what little energy I had. "I'm so tired," I said to Dr. Rawls. "So tired."

"I know you are," the doctor said. "After what you've been through. But just hold on until this conference is finished. We need you sitting here so the media can judge for itself whether or not we're telling the truth."

Carl rapped a gavel for attention. The hum of voices stilled. "We want to thank the media for being here. There is much urgency to this meeting, for Stoney Bedford is far from being well. As a matter of fact, he came here in a wheelchair directly from a hospital bed."

The murmur of voices ran through the crowd. The snouts of TV cameras were aimed at us. Reporters scribbled notes on their pads.

Carl continued. "You are witnessing a great miscarriage of justice. The justice system in the United States is being bent and twisted into an unrecognizable shape. My client, Stonewall Bedford, was released from the hospital just this morning. In the hospital lobby, he was arrested and handcuffed. In a court appearance before Judge Uranus Johnson, Bedford was denied bail, despite everyone present knowing that he was too ill to flee the country and that he certainly did not present a threat or danger to society by being released on his own recognizance."

Carl spoke slowly. He stopped and scanned the media people, as if he was staring down any opposition.

"Our young, ambitious district attorney, Mr. Tighe Boring," Carl said, "recently of the Georgetown University law school faculty, prevailed upon Judge Johnson to deny bail in order to demonstrate to all citizens in America that the law treats every man equally regardless of position, wealth or reputation. It is a ridiculous, political premise in this case and has little, if anything, to do with whether or not bail should have been allowed Mr. Bedford.

"I want you to hear Bedford's personal physician, Dr. Hamlin Rawls, talk about my client's physical condition."

Rawls was angry. He jumped in quickly and succinctly, the movement of his hands and the set of his jaw demonstrating his contempt for those who had mishandled his patient.

"Mr. Bedford is too weak from gunshot wounds to be locked up in jail," the doctor said. "If I had known this would happen to him, I'd have never released him from the hospital. He needs regular doses of his prescription medication and several hours a day of bed rest to fully recuperate.

"He's been locked into a cell with two drug addicts screaming from withdrawal symptoms and a powerful man who brags about killing another man with his bare hands. The only bunk available is a top bunk into which my patient cannot possibly hoist himself in his weakened condition. The two derelicts in the cell have each vomited all over the floor, and, I might add, upon Mr. Bedford here when he lost consciousness and sprawled onto the floor.

"It is inhuman to further add to Mr. Bedford's illness in forcing him to endure such intolerable conditions. One must ask himself what kind of inhuman fiends are we dealing with who would overlook the obviousness of Bedford's illness in attempts to further some outrageous political goals."

"Thank you, Dr. Rawls," Carl said. He turned to the media. "When we are finished with our statements, we'll let you ask questions. Now, I'd like to introduce Mr. Archibald Xerxes from Atlanta. He is incensed by what is happening in this case. Mr. Xerxes has volunteered his services on a pro bono basis on behalf of Stoney Bedford. Mr. Xerxes, the floor is yours."

The tall, handsome Xerxes stood up, fastened pince nez on his Roman nose, straightened his tie and tugged at his coat sleeves. He turned his head slowly from left to right as his eyes swept the media representatives. I had to admire his poise and presence, his showmanship. He was an imposing figure and obviously in command of the situation.

"Oh, what tangled webs we weave, when first we practice to deceive." The voice was cultured, deep and resonant. " 'The whole world,' I believe I heard the D.A. say to Judge Uranus Johnson as the two preened themselves before the television cameras, 'especially this nation's black citizens, is watching these proceedings to see if justice is dispensed fairly and impartially, regardless of a person's status and position in life.' "

Xerxes took the pince nez off his nose and wiped at them with a white handkerchief. "I almost burst out laughing when Boring said those words. Boring? What an apt name for so handsome a man as the D.A. Back to the point. As if any judge in America did not know this necessary emphasis upon equal justice for all. But that is irrelevant to Judge Johnson and Tighe Boring. Oh, and to the U.S. Justice Department. After these great, biased and prejudiced representatives of the mighty United States of America whispered their favorite accusations of racism and hatred on the part of white people into Boring's ear, and Boring jumped up and spouted them off in the courtroom, the judge denied bail to Stoney Bedford.

" 'Because,' as the honorable jurist said, 'because of the volatile nature of this high profile political case . . .' That was Judge Johnson's final reason for ignoring the legal facts of this case and Mr. Bedford's physical condition in rendering his decision. Then the judge left the courtroom with the usual pomp and circumstance granted to those who wear the robes of supposed justice."

Xerxes's face turned sad. He lowered his head, then suddenly looked up. 'Oh what tangled webs we weave. . .' Look at this man." He removed his pince nez and turned to point his right index finger at me. "Stonewall Bedford is a political prisoner, pure and simple. He has been denied bail to satisfy fawning politicians who look at minority groups and say, 'We'd better listen to them. They're angry. They're powerful. They're voters. We need their power on our side. And,' these misanthropes shake their heads sadly and join the great crowd of anguished breast-beaters trying to expunge the nation's supposed guilt, and echo the big lie, 'white people are racists.' "

A stir ran through the ranks of the assembled media representatives. The brilliant flashes from the photographers' flash bulbs and the searching snouts of red-eyed television cameras under the glaring lights added a surreal quality to the courtroom scene. Xerxes threw his head back, raised his fists close to his closed eyes and grimaced as though in pain and desperation.

"The charge that white racism is the most powerful motivating force beating in the hearts of the country's white citizens is poppycock. It smacks of the Joseph Goebbels' 'big lie' technique. In his twisted way, Goebbels was a genius when he said, 'Tell a big lie often enough and people will come to believe it.' Never are the charges of self-love and vanity more fallacious than when you attempt to apply it to that man sitting there whose body is so weak and weary he can scarcely hold his head up."

Once again, he used his hands and head as though appealing to some higher power. "Consider some of the facts. Bedford has paid big sums of money to help five black men go through college and each of them has become quite successful in his chosen fields. Two are ministers; two are attorneys; one is a dentist. I have their names here on this sheet of paper, but Bedford asked that I not reveal their identities.

" 'It's a tradition,' Bedford says, 'that started with my great, great-grandfather. We have continued to help deserving people, not for self aggrandizement, but out of a sense of noblesse oblige.' "

Excited murmuring raced through the fifty of so reporters and cameramen. It was evident that they'd not known this information before now.

"A dangerous man?" The trim attorney in his expensive gray suit threw his head back and laughed. "Stoney Bedford, a man who chairs Forest's rescue mission where more than one hundred and fifty poor, desperate and homeless people will be fed three meals today, given medical treatment and furnished beds for the night. He spends three hours a day there among the people, helping, counseling and encouraging them. He gives $1,000 per month from his own pocket to help finance the mission.

"I want you to see this." He opened a thin, six-inch long leather covered box and held it high so it could be seen. "Do you recognize what this is? It's the Silver Star for valor in battle against America's enemies in the Mediterranean during WWII. Carl Krippendorf, that man sitting there," he pointed to Carl, "owes his life to Stoney Bedford who pulled him from the sea when a German .88 shell blew away his leg and sunk his landing craft off the beaches in the invasion of Salerno, Italy."

He folded his left arm across his chest, cradled his chin in his right hand for a moment, then took a deep breath. "In this case, Most of the laws of evidence, decency and justice have been denied Stoney Bedford. And for what reason? The U.S. Justice Department and the blacks want to make an example out of him because he dared to stand up for his beliefs, dared to defend his home against the assault of murderous thugs; dared to kill those who were trying to kill him. He has paid so dearly for his courage. His wife and son were killed the same night the attackers gravely wounded him. The murderers came at 2 o'clock in the morning hoping that Bedford and his family would be asleep and they could do their killing before any one of the three Bedfords could rise up to defend themselves.

"The attackers paid a price much greater than they ever dreamed. Several of them were killed and as a result, their black political leaders have turned their venom on Stoney Bedford. And the government is siding with them. It's plain that Bedford is a political prisoner.

"We demand that Stoney Bedford, a true American hero, be released without bail immediately." He scanned the media representatives again, this time even more slowly. Carefully he removed his pince nez and slid them into his pocket, then sat down.

A stillness descended upon the room.

Dr. Rawls leaned over and whispered to Carl, "I'm helping Mr. Bedford down and into the wheelchair. Then, we're going to leave this room. This is too wearing on him. I'm afraid of the consequences."

As I held onto the doctor's shoulder and was helped into a wheel-chair, media representatives started yelling questions. Carl and Xerxes would have to answer them.

At four o'clock that afternoon, I was released from jail without posting bail. Carl drove me out to Bedford House where Archie Jones and his wife, Lettie, started nursing me back to health.

Two days later, workmen began erecting two flagpoles on the front lawn of Bedford House, one sixty feet high, the other forty feet high. At 1:30 in the afternoon, the work was finished. I asked Archie Jones to raise the U.S. flag on the taller of the two poles and the Confederate flag on the shorter one.

On Wednesday of the following week, D.A. Tighe Boring held his own press conference to level charges of blatant racism, bias and prejudice against me, Krippendorf, and Xerxes. His remarks received only scant coverage on the evening news, and even Victor Allen's *'Ledger'* showed their disdain by according Boring's blandishments two small paragraphs on the inside pages.

Carl telephoned me as often as three times a day. "Stoney, over a thousand letters a day are pouring in from all across the United States and around the world. Less than one percent of them are unfavorable. Many of them contain money, some of them substantial amounts, to, as they label it, 'help set this patriot free.' "

He was excited and his words were also lifting my spirits. "The people calling and writing these letters offer encouragement and express their admiration for your courage and willingness to fight for principles. The volume of phone calls is so great until I've had to have three additional lines installed in my office and hire two more people to help out the other three. The five do nothing but listen to the callers, record their messages and their names, addresses, and telephone numbers. People are planning to come to Forest in great numbers for your trial, and they're eager to stage counter-demonstrations to nullify the effects of those which we are certain the minority groups will be staging. Already, hundreds of them have arrived in Forest."

Xerxes called daily to help boost my spirits and to assure me that we would win our case. Several times he came to Forest to have lunch at Bedford House with Carl, Julie, and me. He and Carl laboriously constructed my defense for the upcoming trial.

"Stoney," Carl said. "Be certain that Morris Light develops his footage recorded by his cameras of the attack on your home and that he puts it together. In all probability, it may well turn out to be one of the most important pieces of evidence we can present in our defense."

Julie Peel drove me to the cemetery on Wednesday and Sunday afternoons. We were both working our way through the process of grieving. My heart went out to her. The spark was gone from her living. I could see it in the way she walked, in the droop of her shoulders. The radiance that once lighted her beautiful face was gone. Her cheeks always seemed to be glistening from the tears that never seemed to stop flowing from her sad eyes.

Often, the willowy young woman broke down and cried as she stood by William's grave. "Oh, William," she'd sob. "I loved you so much. July 12th was to be our wedding day. I look at the wedding invitations we'd already had printed and weep my heart out."

At times, she knelt and put her cheek against the red clay mound of dirt that covered him. I liked to think I knew what she was going through. I'd sit in a folding lawn chair we'd brought along for me and envision Donna Elaine and William walking heaven's golden streets and singing with the choirs of angels.

I could hear my wife reciting her tales of helping the poor families in the church, see her laughing, feel her body close to mine.

Many times, I wanted to say to William, "Mix us a martini before the evening news, son."

I'd hear him say, "Sure thing, Dad."

At times, I'd have Archie Jones drive me to the hunting lodge far down the rutted dirt road at the back of our acreage. I could be close to my son there where I'd taught him how to shoot and hunt, the same way my father had taught me. There, the roots of our family ran so deep until at night I often imagined I could see various ones of them walking toward the front porch of the lodge. My son and my father were the most prominent ones in the ethereal parade.

At nights, in my dreams, I'd automatically reach my left hand back to clasp Donna Elaine closer to me, only to wake up when I found that I was alone. Always alone.

"Where have all the flowers gone . . . ?"

And daily, the D.A. was freely predicting, to any one who'd listen, that he was going to get a conviction of Stonewall Bedford on charges of murder. He made the mistake of doing that one morning at the restaurant when my old friends in our discussion group were there having breakfast. He was immediately set upon by yelling, arm-waving men. They had to pull two of my defenders off the handsome Boring, but only after they'd torn off his coat and shirt. They said Boring literally ran from the restaurant, jumped into his car, locked the doors and sped away.

I thought of the two older, taciturn men at the council meeting that day who had made the matter-of-fact statement that this and worse things than the incident in the restaurant would happen to people like Tighe Boring. I could not find it in me to feel sorry about evil befalling Boring.

CHAPTER 23

Carl Krippendorf was not his usual calm self on the telephone. "Stoney, have Archie Jones drive you from Bedford House to the hunting lodge. Right away. And please don't tarry. Just go. I don't want the media to have access to you for the next few days."

"Why, Carl? Has something unusual developed?"

"One of my sources called me with information that the Justice department attorneys had fed questions to some of their media lap dogs in order to trap you. If you answer the questions in your usual direct way, you could severely weaken our case. It's a devilish thing, something that shouldn't happen in America. But, I suppose we have to admit that the press is not on our side. And we know the government isn't. That's true. Most of the time anyway."

I was lost in depression's fog. "I'm so tired, Carl. Why can't I just stay home and refuse to let the media inside Bedford House?"

"Stoney, listen to me." He was not happy with my attitude. "Please do what I say. The media know you're at Bedford House recuperating and they will badger you twenty-four hours a day if you stay there. They'll cajole, flatter and lie to you. They'll do anything to trap a person and get the slant they want on a particular story."

"I don't disagree with you, Carl. I've been that route before. Many times. I know the extremes to which reporters will go."

Reporters! They were bloodhounds baying on the trail of a story. I remembered another day they'd been pursuing their story. The day poor Alice ran to escape them, fell in the street and broke her arm. And now she, too, was in her grave.

"Stoney," Carl asked. "Are you listening to me?"

"All right, Carl. I'll go. If you insist."

"I do insist. I want you completely well before the trial starts. Certainly, we want to see you with a lot more energy and a clearer mind than you have right now. Oh, and take your cellular phone with you. The one with the unlisted number. Xerxes and I will need to consult with you as we finish our preparation for the case and plan strategy for your defense."

"Okay, Carl. Morris Light and his assistant will go with me to the hunting lodge. They say they need more footage of this particular time in my life for their documentary."

"Good," Carl said. "That way, you can make certain he's putting together the footage on the attack for our use when we go to trial. Anyhow, the two of them can at least be some company for you while you're there at the lodge by yourself."

My life had changed so much in the last three months, and I, myself, certainly had changed in many respects. In what specific ways, I could not as yet define, but I could feel the turbulence of change churning inside me. Much of the fire in my guts had died out; the same fire that had made me an energetic, viable player in the business world and in the city's power structure. Political office no longer held excitement for me. My zest for life itself had greatly diminished. Loneliness made me want to sit down in some chair and wind the strands of my life inward until there was nothing left. At times, I felt as though I was sleep walking. My wounds had taken more out of me than I wanted to admit. Although I still suffered much pain, I was determined not to get hooked on the painkillers which Dr. Rawls had prescribed for me.

Each morning, I sat on the cabin's long veranda, sipped the strong coffee that bit at my senses, read my worn Bible and prayed. It was the only path that led through the bogs of evil clutching at me, a path which eventually emerged from the darkness into sunlit fields. Meditation and solitude proved the medicine I needed as I struggled to make sense out of what was happening to me.

I tried to find my way back to God again, for I was a long way off and lost. Lost, like the prodigal son. I'd invested my inheritance in things now vanished and lost all I had, but the Holy Father would welcome me home with feasting, song and familial love. If only I could find the road that led back home. Oh, God,. I need to find this road before it's too late.

There were so many stumbling blocks as I lurched along the path towards the place of my being like a crazed man fleeing from some dread monster, a monster I myself had created by unwise actions and mind sets. Had I sacrificed my wife and son on an altar erected to a false God? Or thrown them into the Coliseum's arena for the tearing of their flesh by today's new lions which the Federal government had turned loose to prey upon its citizens? Had I sat above the arena where my wife and son faced the new lions, in the seat of honor, with some members of the long vanished Southern nobility and heard only the distant drums at Gettysburg?

I now wallowed in my own days of reconstruction because of my Southern soul. My mind wrestled my own imagined, modern day carpetbaggers, which were spawned in my darkest thoughts. The tentacles of my conscience reached from the dark fogs of grief to clutch me to these ghosts with unyielding arms.

"Oh, God," I prayed out loud. "Forgive me wherein I have sinned. Help me to remember that each of us has sinned and fallen short of the glory of the Lord. Help illumine my mind as I read and study Your holy word. Help me find the road back home."

At seven in the morning, only the noises of the forest filtered through my thoughts, and these sylvan sounds were heard only dimly. I searched diligently for those passages of holy scripture that might give me some hope for a better life. One morning, I came to some words of Jesus that literally leaped from the pages of the bible and into my heart.

"I am come that they might have life and have it more abundantly." I wondered about the expression on Jesus' face as he said those words, about the tenor of his voice and the ring of authority. If I could just once more go back to the abundance I had in my life only a few short months ago, that would be my greatest joy.

"All things are possible if thou canst only believe." Oh, I believe, Lord. I'm so alone, I have no choice but to believe. I know that my wife and son cannot walk this way again, but perhaps I can rebuild my life on the memories I have from knowing them so richly and for so many years.

"For my God shall supply all of your needs according to His riches in Glory, through Christ Jesus." Oh, God, I have so many needs. My wife and son are gone; my life as I've known and lived it for many years is now no more. Visit upon me some kind of peace that blossoms within myself that I might once again feel as though I'm worthy.

"If ye but have the faith of a grain of mustard seed, ye can say to this mountain, remove hence to yonder place, and it shall be removed: and nothing shall be impossible unto you." I had so many mountains in front of me to be removed. How does the song go? "You always hurt the one you love . . . " I had not meant to hurt my wife and my son, nor anyone else, for never in my life had such motives been a part of my life.

How could believing in principles lead to such a personal holocaust as that which had engulfed me with its flames? When you believe in honor and heritage, and there are those who rear up in your path and yell "Racist", is one supposed to say, "Oh, I'm sorry." and slink off to hide in a state of not believing in anything?

As Speaker of the House, the silver-haired legend, Sam Rayburn of Texas, used to tell incoming freshmen representatives to the U.S. Congress, "To get along here, you must go along." What he was saying was that belief in expediency and not principle was the smoothest path in politics. I could never go along with 'Mr. Sam.' That's the coward's way that has so crippled our great nation until perhaps there is not enough courage left in us to govern ourselves with honor, according to principle.

The devil's song often broke through with clanging jubilation. "Oh, there's no hiding place down here, no hiding place down here. I went to the rock to hide my face, the rock cried out 'No hiding place' . . . "

But I'd touched the caskets of Donna Elaine and William that day in the cemetery. I'd heard their death cries that terrible night Karim and his murdering compatriots had burst into our home behind a curtain of deadly fire.

"No hiding place down here. No hiding place down here . . . " The mountains had not yet been removed, and I had not yet found too many things to be possible for me as I struggled to believe and nourish my faith in God.

I fought against Satan's intrusion, against his cackling glee, but I was still so lost, so far from home. So far from home. "The Lord is my shepherd, I shall not want. He maketh me to lie down in green pastures, he leadeth me beside still waters. He restoreth my soul . . . "

I took long walks in the woods and many times found myself immersed in the overwhelming greenness of early summer. Here and there, fallen logs had impeded the flow of the small brook, creating deep, quiet pools where mosquito hawks darted with their blinding quickness and big fish jumped. Further along the bank's barely discernible trail, startled rabbits bolted from my path and a huge diamond-backed rattlesnake crawled slowly from the pool of warm sunshine that hovered on the trail until he disappeared into the dense undergrowth.

The shrilled symphony of birds as they went about building their new nests was a song of awakening. Several squirrels had found the bare trunk of a dead tree and were busy running along its leafless branches and ducking into the holes to hide and sire their young. Noisy blue jays fussed at me as I walked, trying to hasten my departure from their territory.

Then I heard it. The lonesome cry of the mourning dove. "Daddy," William used to ask me when he was a little boy and we roamed these same woods. "Why is the mourning dove always so sad?"

"I don't know, William. Perhaps his cry is God's way of reminding us that 'Into each life some rain must fall.'"

"When the rain comes, Daddy, I hope I'll always have an umbrella.'"

"You'll have one, son. Each of us has such an umbrella, if we will just unfold it. It's God's love for us."

Late one afternoon, as I sat on the lodge's long veranda, sipping a martini, Carl Krippendorf called me on my cellular telephone. He was excited. "Judge Johnson has set the trial date, Stoney. It's July 5th."

"That soon?" I asked. "That's less than two weeks away."

"Don't worry, Stoney. Archibald Xerxes and I are ready. We've prepared as thoroughly for this case as one could. We hope we've anticipated all of the legal angles and maneuvers and are ready. I'd bet that we have done just that."

"I have complete confidence in you two, Carl. I have to believe in you, because I certainly don't want to go to prison,"

"We know that Tighe Boring, the D.A., will attempt to prove that you had planned days in advance to kill some of the blacks. They'll claim that you are lying; that the two bodies left on the sidewalk in front of your house is evidence that these people were occupying a public space when you killed them. They'll use enlarged photographs of the bodies, your home, your house number. And, of course, the testimony of the police officers who answered the call."

"There were more than two dead people, Carl. They carted the other bodies away, making certain they didn't leave any of them sprawled on the lawn. I've told you what they did with them, haven't I?"

"No, I can't recall that you did, Stoney."

"Roy Bester said they dumped the badly wounded attackers alongside the streets in black neighborhoods where they died before dawn. Their deaths were labeled as drive-by shootings."One very peculiar thing though. All the bullets had been dug out of their bodies

"Damn," Carl said. "That's the work of mad dogs. Dumping wounded men along the street and leaving them to die. Very clever mad dogs though. If you can't find a bullet there's no chance of a ballistics expert tying them to the bullets from your guns."

"So that's the reason Roy told me that some of the bodies were badly mutilated. We're not dealing with people who are attending a Sunday School picnic. They also took the guns out of the hands of the two on the sidewalk so they could claim I shot unarmed men."

"But, we've got a secret weapon they don't yet know about," Carl said. "I've seen the seven minutes of film footage put together by Morris Light. It is very dim, but it does corroborate everything you've told us about the attack. But Judge Johnson may not allow us to introduce it as evidence. And, even if the Judge does allow it to be introduced as evidence, the jury may not accept it as credibile. And Boring could sell the jurors that it's something that's been manufactured from researching old files of documentaries of other times and places."

"I don't know whether or not it will help our defense," I said, "but I'm relieved that at least we have it available."

"But, the film will not give the clear evidence we need. Because it was night and the lighting did not allow for clarity, and because of the distance of the cameras from the action, the people in the film are unrecognizable. They're just shadowy figures."

My spirit plummeted. Another hope dashed. Where was the road back home?

Carl sighed. "It's weight as evidence is not as heavy as Xerxes and I would like. Unfortunately, the only eye witness we have to what occurred is you, and perhaps Light and his assistant. And the jury may or may not believe your testimony."

"Maybe the only things I have going for me are photographs of the bullet holes in my house and the bodies of Karim and the other two blacks that died inside. And, of course, the deaths of my wife and son."

"We plan to build our case on self defense," Carl said. "Traditionally, it's a recognized principle of law that a man has a right to protect his home and person when attacked. At least, that used to be a universally accepted principle. But, these days, one can scarcely rely on members of the jury believing in such things."

"Suppose Boring tries to turn the tables on us and claim Karim and his gang were acting in self defense. That they only returned our fire only after we killed three or four of them?"

Carl laughed. "That's ridiculous. Karim and two of his henchmen were found dead inside your home. If they had been acting only to defend themselves, they would not have smashed their way into the house. And, of course, the ballistics reports show that your wounds and those of your wife and son came from bullets fired from their guns."

"Do you think the jury will believe us when we tell them about Karim's fellow attackers prying the guns out of the dead men's hands and dumping their bodies along the streets in the black neighborhoods?" I sipped at my martini and waited for Carl's answer.

"Perhaps they will; perhaps they won't. At least, Light's film shows the position of the dead bodies. And the number. It's the best thing we have to back up that story. If . . . If the judge allows us to introduce it as evidence."

"And Oliver Hindsmith? The Justice department lawyers?" I asked. "I presume they're still gung ho about making an example out of me for all the world to see?"

"Yes, they've put so much emphasis on this case, until they almost *have to have a conviction.* Boring is their front man, their attack dog. Xerxes and I will try to get the jury to see that the charge of murder is really inconsequential as far as the Justice department is concerned. *They want to deliver your head on a platter as their political offering to the howling mobs.* The prosecution's major claim will be that you murdered the two dead men on the sidewalk and violated their civil rights at the same time."

"Is Boring getting as much pressure from the blacks as I think he is?" I asked.

"Well, Stoney. It's not only the blacks that are exerting pressure. It's liberals, too. Liberal activists. They've flocked here from all parts of the country. They've made it a cause for which they can fight, one to which they can rally the usual bunch of kooks for demonstrations. And the press. I'd have to say that this is their 'cup of tea.' Newspapers, radio, the television networks. Day after day, they trumpet your blind hatred of blacks and use you, your position and power to show that people like you still control much of Southern life."

Anger hit me. "Carl, that's simply not true. If it was, I wouldn't be going to trial for murder."

"The elitists are making a believable case for that thesis, Stoney. Many prominent people from academia. Others from liberal think tanks. They're pontificating daily for the press which eagerly seeks them out as experts. And, of course, sadly, we have our share of Southern turncoat whites who seem bent on wallowing in seas of racist guilt and the felt need for atonement. And they make themselves readily available to the media."

"Shades of France's famous Dreyfus case."

"You nailed it, Stoney."

"Carl, people like me. We're antique relics, the last remaining mastodon of an age of myth that goes back so far no person alive today ever experienced it. Thus, few can understand the thinking and the moral basis a person like me uses to orient his life and actions. We are objects of scorn, objects that must be smashed into fragments."

His voice rose. "People like us, Stoney, are not easily smashed. And that frustrates this pack of hyenas."

"We were supposed to have been finished in April of 1865. And certainly during the harshness of reconstruction. Surely, the recent coming of the sophistication of political correctness should have stamped out even mastodons such as us. But, we'll never blow away, no matter how many years pass, no matter how they oppress us. We'll be here until hell freezes over. We've been entrusted with the tablets of decency handed down from the mountain tops of human freedom. Tablets chiseled out of raw courage and washed in the blood of martyrs."

"You haven't changed much," Carl laughed. "You're still the same Stoney Bedford I've known forever."

"I wonder, Carl. I wonder."

"Oh, I gave Julie Peel your unlisted cellular phone number. She asked me for it. And Harris Woolford wants you to telephone him."

Waves of nostalgia swept over me. "Carl, I wish you were here to join me in a martini. So we could talk about old times."

"Yes, Stoney. I do too. Nostalgic things. Especially that day you pulled me from the water off the invasion beaches at Salerno. And saved my life. Once again, thanks, old buddy."

Julie Peel was crying when she telephoned me.

"What's wrong, Julie?"

"I've been packing away my wedding gown, Stoney. Trying to bury the mementoes of a life that will never be for me."

There was a catch in my voice. "Yes, Julie. July 12th will soon be here."

"I don't know how I can stand it. I go to pieces each time I think about William's death, about the wedding that will never take place. Oh, what will I do?" Her cries of sorrow grew louder.

"Julie, let's you and I get together that day. July 12h, I mean. Go out to dinner and just visit. Okay?"

"I'd like that. It'd be a great comfort to me. William and I had planned each detail of our wedding day. The songs, the music, the getaway. Our honeymoon in Hawaii. And now, it is never to be."

She broke down completely. Great heart rending cries of anguish that started me crying too. I couldn't come up with any words to console her. Nor myself. I missed him acutely. In a hundred ways.

"Our friends have been so sweet," she said. "So understanding. And my poor parents are almost as broken up about it as I am." She was moaning again. There was such anguish in her voice until I wanted to run to her and take her in my arms.

"I know, Honey," I finally said. "It's bad. I cry a lot, too."

We both cried for a few more minutes. No words were necessary between us.

"I went to the cemetery again today," she said. "I carried fresh flowers and put them on William's grave. And one yellow rose. He was always bringing me a single yellow rose."

William had been a romantic at heart. Donna Elaine and I often talked about it.

"I don't know if I can ever pick up the pieces of my life, Stoney." The wails of anguish came again. "I move like a zombie. My work is suffering terribly. What am I to do?"

"Turn to the Lord, Julie. That's all I can advise you to do. It's a slow process, but reading the Bible each day is helping me to regain some small amount of perspective."

"God and I aren't on good terms right now," she said. "I'm angry at him for letting a thing like this happen. William was so decent, so honorable. So sweet. And he had your principles of standing for honor and nobility, speaking up for our Southern way of life. He didn't deserve to die at the hands of vengeful killers."

"Neither did Donna Elaine," I said. We were both crying again.

It was evening. Dusk was coming on. After she hung up, I sat on the veranda of the hunting lodge again. Thinking.

After supper, I phoned my friend, Professor Harris Woolford. "Harris, this is Stoney."

"Hey, man. You been hiding out?" Harris's sense of humor threaded through most of the things he said.

"Yes, Harris. You might say that. Anything to escape that baying pack of media wolves."

"Damn," Harris said. "The wolves are in full cry all right. This case has the whole world excited, Stoney. I've been on television in London, Paris, Tokyo, Hong Kong, New York, Los Angeles, Chicago, Houston, Miami. You name it. I've been there. They call me the expert from the academic world. And someone who knows you closely."

I tried to match his light-heartedness. "And the only thing that will satisfy them is for me to be hanged in the public square?"

Harris laughed. "Hell, no, Stoney. Don't be so down on yourself. Millions of people sympathize with you and are wondering what they hell's going on in the dear old USA. You know what many of them ask me?"

"What?"

"Isn't Stoney Bedford really a political prisoner? The victim the government has seized to throw to the howling minorities? Isn't that the sole motivation for making his trial some kind of a circus?"

I actually smiled. For the first time in weeks. "Of course, Harris. It makes no sense. Right and wrong have been inverted. Why wouldn't our justice system be putting Karim's guerillas on trial? They're the ones who violated the rights of me and my family, the ones who murdered my wife and son?"

"You know how I answer them?" Harris asked. "I resort to my best academic manner and answer, 'Yes, Bedford is a political prisoner.' Then I give them a history lesson. 'The North still hates the South, still has the Southern region of the United States under reconstruction. The only difference between 1865 and now is that the modern day 'army of occupation'' is composed of minorities and attorneys from the U.S. Justice department shrouding their efforts under the mantle of civil rights and the protection of the blacks from Southern white racism. These new militants of 1996 are the carpetbaggers shoving whites off the sidewalks and claiming that Southerners owe them reparations for their years of slavery."

"I'd bet they don't cotton too kindly to your stance."

"Who gives a shit," Harris said. "I say what I damn well please."

"Do they actually put such words in their stories? Does TV use them on their news reports?"

"Man, I've even been on "Twenty Twenty" and "Sixty Minutes." And they did a fair job in their editing of the tape. The commentators ask me, 'Will the North and its politicians succeed in finally erasing what you refer to as 'southern principles of honor and nobility'?

"I answer, 'No.' The more they try to make Southerners suffer under the heels of verbal and political oppression, the stronger the spirit of rebellion. Even Hitler couldn't stamp out resistance to oppression in the people of the countries he conquered. These punitive political actions will not do it to us Southerners either. We'll fight back. You can count on it."

"Damn, Harris," I said. "You're a true friend. I wish you were here so I could shake your hand."

"Tomorrow, reporters from the *'New York Times'*, the *'Washington Post*, the *'Chicago Tribune'* interview me. I've rehearsed what I'm going to say. I'm going to really lay it on them."

"Just imagine, Harris. Something that happened to one person like me in the little old town of Forest, Georgia being of interest in New York and London. I can't quite comprehend it."

"Stoney, this story has all the elements of a Greek tragedy. Whites against blacks; hatred and racism; rising storms of anger; remembrances of the Confederacy; reconstruction terrorism, carpetbaggers, valor and honor. Your courage in challenging the blacks and their demands to pull down the Confederate flag; the opening battle of the declared war by black leaders against the whites; the storming of your home and the murder of your wife and son. These kinds of things pull at the heart strings of thinking people and make them want to stand beside you."

"We have to go to Franz Kafka's novels for the unusual element in all of this," I said.

"Yes, Stoney," Harris said. "The government's turning your trial into an act of political persecution to please the howling mobs. But that wasn't an element in the great Greek tragedies."

"It was in the persecution of Jesus," I said. "He was turned over to the howling mobs for political reasons. They wanted to get Jesus out of the way, He was interfering with the exercise of their power."

"Damn," Harris said. "I never thought of that. I'll work it into my stories in my next press interviews"

"Please understand, Harris. What I'm pointing out is not sacrilege. I'm not comparing myself to Jesus, not by any means. But that's what my

271

own government is doing to me, an innocent citizen. Why? To satisfy the mob's demands for blood. My blood."

"By the way, when is the date set for your trial?"

"July 5th."

Able Erling and I will be there," Harris said. "You can count on it."

CHAPTER 24

Bread and a circus. The Romans knew what the people wanted. I looked around the courtroom and knew that things hadn't changed much over the centuries. Each of those people who filled every single seat were there for the circus. Outside the courthouse, along the sidewalks and spread across the lawn, concession stands were doing a booming business selling to the hundreds who had not been able to get into the courtroom.

Many of those present seemed to be enjoying the spectacle immensely. Hot dogs, hamburgers, pop corn, cold drinks, balloons, buttons, placards, T-shirts—most anything you wanted was for sale. The trashy, tabloid magazines with my picture on the front page in my wheel chair at the cemetery were popular items. Many people had them in their hands as they stood in small groups and discussed certain parts of the magazine's long article. In three areas, men played guitars and sang sad country ballads to those gathered around them.

Others in the crowd exuded no joy. Their faces, the tone of their voices, the way they stood, their gestures, their dress showed their sullen anger. They stood apart and surveyed the scene with cold eyes. They stepped aside for no one. Printed signs pinned to the backs of their shirts or dresses read: "Justice is mocked. The government has betrayed us. We've had enough."

It had taken Carl, Xerxes, Julie Peel and me ten minutes to navigate the seventy yards to the courtroom from the place on the curb where our driver had let us out. A hundred or more black demonstrators jeered as we approached, shook clenched fists and waved posters proclaiming me a murderer.

The crowd pressed in close. Dozens of hands reached out to touch me. Some bold ones waved large Confederate flags and shouted encouragement to me. Two older women in long, antebellum gowns with hoop skirts, wearing bonnets, closed their eyes as we approached them and extended their hands to the heavens to pray for God's mercy on me.

The forest of media representatives dissolved into a surging mass of individual reporters and television cameramen. Each of them seemed determined to get near enough to shout questions at me. I didn't answer.

One woman with a microphone grabbed my right arm and shook me. "Answer my questions, dammit," she shouted. "Why did you shoot those innocent people?" Carl pushed the microphone aside and urged me forward with a firm hand at my back.

Thank God no cameras could follow me into the courtroom. I looked at the section reserved for the five reporters chosen for the media pool. They would share the happenings in the courtroom with all the other media outside. Three artists were sketching scenes of the trial for TV and newspapers.

Victor Allen of the *'Ledger'* sat in the front row scribbling in what appeared to be a short hand note book. He looked up and smiled at me. The arrogant little executioner pretending the face of one who had been redeemed! If there was any way he could do me in, Allen would find it and relish delivering the coup de grace.

We knew that the composition of the jury was crucial to our case and Carl and Xerxes fought every step of the way to ensure, as best they could, that those chosen would be fair and objective. It was an almost impossible task.

The two of them huddled often to use the new jury selection techniques. They weighed the educational background of prospective jurors, their mindsets, their expressed philosophies on being questioned. They used. every peremptory challenge allowed the defense to bar some individuals from being seated. Xerxes questions were incisive and disarming. Three of the prospective jurors admitted that they had already formed opinions on my guilt or innocence and were excused.

Boring was full of scorn and bluster and tried to intimidate four individuals, three women and a man. "Are you proud of your long tradition of Southern independence?" he said to Annette Folman, in a tone of voice that could only be described as mocking scorn.

"We haven't been properly introduced," the trim and beautiful woman said. "Aren't you Mr. Boring?" she asked, brushing her dark hair from her right eye.

The D.A. was taken aback. "I'm not a Southerner," Boring shouted. "And we're not at an afternoon lawn party." He raised his clinched fists and craned his neck backwards in exasperation,

"Oh," the demure woman smiled. "Then that accounts for your boorishness. I should have known. In the South, someone like you would not be invited to our parties."

The courtroom erupted with laughter.

The woman turned to the judge. "Judge Johnson, would you please ask this man who's shouting at me not to blow his breath into my face? It smells bad."

Even Carl Krippendorf and I had to laugh at that. Boring moved back two paces and slammed his right fist into his left palm. Hindsmith, the justice department lawyer, jumped to his feet and objected to "Folman's impudence." The judge banged his gavel and told Hindsmith to shut up, that he had no official status in the case and that he was not to voice any opinion. Johnson then proceeded to lecture the dark haired woman on courtroom decorum. It proved to be a mistake.

"Judge," the woman said. "You have no right to try and patronize me from what you conceive to be your more lofty position. I know my rights. I reject your attempts to belittle me. Please do not persist in such behavior."

The courtroom erupted again with laughter. The judge banged his gavel. "You are excused from duty as a juror," he said.

"Oh, but that's not fair," she said. "I spent my valuable time to come down here as a citizen. You have not yet given me a valid reason for not seating me as a juror in this case. Have you?"

Boring came to Johnson's rescue. "I will exercise one of the prosecution's valuable challenges to excuse this person as a juror in this case."

The woman beckoned to Xerxes. "Is what this man saying valid, Mr. Xerxes?"

"Yes, Mrs. Folman. Under a peremptory challenge, Mr. Boring does not have to give a reason for his not accepting you as a member of the jury in this case."

She shrugged, stood, and looked around the room slowly. "It is my firm opinion, and that of many others in Forest, that Stoney Bedford will not get justice in this court. This is the government's attempt to persecute a citizen just because he's a true Southerner with firm beliefs in honor and principle." She stepped down and walked from the room.

The judge closed his eyes, bent his head and rested it on his finger tips. It seemed obvious that a true, Southern aristocrat had stood her ground with great courtesy and had escaped Judge Johnson's wrath. He could have found her in contempt, but he knew that the hot winds of Southern public scorn would lick at him for years to come if he had tried such a tactic.

Selection of the twelve jurors was completed by noon. My two attorneys and Julie and I sat in a third floor office behind closed doors to eat sandwiches Carl had ordered brought in. A sense of uneasiness diminished conversations. None of us was satisfied with all the members of the jury.

I was being tried for first degree murder, and Carl reminded me once again of the seriousness of my predicament. "Stoney, although I don't believe it will happen, if all twelve of these people agreed to the murder charge, you could receive the death penalty. And that ain't good, my friend."

Xerxes still fumed about the composition of the jury. "I don't like it," he said. "I just don't like it. Some of those jurors have already convicted you, Stoney, regardless of what transpires here in this courtroom."

"What disturbs me," I said, "is that people lied about not having preconceived ideas of my guilt or innocence."

"Five blacks and seven whites," Carl said. "Six men. Six women. And these are the days of a different breed of juror than what we used to get in trials such as this. They don't use the same standards and values used years ago to arrive at their judgments."

"There are at least three, bleeding heart liberals on that panel," Julie Peel said. "And they're all white."

"If you mean that they're not sympathetic to Stoney's defending his home and killing several of the attackers," Carl said. "I'd certainly agree with you. They just don't buy a person's standing up for principles and beliefs. I think it would actually have pleased them had Stoney and his wife and son just sat quietly by and died without one sign of resisting. Like sheep entering the slaughter pen."

"Let's cope with the hard facts of what we are faced with," Xerxes said, wiping his mouth with a paper napkin. "That Helen Rinker will give us lots of trouble," he said. "I know her. She's big in state Methodist church circles. Making speeches. Always pushing liberal causes and yelling that whites are guilty of discrimination against minorities."

"Why, Mr. Xerxes," I said, tongue in cheek. "You're not being sophisticated and politically correct. That's not the popular line to adopt nowadays."

The Atlanta attorney pulled on the French cuffs of his shirt until his cuff links showed beneath his coat, smiled and said, "Most people find me too much like Cary Grant to refer to me as unsophisticated. But, I do know what you mean by those words."

Julie nibbled on the pickle slices on the paper plate. "That crusader from the Unitarian church, associate minister Wright Talbert. He really bothers me. Why, he burns candles on the steps of the courthouse on the night the state executes convicted killers. And if the person executed is black, he goes to the press to announce the innocence of the one on death row. 'The justice system is geared to favor whites and murder innocent blacks,' he's fond of saying."

"That statement is widely accepted as being true," I said. "Whether it's true or not—and I'm certain it's not—there are more blacks in prison and on death row, simply because they engage in criminal activities to a far greater extent."

That young woman in the beautiful clothes," Xerxes said. "April Stuart. She's blissfully wedded to liberal causes. She's a child of the rebellious '60's. She'll be tough to convince."

"I know her family," I said. "She has nothing to do with any of them. Not since she was graduated from Stanford at Berkeley."

"These are the worst sandwiches I've ever tried to eat," Carl said. He threw half of his sandwich back into the plastic box and closed the lid.

"They're not exactly gourmet fare," Julie said.

I turned to Xerxes. "I liked the way you chewed into the prospective jurors, Mr. Xerxes, digging for the truth as to their likely actions. I can see now why you are so feared as a defense attorney. Thank you again for volunteering to assist in my defense."

He waved his right hand and shrugged. "From one unreconstructed rebel to another," he said. "It is I who thank you for your courage to stand up for the great heritage our forefathers left us here in the South."

Julie's anxiety popped out again. "Do you think we can get a 'Not Guilty' verdict?' She dabbed daintily at her red lips with a paper napkin.

Xerxes raised his shoulders slightly, breathed deeply and became pensive. "We'll be fighting for such a verdict each step of the way," He said. I could see the worry on both his and Carl's face, hear the uncertainty in their voices.

"It'll take a unanimous verdict of the jury to find you guilty of murder in the first degree," Xerxes said. "I just don't see that happening. Even one vote to the contrary will mean a 'hung jury' and a mistrial. I would not be surprised to see the charges reduced to second degree murder. That would make it easier for members of the jury to rationalize and come up with a lesser verdict. That could get you a prison sentence and would mollify the blacks to some degree."

"Don't forget the 'violation of civil rights' charge," Carl said. "That's why those damn justice department guys are butting into this case with such energy."

"The civil rights violation is only a side issue," Xerxes said. "Stoney can't be tried for that now, but it can be brought in to establish motivation for their charges of murder."

"How will it play?" I asked.

His eyes widened; his black eye brows arched. Momentarily, his shoulders slumped. "Many people here and in other parts of the country want you put away. So does the press. There's an aberrant streak in the psyche of this country that sees people yelling for the scalp of people like you. It is particularly vicious when it's directed at a person who stands for moral principles and will not bend. Somehow or other, it makes the boomers, those below the age of fifty, uncomfortable when they run into a person who is willing to sacrifice for his ideals and integrity."

"How well I know their philosophy," Julie Peel said. "I'm one of them, demographically, that is. Not philosophically. 'Everyone's a little crooked,' they say. 'All people lie, cheat and steal, at least a little. Don't talk to me about this moral crap. It's a cover up. When you hide behind those high-sounding phrases to restrict the way I live, it's only because you're afraid to admit that you are human.'"

"Julie," I kidded and feigned surprise. "You're one of them and you didn't use the 'S' word nor the 'F' word."

"You're right," she said. "I don't intend to sink to such a vulgar level. I don't have a great need to be like everyone else. I'm set on being my own person, and that does not include being foul mouthed and cheap."

Carl looked at his watch. "It's getting close to one o'clock," he said. "We'd better head back to the courtroom."

I'd already lost so many of the things that had added joy to my living until I just could not bring myself to care too much about the verdict. I had to dig deep inside myself to find the still smoldering coals of fire that lighted my being and would never be entirely snuffed out. It was the gallery of Confederate fighting men in the library of Bedford Place that had stamped their legends into my soul. That, and the sounds of the distant drums and the bursting shells at Gettysburg kept me going. That had been a terrible time for the men in gray, but they had acquitted themselves with honor. I could do no less.

CHAPTER 25

An instant hush fell on the large courtroom as the bailiff bade us rise for the entrance of Judge Uranus Johnson. The exact time was two p.m. The greying judge rubbed his hands across the paunchy stomach hidden beneath his robe and settled into the enormous, high-backed chair. He leaned back, clasped his hands together and peered over the tops of his tiny, reading glasses.

"Mr. Boring, is the state ready to proceed?" he asked.

"We are, your honor."

The District Attorney, his handsome face tinged with a hawk-like arrogance, exuded confidence as he began the state's opening remarks. He stood near the twelve men and women in the jury box, the finger tips of his hands together and nodded, as though in a deep, pensive mood.

"Ladies and gentlemen of the jury. The state intends to prove beyond a reasonable doubt that the defendant, Stonewall 'Stoney' Bedford murdered two, innocent citizens, Alonzo Derkin and Tug Canton, in cold blood. He had planned the killings for weeks. As we used to hear said so often in the south, sadly I might add, he was going 'to kill himself some niggers.'

"Those are such ugly words until it pains me to even think about them, much less say them out loud so that compassionate, responsible people can hear them. We will present evidence and witnesses to prove the fact that Bedford suffers from delusions of grandeur in that he imagines himself a Confederate general living back in the 1860's and fighting for the lost glory of a defeated army of rebels. An army of vainglorious slave masters who were trying to break up this great country by seceding from the union so that they might continue the institution of slavery."

"You tell them, brother," a black woman in glittering white caftan moaned. "That's the truth. You tell them, brother."

Judge Johnson rapped his gavel sharply and said, "Order in the court. This court will not tolerate such outbursts as that. If you persist, the bailiffs will remove you from this room. Have I made myself understood?"

Tighe Boring waited patiently. When quiet fell again, he clasped his hands behind his back and began pacing, ever so slowly back and forth before the jury box. "You will hear the plans and strategy which the defendant, his wife and his son developed to prepare for the killings; see the weapons with their star light scopes and laser sights for night fighting with which they were armed; learn how they lay in wait for the victims to appear; and view the one inch thick steel shields the three had ordered cut from discarded steel tanks and behind which they hid to insure their own safety.

"The three Bedfords planned to kill others but not to be killed themselves in case any of their victims thought about fighting back to preserve their own lives. Stonewall Bedford, on that night, became a Confederate general in charge of his tiny band of deadly killers."

Boring waved his right hand towards two long tables on which were displayed the rifles, pistols and shotguns with their special scopes and laser sights. Dozens of empty shotgun shells and spent rifle and pistol casings, plus several boxes of unopened shells and cartridges took up half of one of the two tables. They'd seized the weapons from my home that night I almost died from my own wounds.

The four shields were displayed behind the tables on which the weapons were spread. The pock marks of dozens of bullets marked the upper half of three of the shields. The fourth one had no bullet indentations. It was the one behind which Donna Elaine had crouched as she hid in the bedroom closet.

On the corner of one of the tables lay the canister, which contained Morris Light's film footage of the actual attack.

The District Attorney knew that he had released the hounds of hell in the minds of the jurors and he intended to urge them on in their wild race through the imaginations of those who would decide my guilt or innocence. He walked to the tables where the weapons were displayed.

"I want each member of the jury to see through one of these special scopes which allowed the defendant to watch every movement of the victims, even on the darkest of nights. Then, I want you to consider in your mind the methodical madness that ruled Bedford's mind that fatal night and even unto this day, unto this very moment."

He waved his hand towards me. I knew that the constant pain of my wounds had pinched my face into an unpleasant mask. I tried to change the expression so that it became impassive, but I failed.

Boring walked to the jury box. "Many of us are hunters and have scopes on our rifles, but we don't hunt at night. With a star light scope, there's only one animal you hunt at night, and that animal is a human being."

He shook his head to signal his resignation. "And those laser sights on the Glock pistols. When the dot's on the target, all that's necessary is the squeezing of the trigger. It's hard to miss. These weapons and objects I'll ask jurors to examine will be entered as part of the state's evidence."

He handed one of the rifles to one of the jurors seated on the front row of the jury box, a droll, sour-faced, taciturn man whose arms were so skinny and small until I wondered if he was strong enough to hold the weapon.

"Your honor, if it please the court, I'd like to have the lights dimmed to the lowest level in order that each juror can see the deadly effectiveness of this weapon when it's used at night."

"Permission granted," Judge Johnson said.

Boring turned back to the members of the jury. "When the lights are dimmed, I want each of you to sight through the scope on the weapon as it is passed from one juror to the next It's an important piece of the state's evidence in this trial of the defendant.

"Now, Bailiff, the lights, please."

Slowly, the light in the room dimmed until we sat in almost total blackness.

"Oh, Lord, it's terrible." The voice was female and prayerful. "Even I could kill with this thing."

"Such weapons as this ought to be against the law," a man's voice said.

"I hate guns," another woman said in a loud voice. "With one like this, the victim wouldn't have a chance."

"It's just a star light scope," another man said. "All of our men in Desert Storm had rifles with scopes like this. It's nothing special."

"Hopefully," a strong woman's voice said with measured slowness. "Americans will always have the right to own guns with which to hunt—or defend themselves if they are attacked."

"Now, Bailiff," Boring commanded. "Turn up the lights, please."

Boring used both his hands to smooth his stylishly long hair down the back of his neck. Without thinking, I ran my right hand through my thinning hair. Carl nudged me and whispered, "Watch Boring. He's putting on a damn good show. Playing to the gallery."

"Judge Johnson," Boring said, addressing the bench. "With your permission, I'd like to have each member of the jury walk, single file, by those four steel shields, since they're too heavy for me to bring to the jury box. And, as they do, they can inspect the other weapons and shells and ammunition and empty casings lying there on the tables. As well as the pistols with lazer sights."

"You may instruct the jury to do just that, Mr. Boring." The judge was still peering over the edge of his small reading glasses, like an owl with unblinking eyes waiting for dusk to come so that he could silently fly his swift, nightly hunting forays for food. Today, I'd decided that he was more like an owl than an anteater.

The procession resembled grade school children lining up for their turn on the play ground equipment. Several touched the shields with their finger tips and inspected the pock marks left by the bullets fired the night the assassins stormed my home. A few picked up one of the pistols with laser sights and imagined they were sighting through it. Two of the women counted the spent shells and empty rifle casings, shaking their heads as if recoiling from the whole story. They did not touch nor ask about the cannister of film. One by one, they returned to their seats in the jury box.

I looked around the courtroom at the people. Caught up as participants in a live performance, they were transfixed by the actions taking place before their very eyes. They'd seen similar stories many times, at a distance, on television or in the movie houses where they were passive outsiders looking in, but now they were seeing the real thing up close. They could almost touch the actors, see the stars and supporting players sitting quietly in their chairs or on their feet moving about the stage, delivering their lines in sonorous voices. The live drama had the spectators in the courtroom sitting on the edges of their seats, wondering what was coming next.

I could picture the imaginary director's camera trained on the district attorney performing center stage. Boring again clasped his hands behind his back and paced slowly back and forth in front of the members of the jury as he resumed the presentation of the state's case.

"This is a story straight out of the annals of Hollywood filmdom," he said. "The threads of the story reveal the fabric of today's life in the South as it really is. You will hear a recital of the long history of Bedford's prejudice and oppression of black people."

I almost leaped to my feet to shout "Liar." The prosecutor's intelligent, piercing mind was cleverly stacking the deck against me, invoking the ancient pictures of the South's overseers of slaves with their whips cracking across the backs of pliant black people who were begging for mercy. It was a false myth built by the turncoat writers Erskine Caldwell,

Truman Capote and Tennessee Williams, and Hollywood screen writers. The truth is that no Southern plantation owner would have treated his slaves in such a fashion. On the contrary, they cared for and ministered to them to keep them well and reasonably happy. A "Simon Legree" on any plantation would have been immediately exiled and chased away by the master of the land upon discovery of such cruel actions.

In the jury box, Alice Rinker and April Stuart were nodding their heads in agreement. The svelte "child of the sixties" acted bored by the whole thing. The five black jurors wore masks of impassivity. Their emotions did not show on their faces. The thin, wasted Methodist activist and the Unitarian minister were both listening intently, their finger tips together and touching the point of their chins.

Boring was splashing broad swatches of verbal color onto the canvas of my trial, but these jurors were painting their own pictures that would determine how they'd vote on my guilt or innocence.

"A ballistics expert will testify that the bullets that killed Alonzo Derkin and Tug Canton came from Bedford's rifle and his Glock automatic pistol, both fitted with night vision scopes or laser sights. The better to kill with at night."

Carl leaned over and whispered to me, "I've heard nothing so far that we didn't expect."

Boring was a powerful showman, no doubt about it. Hugh Hindsmith, the black justice department attorney, and his two assistants, sat at a table five feet behind Boring's table. Hindsmith's arms were folded across his chest, his fingers interlaced, his gold Rolex glinting in the light. There was a look of smug satisfaction on his face. He was a page from Orwell's "1984", the agent of "Big Brother", the all-powerful government, bent on persecuting and controlling its citizens. A man like Hindsmith would be the authoritarian voice of "Big Brother" as painted in "1984", reading the warnings and commands which governed the lives of the robot-like citizens who'd lost all hope.

Boring's powerful voice cut through my thoughts. "The jury will see that Bedford felt his position, his status as one of the chiefs of the city's white power structure, threatened when minority citizens dared demand the removal of the Confederate flag that flies over General Lee's monument on city hall grounds. You will see that, beyond a reasonable doubt, his hatred of those he felt inferior to him, those who refused to submit themselves to his rigid opinions of what constitutes right and wrong, gave him the motivation he needed to shoot innocent people standing on public property, the sidewalk in front of his big, fancy home in an exclusive, all-white neighborhood.

"That cannister you see over there on the table is supposedly filmed footage of the actual attack on the night of March 12th on Bedford's house by armed men. It is a carefully perpetrated fraud spliced together by a man skilled in doing such things. When the time comes, you will be shown the footage. At that time you can determine for yourself how valid it may or may not be. That is, if Judge Johnson decides to admit the film as evidence, which remains to be seen."

"I'll announce my decision soon," Judge Johnson interrupted.

Boring had been caught by surprise. "I'm certain you will reach the right decision, Judge Johnson."

"How dare the prosecutor infer otherwise," the judge said sternly. "You above all people should know the limitations of what you can and cannot say in this courtroom."

Boring's handsome face reflected his chagrin. "You certainly have my sincere apology, Judge Johnson. I'll endeavor to be more careful."

"You may continue," the judge said.

It took the D.A. a moment to remember where he had been derailed from his presentation. He gestured towards me. "You will be shown that the defendant fired the shots that killed Derkin and Canton. The evidence and testimony we present will prove that Bedford should be found guilty of murder in the first degree and sentenced to death."

Boring turned to Judge Johnson. "Your honor, that concludes the prosecution's opening statement." He walked to the empty chair at the prosecutor's table and sat down.

"Thank you, Mr. Boring," Judge Johnson said. "And now, the defense may present it's opening statement." He waved his hand towards the table where we were sitting, as if it were some tiresome procedure he was reluctant to have to go through.

The low hum of voices sounded like the drone of blow flies hovering around a suddenly discovered corpse that had been too long dead and too long hidden. The stories written on the individual faces of those in the courtroom told of their buried feelings. I saw the grim faces of men and women I'd known for years. Their unwavering allegiance to the Confederate flag and the emotions it sparked in their hearts was punctuated by the set of their jaws and the defiant gleam in their eyes.

Outspoken, Sammy Lewellyn, straight, thin, strong, and proud of the long gray line from which he was descended. Martha Lou Vickers, United Daughters of the Confederacy, with her quiet courage and polished speaking skills that had rallied women throughout the state to stand with us.

There were other, less friendly faces, the faces of people who had disavowed those very philosophies which had brought me into this court-room. I knew their families and had shared the grief their actions had brought to parents whose only sin (in their children's eyes) was reverence for the forces that had shaped us as proud people and a state whose sons had fought so valiantly to establish the South as a free and independent nation.

Byron Milken, suave, sneering apostle of "pulling those poor, uninformed, Southern relics of bygone days into the twentieth century." Annette Folman, brain-washed Georgian beauty who had gone off to Kent State University in the early '70s and joined every demonstration against tradition the marijuana or coke crazed long hairs organized. Why she had bothered to return to Forest could not be determined by most of us, since her hatred of her origins was an invisible cloak wrapped around her every action.

Morris Light and his assistant, through special permission granted by Judge Johnson, were on a small, high balcony in the back of the courtroom. I knew now why Light was a success at producing documentaries. He was willing to go the extra mile and work the long hours to get the film footage he needed to piece the complete story together.

Last night my dreams had eased in to carry me to places I'd inhabited long years ago. Sometimes, they carried me to strange settings occupied by old friends, and I knew that we had never been in those places together and that the pictures parading through my restless mind were a composite of my hopes, fears, pressures, grief and loneliness.

Often, I was back in 1943 off the beaches of Salerno, Italy, climbing down a cargo net draped over the side of our amphibious LST and dropping into one of my squadron of twenty-seven circling small boats, LCP's, filled with taunt-faced infantrymen who'd soon be on that beach fighting the Germans. When the bursting shells, the screams of dying men, the spurting fountains of blood from the wounded forced me to sit bolt upright, I'd gotten out of bed and sat for a long time at the lodge's scarred dining table and sipped hot tea.

I had deluded myself into thinking I could be a viable player in this controversy over the Confederate flag. Now, I knew that the dice I had rolled had been shaved by a hurrying world with changing attitudes, that the dice showed "snake eyes," that the opposition was not willing to give me a fair break.

I gazed out the tall windows of the courtroom at the red skies and the lengthening shadows of the late afternoon. The night would be one of those early spring nights that could chill you to the bone, if you were careless enough to venture out without a sweater or jacket.

Archibald Xerxes stood up at the table where we were seated and prepared to present the defense's opening statement. He removed his pince nez and placed them in his shirt pocket. He'd bring them out for use when he had some document to read. The tan on his lean, handsome face stood out more sharply against the touches of gray creeping up his temples and beginning their march into his thick mop of black hair. His Armani suit, the white, brocade shirt with French cuffs, the gold cuff links that gleamed in the lights, the red silk tie and the red, silk handkerchief tucked neatly into the top pocket of his coat—Xerxes looked every bit the general ready to launch our legal attack upon the enemy forces.

He too was a skilled actor, every bit the equal to Boring. He knew how to use his commanding presence to fill the stage in front of the jury box. His voice was that of the low and resonant cello in a mental symphony. "Ladies and gentlemen of the jury," Xerxes said. "My client, Stoney Bedford, the defendant in this case, should not be on trial today in this courtroom. He should never have been indicted by the grand jury. He certainly should not be charged with first degree murder—or with any murder at all.

"There was not even probable cause for doing so. This case is pure and simple a political case, pressured onto this court by blacks and the U.S. Justice department in the name of 'political correctness.' Oh, it's cleverly disguised. I'll grant you that. It is wrapped in cries of 'racism' and 'bigotry' and the unannounced enhancement of vote-getting possibilities by the political party now in power. Be that as it may, we recognize it—or at least many of us do—as an attack by blacks and liberals on the South and it's traditional way of life. Stonewall Bedford is the pawn in this political chess game.

"'Pull down the Confederate flag' they cry. 'It's a symbol of slavery." Those are the stereotypical shouts of 'Wolf' by frightened people dodging their own mental shadows. You hear these false cries largely because the people of this section of the nation have not yet bent to the liberal will. Southerners are seen as standing defiantly in a circle of steel, committing all sorts of unforgiveable acts in the name of personal liberty and freedom. Horror of horrors! These defiant people have not been shaped into the pliant mold envisioned by the enlightened establishment who rule our every act. How dare they resist such indoctrination those who shape national thought ask? They must surrender once and for all—unconditionally—as they should have in 1865 and the years of reconstruction that followed.'"

Xerxes straightened his back, tugged at his French cuffs, jutted out his chin and said, "Well, we too have our battle cry. Our answer is, 'We will never surrender. Never . . . Never . . . Never . . .' "

He slapped the railing of the jury box with the flat of his hand. The loud noise of this unexpected maneuver brought startled sound and movement from jurors, the judge, the prosecutor's team and many in the court room.

"First degree murder."

Xerxes snorted in disdain, turned his back and walked a few steps away from the jury box, raised his voice and pointed at me. "Stonewall Bedford did not even know the names of the so-called victims. Tug Canton and Derkin . . . Derkin . . . Oh, Alonzo Derkin. It is difficult for me, at times, to recall their names. There were so many who mounted the attack that dreadful night of March 12th.

"The question should be, 'Who murdered who', or as my wife would correct me, 'whom.' When the police did finally arrive at the scene, in front of Mr. Bedford's beautiful home in one of our exclusive suburbs—oh, I'm sorry. I remember now that to live in a house such as that in which the Bedfords lived, automatically marks a man or woman as suspicious in present day society. But when they did arrive, they found a gravely injured man inside his own home, clutching the body of his beautiful dead wife and moaning her name, 'Donna Elaine, Donna Elaine.'

Xerxes' voice broke. "It was one of the saddest scenes imaginable. They told him they had to pry the dead body of his wife from his arms." The handsome lawyer of Greek descent flipped a handkerchief from his pocket and dabbed at his nose and eyes.

"And yet today, they have Stoney Bedford on trial for murder.

He shook his head and paused. The rays of the lowering sun now cast parallelograms of gold across the stained wood floor. "His only son, William, had also been murdered by the killers who came in the dead hours of the night. At 2 a.m., precisely.

"Let me ask you a grave question. In America, is it not a recognized principle of law that a man has a right to protect himself, his family and his home from attacks by murderous thugs? There can be no disagreement by anyone as to the validity of this principle. That's the reason the second amendment preserved for its citizens the 'right to keep and bear arms.'

Stonewall Bedford tried mightily to defuse the tension ignited and fanned into flames by black political leaders and the media. His efforts were rebuffed with sneers and derision. He sought the help of two black ministers who should have been his friends since he paid their way through college. Wash Washington and Blue Combs turned away for fear they'd be called 'Uncle Toms,' a kiss of death in the minority community."

Xerxes turned his head in the direction of Washington and Combs, nodded and raised his right hand in a salute of sadness. He paused, shook his head in recognition of the complexities which interlaced this trial with garishly colored threads. Then he breathed deeply.

"Police Chief Dennis Crowe refused to help the Bedfords, dismissing their pleas as overreaction. Let's see. How did he sum it up? 'Black leaders are too intelligent to be involved in such stupidity.'

"They're far to intelligent to openly organize such an inflammatory event. Yet, Stonewall Bedford knew the exact time the attackers would storm his house, his castle. The three Bedfords refused to run away from the fight. To them, standing for their rights was a thing of honor.

"Bedford, his wife and his son were ready when the silent attackers stopped their cars in front of their home, exited with their AK 47's and paused to wait for their comrades to assemble before launching their charge. That was their first big mistake. The Bedfords struck first and scored heavily. But there were too many of the attackers. The fire fight blazed furiously, briefly. Then, it was over.

"Inside Bedford's home, Black Muslim Abdul Karim and two of his fanatical co-conspirators lay dead, killed by a man, his son and his wife who were defending their own home. Outside that home, five more of the attackers lay dead, but the four who escaped death in the fire fights, dragged three of the five into their long, black Cadillacs and fled. But before they left the scene, they dragged two of the five dead men from Bedford's lawn and deposited them on the sidewalk.

"I suppose they engaged in this callused action to make their case, built around the right of people to inhabit public property such as sidewalks and streets without fear of harm coming to them."

He stepped to the table where we sat, winked at us, poured himself a glass of cold water from the pitcher and drank it slowly. Then, he resumed making the defense's opening statement.

"That cannister of film over there on the evidence table." He walked over and picked up the small, black cylinder that contained Light's footage of the actual attack. "You will see the hopelessness in the prosecution's case, for you can count the number of bodies on that lawn for yourself. You can see where the bodies lay. You can see the attacking survivors remove their dead from the lawn. You can watch them drag two of the dead from the lawn to the sidewalk. I'm certain that after you view the film, you'll see the falsity of the prosecution's assumptions.

"Now, what do you think the attackers did with the bodies of the two, possibly three, they pulled into their cars before they sped away? They took them to the streets of neighborhoods racked by drive-by shootings and dumped them. Most people who read the newspaper or watched TV news, saw only that more 'victims' had been added to the total of drive-by shootings and killings and shrugged their dismissal of the affair. 'Well,' they said, 'I see where they found more dead men over in those wild and wooly streets of Cransford.'"

I glanced at the spectators. Many of them had their elbows propped on the arms of their seats, transfixed by Xerxes' words. A dramatic spectacle was unfolding before them and they were enthralled. Even Judge Johnson, his small, drug store reading glasses on the tip of his nose, peered intently over the top of the glasses.

"Isn't it a sad day in America when we grow tolerant of this methodical genocide of a whole race of people?" he asked "How can we dismiss such barbaric conduct in America? We can't and we should not."

Xerxes sighed loudly. You could detect a wisp of sadness in his manner. He was right. Americans had been exposed to such killings over such a long period of time and on such a large scale until we had grown almost insensitive to the headlines in the morning newspaper.

The bold Greek took his time. Slowly, he walked to the strip of carpet in front of the box in which the jurors were seated and began to pace. "The defense will prove that Stonewall Bedford is one of the fairest, kindest, most decent men ever to walk these red clay hills of our native Georgia." He looked towards the table where the justice department lawyers sat. "Well, he is that kind of man to most of us who are natives of this greatest of all the states, Georgia."

He turned to face towards Judge Johnson. "Bedford is a man who stands as tall as a solitary, lofty pine in defense of individual liberties. He has never been a man motivated by racial hatred, nor bias nor prejudice. Yet these accusations rolled so easily from the district attorney's tongue earlier. I wonder if he knows what character assassination is?

"Stoney Bedford is Southern to the core and, like the majority of us, he's proud of it. Oh, we know that we have turncoats in our midst and they're to be pitied. They are truly 'people without a country.' They should seek a climate more friendly to their philosophical views, for they will never be allowed to live peacefully here. They have disavowed us; we have disowned them. The colony of their friends is indeed a small and ragged group.

"As I was saying, Bedford is Southern to the core and like most of us, he takes challenges as an intensely personal thing. Furthermore, a true Southerner will fiercely defend his honor, his heritage, his home and his family against any attack and he will do so with daring, bravery and nobility.

"This is what he was doing on the night twelve attackers stormed his residence and met such fierce resistance. Some of the charging men were killed in self defense. In that same action, Bedford's own wife and son were also murdered. Yes, Stoney Bedford fought with great skill and honor against those who try to force the removal of the Confederate flag everywhere in our Southland. If these historical revisionists have their way, all trace of the Confederacy and its flag will gradually disappear from even our history books, much less from the flagpoles that mark monuments to our generals and the Confederate soldier who fought fiercely to get the Yankee foot off his neck.

"I say to you that you will never pull down all the Confederate flags in our Southern homeland. You will find them flying for the next 1,000 years."

A murmuring broke out in the still chambers. Several "Amens" went up as a second to Xerxes' expressed sentiments. The judge rapped his gavel. "Order in the court. Order in the court." His voice was stern and authoritative. The owlish face was that of a predator ready to swoop down upon any person who dared to utter a sound.

Xerxes paused and slowly scanned the people in the jury box, then the judge, the prosecutorial staff and the audience. His body was coiled and tense, ready for the charge up Cemetery Ridge at Gettysburg.

He walked to the table where the guns and ammunition were displayed. "These weapons, these protective steel shields? To any thinking person, they represent resourceful, inventive moves by people who knew with certainty that Abdul Karim and his thugs were going to come after him and his family.

"Yes, he had informants in the black neighborhoods who told him the specific details of what Karim and his crew were planning to do. He begged his wife, Donna Elaine, to go to her mother's home in Ames, Georgia, so that she might escape the threatened danger. But, like her husband and son, she was a woman of courage, and Southern to the core. 'No,' she said. 'I will not. I stay here where I belong. Beside you and my son. And, if you two are killed, I will have very little left for which to live anyway.'

"He and his wife and son could have fled, left their home, sought hiding places elsewhere. But no real American likes to be intimidated and forced to leave his own home.

"His third choice? Stay and fight. Prepare thoroughly for the battle you know is coming. Lay out plans and strategy. Plan and fight to stay alive and make the attackers pay dearly for their unjustifiable acts."

For the first time in the trial, I saw the older, grim faced man and his balding companion in the spectator's gallery. Even from a distance of fifty feet, their eyes glowed like beams of black light. I thought about the silent men in camouflage outside on the courthouse lawn, their faces impassive, their rifles clutched in their hands.

"You will hear recordings of death threats Bedford and his family received over the phone and read those which were mailed to him. You will hear citizens testify of his tireless fight to aid the poor and homeless and attest to his ingrained sense of fairness, honor and nobility.

"Stoney Bedford is no murderer. He is a political prisoner, much like that poor soul depicted by Franz Kafka in his great work *The Trial*. If you haven't read it, you should. And the government? George Orwell in his disturbing work titled *1984* painted a graphic picture of what the government today is attempting to do to one of its more honorable citizens. The age of 'Big Brother' is indeed here, and thousands of our countrymen are crying out for relief from his prying into our private lives, from his unjust actions."

Xerxes pulled both his hands up to his shoulders and shuddered. "We're scared, too," someone in the gallery yelled. Judge Johnson's head snapped up. He banged his gavel and yelled, "order in the Court! Order in the court! There must not be any more such unseemly conduct."

The golden-tongued Greek turned to Judge Johnson. "Just a citizen's cry for help, Judge."

"Proceed, counselor," the judge ordered.

"Stonewall Bedford had no motive to murder any person. He doesn't hate black people. On the contrary, the Bedfords, for a century, have paid the expenses of college for young black men. The defendant himself can number five such men he and his wife have helped with generous amounts of money and friendships

"He did have every right to repulse those who came to kill him on the night of March 12th. American citizens have a right to defend their homes, and he did so—at great price to the attacker and himself."

The crying of a few women in the audience was plainly audible. Even two or three men had tissues to their noses and were blowing into them gently.

"Militant minorities," Xerxes continued, "and an all powerful central government do have their motives for pressing forward with this fraudulent—albeit politically correct trial. This strange new breed of persecutor of free people concluded that person who stands so resolutely in their paths, as has the defendant, must be removed from the scene by any possible means."

He carefully placed his pince nez into his coat pocket, straightened up to his full height, buttoned his suit jacket and pulled his French cuffs down. "There is no case here against the defendant. There is only political oppression and chicanery. On those grounds, the defense moves for dismissal."

Xerxes had caught us all by surprise. An excited murmuring swept through the courtroom. People were shuffling their feet, changing positions in their seats, whispering to those close by. The judge's mouth had fallen open. Boring had leaped to his feet, as had Hindsmith. The media section was abuzz with activity.

The brilliant defense attorney folded his arms in defiance and looked at the judge who was still shocked and amazed. Judge Johnson suddenly snapped upright in his black leather chair, pushed his drugstore reading glassed back upon his nose. His face betrayed his confusion as he groped for words to meet the challenge of this upstart attorney.

Johnson finally found his voice and began banging his gavel. "The defense's motion is denied. The trial will proceed." He banged his gavel as he struggled to regain his composure and his control of the proceedings.

"I find your motion quite unusual, Mr. Xerxes." The judge's voice had regained its sternness.

"Unusual or not," Xerxes said, "It is within my perogative to move for dismissal. Legal scholars will argue with great erudition the validity of your ruling, Judge Johnson. Further, they will question all aspects of this trial for years to come. We want the entire world to see and know that this trial is fiction at its worst "

He looked at me and winked. I noticed that Carl was grinning and that Julie was smiling.

"With that observation," Xerxes said, "This completes the defense's opening statement," your honor

Judge Johnson looked at the large clock on the back wall of the courtroom. "Due to the lateness of the hour, if it is agreeable to both the prosecution and the defense in this case, I will adjourn court until 9 a.m. tomorrow. Do each of you agree?" he asked and nodded to Boring and Xerxes.

"I agree," Boring answered.

"The defense agrees," Xerxes said.

Xerxes' brilliant maneuver had raised our spirits, had actually given the four of us something to chuckle about at dinner that night.

We were secluded in the private room of Berlein's, Forest's finest restaurant. As we waited for our steaks and sipped on a fine California Cabernet, Carl laughed and slapped the table.

"Damnedest thing I've ever seen," he said. "I've got to hand it to you, Archibald. I thought old Johnson was going to explode."

"Hell, I was so surprised that I almost fell off my chair," I said. "A beautiful move, Xerxes.

I turned to Julie and Carl. "To Xerxes. A toast. I salute an intelligent mind."

"I feel like dancing around the room," Julie said, sipping her Cabernet.

We did not tarry long over dinner. We slipped out of the restaurant's side door.

Tomorrow was facing us and we'd need every ounce of physical and mental strength we could muster.

That night, I dreamed that I was being strapped to a guerney and rolled towards the execution chamber.

CHAPTER 26

"Something evil this way comes."

When the court reconvened the next morning at 9 o'clock, I sensed that something was wrong. Some shapeless form of darkness and evil was trying to coalesce in the courtroom to wrestle with our efforts in my behalf. Anxiety welled up inside me and I was reminded of my navy days in World War II when I knew that our ship was headed for an invasion. I studied the faces of those at the prosecutor's table, seeking some clue.

Boring had the handsome, assured face of a gigolo who knew that his prey had been weakened and would soon fall into his rapacious clutches. Hugh Hindsmith and the other two justice department attorneys were smiling like the cat who had just eaten the canary.

I leaned over and whispered to Carl. "Unless I miss my guess, they're going to spring something big on us. Something unexpected."

"Yes," he said. "I get that distinct feeling, too." He nudged Xerxes and whispered to him.

The dapper Greek slid his chair back and eased over to me. "I'm concerned, too. What do you think is up?"

"I wish I knew," I answered. "Whatever it is, we'd better be ready to roll with the punches, because I think they're going to try for a knockout."

"Over our years in courtroom, Carl Krippendorf and I have been punched hard so many times in courtrooms like this, until you can count on our not showing any surprise, even though we might feel uncertainty inside. We do know how to counter punch."

"Whatever happens, we'll land on our feet," Carl said. "Like the proverbial cat with nine lives."

"Don't forget, guys," I said. "I'm no cat. I have only the one life and it's that life that's at stake. If I'm judged guilty of first degree murder, I could be sentenced to death. And that thought doesn't exactly make me feel comfortable." I rubbed my chest with my right hand.

Judge Johnson rapped his gavel. "This court is now in session," he said. He waited for the hum of voices to die down and for the spectators to settle into more comfortable positions in their seats.

"Is the prosecution ready to proceed with this case?" he asked.

"We are, your honor," Boring said. "But first, we'd like to ask the court to rule on what we consider a very important point."

"Oh," the judge said. "And what might that be?"

Boring's voice quickened with enthusiasm. He was ready to spring the trap. Ready and eager. "The defendant was indicted by the grand jury for the murder of Alonzo Derkin and Tug Canton, two innocent human beings who were shot down in cold blood in front of the defendant's home while they stood talking on a public sidewalk. I have reread the transcript of the indictment and can find nothing in it referring to an Abdul Karim and two other men who died when they broke into Stonewall Bedford's home. Most of us know why the indictment did not deal with this matter. The law protects any citizen when people storm into a person's home firing any kind of a weapon."

"Mr. Boring, I don't yet see the point you are trying to make," Judge Johnson said. "Would you please come directly to the point?"

"The prosecution will call witnesses who will testify that Derkin and Canton were not with Karim and the others, but were at Bedford's home fifteen minutes before Karim and his people showed up. The two murdered men did not even know Karim and his crew of Muslims. In light of this, we ask the court to rule out any reference to Karim and his Muslims in this trial, since it would be irrelevant to the case."

Xerxes jumped to his feet. "Objection, your honor. The defense will present a video to show to testify that Canton and Derkin were two of the twelve attackers who stormed Bedford's home on the night of March 12th. Derkin and Canton had automatics in their hands and were actually killed in the middle of his front lawn as they ran toward the house, firing their weapons. We also now have witnesses who will testify to this fact."

Judge Johnson leaned back in his chair for a long while as he pondered his ruling. "The objection is sustained," he said. Each side will have the opportunity to prove their statements. But I warn both of you that your proof must be believable and your witnesses must be credible. I will not tolerate the cheapening of the judicial process through perjured testimony or manufactured evidence. Is that clear?"

Both Boring and Xerxes answered in the affirmative.

"Mr. Boring," the judge said. "You may proceed with your case."

"Thank you, your Honor," the district attorney said.

His shoulders had slumped to a measurable degree, reminding me of a punctured automobile tire from which the air had rushed. The ringing tone of assurance was now missing from his voice.

"I call Black Muslim Mueschle Jabbar to the witness stand," Boring said.

I remembered the February day I first saw him in the hall outside of the city council's meeting room. Jabbar was tall, trim and erect, like an army colonel about to dress down his troops who hadn't measured up to expectations. He wore an expensively tailored black suit, white shirt and a red bow tie, as he had on that first day we met. He still carried himself above the crowd; his eyes still glowed with that piercing cynicism. He was a warrior to be admired and feared.

The tall man was quickly sworn in.

"Please state your name and address for the record," Boring said.

"My name is Mueschle Jabbar. I live at 4712 Albion Street, Apartment 65, Forest, Georgia."

"I believe you know the defendant, Stonewall Bedford."

"Yes, I've had the dubious pleasure of meeting Bedford." He looked towards me and sniffed his dismissal.

"Bedford is on trial for murdering two citizens, Tug Canton and Alonzo Derkin, who had the 'unmitigated gall' to stand on the sidewalk in front of his home." A twitter of laughter fluttered through the spectators. "Were you acquainted with either of the two victims?"

"No," Jabbar answered. "I knew their names but I'd never been introduced to them nor had any social contact with either of the two."

I gasped. My hand flew to my open mouth. Hindsmith smiled broadly and glanced in our direction.

"That's strange," Boring said. "The defendant claims that they accompanied you and nine others to his home on the night the murders took place."

"That's not true," Jabbar said. "When the seven of us arrived at Bedford's home that night, there were two dead black men lying on the sidewalk. That's when we knew we were in trouble, that they were waiting inside their home with automatic weapons. They opened fire on us immediately."

"No further questions," Boring said. "Your witness, Mr. Xerxes."

Jabbar drew in a deep breath, folded his arms across his chest and scowled. He was ready to do battle with Xerxes.

"Mr. Jabbar," Xerxes said. "Are you aware of the penalties for lying on the stand after being sworn in 'to tell the truth, the whole truth, and nothing but the truth, so help you God'?"

"Listen, you white devil," Jabbar sneered. "I will not allow you to bully and intimidate me and accuse me of lying. Is that clear?"

Xerxes turned to Judge Johnson. "Your honor, will you please instruct the witness to answer the questions without giving vent to his rage and hatred?"

"The witness will please contain himself. You must confine your answers to the question."

"Judge," Jabbar said. "This is a new day in America. Black people no longer have to bow down to the 'white Massa.' America will soon learn that new standards of justice and procedures during trials will be instituted because of the demands of its black citizens. Furthermore, I have a right to be treated humanely in this courtroom. I demand that my rights be protected. Nor will I let this, this 'dapper dan' of an attorney, berate me."

"Isn't it true, Mr. Jabbar?," Xerxes asked, "that when the twelve of you attacked the Bedford home, that three members of your attacking force were killed inside the house?"

"There were only seven of us who had a fire fight with the Bedfords that night," Jabbar said. "Not twelve. And yes, three of our group, including our leader, Abdul Karim, were killed inside Bedford's house."

"Isn't it true that before those of you who lived through the attack left Bedford's home, you pried the guns from the dead hands of Canton and Derkin, pulled their bodies down to the sidewalk, picked up your three wounded comrades and hauled them away?"

Jabbar threw his head back and laughed. It was a laugh of sarcastic dismissal. "Man, you sound as though you've snorted too much of that white stuff. Two black men were already dead and lying on the sidewalk when we drove up. Derkin and Canton I suppose, although I don't know and could not identify them. They had no weapons in their hands. And hauling three wounded men away? There were no wounded comrades for us to haul away."

"If you didn't haul away three of your wounded comrades, why did police discover one of your dead comrades in each of the three different sections of the inner city? And the three have been identified as members of your Muslim group."

"Oh, yes," Jabbar said. "That's so sad. Three of our brothers. Unfortunately, blacks do kill blacks in senseless shootings. We decided that some hopped up kids were out to prove they were men. That's the way they do it, you know. Get a cheap Saturday night special, drive down the street and shoot innocent people. Even though the Muslims strive mightily to instill self respect and discipline in our neighborhoods, we don't always succeed."

"Your group hauled these three away from the Bedford's home and dumped them to die in order to divert suspicion from you and your group of attackers. Isn't that what really happened, Mr. Jabbar?"

"I told you once that that's a lie," the hostile Jabbar bristled. "How many more times am I going to have to tell you? You're trying my patience." He turned to Judge Johnson. "Judge, can I be excused? I will not be badgered by this man any longer."

"I fail to see where the defense attorney is badgering you, Mr. Jabbar," Judge Johnson said. "The procedure he's using is fair and customary."

"No further questions," Xerxes said. Judge Johnson looked relieved.

"I have no further questions at this time," Boring said. "The prosecution reserves the right to recall Mr. Mueschle to the stand if deemed necessary. Or any of the other witnesses who are called to testify in this trial."

Jabbar rose slowly from the witness chair, thrust his right fist into the air and shook it, then walked slowly back to his chair.

"Right on, brother!" The chorus came from several throats.

Judge Johnson rapped his gavel and called for order.

Boring stood up. "The prosecution calls Bill Yorkin to the witness stand."

Yorkin was William's friend who had cut the steel tanks apart to fashion the protective shields for my son, my wife and me. He owned Yorkin's Welding Service in the city.

The questioning began.

The district attorney walked across the room and touched one of the three shields. "Mr. Yorkin, have you ever seen these four steel barriers which the Bedfords used as shields the night of the fire fight between them and Karim's group?"

"Yes sir. I cut them out of steel tanks with a welding torch and delivered them to Mr. Bedford's home. I even helped my friend William carry them upstairs. They're pretty heavy you know."

"They are heavy, Mr. Yorkin," Boring laughed. "On what date did you deliver them to the defendant's home?"

Yorkin consulted a yellow sheet of paper with lines on it. Probably a delivery invoice. William's signature would be on it. "The date was February 26th of this year. 1996."

"Let's see," Boring said. "February 26th. The murders were committed on March 12th, fourteen days after you delivered them to Stonewall Bedford's home. Thank you, Mr. Yorkin. Your witness, Mr. Krippendorf. Or Mr. Xerxes. Whoever."

"The defense has no questions for Mr. Yorkin," Carl answered.

"Next," Boring said, "the prosecution calls Hunt Whitaker, Forest's leading gunsmith and recognized authority on weapons."

Whitaker, if he were twenty years younger, could have played defensive tackle for the Atlanta Falcons. There's not an ounce of fat on his 5''8'' frame. Just bone and muscle, two hundred and eighty pounds of it. Three evenings a week he's at the Athletic Club, pressing weights. I've been told he could dead lift 400 pounds. His face had the set of a bulldog whose teeth had latched onto someone's arm. He'd not let go until all hell freezes over.

"Mr. Whitaker, I understand that you do modifications of guns for hunters all across the United States and in several foreign countries. Is that correct?"

"Counselor, I can save this court time and trouble," Whitaker said. "I sold and mounted the sights on those guns of Mr. Bedford's. They're for night shooting, and I told Bedford they were a damn good idea. As many crazies as we have running around in Forest and throughout the country, a man needs guns to protect himself. To stay alive. We are guaranteed the 'right to keep and bear arms' under the second amendment to the constitution, but the gun haters are chipping away at that right."

Whitaker was in love with guns and knew what they were for and the jobs they could perform in the right hands. He was launched now and could not be stopped.

"I'm glad Stoney and William had those guns when those thugs attacked his home and killed his wife and son. The Bedfords killed three of them inside their home, including the group's high mocus, Karim, two more on the lawn and three more of their group who were picked up and hauled away by the survivors. The three were dumped in black neighborhoods to make it appear that other blacks killed them in senseless shootings."

Boring held up his hand. "Judge Johnson. I ask that all of the uncalled for sermonettes preached by Mr. Whitaker be stricken from the record. That would be everything from 'they were for night shooting' on through to the end of his tirade."

"Yes, counselor, I agree," said the judge. He ordered that the portions of Whitaker's testimony referred to as "sermonettes" by Boring be stricken from the record.

"No further questions for this witness," Boring said.

Carl Krippendorf used his cane to make his way to the witness box. I knew the pain that stayed with him constantly. "Mr. Whitaker, did William Bedford tell you why he wanted the laser sights and star light scopes mounted on those weapons over there on the table."

"Yes, he did," Whitaker said. "He and his family had been getting death threats on the telephone several times a day. Then, a reliable source told Mr. Bedford in person that Karim and his group were going to kill him as the opening strike in their declared war against whites. They were using the flag as their pretext. Wanted to stir up blacks everywhere through making an example out of Stoney Bedford for the whole world to see. They needed a victory and eliminating Bedford was to be it."

"No further questions for this witness," Carl said.

Boring was smiling when he stood up. He placed his left fist in his right hand, flexed his shoulder muscles, then folded his arms across his chest and used dynamic tension as a technique to relax his body. "I call city council member DeLong Tolman to the stand," he said.

Carl leaned over and placed his hand on my knee. In a soft voice, he said, "He'll use Tolman to try and prove you have shown by your words and actions an established history of prejudice against minorities."

I felt my stomach muscles tighten as I watched Tolman swagger towards the witness stand. I raised my eyes to look around the crowded room and caught sight of Professor Harris Woolford and Able Erling in the audience, sitting in the same seats they occupied each day. Both knew that they'd probably be called as witnesses later during the trial. Harris grinned at me and waved slightly with the tips of the fingers of his right hand.

"Mr. Tolman," Boring began. "How long have you served on the city council with the defendant Stoney Bedford?"

"Too long," Tolman sneered. "Far too long."

"How long," the district attorney insisted.

"Ten years."

"From your experience, how would you characterize the defendant's feelings toward black people?"

Xerxes leaped to his feet. "Objection, your honor. The prosecution is trying to lead the witness."

"Objection sustained," Judge Johnson said. "Rephrase your question, Mr. Boring."

"Does Bedford like or dislike black people?" Boring looked at the jury, arched his thick eye brows and pursed his lips.

Tolman laughed. "Anyone who reads the newspaper or watches news reports of council meetings on TV knows that Bedford hates blacks .It's his actions, the things he says, the phrases he uses in debating. His speeches always includes slurs against minorities and the way they see certain things." He paused. "But I envy his ability to speak. He is powerful."

"That's interesting, Mr. Tolman," Boring said.

"If you need further proof, witness his railing against my motion in council meeting to ban the flying of the Confederate flag over that stupid statue of General Lee. He knows it offends black people and that we see it as a symbol of slavery"

"Objection, your honor," Carl Krippendorf said, rising to his feet. "How does the witness know that the defendant knows that flying the flag offends blacks. Isn't it possible that Mr. Bedford's objection to pulling down the flag arises from his own philosophical beliefs in the nobility of the cause for which that flag stands?"

"Objection sustained," Judge Johnson ruled. "The witness is instructed to forego his personal opinions and proceed to outlining for the prosecution the defendant's remarks that bespeak racial animosity."

"Thank you, your honor," Boring said. "Mr. Tolman, what are some of the things Bedford has said that would offer proof of your belief that he is a racist?"

"Well, after the elections of November, 1994, when the Republicans took control of both houses of the Congress, he laughed and said to me: "Well, Tolman. We got you blacks where we want you now. We are going to stop your abuse of the welfare program; we're going to stop giving $450 a month checks to children in the black community who are coached in how to act crazy at school so they can qualify for such payments; we're going to make those black teenagers who get pregnant go to work instead of riding the welfare program; and we'll teach all of you the dignity and necessity of working if you want to have a roof over your head and eat."

"In other words, he saw the Republican control of Congress as a way to punish black people?" Boring asked.

"Objection," Xerxes cried. "That is a leading question. I'd remind the district attorney and members of the jury that any reform provisions in welfare apply to white people as well as minorities."

"Objection sustained," the judge ruled.

"Did you know the two murdered men, Canton and Derkin?" Boring had changed tactics.

"Yes," Tolman replied.

"When is the last time you saw them alive?"

"On the night of March 14th, 1995."

"Tell us about it," Boring said.

"Norris Cape and I were still angry over the defeat of the motion to ban the flag. We decided, along with Tug Canton and Alonzo Derkin, that Bedford's neighbors needed to be reminded of the kind of man Bedford is. The kind who had brought lots of trouble to their exclusive neighborhood. The four of us hand lettered some protest signs on white cardboard, stapled them to sharpened wooden sticks and drove to Bedford's house. We were going to drive the stakes with their signs into the neutral ground between the sidewalk and the street."

"Did Karim and a group of his Muslims go along with you to Bedford's house?" Boring asked.

"No, they did not."

"What happened when you got to Bedford's home?"

Tolman began to shake his head as though in sadness. "Canton and Derkin rode on the passenger side of my black Cadillac. The moment they stepped out of the car, they were killed by rifle fire from the top floor of Bedford's house."

Several of the spectators gasped. A murmuring arose in the chambers. The prosecution had scored heavily in its case against me. We'd have to find some way to prove that Tolman was lying. Light's video of the attack would substantiate our story—if the judge ruled it admissible evidence. If he didn't, our efforts had suffered a real blow. A sudden chill passed through me, I bowed my head and rested it lightly on my left fist.

"Were they on the sidewalk when they were killed?" Boring asked.

"Yes," Tolman said and clenched his hands together.

"And what did you and Norris Cape do?"

"We got the hell out of there," Tolman said. "We didn't want to be killed the way Canton and Derkin were slaughtered."

"No further questions," Boring said. "Your witness, Mr. Krippendorf."

Carl made his way slowly to the area in front of the witness stand. Tolman's face was impassive.

"Mr. Tolman, I'm puzzled," Carl said. "Perhaps you could help my befuddled mind."

"I wouldn't even try," Tolman chirped. "It's hopeless."

Laughter rustled through the audience, like leaves skipping down the sidewalk before a cold, autumn wind.

"I know, Mr. Tolman," Carl said. "I'm a sad case, but didn't Mr. Bedford help you get a branch library for one of the areas in your district 9. Boxville, I believe. He made the proposal to the city council, got behind it and persuaded other council members to vote for it. Isn't that correct?"

"Yeah," Tolman answered grudgingly.

"And didn't Bedford take the lead in getting a new building erected for the food stamp office on Lincoln Lane? To make it easier for food stamp recipients to get to the office and find a parking place?"

"Yeah," Tolman said. "But Bedford's clever. He was just trying to work us black council members into a position where we'd feel as if we owed him our votes."

"Oh, I see," Carl said. "He did it but you resent his doing it?"

"I didn't say that," Tolman said.

"And the $200,000 for a new city park in councilman Norris Cape's district. Wasn't it Bedford's idea? Didn't he take the lead in selling it to other council members? Wasn't the vote on the park a unanimous vote?"

"Yeah."

From long experience, I could tell that Tolman was not happy at all with the way the questioning was going.

"Did you know, Mr. Tolman, that Councilman Bedford paid the expenses for five black men to attend college and make it through to graduation? Two attorneys, one dentist and two ministers?"

A hush fell on the courtroom.

It took a few seconds for Tolman to reply. Finally, he said, "Yeah. He's a rich man and rich people have the money to buy the souls of some of our weaker brothers. And, when they do something like this, they feel less guilty about having kept blacks in slavery. Out in the black neighborhoods, we call people like those five, 'Uncle Toms.' They are not respected in the black community."

"Oh, why is that, Mr. Tolman?"

"Such people side too many times with whitey against their black brothers. It's just something they think they owe whites in return for the money to send them through college. Fortunately, we don't need to turn to whiteys any longer and beg for help to go to college. We've got Pell grants to pay our way now."

"Pell grants?"

"Yeah. The government is finally assuming its responsibility to help blacks by giving us college money. It's a step towards reparations for the years we spent in slavery. And, we are going to demand even more. Black people will pressure the government and citizens until reparations—and generous ones at that—are forthcoming."

"Oh," Carl said. "The taxpayers are now, through these Pell grants, paying for the things which people like Stoney Bedford did voluntarily?"

"Yeah," Tolman said. "Now, we can go to college in style and not owe white people anything. Black people are entitled to go through college free."

Carl changed tactics. "Tell me, Mr. Tolman. Do you hate white people?"

Boring objected. "The attorney for the defendant is asking an irrelevant question, a question whose answer will have to be subjective."

"Objection sustained," Judge Johnson said.

"I don't mind answering the white man's question," Tolman said cheerfully. "You damned right I hate white people. When you've been kicked around for two hundred years or more, the way blacks have been, you learn to hate. But now, the tables have been turned. Us blacks have the power now. Politically and economically. We're not afraid of white people anymore. We've declared war on whites—and we will win this war."

"War?" Carl asked.

"That's right, white man. War. We want what you whites have. And we're going to take it. That's the only way we'll ever get what we're rightfully due."

"That's a very interesting philosophy, Mr. Tolman. Did you ever think about black people working in the same economic and social system in which whites work and earning their way to a better living, to a greater share of the world's goods?"

"Hell no," Tolman said. "Whites exclude us from the system. And when we do work inside of the system, it takes too long to get any where.

The government owes it to us. We want it now, and if you don't give it to us, we'll take it by force."

I looked at Boring. I could see that he felt very uncomfortable with Tolman's performance. His jaws were clenched, his face was a mottled red. Hugh Hindsmith had his head in his hands and was looking down at the papers in front of him.

"Mr. Tolman," Carl said. "Could you clear my mind on something? Mr. Bedford has repeatedly told Mr. Xerxes and me, that Canton and Derkin were members of the Karim group that assaulted his home on March 14th. Yet you say you and Norris Cape brought them to the Bedford home that night. Are you certain that the testimony you have given this court accurately reflects what happened that night?"

"Listen, white man," Tolman sneered. "It's Bedford who's lying. I don't need to. I know what I did that night. I ain't gonna sit here any longer and take such crap."

"No further questions, your honor," Carl said. "We do reserve the right to further question Mr. Tolman, as well as any of the other witnesses who have or will appear for the prosecution. Or for the defense also."

Black Muslim leader Malcolm XIV took the witness stand. He testified that black ministers Wash Washington and Blue Combs had told him that "that old white racist Bedford was bragging and telling others that he would 'kill some niggers if they tried to pull down the Confederate flag.' "

"He's helping our case," Xerxes told me in a soft voice.

Malcolm XIV was cold and arrogant when Xerxes questioned him about what the ministers Combs and Washington had reportedly told him.

"I know what I heard," he said, his voice flat and devoid of emotion. "It was common knowledge in the black community that Bedford was a man who'd kill you if you looked cross-eyed at him. We also knew, if a black man didn't bow and scrape to a rich white man like Bedford, as such people expect the blacks to do-and still expect us to do to this day—that those who did not bow down would find all kinds of obstacles thrown into their path, no matter what you tried to do. It's just an unspoken rule white people use against what they call 'uppity' blacks.' "

A nervous twitter fluttered through the crowd. A woman with contralto voice moaned, "Oh, no. White people don't have that kind of agenda when dealing with blacks."

Judge Johnson banged his gavel and called for order."One more outburst such as that and I'll clear this courtroom."

"Are you still one of the troops of the great Merciful Ayatollah of Philadelphia?"

Malcolm XIV bristled. "Yeah, white man. And I'm proud of it. Nobody shoves us around."

"Does your leader, the Merciful Ayatollah, still preach that his disciples are at war with white people?" Xerxes asked.

Malcolm assayed Xerxes coolly and diffidently. "Not only have we declared war on whites," Malcolm said coldly. "We are fighting that war—and winning it. It's we blacks who are intimidating you white people now. You're scared as hell. Almost pissing in your pants. You give in more to us each day. And it will become worse. There's no escape for you."

"Why do you and the Merciful Ayatollah hate whites?" Xerxes asked. "As your leader had said in his books and as you have expressed today on the stand?"

Malcolm XIV laughed. "That's a stupid question. You white people brought blacks to this country in chains as slaves and despite the Civil War, you still treat us as slaves. When we win our war against you—and we will win it—we'll run things and whites will work for us. We'll have the things you have and you'll be poor. Like most blacks are poor now." He raised the clenched fist of black power. "But you whites won't pay any attention to our declaration of war—until it's too late." The clenched fist shot up into the air again.

Many in the spectator's gallery were disturbed. The judge did not stop the low, angry hum of voices.

"Thank you, sir," Xerxes said. "You've revealed some startling information to this court. And to the world, hopefully. No further questions, your honor."

"I call Sister Eleanor Rose to the stand," Boring announced crisply.

The white-haired little old woman smiled and nodded to two of the jury members as she made her way to the witness stand. She had lived long enough to learn the manner of oblique avoidance with which older blacks face the world they see as ruled by whites.

"Sister Rose," Boring said. "Have you had occasion to observe the defendant up close in his relationships to others?"

"Yes suh, I knows Mr. Bedford well," she said softly.

"Would you tell the court about these occasions?"

"In 1993, at the mission we blacks founded out on Aqueduct Street, Mr. Bedford insisted he be allowed to help us prepare and serve the Thanksgiving dinner to the poor and the homeless. To keep him quiet, we put him in the kitchen to help prepare the meal.

"The folks we feed don't have no place else to go. They'se forced to seek out the free food we provide in our feeding program. Them that comes are all black because whites won't give us homes and feed us the way they should."

"What did he do to help, Sister Rose?"

The frail little woman smoothed the cheap print dress she wore. "Well, I 'pose I'd better tell you. That man took over. Ordered the kitchen help around with such mean ole words they came and axed me to stop him. Treated them like they'se nobody. I had to move him to the serving line in order to calm the kitchen help down."

"Those are harsh terms you've used, Sister Rose? Could you tell us more?"

"That man is sumpin' else." She chuckled. "Yes sir, he sho' sumpin' else. Called the kitchen help by their first names. 'Mary,' he'd say. 'You do this.' Then 'Henry, you take care of that over there.' Well, black peoples deserve to be treated in a dignified manner, too. We should be called 'Mrs.' and 'Mister' jes like white folks."

"When he was serving food on the serving line, what did Mr. Bedford do?"

"Lawd, that man is one more stingy white man. He'd put small amounts on their plates and tell them 'You can come back for seconds if you want to.' Well, going back for seconds makes most folks 'shamed. I tells the servers I'd rather put too much on the platters and have to throw some of it out. That way, them poor folks ain't 'shamed."

"Has Mr. Bedford ever attended one of your candlelight vigils on the nights the state executes a black person?"

"He did for a fact. He sho' 'nuff did. Not jes' once, but twice. And both times, as we prayed, he interfered with our vigil and persecuted those of us holding dem lighted candles."

"What'd he do?" Boring asked.

"He'd bring a dozen white folks with him and they'd kneel down and light candles. Then Mr. Bedford would pray out loud for the murdered victims of the man to be executed."

"Oh, how loud?"

"Loud enough so that those of us praying dey wouldn't execute dat po' prisoner who could not fasten' our 'tention on de Lawd."

"Your witness, Counselor."

Xerxes walked to the witness stand. "Sister Eleanor Rose. Tell me, Sister Rose. In what Catholic order have you been designated as a sister?"

Sister Rose frowned and twisted a handkerchief in her small, bony hands. There was a frantic look on her face as she turned towards Boring who couldn't help her. "Well," she said. "I'se not a member of one of dem 'ficial Catholic orders. The name 'Sister' is jes a name I picked up along the way. I've been helping to feed po' folks a long time."

"Oh," Xerxes said. "But the name does make it easier for you to raise funds for your feeding program, doesn't it?"

"Yes suh," she smiled. "I've helped the poor so long, until lots of folks see me as one of the Lord's special angels."

"Tell the court, Sister, if you will. Don't most of your funds to feed these homeless and poor blacks come from generous white people?"

She twisted her handkerchief and cleared her throat. "Well, I 'pose you could say dat. But white folks don' need no hep. White folks are the ones who have the money and they ought to give it to me to take care of these po' folks. After all, they'se 'sponsible for most of the folks who come to eat with us being homeless and poor."

"Oh, how's that?" Xerxes asked.

"Everybody knows white folks keeps us beat down here in de' South."

"Tell me, Sister Rose. How much does Mr. Bedford contribute annually to your feeding program?"

"Five thousand dollars. But, he ought to give more."

"That's an interesting observation, Sister Rose. Did you know that Mr. Bedford is president and chairman of the board of the Forest Rescue Mission that feeds, gives lodging to and encourages several thousand rootless, homeless poor people each year, both white and black?"

"Yes, I knows dat. I also knows that dey heps more white folks than po' black."

"Well, Sister Rose. Don't white people who are down on their luck deserve help, too?"

"I 'pose so. But they'se white. They'se can work their way out of poverty. Black people don't hardly ever make it out."

"No further question, your honor."

Julie Peel was fuming. She leaned over and whispered to me, "That woman is a gold plated phony. Masquerading as some saintly figure. Using poverty and poor people to further her own political agenda. Why people don't see through her is more than I can understand."

"She'd rather lie than eat," I told Julie. "Only she does it so expertly that she's believable."

"The tide is running against us," I whispered to Xerxes. I could sense that he and Carl had lost some of their optimism, though they had succeeded in bringing into sharp focus many of the weak points in the testimony of the prosecution's witnesses we'd heard up to this point.

For the first time, I allowed myself to think about being confined to prison for the rest of my life. I could think of nothing so ignominious as coming to the end of my days and dying in a barren prison cell among people who would scarcely notice my passing.

CHAPTER 27

At times during my trial, I realized I was no longer capable of standing as the stalwart defender of personal liberty. I could scarcely defend my own liberties; that is, if I had anything resembling liberties left to me. As hard as I tried, I couldn't relax. Every muscle in my body ached; every nerve felt as though it had been stretched taut and would snap unless tension was relieved. My mental processes faded into and out of swirling mists of grey fog that slowed my answers to the simplest questions and dimmed my mental acuity to a level where I barely functioned.

How long can a person endure the highly charged emotional encounters of being tried for murder which he didn't commit? How long can he spiritually ward off the assaults on his personal integrity that continue day after day with increasing intensity and not become depressed? The circles of my world were growing more narrow by the day, tightening, ever tightening, until I could do nothing it seemed except stew in the cauldron of witches' brew that the gleeful, cackling hags stirred constantly. They were always there in the hidden darkness of my mind.

"Bubble, bubble, toil and trouble . . . " I searched desperately for some peace of mind, but it was as elusive as running through the meadows chasing the end of a rainbow. Most of the times, the pot of gold stayed beyond my reach. For my tormented soul, life's paradise had been lost.

It was July down South and the world was a shimmering green covered with the distant haze of summer's mysterious shroud. July's canvas, with its brilliant blue skies, was colored with memories of long summer days, boyhood fishing holes where a big one might be lying in wait in the deepest parts, ice cold watermelon and Independence day parades with brass bands and flags and patriotic speeches. And most of all, the long, lazy summer afternoons beckoning me to joyful exuberance.

Dawn's light came earlier each day and the sun brightened the skies until 8:30 or 9:00 o'clock in the evening. Yet I could not stop to rest my harassed spirit, to feel again the conspiracy of summer, to dream of life's flashing jewel tones, to listen to the symphony of the cicadas that began at dusk, or to bask in remembered joys. I could find no place where the shrill cacophony of hatred and the intrusive snouts of television cameras and the shouted questions of reporters did not follow me.

I felt like a hunted animal, fleeing through the forest, stumbling, falling, becoming entangled in the clutching vines, finding myself almost too tired to continue running. But behind me, back there on the trail, the exultant cries of the pursuers drew closer, ever closer. With great effort, I'd once again arouse myself from the black fogs of resignation and begin again to run. I had no choice. I must keep running, running . . .

I was still not completely well from my wounds and the long days in court drained me of energy. I had to stay alert every minute, listen intensely to every word, make judgments, scribble notes, make self-correcting course changes. These things completely absorbed me. The end of the day did not bring relief from these burdens, for once I exited the court chambers, I faced a different world, peopled by strangers demanding that I dance to their raucous tunes.

In order to find some place where I could hide out from the press, the demonstrators and those whose anger was often expressed in shouted curses, we had to devise ingenious plans of escape.

Each day; a circle of policemen met me at the door that opened into the hall from the courtroom and held the crowd at bay as we made our way down the corridor to the elevator. Men and women shouted, pushed, shoved and literally clawed at the officers in efforts to tear at me. Men with TV cameras scurried backwards as we walked, shouting questions and continuously filming, recording every movement.

"Never, never, never answer any questions from the press during the course of this trial," Xerxes cautioned. "Never, never, never."

The fastidious, charming Greek always held my arm as we hurried along. Carl could not keep up, so he would leave five minutes before the rest of us exited the courtroom. To clear the way for Carl's slow progression, two police officers, one on each side of him, kept the crowd at bay as he headed downstairs to his automobile.

Once the officers and I left the elevators and burst through the doors to the outside world, the frenetic efforts of determined reporters and people increased to frightening levels of noise and threatened physical assault. At times, the officers had to use their sticks to beat back some of the angrier individuals who somehow had centered their intense focus on me as a despicable straw man on which they could rain their frustrations.

"Killer! Bastard! I hope they hang you!" The same shouted, daily litany escaped the throats of the long-haired, unkempt strangers who had come from many different parts of the country to, as they often yelled, "Help put you away." Inevitably, one or two of them would get near enough to spit into my face as we rushed towards Carl's automobile which Harris Woolford made certain waited for us each day at the curbside sixty feet from the door.

I'd been haunted by remembrances of their faces as we pushed through the crowd that first day. I invariably searched for the silent, impassive men in camouflage hunting clothes who held their rifles across their chests with clenched hands. At times, I'd be pushed and jostled close enough to some of them to hear their words: "We're with you Mr. Bedford. When the time comes, you can count on us. We're tired of the government persecuting its citizens the way they're persecuting you."

As we pulled away, some in the crowd always beat on the windows of the car with their fists, shouting and cursing. Twice, one tenacious protestor sprawled across the hood of Carl's automobile as we drove away and had to be dragged off by police officers.

"This insanity," Carl would curse. "Damned mad dogs. Infected with some strange philosophy that has driven them mad. Just like rabid dogs. And it's not even the dog days of August yet."

It was unnerving to look back and always see automobiles and vans loaded with television people and reporters trying to follow our automobile. I was afraid. "Carl, it's a game of 'hide and seek,' " I'd usually say. "How in hell can we escape them and find a hiding place?"

"Watch this," he'd answer. He increased the Lincoln Town car's speed, cornering rapidly, turning and twisting along unfamiliar streets. He was a skilled driver and usually lost the pursuers by turning into the driveway of a friend's home and wheeling onto the apron back of his carport. There, we were hidden from the street and could escape the pursuers.

Two blocks from Carl's house, Harris Woolford waited in his car. Able Erling accompanied him. I'd exit from Carl's car and quickly climb into Woolford's back seat and huddle on the floor board for several blocks. I alternated between Erling's, Woolford's and Julie Peel's homes. Only Xerxes and Carl knew my location.

I felt comfortable and safe with Harris and Able. Able had a pool hidden from view by an eight-foot high wall of sharpened wooden stacks laced close together. On the nights I had escaped the pursuers and was hidden away at the council president's home, we three would put on our bathing suits and swim for at least a half hour. Then, we'd sit around the pool sipping martinis and reminiscing.

"The flag's still flying at city hall," Able said one evening, a big grin on his face.

"Oh," I said. "I've been so sick, so busy with my defense, until I'd forgotten to ask about it."

"Yeah," Harris laughed. "The two men appointed to the council to fill your seat—and Lampkins'—are as dedicated as we are to keeping the Confederate flag where it has flown for many, many years."

"Tolman, Cape and Dines?" I asked. "Are they still raising hell?"

"Surprisingly," Able said, "they've toned down their rhetoric since your March 12th troubles. They seem a little more subdued. They seem to want to get along. They're less fiery in their objections."

"But they're still a pain in the ass," Harris said. "The glasses through which they view the world are darker in color than we ever imagined."

As we ate dinner, Harris played tapes of some of the big bands of the '40s and '50s. Glenn Miller. Tommy Dorsey. Harry James. Guy Lombardo. Songs that tugged at your heart strings with romantic remembrances—or your feet if you loved to dance like Donna Elaine and I did. "Moonlight Serenade." "One O'clock Jump." "Sugar Blues." "I'll Never Smile Again."

"We're sorry you're having to go through this inquisition," Able said. "It reminds me of "The Crucible" and Salem's witches."

"Yeah," Harris said. "How many more stones can they pile onto you before you die, Stoney?" He poured more burgundy wine for each of us. "I remember the witches museum in Salem. One of the favorite torture devices used by the inquisitors was tying the victim down, putting wood on top of him, then piling on stone after stone, hoping the weight and the pain it caused would force a confession out of the accused."

"But one poor man knew he hadn't done anything wrong, that he wasn't a witch," Able said. "His answer, each time his tormentors asked him to confess was to cry, 'More stones. More stones.'"

"This trial of yours, Stoney," Harris said. "It's a government witch hunt. Your tormentors have you strapped to the rack. They're piling on more stones and asking you to confess to wrong doing."

"What the hell is this world coming to?" Able asked. "This is supposed to be America where things like this don't happen. But, it is happening. Franz Kafka and George Orwell's pioneering works predicted these things. Now, they're here and people still don't believe it."

I got up and walked to the draperies. I lifted each one of them and peered behind the folds as though looking for an imaginary enemy. I looked through the window at the outside world cautiously, then ducked away from the glass. Then, I eased across the room and peeked around the door facings of each of the two doors that led from the dining room into the hallway . I drew back quickly and flattened myself next to the wall.

Harris and Able jumped to their feet. "What'd you see?" Able yelled.

"Sh-h-h," I whispered and put my right index finger to my lips. "Big Brother is watching us."

"Shit man," Harris laughed. "You scared the hell out of me."

"Big Brother," Able said, shaking his head. "Orwell wrote that the government's all-seeing eye would follow us everywhere we went, even into the bedroom and the bathroom. There would be no escape. Yes sir. Big Brother is watching us."

Boring was somehow different in the court the next morning. Some of the bounce seemed to be gone from his step; his voice was not ringing with the confidence it had a few hours ago. The tedious process that kept all of us mentally on our toes was beginning to wear on him.

"I call noted psychiatrist, Bellows Windhorst, to the stand."

We had studied the list of witnesses and had a general idea of what to expect from Windhorst. He was young and energetic, deeply tanned and obviously swimming in pools of narcissistic self-love. His sense of self importance inflated his manner and speech like the heater in a drifting, hot air balloon. As an expert witness for the prosecution, his fees for appearing were several thousands of dollars. And he loved every minute of his time in the spotlight.

His pencil thin mustache made his face appear to be a charcoal character sketch similar to those drawn by the hungry artists that haunt the famed Jackson Square in New Orleans.

"Tell the court, Mr. Windhorst, what my office has asked you to do." The smug smile once again lighted Boring's face.

"Mr. Boring," the young man said, his chin raised to give him an air of sophistication. "You asked me to do deep psychological research on one Stonewall Bedford based on available evidence. I was commissioned to develop a profile of the defendant. I have done just that and it isn't flattering, to say the least."

"How did you conduct your research, Mr. Windhorst?"

"Bellows," I said to myself as I sized up the vain young man siting on the witness stand. "Bellows. A furnace. Hot air blowing on molten metal to cool and help shape it. I'll bet that all we're going to hear is hot air conjured up in the tortuous recesses of a mind craving money, fame and power."

Windhorst told of researching my family background, business success, marriage, church and community activities and minutes of Forest City Council meetings. He held up a thick file of newspaper clippings and called it a catalogue of my published statements. Then he told of hours of tape recordings made from interviewing people who knew me.

"The profile, Mr. Windhorst," It was now clear that this psychiatrist was a key player in the prosecution's case.

"It isn't a pretty picture, Mr. Boring. But, here goes. Stonewall Bedford suffers delusions of grandeur. He's lost back there in time some-where in the 1860's. There are portraits of Confederate generals hanging on the walls of his plantation home, Bedford House. Many times, he goes there, closes the doors to the library and actually talks to these long dead ancestors whose portraits, to Bedford, are illusions of reality. He's been known to remark over the years that he hears the distant sound of the bursting shells at Gettysburg, the muffled roll of the drums, the shouted commands of Confederate officers to '*char-r-r-ge.*' "

Windhorst was playing his role to the hilt, posing his handsome face in different angles, punctuating his statements with just the correct tone of voice and inflections, sweeping his hands into the air in well practiced gestures. His verbal characterizations of me were the slashing blows of a hatchet man. He was earning the large fees being paid him from taxpayer funds.

"When he loses himself in Pickett's charge at Gettysburg," Windhorst said, a touch of sadness in his clear voice, "he keeps saying, 'The high ground. If only we could have held the high ground, we'd have won that day at Gettysburg.' Mr. Bedford is known for expressing his grief that he wasn't at Gettysburg to fight for the Confederacy."

Boring was scratching the back of his head. There was a perplexed, quizzical look on his face. "Your words are drawing a frightening picture for this court, Mr. Windhorst."

"It gets worse, Mr. Boring. His friends have told me that each time he sees a Civil War movie, documentary or historical sketch on television, he keeps saying, and I quote the exact words from an anonymous source, 'If only we had won. If only the South had whipped those Yankee bastards. The world would be so much better off and the South would be a free and separate nation where individual freedom is more highly valued and the interference of the government in people's lives held to minimum essentials. We'd not have the Northern boot continually pressing down on our lives, demanding that we grovel before them.'"

Windhorst was playing on our emotions, appealing for sympathy. "I do not wish to cause Mr. Bedford pain," he said to Boring. "Are you certain you wish me to continue?"

"Indeed we do," Boring said. "Indeed. Please do continue."

"He's the typical noble Southern patriarch. He expects his position and heritage to gain him deference from most people. 'By right of birth', he's fond of reminding people. It angers him when others look upon him as only an equal and proceed to treat him as such. His 1860's thinking is that of a landed slaveholder. His reverence for the Confederate flag tells us that he's never given up on the Confederate cause; that he's still fighting the Civil War. Only now, as he wages his private war, there is no opposing army of men in the union blue. By transference, the enemy in 1996 is the black man, in endless phalanx, threatening him and his world. This new enemy must be defeated, annihilated, broken. He's one of Pickett's troops charging up Cemetery Ridge."

"Your insight is refreshing, Mr. Windhorst," Boring said encouragingly. "In your research, did you find reasons that such a man would readily kill black people?"

"Objection, your honor." Xerxes had risen quickly from his chair, his pince nez still clasped to his nose. "All of this psychiatric pap is pure conjecture. The figment of the misshapened imagination of a man deeply immersed in the black pools of narcissism, relishing the numerous streams of self love he ladles over himself."

Judge Johnson peered over the tops of his drug store reading glasses and said, "Objection overruled. This expert witness may proceed to answer the question."

Carl leaned over and whispered to me, "Johnson's giving us excellent grounds to appeal our case—if the jury returns an unfavorable verdict."

"What he's telling the court is almost an exact replica of what I've read in journals of psychiatry," I whispered. "Only the names have been changed. It's grade school, B picture psycho babble. But, look at the members of the jury. They're entranced."

Windhorst nodded at the judge, straightened his red silk tie, craned his neck against a shirt collar that appeared too tight and continued. "Mr. Bedford cannot accept the fact that men like him can no longer intimidate black people, but that the white man himself is now running scared. He's obsessed with a love of guns and shooting. He and his son, William, used to shine and polish their gun collection—which is considerable—for hours at a time. Lovingly, I might say.

"Remember, now, in Bedford's view of the world, the black man is the enemy who is assaulting Confederate positions and routing Southerners from their entrenched sociological and psychological positions. The attackers are no longer the blue coats of the Union army. Now, it is General Stonewall Bedford who must storm Cemetery Ridge in suicidal sacrifice for lost causes.

"It is he who must kill the enemy. He has many guns; he's skilled in their use; the enemy is out there; he hears and sees them and knows he must destroy them. He is the force standing before this new enemy and recreating again, in his mind and by his actions, the world in which he'd much prefer to live. His task is simple. As a soldier in Confederate gray, a Southern general by birth and position, he must kill the enemy when they come against him. That is what he did to the blacks that night who dared occupy the public sidewalks and street in front of his big home in a 'white man's neighborhood.' "

Boring had gotten the picture of me he wanted of me painted for the whole world to see and remember, the blacks and grays of a Stonewall Bedford disconnected from reality. He was relying on Windhort's having lodged this deeply in the minds of the jurors. It was the picture he needed jurors to remember if he was to be successful in his prosecutions of me.

The pride and satisfaction of his own peacock preening glowed in his face and energized his body. Windhorst's verbal brush strokes, invented and patched together from psychological jargon that gave it credibility, had painted me as a "Dorian Gray" lost in the fogs of a demented mind, hunting the black man as prey, methodically killing with Hitlerian precision.

"No further question," Boring announced. "Your witness, Mr. Krippendorf."

Carl limped to the witness stand in front of Bellows Windhorst, the psychiatrist. "You have quite an imagination, sir. I see that the pupils of your eyes are dilated. Tell me. Did you have your morning snort of coke before you took the witness stand today?"

Windhorst laughed. "This is the 1990's, Mr. Krippendorf, not the 1950's. Many of us use drugs for recreational purposes. It is an accepted thing in the modern world in which we live." He was protecting his sophistication with an air of insulting irreverence.

"Please answer my question, sir. Did you snort the white powder in the men's room this morning, just before you came into this courtroom? Careful now. I have a note that was passed to me saying that you did just that. And the source is very reliable."

"Yes. Coke calms me down; makes me think more clearly; sets my imagination free; helps me to articulate clearly."

"Oh, then you freely admit to the daily use of coke?" Carl asked.

"Yes. And I'm not ashamed of it. It's a great help in sharpening my mental faculties."

"Well, Mr. Windhorst," Carl said. "Your imagination certainly has been freed from its moorings the last few minutes. It is wonderful what snorting coke has done for your ability to draw illusionary pictures of Mr. Bedford. But, I'm puzzled. As I usually am when communicating with the sophisticates of your generation. Your words sounded like memorized phrases taken directly from articles in the trade magazines of your professions." He held up a magazine published for psychiatrists "Have you read this latest issue?"

"It's in my office, but I've been far too busy to read to it," Windhorst said. "I have so many clients who need my help and counsel."

"I just wondered, Mr. Windhorst. Here's an article that talks about people inventing more desirable worlds in which they'd like to live. You used some of the phrases in this article to describe the defendant. Tell us, now," Carl cajoled. "Didn't you copy some of these phrases for use in your report to this court because they sounded great and it made your job of researching a psychological profile on Bedford easier?"

"I most certainly did not," Windhorst bristled. "Those phrases are used by many psychiatrists who've diagnosed people with the dementia from which Bedford suffers."

Carl changed tactics. "Fascinating thing, the imagination." Carl rapped the steel of his artificial right leg with his heavy cane. The younger man on the witness stand was startled. "Do you know what makes that sound, Mr. Windhorst?"

"No," he shuddered, hunching his shoulders together and frowning. "Whatever it is, it's dreadful."

"You told us about Bedford's imagined enemies. That sound," Carl rapped his cane against his steel leg again. "That sound is the result of the work of the real enemy, Mr. Windhorst. The Germans—and they were not imaginary—they were the real enemy we encountered when we invaded Italy at the beaches of Salerno in World War II. The real enemy blasted this leg of mine off with a German 88 shell. Blew my landing craft to pieces. That man there, Stoney Bedford, the real Lieutenant Bedford, dove into the water and saved me from drowning. He risked his own life and was awarded the Silver Star for valor. That's the man you say is lost back there in the 1860's at Gettysburg. Did you take that into consideration when you were doing your profile of Stoney Bedford?"

"Oh, no one wants to hear those old war stories," Windhorst said, a broad smile revealing his long upper gum line. "As a nation, we've grown beyond such an elementary state of mind. The United States should feel guilty that they deliberately used fire bombs on German cities and civilians and killed thousands of innocent people. As a nation, we should suffer piercing remorse and guilt for violating every law of decency by dropping the A-Bomb on Hiroshima and Nagasaki. Those poor, poor people. That's the same mentality that drives Bedford to hating and killing our black citizens."

Carl Krippendorf's voice took on a sharp edge. "War stories, Mr. Windhorst? No one wants to hear tales of World War II any longer? Twenty years ago, thirty years ago, back there in the '60's and '70's, perhaps what you say would have fitted your mentality, the mentality of the spaced out generation of hippies and flower children. You and the howling mobs of revolutionaries who were too busy tearing the country apart."

Carl struck his artificial leg again with his heavy cane. "There are many of us who have a fierce love for America and the freedoms we have purchased with our blood and sacrifices. Your blythe and immature statements about national guilt does not describe the public pulse of today. Millions of Americans are rediscovering patriotism and pride in America.

"The revisionists of history," Carl sneered. "I believe they call them deconstructionists, would erase every last memory and record of our American heroes and deface or tear down our national shrines which are so dear to our hearts. But fortunately, these revisionists, these deconstruction-ists, are in full retreat. That's why people like Stonewall Bedford resist efforts to erase a beloved symbol such as the Confederate flag."

Windhorst was squirming in his chair. "Your honor," he asked Judge Johnson. "Do I have to sit here and listen to this ancient rhetoric from a total has-been?"

"The defense is making valid points concerning the beliefs that motivate the defendant. You may continue, Mr. Krippendorf."

"Thank you, Judge Johnson. Mr. Windhorst, some of us, people like me, Stoney Bedford and Archibald Xerxes, and many other people sitting in this courtroom, are not ashamed to glory in our cultural heritage such as that part we Southerners venerate that is represented by our Confederate flag and the heroic valor of our men in gray in Civil War battles."

Windhorst held up his hand. "This is a new age we're living in, Counselor. Such ugly pages as those that record Civil War battles should be erased from school textbooks so that future generations will not even know of them. We need to be less provincial and more worldly-wise to live in this global age."

"Oh, that's interesting," Carl said. "It would make you a happier citizen if you could revise our history books?"

Windhorst laughed. "We have already erased many of these tragic errors from our history books. Our generation has worked hard to present a more enlightened approach to United States history and we're rather proud of our accomplishments. People of my same global outlook now control many of our textbook publishers and even the Smithsonian museums. It's just a question of time before our hidden erasers completely remold our history as a country."

Righteousness and smugness glowed in Windhorst's voice and showed on his face.

Carl frowned. "I've read some of these revisions, Mr. Windhorst. And you are correct. They have erased from the modern school textbooks in use in our classrooms many of our national heroes. In one text book, Martin Luther King gets ninety-three mentions and George Washington and Abraham Lincoln only one each. And you are proud of these approaches to revising our national history?"

"You bet I am. To people of my generation, people such as Washington, Lincoln, Davy Crockett, Pershing, Eisenhower, Churchill l—they're no longer important in this new age. No. Timothy O'Leary, the Beetles, Kurt Cobain. These are the real role models our country needs to emulate in order to move into this sophisticated age."

Wisely, Carl waited for the crowd's furor to run its course. He stood in front of the witness box shaking his head in amazement, as though new insight had flashed from Windhorst's tongue and penetrated his reluctant mind.

Windhorst rambled on. Carl let him hang himself. "And in rewriting our battle history, they teach that America is responsible for starting wars and that we owe national apologies to the Germans and the Japanese.

"I understand that you refer to yourself as a citizen of the world, Mr. Windhorst. Is that correct?"

"I certainly do. Nationalism as represented by our flag is a philosophy of sin and disgrace. It leads to wars and genocide. Just like the Confederate flag. It's the South's expression of nationalism of the worst sort, based on keeping minorities subjugated."

"Are you married, sir," Carl sighed.

"Not any more, thank goodness." The wide smile came again. His chin raised as if in discovery of some great truth.

"Let's see," Carl said. "You've been married twice?"

"Oh no. Three times. These days, when two people get married and become bored with each other, as is so often the case, they walk away from their flimsy union. They seek a quick and easy divorce that makes them free again to get on with their life. I've never found anyone I could be compatible with yet. But, I keep trying." He smiled with satisfaction at his openness.

Carl consulted some notes. "Let's see. Edith, your second wife. That was her name wasn't it?"

"Yes. Edith was her name."

"That night she was killed. Let's see. You were booked for DWI and running a red light. She was buried and you did not see fit to attend her funeral. Is that right?"

"Well, my collar bone and left arm were broken in the same accident," the trim young man protested. "I just didn't feel well enough to go. Besides, funerals are so boring and depressing."

"But you are alive. Edith was killed in the accident. So was the young mother who was driving the car you broadsided in the intersection. And her two small children."

"But the people in the other car I hit don't count. They were black people on welfare. They had little if any future. The world is better off without them." Windhorst spoke with conviction.

"Four people died because you were drunk. Hopped up. And the world is better off, because they weren't really significant. If you ran a profile on yourself, Mr. Windhorst, similar to the one you so eagerly presented to this court, I wonder how it might read?"

Windhorst laughed. "Oh, my venerable friend. I'm a psychiatrist. Such things do not apply to me. I'm above such mundane things."

"No further questions, your honor." Carl rapped his cane across his artificial leg again, looked at the tall, young man with the pencil thin mustache, shook his head in dismay, then walked with uneven gait back to the defense's table.

Boring called a man to the stand who must have been every bit of 6'10" tall. He wore an open collar sport shirt and appeared nonchalant about the proceedings. "Tyler Wink is a ballistics expert with the FBI. He is here to verify that the bullets which killed Canton and Derkin came from those two rifles on that table over there. Rifles belonging to Bedford."

Wink's testimony was dry, factual and to the point. Neither Carl nor Xerxes bothered to question him.

"I might point out, Judge Johnson, that Mr. Wink has also verified that the bullets which killed those three black men inside of Bedford's home came from those same weapons. And, that the bullets which killed Mrs. Bedford and William came from the pistols carried by Karim and the other two who died with him inside the house."

"When will you be finished presenting the state's case, Mr. Boring?" the judge asked.

"Judge, there may be other witnesses the prosecution finds it necessary to call, but if they're not on the prepared list already in the court's hands, naturally I'll seek your permission to call them. But, I can inform the court today that the prosecution does have one additional witness I plan to call," Boring replied. "A surprise witness who has new information of vital importance in this case. When court reconvenes in the morning, counsel for the defense and I will huddle with you and seek the court's approval."

Johnson had had enough for the day. "The lateness of the hour leads me to declare a recess in this case until tomorrow morning at nine o'clock." The judge banged his gavel, a bit too loudly I thought.

CHAPTER 28

The four of us, Carl, Archibald Xerxes, Julie Peel and I had finished dinner around Bedford House's long oval, mahogany table. The Cabernet Sauvignon we'd had with our meal had helped to relax us some, but the conversation was still not flowing freely. Each of us was still uptight over our day in court. It had been long and wearing and had called forth the protective covering people scramble to put on when psyches are battered into uncertainty.

"How about an after dinner brandy?" I asked.

"Excellent idea," Xerxes said. "Do you have Three Star Hennessey? Cognac?"

"You are a man of good taste, Mr. Xerxes," I said. "I just happen to have some Hennessey."

"I'll take some too," Carl said. "Perhaps it'll help to revive me. I'm beat. What little energy I had has been drained."

"Pour me some, too," Julie said. "I love to sip an after dinner brandy. Slowly. It's one of the things William and I used to enjoy together." If anything, the sadness on her face enhanced her beauty. She was a lady of steel, flexible enough to bend before adversity but never break.

Xerxes had stood to inspect some of the paintings that lined the walls of the big diningroom. "We must devise our strategy for tomorrow," he said, watching me pour the Hennessey into the crystal brandy glasses. "DeLong Tolman's testimony today was very damaging. We know he's lying, but the members of the jury don't."

"How can we discredit his testimony," Julie asked. "Is there a way for us to attack his credibility?"

"Light's film will prove that Tolman's lying," Carl said. "If the judge agrees to let the jury see it. If the picture quality is bright enough to identify faces. If the prosecution does not succeed in discrediting the footage. If; if, if . . ."

"We have to come up with something else," Xerxes said. "Just in case all those 'if's' Carl just named come to pass. The Muslim, Jabbar, corroborated Tolman's assertions that Canton and Derkin were not brought to Stoney's home as part of the attacking force. Unless we can find some way to tear Tolman's statements apart, we're going to lose this case."

We sat in silence around the table for a long while, sipping our brandy. Things looked bleak for me. I looked around the diningroom at the things I loved and thought about the world I gloried in—Bedford House with all of its memories; the hunting lodge that helped me to escape to a simpler life; the touch, feel and smells of the land of my birth which mesmerized me. If I go to prison, this world would be left behind me as the prison gates clang shut. I'd be a man without a country. A cold shudder shook me so that my brandy almost sloshed from its goblet.

"Boring's surprise witnesss tomorrow," Carl said. "I'm worried. I wonder who it could be?"

"Whoever it is, we'd better be prepared," Xerxes said. "And Carl, you and I must shift our legal minds and skills into overdrive in finding ways to tear down Tolman's lies and build credibility for Light's film of the actual attack of March 14th."

Mrs. Jones came into the room and handed me the cordless telephone. "It's Mr. Bester. He says it's important that he talk to you."

"Thank you, Mrs. Jones. Yes, Roy. How are you?"

"Okay, Mr. Bedford. I watched the news reports of what happened in court today. I know who Boring's surprise witness is."

"You do? Who is it?"

"Layla Jenkins."

"Jenkins? I don't believe I know Layla Jenkins."

"Twenty years ago, your wife had her mother as a cleaning woman. Nashta Jenkins. Layla, the daughter, was fifteen at the time."

"How can they wring a surprise out of those facts, Roy?"

"She's going to testify that you came home the morning of June 20th, 1975, for coffee and that you took her upstairs and raped her. Three times."

"Damn, Roy. That's a point blank lie." I could feel the flush of anger blurring my mental clarity. "Where was my wife on that particular day?"

"Supposedly at the church doing volunteer work."

"The girl's mother. Why didn't she stop me since I was supposedly raping her daughter?" I became conscious that my left hand was rubbing circles around my chest in efforts to rub away the tightness.

"Layla Jenkins will testify that you gave her mother an extra fifty dollars and threatened to tell the police she had stolen some of Donna Elaine's jewelry—if she protested your having sex with her daughter."

"It's a nightmare, Roy," I said. "If I raped her, why hasn't this Layla Jenkins come forward and told someone a long time ago?" The left side of my body where I'd been wounded started throbbing. It still did that when I was tired and under stress.

"She claims she's been going to psychology group therapy sessions for sexually abused women. These sessions have given her the courage to finally come forward and tell her story. Not to mention the $15,000 that Hugh Hindsmith has paid her to do this. Hindsmith himself concocted the story and has rehearsed her in how to effectively present it to the jury."

"Thanks, Roy," I said. "You're a real friend, and I deeply appreciate it."

"That's not all," Roy said.

"You mean there are more surprises?" I took a deep breath and sipped at the cognac.

"This time, we can pull a surprise on Boring and Hindsmith," Roy said. "LaJuana Tolman, the estranged wife of Delong, is in my office right now. She said she had proof that Delong was with her all night on March 14th. That he couldn't have driven Canton and Derkin to your home in the city."

I rose quickly to my feet. I wanted to cheer. "Roy, this is the best news we've had all day. Will she testify for the defense tomorrow?"

Roy's voice was positive. "Yes, she'll do it. And with good reasons. Delong is eighteen months behind in child support payments. He comes to her house once a week for all night sexual bouts. Beats her with his fist if she expresses reluctance to accommodate him."

"Hold on a minute, Roy. While I ask Carl and Xerxes what we should do to make certain she's in court tomorrow."

"Wait a minute," Roy said. "You won't have to do anything. Mrs. Tolman is spending the night in our home. My wife is preparing dinner for her now. She will ride to the courthouse tomorrow with me. We'll hide out in one of the vacant offices several doors down the hall from the courtroom. That way, DeLong won't see her. You can call her as your surprise witness."

"Roy, we're indebted to you." My heart was so overflowing with gratitude I was close to becoming maudlin.

"You needed the help, Mr. Bedford. You helped me when I needed it. For six long years. It's the least I can do."

"What was that all about?" Carl asked after I clicked the button that disconnected the phone.

I told the other three about Layla Jenkins and LaJuana Tolman. The mood around the long oval mahogany dining table changed. The excitement over the possibilities of discrediting Tolman's testimony brought new hope.

"I've been wanting to tackle that DeLong Tolman again," Carl said. "Now, we can tear him apart about his supposedly taking Canton and Derkin to your house that night. The lying bastard."

"It looks as if Mr. Tolman is facing charges of perjured testimony," Xerxes said. "If we can make his wife's testimony stand up under the abuse that will be heaped onto her. Boring and Tolman will froth at the mouth when they see Tolman's wife walking towards the witness stand. And after the day's over . . . I shudder to think of what might happen to the poor woman."

Carl brought us crashing down to earth again. "But we've still got the matter of your supposed rape of a fifteen year old twenty years ago," Carl said. "And with the headline emphasis on child abuse these days, members of that jury are not going to take kindly to Jenkins' story."

"It could blow our case sky high," Julie said. "We simply have to prove where you were on June 20th, 1975. Can we do it?"

Each of us sat quietly for a few minutes. I poured more brandy for Carl, Xerxes and myself. Julie, drumming her long fingers on the table's polished surface, declined. Suddenly, the thought struck me. My tax files. I'd never thrown them out. I had them stored in boxes for each of the last thirty-five years. And in each of those boxes there was more than just tax records. I had carefully kept Donna Elaine's daily calendar for each year as well as my own daily appointment calendar which I kept on my desk at the office of the convenience stores we had owned. A man could never be too careful about such things, for any business man fears that the IRS will descend on him for an audit. I had convinced myself that it was just best to save such things, even though Donna Elaine had fussed mightily about the amount of space the stored records took up.

I jumped to my feet. "I know how we can prove where I was June 20th, 1975."

"Damn, Stoney," Xerxes said. "You scared hell out of me. I thought you were having a heart attack. Tell us how we can prove your whereabouts."

"I'll show you. Have some more brandy while I'm gone. I'll be back in five minutes." I walked hurriedly down the long hall to a large room I'd converted into an office when I moved away from the house in which Donna Elaine and William had died. I had moved most of my old tax records out here to Bedford House. I prided myself on being highly organized and keeping excellent records.

I unlocked the room where the records were stored. Accordion folders for each tax year were in sturdy boxes, stacked in ascending order. The year 1975 was scrawled across the box in bold strokes from a magic marker. My heart jumped. There it was. I opened the bulging accordion folder, saw my business appointment calendar for 1975 as well as Donna Elaine's appointment calendar for that year.

Quickly, I thumbed through the months. June. Let's see. June 20th. Hell, I wasn't even in Forest, Georgia. For three weeks, beginning June 8th of that year, William, Donna Elaine and I had been touring the West. Nevada, Utah, Idaho, Montana, Wyoming. Las Vegas, Sun Valley, Crater of the Moon. Yellowstone Park. Big Sky Country. Custer's battlefield. The Oregon Trail.

I had definite proof that I was there on the dates in question. Airline ticket stubs. Motel bills. We'd flown home to Atlanta; our flight was late; we had arrived in Atlanta around midnight; then we drove home on June 29th. I had unlocked our front door at two a.m. in the morning.

I let out a whoop and ran back to the diningroom to show the treasures to the others. Soon, we were laughing and slapping each other on the back and exulting over our good fortune.

"Damn," Carl said. "What a stroke of luck. Perhaps the tide is changing for us. It sure in hell hasn't been going our way so far."

"I can't imagine anyone keeping tax files for twenty years," Xerxes said. "Pour me more brandy, Carl."

Julie grabbed me and we waltzed around the room as she hummed "The Tennessee Waltz." She had remembered that the song had special meaning for Donna Elaine and me.

CHAPTER 29

The next morning when court reconvened, Tighe Boring called as his first witness, Dr. Ufert Ulman, dentist, from Augusta. Dr. Ulman was one of the five blacks I'd sent through college. He was my friend. We'd always been able to communicate. After the deaths of my wife and son, he'd come to see me and we had visited over dinner for a long time. I had been touched by the genuine sadness he demonstrated. Why was Boring calling him as a witness? Anything Ulman would say would help my defense."

"Do you know the accused?" Boring asked.

"Yes," Dr. Ulman said in a strong, clear voice. He looked at me, then said, "Quite well."

"Tell us how you came to know Bedford, Dr. Ulman."

"I worked for him in one of his convenience stores several summers. After work, I'd go to his home and cut his yard."

"Did he assist you financially in going to dental school?"

"Yes" Ulman said. "Quite liberally, I might add. And I owe him a lot." He was of medium build, trim and easy going.

"Why didn't you return to Forest to set up your dental practice?" Boring asked.

Ulman smiled. "To tell you the truth, I didn't want to live anywhere close to Mr. Bedford."

My mouth must have fallen open with shock. Ulman had thought he could establish a bigger practice quicker in Augusta. I had agreed that this was a wise move and Donna Elaine and I had given him $8,000 to help him buy equipment and set up his office.

The D.A. was leading him on. "Why is that, Dr. Ulman?"

"After I finished college, he wanted me to register to vote as a Republican. When I refused to, he became enraged. Called me disloyal. Said I owed him more than that. He'd been drinking heavily that evening when the incident happened. 'You ought to still be in cotton fields, Boy,' he yelled. 'If it hadn't been for me, you would be. You know what you've become? An uppity nigger. Just plain nigger.'"

I whispered to Xerxes, "The man is lying through his teeth. Somehow or other, Hindsmith has bought him off."

"It has all the hallmarks of being something those justice department lawyers have cooked up," Xerxes said. "They're determined to put you away. They're skilled in Orwell's 'Big Brother' technique."

"Franz Kafka's *'The Trial'*," I said.

Boring was making the most of his golden find. "Is there more to the story?" the D.A. asked.

"When I tried very calmly to take up for my rights, he threatened to get his pistol and kill me. Wouldn't let me leave his livingroom. His wife calmed him down and told me to go quickly. I haven't seen him since that night eighteen years ago."

Boring was nodding his head up and down, encouraging the witness to continue. "Did he say anything else?"

"Yes sir. He said he'd killed uppity niggers before, just like his daddy before him. And his daddy's daddy."

None of the Bedfords had ever killed a black person. None of us ever referred to Negroes in such derogatory terms.

"Did he think his helping you through dental school bought your soul?"

"I would have to say he thought he owned me. That's why I'm saving money to pay him back every dollar he spent to help me through school. When I get that done, I won't have to think of Stoney Bedford ever again."

"On cross examination, ask Ulman about being busted for drugs," I whispered to Carl. "And about the $8,000 I gave him to set up his office."

Ulman seemed to be his relaxed, easy going self as Carl began his questioning of him. "Doctor Ulman, Mr. Bedford and I are chagrined to hear such testimony from you, especially since none of the things you have testified to ever occurred."

"Oh, yes they did, Mr. Krippendorf."

"Do you have any proof that these purely imagined events between you and Mr. Bedford ever took place?"

Ulman's sunny disposition disappeared instantly. "Yes," he bristled. "His wife. She's the only one that kept him from killing me that night."

"How convenient, Dr. Ulman," Carl said. "She is not here to corroborate your story. As you well know, Mr. Bedford's wife has been dead now for several months."

"I can't help that, " Ulman snapped. "I've told the truth about that incident."

"Let's see, Dr. Ulman. You said you didn't want to move back to Forest to set up your practice. The reason, I believe you said, was that you didn't want to live anywhere close to Mr. Bedford."

"That's true."

Carl persisted. "Wasn't the real reason based upon your reaching the conclusion that you could develop a bigger practice quicker in Augusta?"

"No, that wasn't the reason," Ulman said.

"Didn't Mr. Bedford and his wife give you $8,000 to buy your equipment and help you set up your office in Augusta? Be careful how you answer that, Doctor, because Mr. Bedford has the canceled checks and the invoices for the equipment he and his wife bought for your office. And I wouldn't want you to perjure yourself."

"Oh, they gave me the money as a loan," Ulman smiled.

"A loan? Eighteen years ago? Have you repaid this loan?"

The color drained from Ulman's face, turning it pale. His jaws were clenched.

"No, I haven't repaid Mr. Bedford yet. But I've been intending to do that."

"Let's see, Doctor," Carl said. Haven't you been netting over $100,000 a year from your practice?" Carl was taking a flyer, trying to smoke out the truth. It worked.

"Well . . . " Ulman was trying to choose his words carefully. "Yes, my practice has been quite successful."

"And after eighteen years, you haven't repaid Mr. Bedford? You said it was one thing you intended to do; that it would give you great joy and free you from any obligation you might feel to the Bedfords. The truth of the matter is, Mr. Ulman, someone coached you in your testimony here today, didn't they? You never intend to repay the money the Bedfords have so generously invested in you."

Ulman was no longer the cocksure, successful dentist he had been prior to assuming the witness stand. Boring was on his feet.

"Objection, your honor. The attorney for the defense is trying to lead and intimidate the witness. He is making a serious charge by even asking the question."

"Objection overruled," Judge Johnson said. The judge's stare over the top of his cheap reading glasses became even more fierce. Anger painted his cheeks red. "I find the questions quite pertinent and the Doctor's answers very revealing. If his testimony does turn out to be perjured, I will invoke the harshest penalties provided by law. Doctor Ulman, please answer Mr. Krippendorf's question."

"I do intend to repay the money," Ulman said. "But I've got two children, a big mortgage and many other things that seem to eat up the money I make."

"That car of yours out in the lot," Carl said. "It's beautiful. And very unusual." Carl was flying blind again. "Would you tell us about it."

"That's private business, Mr. Krippendorf. A dentist has to own a good automobile."

"Judge," Carl said. "Would you please instruct the witness to answer. The question is quite relevant."

Johnson instructed Ulman to answer the question.

"It's a Jaguar. Red. 1995. There's nothing wrong with owning a car like that."

"No, Dr. Ulman. Not as successful as you are in your dental practice. But, since you want to pay Mr. Bedford back for his years of generosity to you, wouldn't it make good sense to first repay him instead of spending almost $60,000 for a hot car like a Jaguar? With all the extras you required the dealer to add?"

Ulman looked towards Hindsmith and shrugged his shoulders. He was obviously unsure of himself. Finally he blurted out some angry words. "I've got a right to drive the kind of automobile I want to, and you can't criticize me for it. I resent your implications."

"Implications?" Carl asked. "Look at the things you implied in the wild tales you told about my client, Stonewall Bedford. You have implicated yourself with your own actions. You have revealed the glaring, unvarnished truth about your motives. I ask you—and at the same time warn you to be careful of perjuring yourself—there is no truth to the things you said about Mr. Bedford threatening you with a gun is there?"

Ulman looked towards Hindsmith and the other two justice department lawyers again. His eyes pleaded with them to help him out. The three busied themselves in deep concentration on the stack of papers in front of them.

"I have told the truth here today," Ulman said slowly. "People such as the privileged Bedfords want people of lesser statue to bow down to them, to defer to their wishes. I'm not about to do that."

"What was the date that this supposed incident occurring between you and Mr. Bedford?" Carl asked.

I suspected that Carl was prepared to take another flyer to get at the truth. He was remembering my discovery of the records that would later be used to reveal Layla Jerkins' lies.

Ulman wrinkled his brow as he tried to come up with a date. "Let's see. Eighteen years ago. That would be 1977. And it was shortly after my graduation. I'd say it was around the first or second week in June."

Carl turned towards me and winked. I knew that when I went home tonight, there'd be more digging through my long-kept tax records. We'd prove tomorrow that the good doctor was lying, if for no other reason than the incident he had spun from his willingness to lie, for whatever motives, never happened.

"Let's see, Doctor Ulman," Carl said. "Have you had any experience with drugs?"

"No way, man," Ulman snapped. "No way."

"That's interesting, Doctor. Very interesting. Don't police records show that you were arrested and charged with selling drugs? Not one time, but three times?"

"How'd you know that?" Ulman asked. It had been an automatic response slipping from a surprised mind.

"Oh, we know lots of things, Doctor. You want to tell us about it or shall I consult my files on you?" Carl pointed to the table where the three of us sat. There were several thick file folders on top of the desk.

I hoped his bluff worked. Ulman's calm face had turned stormy with repressed anger.

"You damned white people. Always putting us black people down. Everybody makes mistakes in life, but that doesn't mean a man can't straighten up and fly right. Why don't you get off our backs. You've probably done worse than I've ever done."

"The drug charges, Doctor?"

"The first incident happened right after I was graduated from Meharry Dental School. The cops framed me. We were having a party and getting high. Just an innocent party. The police busted down the door and carted me off to jail."

"The truth of the matter is, you were running a crack house, weren't you? And raking in the money hand over fist. How much time did you do?"

"None. I got off on probation."

"And went immediately back into business?" Carl asked.

"Well, the money was so good," the doctor said. "And my wife was hooked. I did a year for the second and third times. And four years probation."

"You are practicing dentistry now, aren't you Doctor?"

"Yes. The Justice Department helped me to get my license back."

"The Justice department? Was it that man over there, Hugh Hindsmith, who helped you get your license back?" Carl pointed his right index finger at Hindsmith who was squirming in his chair.

"Yes. It was Mr. Hindsmith."

"No further questions of this witness, your honor."

Boring and Hindsmith were in whispered consultation. You could hear a loud buzz of voices around the courtroom. I turned to look at part of the audience. An older, grim-faced man was waving his fist towards the witness. It was the same, older, angry man who'd said that day months ago, before the meeting started, "We've had enough,"Several people were shaking their heads in disgust. Three women held tiny Confederate flags fastened to pencil thin poles in front of their faces. Their heads were bowed, their eyes closed, their lips moving in silent monologues.

Many of the spectators had obviously concluded that the trial was a mockery. A low, mournful sound from a hundred throats took a few seconds to register on Judge Johnson. He adjusted his unattractive store reading glasses and peered angrily around the room. He could not pin down the specific people who were doing the sad humming. It frustrated him, but fortunately, he waited and kept his anger under control. The sound died down. The judge seemed relieved to feel as though he was once again in control.

Carl whispered to me, "And now, our handsome and suave D.A. is going to play his trump card. He thinks. From a deck that's been mouldering for twenty years. Miss Layla Jenkins."

CHAPTER 30

Boring knew how to pump himself up. His air of authority and his pompous manner had returned. He fiddled with the knot of his expensive, red silk tie, craned his neck, pulled down his cuffs, took a deep breath and threw his right hand into the air. With his finger tip, he pointed to a beautiful, black woman in her thirties.

"Judge Johnson, in your chambers this morning before court reconvened, agreement was reached between both the prosecution and the defense for the calling of a 'surprise' witness. The prosecution now calls that 'surprise' witness, Miss Layla Jenkins, to the stand."

With majestic ease, the slim, shapely woman walked to the witness stand and was sworn in. Her blue silk dress with it's long, V neck was a page from *Vogue* magazine.

"State your name and address for the record please," Boring said.

"I'm Layla Jenkins, 1220 Desert Palm Road, Los Angeles, California."

Her voice was clear and musical. Julie, her pale face and clear blue eyes alight with curiosity, leaned over and whispered, "The woman is a consummate actress. She's been trained in theatrics somewhere."

Boring pointed at me. "Do you know the defendant, Stonewall Bedford?"

Jenkins lowered her eyes, dropped her head towards her chest and said, "This is painful for me, Mr. Boring. Yes, I do know the defendant."

"Why would your coming here to testify be painful, Miss Jenkins?"

She did not answer the question immediately. She seemed to be having trouble finding the right words. "Because of what Stonewall Bedford did to me twenty years ago, I've been in therapy for the last seven years. Therapy for sexually abused women. It was my only hope. I had to face up to what happened to me and seek counseling to chase away the terrors that haunted my mind."

Boring himself was no slouch as an actor. He waited for her words to sink in. "Twenty years ago? Let's see, you would have been how old at that time?"

"Only fifteen."

"You say the defendant did something to you? Would you please give us the details?"

Her face was wreathed with sadness. She used the twisted tissues she held in her left hand to wipe the corner of each of her eyes, being careful not to smear her mascara. She broke into sobs. "It's so difficult to find the words to tell the court. But, I'll try. My mother was a maid at the Bedford home. You know. Cleaning, scrubbing, cooking, making beds. I had gone with my mother to the Bedford home that day to help her. She hadn't been well and yet we needed the pitiful sums the Bedfords paid for such menial work."

She sobbed even louder and dabbed at her eyes again. The V neck of her blue silk dress showed enough of her quite large breasts to pique any man's curiosity.

"Please continue, Miss Jenkins." Boring's voice had softened and he had lowered his tone to fit the mood of the scenes being played out on the stage. He feigned great pain at Jenkins' words.

"Mr. Bedford came home about 10 o'clock in the morning, as he said, 'to drink coffee.' I became conscious that he was staring at me and using his tongue to moisten his lips. I couldn't help but sense what was happening. I mean, a girl knows when someone in the same room has sex on his mind. I was coming of age in those years. The hormones were flowing. I was keenly aware of such things. Mr. Bedford's mood became that of a tiger in heat looking for a mate."

She seemed to break up again and lose control of her voice and emotions. Her sobbing turned into loud bawling like a mother weeping at the wailing wall for a dead child. The judge shifted uneasily in his chair. The low murmuring arose again in the crowd. I noticed the three women with the tiny Confederate flags lowering their heads. closing their eyes and letting the flags hide their faces.

"You, your mother and Mr. Bedford were there in the kitchen. What happened?"

"He walked over and put his arms around me. 'Mighty pretty daughter you got here, Nashta.' Then he said to me, 'I bet you run all the boys crazy with this body of yours.' He . . . he . . . he put his hands on my breasts and started kissing me. Then, he dropped his hands to the cheeks of my ass and pulled me towards him. 'You got me worked up, Layla girl. I'm going to take you upstairs and really explore this body of yours.'

"No, Mr. Bedford, I pleaded. I'm just here helping my mother with her work. I've never done anything like that before. Please let me go."

The accompanying sobs came again. She could turn the fountain on seemingly at will. The sound effects emphasized her heart break. "When he heard that, he really got excited and started rubbing his, his, his penis. I could see it bulging in his pants. He said, 'I've been wanting to—she turned to the judge and said, 'Forgive the ugly words, your honor'—fuck you since you were twelve years old. A white man loves to fuck pretty young nigger girls."

Several in the crowd emitted audible gasps. Three black women sitting on the front row and dressed in long white gowns, closed their eyes, joined hands, began moaning and started swaying side to side.

Jenkins threw up her hands and turned her face away from the 'horror' of it all, like a frightened young maiden fleeing the 'terrors of the dark forest.'

"Your mother?" Boring asked. "What did she do?"

"Remember, this was twenty years ago and things were much different then. Older black women were scared of their 'white masters' like Mr. Bedford. Mama pleaded, 'No, Mr. Bedford. She's just a child. Please don't do this to my daughter. Do it to me instead.'

"He laughed at her suggestion like it was some big joke. 'Over the years, I've already had enough of you, Nashta. I want this fresh, young girl here. Maybe she hasn't even been broken in yet. Oh, boy. If she hasn't, that'll make it worth a hundred extra dollars for you, Nashta.' "

"He grabbed my hand and starred pulling me towards the stairs. 'C'mon, Layla. Let's go have a good time together. Oh, Nashta, here's $50 now. If she's really 'fresh meat', well, there'll be another fifty. Maybe even a hundred. She'll be worth it."

"I was scared of the man. A young Negro girl is seldom in a position to keep a white man from doing anything he wants to do to her. He pulled me upstairs, had me undress and take a shower, then get on the bed. He got naked and lay down beside me. At first, he just kissed me and played with my body and moaned. Then, he got on top of me and forced his big, hard penis into my, well, you know, my pussy. It hurt something terrible. I had never done it before and this excited him.

"The words he used were so ugly I'm ashamed to say them." She made a pretense at being shy and embarrassed. 'Oh, boy!. A maiden head. Fresh meat!' He yelled and hollered as he plunged deep into my body. He began having an orgasm. Pumped all his sperm into me. I was so scared, so full of shame until all I could do was lie there and cry."

" 'Do you like it, Layla?' he asked over and over as he humped and moaned and pinched my titties. 'I know you do, because all you nigger girls are running around with hot pussies. Fucking. You were born for it. Made for it. And why not? It's so good. It's so good.' "

"Was that the end of it, Miss Jenkins?" Boring asked.

"I wish it had been, Mr. Boring. But he got on top of me two more times in the next hour. Kept kissing me, hunching into me and asking me if I was 'coming.' Each time, he pumped his white man's sperm into me. Kept saying he wanted to give me a baby. Said that'd make him so proud. Finally, he was exhausted and let me get out of bed and put my clothes on. He made me wait in the room with him while he got dressed. Then, I walked downstairs with him where he told my mother how much he had enjoyed fucking me. He gave her another fifty dollars and told her to bring me back with her again next week and there'd be another hundred dollars. And fifty dollars for you, too, Layla."

"He didn't give your mother the extra hundred dollars he'd hinted at?"

"No, sir, Mr. Boring. But then, we knew he wouldn't."

"Where was his wife?" Boring asked. "I mean, when he was raping you?"

"Oh, Miss Donna Elaine was always up at the church trying to help poor white folks who were down on their luck. She hardly ever got home before three in the afternoon."

"Did you ever go back to Mr. Bedford's home again with your mother?"

"No, Mr. Boring. My mother and I moved away from Forest two days later. We were so frightened and so ashamed of what had happened. I did have his baby. Gave it to my grandmother to raise. What he did to me kept me from ever getting married. I just couldn't tell my future husband about what a white man had done to me."

She then related a long story of how she finally realized that therapy was necessary. Her psychiatrist had helped her to dig through her buried memories and recall June 20th, 1975 and honestly face what had happened with a mature perspective. He had even encouraged her to come forward and tell the story as a soul cleansing technique. "It's been a long, tough road, but thank the Lord, I'm making it. I'm making it." She lowered her head again for several seconds."

I looked at the twelve people in the jury box. Alice Rinker and two other women were crying. One was biting her quivering lips. Three of the men were shaking their heads, but there was no way I could discern the effect that Jenkins' story was having on them. I smiled to myself and wondered what they'd do when we exposed this woman's perjured testimony.

"The defense keeps telling us that Mr. Bedford is a kind and generous man of great moral rectitude," Boring said. "Could he really have raped an innocent girl like you? Isn't that difficult for most white Southerners to believe?"

"Oh, having sex with black women is just a part of growing up for white men in the South," Jenkins said. "It's sort of an initiation ritual. The white community sees nothing wrong with it. That's why Mr. Bedford's friends keep telling you that he's a Christian man with the highest character. To them, violating black women sexually is exciting. It's just having a little fun that they say hurts no one. It's almost the same thing when whites shoot black men. It's not anything to get excited about."

"No further questions, Judge Johnson," Boring said. "Your witness, counselor."

Carl's walking stick thumped the floor loudly with each step he took. "My name is Carl Krippendorf, Miss Jenkins. You certainly know how to make a dramatic scene unfold. You've studied for the theater, haven't you?"

Jenkins smiled. "Yes. In Hollywood they seem to think I'm a fine actress. I'm in my second year in the weekly network TV series, 'Going For Broke.' The show's ratings are quite high."

"I know that pleases you, Miss Jenkins." Carl was baiting her before he sprung the trap. "Refresh my mind now. What was the date that my client took you upstairs at his home and raped you?"

"June 20th, 1975. It was so terrible until the date is burned into my mind."

"Yes," Carl said. "To be deflowered as an innocent girl of fifteen by being raped is a terrible thing. It would scar a person forever. Can you tell me how you remembered the date and the time so precisely, after twenty long years?"

"I remember it each day, even up to this very minute sitting here in court" She sobbed for several seconds. "It's in my school girl's diary. It's just a thing anyone would remember."

"Yes, most any of us have a special memory of the dates for traumatic occurrences in our lives," Carl sympathized. "Life is so full of the small, hour-to-hour things we need to be doing each day until we soon forget what we had for lunch yesterday."

There was laughter in the courtroom.

"It's the same thing with men as successful in business as Mr. Bedford was. He has so many things happening in the course of his work each day, he keeps a desk calendar to record less consequential things. Such as 'See salesman Henry Jones at 2 p.m.'; 'pick up son after basketball practice at 6 p.m.' Do you keep a daily calendar of 'Things to Do' Miss Jenkins?"

"Of course, everyone does, Mr. Krippendorf. But, I don't see what all of this is leading up to." She looked at her watch. "I don't have all the time in the world. I've got to drive to Atlanta after I'm finished here and catch a plane back to the west coast."

"Yes, time is valuable to important people like you, Miss Jenkins. I'll try to hurry things up."

The radiance of the beautiful Miss Jenkins' face, so assured and pleased with herself a few minutes ago, was disappearing by the moment. The first signs of fear were showing up.

"June 20th, 1975," Carl repeated. "That's the date Mr. Bedford raped you and you're certain of that?"

"Yes." Jenkins was hesitant about elaborating further. The mounting fear creeping up inside of her was now reflected in her voice and on her face. She did not find it necessary to carefully choose her tone of voice. Her emotions were now choosing for her.

"Would you say that it's impossible for a person to be in two places at the same time, Miss Jenkins? Especially when those two places are separated by fifteen hundred miles?"

Jenkins did not answer.

Carl turned to the table where we were sitting. "Mr. Xerxes, would you hand me that file folder on the desk in front of you? I walk so slowly, you know."

"Certainly, Carl."

"No, I've changed my mind," Carl said. "Would you please bring me that entire box labeled 'Tax Records, 1975' and stand here and hold it for me."

Xerxes stood up, lifted the box and walked slowly towards the witness stand. He propped the bottom of the box on the railing and held it so that Carl could conveniently reach any of the items.

"Miss Jenkins," Carl said. "In this box, we have all of Mr. Bedford's income tax records for 1975. These records attest to the fact that Mr. Bedford is a careful and methodical man. Believe me, when it comes to the Internal Revenue Service, you can't be too careful in making certain you have every scrap of paper necessary to substantiate your income tax returns. Any business man will tell you that including your daily desk diary—as well as his wife's daily social calendar—as part of those income tax records is very wise."

Jenkins was no longer acting, Her shapely legs were now tensed so she could spring for the door and escape from this place as soon as she could. Even her knees were leaned towards the exit doors. Her hands gripped the arms of the witness chair. Panic and pain contorted her beautiful face. Every fiber in her body was telling her to flee to avoid the fire that Carl was heaping upon her.

"Ah, here it is," Carl said. "The diary where each of his 'Things to Do' are recorded for each day of the year. Oh, it's not as intimate as your school girl's diary, and certainly not as refreshing. June 20th, 'that terrible date burned into my mind' is how you described the day Stonewall Bedford raped you in the upstairs bedroom of his big house."

Carl thumbed through the pages. He was in no particular hurry. "April 15th, 1975. Let's see. Bedford wrote on this page, 'Mail U.S. Income Tax Return.' Did you mail your income tax return on that date, Miss Jenkins? Oh, I'm sorry. You were only fifteen at the time and not quite ready to begin paying income taxes. 'June 1st. Pick up airline tickets for Salt Lake City.' Wonder if his diary reveals when he's flying to Utah? Wonder who's going with him? 'June 5th. Have secretary phone for hotel and motel reservations June 9th through June 28th. Two rooms. One for wife and self; one for William.' "

Jenkins' eyes were darting glances towards the table where the prosecuting attorney and the justice department lawyers were sitting. She desperately needed help. The step by step building so carefully constructed for her testimony was crumbling, imploding, and she was still trapped inside it. She would be crushed to death.

"Look here, Miss Jenkins." Carl held the open diary in front of her face. On each page of this diary, from June 9th through June 29th is written, 'On vacation out West. Salt Lake City, Sun Valley, Crater of the Moon, Jackson Hole, Wyoming, the Grand Tetons, Yellowstone National Park,

Yellowstone Lodge, Old Faithful, Montana, Custer's battlefield, the Oregon Trail. And on June 29th, fly home to Atlanta. Drive to Forest.'

"Here are the pages for those same dates of Donna Elaine Bedford's calendar. Look, she has the same notations on the dates June 9th through June 29th."

The spectators were on the edge of their seats, leaning forward, hanging on Carl's every word. Judge Johnson peered over the edge of his tiny reading glasses, a displeased look on his pudgy face. Boring's head was leaning on his hands. His eyes looked down at the notes in front of him. Hugh Hindsmith wore a pinched expression on his face.

"Oh, he didn't go on that trip," Jenkins said. "He changed his mind. Canceled his plans. You're using these phony entries to try and cover up what he did."

"Let's see. If the defendant raped you in Forest on June 20th, how could the three of them, Bedford, his wife, and his son, have been spending four days at Yellowstone Lodge in Yellowstone National Park on the very day he was supposedly raping you and saying those ugly things to you? I won't repeat them, for most of the people in this room are still genteel and high principled. They don't use words such as those you say Mr. Bedford used when raping you. Oh, I'm sorry. When he was supposedly raping you."

I could tell that Carl was immensely enjoying the destruction of the witness' composure and credibility. To tell you the truth, so was I.

Carl held up copies of the paid bills for the stay at Yellowstone lodge. "Here is confirmation of their stay at the lodge. June 18th, 19th, 20th and 21st. Here's the receipt for the payment for their rooms. There are also receipts in this box from each of the hotels and motels at which they stayed during their three week vacation out west. And here are the airline ticket stubs for the flight to Salt Lake on June 9th, 1975, and the return flight from Salt Lake to Atlanta on June 29th."

He pointed to each document that confirmed his words. "Miss Jenkins. Stonewall Bedford could not possibly have raped you on June 20th in Forest, Georgia. He was fifteen hundred miles away. Who paid you to come here with this atrocious lie about the defendant? Is that person here in this room?"

"I don't care what you say," Jenkins said. Her crying now was not theatrical. "I know what he did and when. And he did it! Ruined my life. Forever. Black women don't have a chance in this white man's world."

She jumped to her feet and lunged away from the witness stand.

"Just a minute, please," Carl said. "I'm not finished yet. Please return to the witness stand."

Jenkins returned reluctantly to the witness stand. She was bawling now in a sad, hoarse voice.

Carl waited until she grew quiet. "Tell us, Miss Jenkins. Is the $15,000 you were paid to come here and tell these lies worth the years you will spend in prison for perjured testimony?"

Boring was on his feet protesting. "Objection, your honor. Objection. Counsel for the defense is trying to intimidate the witness through frightening her. None of us know about the alleged $15,000 payment. Nor do we know if this distraught young woman has perjured herself. And certainly, we have no way of discerning, at this moment, if the documents shown us by Mr. Krippendorf were put together in the last twenty-four hours or—if they were really from records that had been stored for twenty years. That's stretching the imagination."

"Objection sustained," the judge ruled. He turned to Carl. "Counsel for the defense must abandon this line of questioning."

"Your honor," Carl said to the judge. "We'd like to enter these records as evidence. I have no further questions for this witness."

Applause broke out. Some people were waving their arms in jubilation. The judge patiently let the relief that some of the spectators felt vent itself. After a while, he pounded his gavel.

"I have warned all parties that I intend to deal severely with perjured testimony," he said. "A witness takes an oath to tell the truth when they place their hand on the Bible. It seems obvious that not all witnesses have told the truth."

He was an angry owl peering unblinking over his store-bought glasses. A hush fell over the court room again.

I looked at several of the faces in the crowd. In some of them I thought I detected new hope building for a favorable verdict in our case, but then, I looked at Alice Rinker's face and my heart sunk. The cold, dispassionate anger had returned.

Boring rose up from his chair and said simply, "The prosecution rests."

CHAPTER 31

Xerxes was a commanding figure as he walked towards the jury box. "Ladies and gentlemen of the jury," he said, his voice rich and resonant. "I remind you once again that the defendant in this case, Stonewall Bedford, should not be here on trial. He should never have been indicted by the grand jury. There was not even probable cause for doing so. This case is a political case, pure and simple, a case pressured onto this county and this court by blacks and the United States Justice department in the name of political correctness. First degree murder?" Xerxes sniffed with great disdain. "Stonewall Bedford was doing what any red-blooded American worthy of his salt would have done. Defending his home and his family from attacking killers."

The dapper attorney paused and slowly scanned the people in the jury box, the Judge, the prosecution and the audience. His body was coiled and tense, ready for the charge up Cemetery Ridge at Gettysburg with the rest of us Southerners who still remembered honor and nobility.

"The defense calls its first witness, the honorable Craig Weynel, dean of the University of Georgia Law School in Athens, Georgia."

A small, round faced man entered the courtroom and walked to the witness stand with courtly dignity. He was sworn in.

"Dean Weynel," Xerxes began. "Would you give us your learned opinion of this case, perhaps comment on its validity as a matter for the courts?"

Weynel laughed. "Case? What case? There's no case here that is valid. What is occurring here is a travesty, a political case, as you have pointed out in the press. Certainly, it is disguised as a valid case, dressed in the legal paraphernalia of a trial and conducted seemingly within the legal framework of the law. But any legal analyst would quickly point out that the law's framework as we are seeing here has been bent and distorted to accommodate current fads of political correctness. It's shape is Kafkaesque, to say the least."

Craig Weynel talked with the surety of a man in his lofty position, a man esteemed nationwide for his study of justice and the law. Three million copies of his books were in print. Several times a year, articles under his byline appeared in the most authoritative and esteemed law journals.

Weynel was plainly disturbed. "How can you indict a man for defending his home against savage attacks by killers? Why, a man's right to protect his person and property is one of the cornerstones of our system of jurisprudence.

"And first degree murder?" Weynel burst out laughing. "How could citizen members of a grand jury be pressured into an ignoble indictment such as this. Bedford did not know the people who were coming to kill him He had not chosen certain people to shoot and kill before he turned his weapons on others in the assault party. He did not go in search of two specific people named Canton and Derkin in order to kill them. In first degree murder, the plan to commit such a crime must be hatched against a specific person or persons and harbored for hours, days, week, months or years before the act is committed. That is not the case in this trial."

The noted scholar and law school dean stopped, leaned back in the witness chair and smiled a challenge to anyone who deigned to try and pry a hole in his statements. "What a coincidence that Canton and Derkin supposedly showed up just fifteen minutes before Karim and his crew, with signs to begin picketing. Or so we are told. In the dead of night? Who would believe such a fairy tale?"

The stillness in the room was not disturbed by so much as a rustle of papers or a whisper of voices. "Americans expect more out of their courts of law than what they are seeing here," Weynel said. "This is a farce. I know the judge in this case. And the prosecuting attorney. What is transpiring in this courtroom will assuredly become a matter that weighs on their consciences in the days to come. And a matter that will be trumpeted abroad in the media as the transpiring of an Orwellian nightmare."

"Thank you Dean Weynel," Xerxes said. "Your witness, Mr. Prosecutor."

Tighe Boring seemed his usual, jaunty self as he walked forward. "Dean Weynel," he said. "It's good to see you again."

"Forget the insincere courtesies Boring and ask your questions," Weynel snapped.

Boring was taken aback. He didn't quite know how to react. "Dean Weynel, millions would see this case as tinged with blatant racism. Don't you think that blacks have the right to be deeply offended by the flying of that symbol of slavery, the Confederate flag?"

"No, Boring. I do not. And you are quite wrong in calling the Confederate flag a symbol of racism. That is a liberal cliche. The flag most assuredly is not such a symbol. Black people did not develop that attitude of their own volition. They were taught that about the Confederate flag to serve the political purposes of their opportunistic leaders."

Weynel's impatience with Boring was plainly evident. He was the professor in a law school class lecturing to students who would be held accountable for hearing and remembering the points he was making.

A sly smile prefaced his next remarks. "How does the song from 'South Pacific' go? 'You've got to be taught to hate, before you are six or seven or eight, you've got to be taught to hate . . . ' And if our intellectually inferior leaders who teach hatred of whites to minorities for their own political gain continue such insanity, a genocidal maelstrom of fire will be turned loose in our country."

He slowed his torrent of words, removed his glasses and wiped his eyes. "It will be a tragedy of such magnitude as is unimaginable. Once the fire is turned loose, it will be a fire that will never be contained, a fire that will consume all of us. That's what has happened in Somalia, Burundi and Croatia. Citizens killing other citizens because they are different in beliefs, values and ideals. Nobody wins such a war; everybody loses. And happily, if a happy note can be found in such tragedies, the leaders who foment such a war are usually decapitated by those whom they've taught to hate and the same people they led into battle. Their heads are displayed on stakes and their bodies burned on the pyre."

The D.A. was quiet; the judge was silent; the spectators in the courtroom were transfixed by Dean Weynel's words.

"Boring, as the District Attorney, you should know that this case is not about the flying of the Confederate flag. That's a red herring to throw the average citizen off track and hide the deeper meanings of what this is all about. It also gives the vultures of the media a helpless carcass around which to circle and to call each other to the feasting. This case is about politics and pressure groups; about the central government moving with power and ferocity against a man of principle like Stonewall Bedford; it's about those in power coming up with a human sacrifice to toss to the howling mobs to temporarily assuage the boiling hatred of blacks for white people."

Weynel's small round face showed his love for puncturing the balloons of the pompous. "But then, Boring, I wouldn't expect a nincompoop like you to know the difference. You should never have been graduated from the University law school and turned loose to prey on the public under the pretext of possessing legal skills."

The prosecutor's face had turned beet red. "No further questions, your honor." He hurried back to his seat at the prosecutor's table and collapsed like a deflated balloon.

The law school dean rose from the witness chair, slowly, and deliberately straightened his tie and coat, then ambled towards the court room door, nodding and smiling at people as he walked. I wanted to stand up and cheer. I found it difficult not to burst out laughing at the dejected Boring who had been cut to pieces by an intellectually superior mind.

Xerxes did not want to diminish the effect of Dean Weynel's words. To kill precious time, he pretended to be consulting notes on a sheet of paper. After a while, he looked up and said: "The defense calls Gary Wilhelm, president of the Chamber of Commerce."

Wilhelm was relaxed and easy going. "Thank you, Mr. Xerxes, for the opportunity to testify on Mr. Bedford's behalf."

"You're quite welcome, Mr. Wilhelm. You haven't always felt that way about the defendant have you?"

"No, I haven't" Wilhelm answered. "The first day he made those bold statements about the flying of the Confederate flag, I was terribly upset. You see, at the university, the professors taught us what they called a more sophisticated view of The War Between the States. Naturally, I was caught up in such nonsense. This entire episode has been a bitter learning experience for me."

"Could you explain part of the reason you have changed your opinions about this controversy?" Xerxes asked. "How you came to the conclusion that Stonewall Bedford was not a man lost in the 1860's?"

"As the conflict flamed higher," Wilhelm said. "I called a meeting in the Chamber offices to see what community leaders might do to resolve the conflict. That's when I changed my mind about Stonewall Bedford. I've since found him to be one of the fairest, most objective men I know."

"Why is that, Mr. Wilhelm?"

"In the meeting that day," Wilhelm said. "He and Carl Krippendorf were the only two people who made any sense. Abdul Karim, Delong Tolman, State Senator Willie Sanders—all they did that day was to rant and rave and yell 'racism.' Karim and Tolman actually started yelling 'Pull down that Confederate flag,' and 'It's a symbol of racism.' To the Senator's credit, he was far less volatile. But none of the three offered any constructive solutions to the problem, nor did they seem to want to understand and compromise."

"Tell us what Stonewall Bedford did that day," Xerxes prodded.

"He very calmly defended his Southern upbringing and outlined very sensible reasons as to why the flag should be flown. Then he showed us pledges totaling $100,000 from twenty prominent Forest business men to be used to build a monument to Dr. Martin Luther King on city hall lawn near the monument to General Lee. Not only that, he offered to chair the committee to raise the remaining funds needed."

Xerxes whistled in amazement. "The defendant offered to do that?"

"He certainly did. I was so impressed with Bedford's plan until I pledged $50,000 for the project on behalf of the Chamber of Commerce."

"And what were the reactions of Karim, Tolman and Sanders?" Xerxes asked.

"They railed against the idea and became even more angry. It became clear to me that they had a hidden agenda; that they were not interested in a compromise. All they seemed bent on doing was fomenting racial turmoil in the minority communities."

"Your witness, counselor." Xerxes bowed to Boring in courtly manner.

Boring ran his fingers around the inside of his shirt. The right side of his mouth curled down enough to show his discomfort.

"Mr. Wilhelm, isn't Stonewall Bedford one of the biggest financial contributors to the Chamber of Commerce?"

Wilhelm smiled. "He is quite generous. Yes."

"Could that have anything to do with your, shall we say, dramatic change of heart about this Confederate flag business?"

"No, of course not, Mr. Boring. Stoney Bedford is not a petty individual. He can differ with you without resorting to anger and concretized thinking. He'd continue his chamber membership regardless of what I thought. He's that kind of a person, what we call 'a big man.' He doesn't hate you when you differ with him, nor does he carry grudges against people around on his sleeve."

His level, even tone of voice never changed. "I thought his plan to resolve the conflict over the flying of the flag showed his true stature. It would have brought favorable publicity for our city of Forest all over the United States."

"No further questions, your honor." Boring had evidently concluded that Wilhelm was an effective witness for the defense and had decided to back off.

Xerxes called Nelson Withaus, wealthy real estate developer and gun collector as a witness. "Thank you for coming here today, Mr. Withaus. We need your expert views on gun collections."

"Glad to be here, Counselor."

"You are renowned as a gun collector and an expert on firearms of all types. Tell us about this hobby, Mr. Withaus."

Withaus was beaming. "I have almost two hundred guns of all kinds in five rooms of my hilltop home outside of Forest. My father gave me my first gun, a 20 gauge shotgun, when I was thirteen, but he was very careful to teach me how to use it safely. I fell in love with hunting and guns. I've hunted in many locales and for many different kinds of animals. Grizzlies in Alaska; lions, tigers and elephants in Africa; big horn sheep in the Rocky mountains. You name it. I've hunted it and killed it. And enjoyed every minute of it."

"Mr. Withaus, do you know Mr. Bedford?"

"Yes sir. Quite well. We've hunted ducks and geese together in the coastal marshes of south Louisiana. Boy, those Cajun guides can cook. We ate together, drank lots of good whiskey together and laughed together. Never met a finer man than Bedford."

Xerxes was an actor. He went into his perplexed routine. Scratching the back of his head. Arching his eyebrows. Letting a quizzical look settle onto his face. "The D.A. and several witnesses in this trial have imputed a killer mentality to Stonewall Bedford because he likes guns and hunting. Do you have a killer mentality, Mr. Withaus?"

"Hell no, Counselor. As United States citizens, we have a right under our constitution to keep and bear arms. And it's a precious right. The news media and the misinformed, bleeding heart liberals in the United States are trying to take away this right from us, but thanks to millions of aroused citizens and the National Rifle Association, they're finding the going rough. But, they keep hacking away at it. And we've got a silly, grinning president who has thrown in with the gun haters. For political reasons, I'd say. Who knows what the future holds?"

Withaus drew himself up to full height, squared his shoulders, and jutted his jaw out in defiance. "Killer mentality? That's a big laugh. Bedford doesn't have one, nor do I. I tell you what we'll do though, if you come after us to kill us. We'll blow your damned head off without any sign of remorse. Those fanatics that attacked Bedford's home? They are the ones with the 'killer mentality.' "

Nelson Withaus was not reluctant to state his views. "The 'Merciful Ayatollah'," he snorted. "I've heard him say on TV that the blacks are at war with whites and that he's training his own troops. When they attack us, what the hell are we supposed to do? Stand there like dummies and let them mow us down? To hell with that noise. You come after me with guns and it's either you or me, friend. And I hope it's you, because I don't want to shuck off this mortal coil just yet."

Many spectators in the audience were enjoying Withaus' performance, his good common sense, his forthrightness. "Bedford killed seven of the bastards who stormed his home that night, and I applaud him. I wish I'd have been there to fight alongside him. Sadly, the attackers busted in and killed his wife and son and that's a terrible thing. It was the work of mad dogs. Yet I don't hear this court even talking about Bedford's great losses, nor his rights in this matter. What's this country coming to?"

"I need to ask you a serious question, Mr. Withaus. Some witnesses have characterized Bedford as suffering from delusions of grandeur, as imagining that he's a Confederate general at Gettysburg. Would you agree with their conclusions?"

I thought Withaus would double over with laughter. Finally, still chuckling, he said, "Hell, what true Southerner has not mourned the South's fate? I wish I had been there at Gettysburg to fight alongside our boys. If we'd won there, the war would have been over and the South would have triumphed. If only we could have taken and held the high ground that day. If only . . ."

"I've heard Mr. Bedford use those very same words, Mr. Withaus. Do they mean that the two of you are both slightly, as I've heard it said, 'off your rocker'? I believe the popular jargon of the day is 'he's not playing with a full deck.' "

"Listen friend," Withaus said. "I'm an unreconstructed rebel and proud of it. That Confederate flag is not going to be taken down. All I have to do is send out the call and there'll be ten thousand of us with guns streaming into Forest from every part of the nation, forming circles of defense around General Lee's monument and our flag.

"If you'll observe the crowd outside this courroom, you'll see that some of our troops are already here. And thousands more are ready. All that's necessary is for the call to go out.

"There are many thousands of us who still walk proudly as Southerners, who remember the sacrifices of the boys in gray during the Civil War, who are proud of what our forebears bequeathed us. And, we're not going to let you or any other bunch of raving fanatics make us feel guilty about being a Southerner."

"Do people in other parts of the country feel the same way?" Xerxes asked.

"Millions of them, Counselor. Southern nobility, honor and courage are admired around the world." Withaus stroked his chin. "Another strange thing is happening as a result of this farce here you call a trial. The persecution of Bedford is reinforcing the beliefs of other thousands of our citizens that people are no longer free in the United States; that the government has gone too far; that citizens need to form in militia groups for self preservation."

"No further questions, your honor. Your witness, Mr. Boring."

"I have no questions for Mr. Withaus," Boring said.

"Judge Johnson," Xerxes said. "May Mr. Krippendorf, myself and the prosecutor approach the bench?"

"Concerning what?" the judge asked.

"About your decision as to whether or not to permit the jurors to view Morris Light's video of the actual attack on the Bedford home on the night of March 14th to the jury."

"There are grave questions concerning this film footage," Judge Johnson said. "I have viewed it myself. Several times. I want to see the three of you in my chambers immediately to discuss and decide on the matter. I declare a recess in this case until one o'clock this afternoon."

He banged his gavel, rose from his chair and left through the door immediately behind him. The others followed.

CHAPTER 32

Well over an hour passed before Xerxes and Krippendorf rejoined Julie Peel and me in the small room upstairs in the courthouse. It was where we could hide and escape the pressure briefly—and pick at the food we'd had sent in for lunch. The two attorneys were elated. Their faces were brighter, their steps livelier, their voices assured.

"It was a knock-down, drag-out fight," Carl said, "but Johnson has agreed that the jury can see Morris Light's video of the actual attack. I feel like dancing—if I could move fast enough. Johnson's ruling will help our case enormously." He smiled, one of the few times he had smiled during the trial. Winning, for Carl Krippendorf, was an all consuming desire, and now winning our case seemed a possibility.

"Boring waged all-out war against letting the jury see the video," Xerxes said. "Frankly, the judge wavered and almost decided against it, but the arguments we presented in favor of allowing it to be shown were more persuasive than Boring's." He tugged at his French cuffs until they were protruding at least an inch below the sleeve of his dark blue pin stripe suit. The ruby cuff links were dazzling.

"And we learned a lot in the judge's chambers," Carl said. "Boring's arguments against showing the video revealed what tactics he'll be using in the courtroom to discredit the film. But, the jurors may not be as easily convinced as was the judge. We've got our work cut out for us."

"They're carting a big screen into the courtroom in order for the jurors to see the video of the attack film," Xerxes said. "We'll call Morris Light as our first witness when court reconvenes. He'll introduce the video and narrate it."

"Stoney," Carl turned to me, the smile missing from his face. "Seeing the film might be too traumatic for you. It will bring back many powerful memories. What do you think?"

"Oh, no," I said quickly. "I was there that night when they mounted the actual attack. The rerun can't be too much worse. Of course, I'll shed some more tears."

"Me, too," Julie said. "It seems that crying is mostly what I've been doing these last few months. It will be good to see William again, alive, as

357

he was when the scenes were filmed, if only for a few brief moments. Oh, how I loved him. Tomorrow would have been our wedding day." The beautiful, willowy woman was crying as she talked.

My mouth fell open. I had completely forgotten that July 12th would have been their big day. And Donna Elaine's and mine. We'd planned an afternoon wedding in the garden at Bedford House. Now the roses grew there to blush sight unseen in the Southern air. I'd make certain Julie had a long-stemmed yellow rose to hold in her hands tomorrow. As William would have done.

Once Morris Light was sworn in as a witness and seated, Xerxes asked him to explain how and why the attack had been filmed. He told of our meeting back in February in the liquor store and how he persuaded me to go along with the idea for a documentary of our lives, the events and our actions during the times surrounding the flag controversy.

"Tell us about your experience in this field with PBS, Mr. Light," Xerxes prompted him.

"Making documentaries for PBS has consumed most of my waking moments for the last fourteen years. It's a long, tedious process and I had served my apprenticeship with one of the other major television networks for four years prior to becoming affiliated with PBS."

"Were your documentaries realistic? Were they worth the public's time to watch them?" Xerxes asked.

Light seemed surprised by the question. "Yes, Mr. Xerxes, my eight documentaries were highly commended. They won thirteen major awards in the United States and throughout the world."

"Would you explain to the court and the jury how the footage they will see was made?"

"Mr. Bedford had told me several hours ahead of time when the attack would come," Light answered. "He insisted that my assistant and I not be present. 'I don't want your deaths on my conscience,' he repeated in answer to my arguments to be allowed to stay in the thick of the fight. I told him I had been with the guerillas as they fought the Russians in Kazachstan, but he wouldn't listen."

"Then how did you arrange to film the attack?" Xerxes asked.

"My assistant and I are old hands at rigging cameras in every conceivable position and from many angles," Light answered. "We hung automatic cameras throughout Bedford's home, in the trees out front and in the back of his home, and on light poles at each end of the block and across the street from the residence. Then, without his neighbors knowing it, I hid behind his fence across the street from the house with a camera. My assistant took a camera and hid behind the backyard fence of one of the neighbors whose property adjoined Mr. Bedford's."

"How did you take all of this footage of the actual attack and put it together?" Xerxes asked. "I mean. All those different cameras and that much footage?"

"Any film maker worth his salt knows how to view hour after hour of film, select the footage that best tells the story clearly from beginning to end, then cut and splice the footage together. All of my hidden cameras took enough film that night to last two hours. I chose the segments that showed the Bedfords inside their home fighting off the attackers; then I spliced in the footage of the actual attack. It shows the twelve men as they arrived at the Bedford house in their three automobiles, got out of the cars with their automatic weapons and began firing at the Bedford house. You can see the men running to assault the Bedfords from the front and break in from the back of the Bedford home. It's quite a story. It's as dramatic and exciting as any battle I've ever filmed."

"Are there some bad scenes in the footage?" Xerxes asked. "Sad shots of people dying?"

"Objection, your honor," Boring shouted. "The jurors can decide these things when they see the film. If they can believe it when they see it."

"Objection sustained," the judge ruled.

"Could an expert be successful in discrediting your video as, well, as a fake?" Xerxes asked.

"The footage in the video is certainly not a fake," Light bristled. "It's as real as," he looked around the courtroom, "as real as that fly crawling across the judge's hands."

Johnson moved his hand quickly as laughter rippled through the courtroom.

"But could it be successfully attacked as something a clever man such as yourself could, let us say, manufacture? A production that could be lifted from movie film stored in archives and spliced into your footage?" Xerxes questions struck at the heart of what we all knew would be the prosecution's line of attack.

"With such exciting footage as that which we shot on the night of March 14th, footage that shows men with blazing guns firing on the Bedford home and charging from both the front and back; scenes of Bedford, his son and his wife inside the house firing back and fighting to stay alive; Karim and two of his henchmen smashing into the upstairs from the roof of the first floor in back; people falling dead from the withering gunfire, their bodies sprawled in grotesque fashion—why on earth would I want film from some long-ago movie or documentary stored in some archive? Nothing in those stored canisters in Hollywood can equal the drama of that night. And we have the film of every phase of it, film featuring people that many of us knew intimately."

Xerxes turned to Judge Johnson. "Do we have the court's permission for Mr. Light to walk to the evidence table, get the film and insert it in the VCR?"

"Permission granted," Johnson said. "Bailiff, when Mr. Light gives you the signal, please dim the overhead lights."

"I neglected to tell Mr. Xerxes that you will hear the actual sounds of gunfire and the voices, shouts and screams of the people who are the major players in this documentary," Light said as he inserted the video into the VCR. He signaled the Bailiff. The lights were dimmed.

The video's opening scenes showed William, Donna Elaine and me in our positions upstairs in front of the dormer windows. In the dim light of the hallway, you could sense the tension in the positions of our bodies, the quickness of our movements. We talked in quick phrases.

From some deeply buried well of fear, I head the furies warning me. *"Something evil this way comes!"* A cold shiver ran down my spine.

On each frame, the date and time were plainly visible March 14th, 1:55:00 a.m. Second by second, the time kept changing. 1:55:29 a.m. 1:55:30 a.m. 1:55:31 a.m. The rifles, pistols, shotgun and ammunition stacked around our shields were plainly visible. William and I, when we saw the large, black cars coming, put down our night vision binoculars and picked up our AK 47's. We sighted through the star light scopes.

"This is it!" William said, a ring of finality in his voice.

"Here they come." I announced quietly. "If they get out of their cars with weapons, let's fire first. Honey," I said to my wife, "dial 911."

The dim light inside the house made it difficult to tell who we were on the film. Donna Elaine, in pants and jacket, was the shortest; William easily the tallest. I noticed how long my son's arms were and that my hands shook visibly. The difference in our voices was easily recognizable.

The three big cars moved slowly down the street, their headlights off. They stopped in front of the house. The two right side doors on each vehicle opened and four tall men emerged from the automobiles with their AK 47's at the ready. They said nothing. Their figures were shadowy; their faces indistinguishable.

Sitting there in the darkened courtroom, I could feel my pulse starting to race. I reached for Julie Peel's hand and squeezed it. The tightness in my chest closed on me like a vice.

"Shoot them through the head," William said. On the large screen onto which the pictures were projected, you could see the ease with which he moved.

"Yes, they won't be expecting that," I said. "They think we're sleeping. If we work quickly, we can take out four of them before they can react."

The film showed several seconds passing. "Let's do it," I said

The men William and I shot through the head dropped like clay figures in a shooting gallery. Several of the attackers started running up the driveway. The night came alive with the red streaks from the attackers' guns and our return fire from the upstairs windows.

The film cut back to me. I grabbed my Glock automatic with its laser sight and started firing at the legs of the men who ran across our front lawn. William's Glock spurted towards the running figures. Two of them fell onto the grass and writhed in pain. Their shadowy figures were plainly visible on the front lawn.

Some of the killers began firing AK 47's from the protective covering of the other side of the parked automobiles. The red streaks were a deadly, beautiful curtain in the moonless night.

William left his station in the far dormer window and ran to his steel shield in the upstairs bedroom that faced the back lawn down the gentle slope towards the lake. The bullets were ripping through the walls of the house and spattering against the steel of my shield

"They've broken in downstairs, Dad," William yelled. The camera showed him running to the top of the stairs, firing his Glock. Then, he grabbing his shotgun and squatted behind the shield. You could hear and see the glass shattering in the French doors off the patio. William fired the shotgun twice. The sound was deafening.

"Come on, you sons-of-bitches," William yelled. "We'll give you more than you bargained for."

The screams of pain stirred murmurs in the courtroom. Julie Peel was crying and yelling, "No. No. No."

The cameras showed the men propping a ladder against the back walls that led to the top of the roof just beneath the windows of the upstairs bedroom. Once they gained access to the roof, they used the butts of their AK 47's to shatter the window glass. I turned and started running towards the sound of the breaking glass. My Glock automatic was spraying the room.

I heard the death screams of William. As I turned towards my son's screams, I shot Karim at close range. I ran to the stairs. William was dead, sprawled along the stairs like a broken toy.

At the defense's table where we sat, Julie Peel jerked her hand from mine and began to yell, "I can't watch it anymore. William. My William. Now, we'll never be married. Tomorrow was to be our wedding day."

In the video, I screamed, "Donna Elaine, Donna Elaine, Donna Elaine." I screamed in rage and agony and disappeared into the closet where I could be seen finding her dead body.

The outside cameras plainly showed the surviving members of Karim's attack force picking up the wounded and dumping them into the back seats of the three automobiles. Then they dragged two of the dead men across the grass and deposited them on the sidewalk. They made certain that no weapons remained behind. The big, black automobiles sped away.

On the monitor's screen, police cars with their flashing lights screamed down the street. Uniformed officers jumped from their cars and ran to my house. The next scenes inside our home were brighter. By then, Morris Light and his assistant had run back to our house and were using cameras with lights to continue their filming. Some of my neighbors had joined the police inside the house. There were pictures of the dead. William, Karim, and two of Karim's henchmen. I was holding my wife's body in my arms and rocking and crying for help. Finally, they were able to pry my arms loose and take Donna Elaine away.

The last few seconds of the video showed me in a wheel chair at the cemetery on the day of the funerals of my wife and my son. The thin, fragile Julie Peel, dressed in black with a veil over her face, pushed me to the graves of my son and my wife. You could hear the minister intone the words, "From dust to dust . . . "

The green carpet of grass did not cover all the clods of red clay dug from the ground to hollow out the graves. The silver of the tubular metal frame on which their coffins sat on the broad, black straps gleamed in the bright sun. I touched their caskets in final, reluctant, parting embrace. The camera zoomed in for a close up of my pale, white face. Streams of tears trickled down both my cheeks. The video ended.

"Bailiff," Light said, "you may turn the lights back on."

Julie Peel was sobbing quite loudly, her head resting on her folded arms. I glanced at the spectators. Many of them were also crying.

The judge's head seemed to have moved closer to the surface of the polished, level space in front of him. I could see his eyes quite plainly above the small eye pieces of his cheap glasses His gavel rested on its side, cradled in its holder.

Boring had his handsome face propped on his doubled up fists. His elbows rested on the table as he stayed motionless. He stared straight ahead. At the table five feet behind Boring, Hindsmith and his Justice department cronies sat unmoving, their faces as blank as newly cleaned school room blackboards.

Morris Light was still seated in the chair on the witness stand. His face seemed to reflect the satisfaction he must have felt about the video of the attack. He had spliced together a powerful drama from the several hundred feet of film taken by the hidden cameras.

After a long period of silence, Xerxes rose slowly and walked to the witness stand. "I don't know what to say, Mr. Light, after viewing your video of the attack by Karim and his crew on Mr. Bedford's home."

"There's little to say," Light answered. "The film speaks for itself."

The dapper Greek took in a deep breath and exhaled slowly "Forgive me, Mr. Light. I'm so tensed up after viewing the film until my thought processes are not running as freely as they usually do."

"What about me?" Light asked. "I had to view it hour after hour as I was editing it. The Bedfords had come to be dear friends over the weeks since that first day at council meeting when Karim and Tolman demanded the removal of the flag."

"Yes," Xerxes said. "I can certainly understand your feelings."

"Objection, your Honor," Boring said as he stood up. "This love feast between the witness and the defense attorney is sickening. Would you please instruct Xerxes to move forward in his questioning or excuse the witness?"

Johnson was angry. He rapped his gavel five times. "Objection overruled. I cannot understand how even you, though you are the prosecuting attorney, could fail to be moved by what we've all just seen. This is my third time to see it and it still leaves me depressed. You do yourself little credit with such actions." He turned back to Xerxes. "You may continue, sir."

"Thank you, Judge Johnson. Mr. Light, does your film prove that there were no dead men on the sidewalk when Karim and his fellow attackers stopped in front of the Bedford home?"

"Yes, it does."

"You were across the street with your hand-held video camera filming before, during and after the attack. Did you see a lone car drive up and stop in front of Bedford's home at approximately 1:45 a.m.? We have testimony that a car was there at that time and that two men got out of that car and stood on the sidewalk?"

"No. No car came. I read in the newspaper where DeLong Tolman said that he and Norris Cape brought those two men to Bedford's house at least fifteen minutes before Karim and the others came and that Stonewall Bedford killed them. That is a bald-faced lie. Tolman perjured himself."

"Boring jumped to his feet. "Objection your honor. I ask that last statement of this witness be stricken from the record. The witness is not within the bounds of legal propriety in making such a judgment."

"Objection sustained," Johnson ruled. "The witness is instructed to leave such judgments to the court."

"I thought the date and time on the footage lent greater authenticity," Xerxes said. "Were your cameras equipped to do that at the time the film was being taken or did you add it later in the film laboratory?"

"On scenes where time is an important consideration, my cameras are programmed to automatically add the date and time to the film."

"Why wasn't there more light so the figures could more easily be recognized?" Xerxes asked.

"It was a dark and moonless night. But surely the setting, the street, the house, the people inside let the viewer know what is happening and who the people involved are."

"The pictures of the bodies of Karim and the others," Xerxes said. "There's little doubt as to who they are."

"Yes. My assistant and I had the lights inside the house as well as those on our cameras to make the actions and people in the last sequences more visible."

"No further questions," Xerxes said. He walked back to the table where we were and sat down. "Your witness, counselor."

Boring took over. He was smiling and assured.

"Let's see, Mr. Light," he said. "I've made a few notes here as you've testified and as the video was being shown. You are a skilled technician. You've put together a great piece of work. Let's see. You said that you had to work hour after hour in your viewing and cutting room selecting the events to be spliced together to make the story come alive. Was that a tedious process?"

"Yes it was counselor."

Boring nodded and made a great pretense of deciphering his notes. "Let's see. All together, from your testimony, I've counted sixteen years of experience you've had in developing the great skills which have become so apparent here today in this courtroom. Sixteen years? Is that figure correct?"

"Yes."

"Over those sixteen years, have you ever borrowed footage from other movies and documentaries and spliced them into your documentaries?"

"Yes. That's a common practice."

"And with the advent of digital equipment and the use of computers, is it not now possible to take such borrowed footage and transfer the people depicted in that footage to a different location of your own choosing?"

"Yes, that is now possible, but it certainly was not done in the video you've just seen."

"Mr. Light., I'm not at all certain of that. You are a skilled technician. You have said that you could do such a thing. Did you not?"

"Yes, I am familiar with the technique."

"And you have used such techniques in some of your documentaries which have been shown on public television?"

"To a limited extent. Yes."

"Mr. Light. Did you see that great motion picture, 'Forest Gump'?"

"Yes I did."

"Did you see Gump addressing that dirty, unkempt crowd of thousands of protestors at the Washington monument and around the reflecting pool during the Vietnam war?"

"Yes."

"Forest Gump wasn't really there, was he, Mr. Light?"

"No, he wasn't."

"But it came across as being very real, didn't it, Mr. Light? I mean, most any of us could actually believe that Gump had been transported, through some magic, back in time to the early '70's to address those protestors? Isn't that true?"

"Yes, it did look real."

"Gump's picture was taken on some Hollywood film stage and then transferred to old films of protestors taken years ago by the Washington monument. Wasn't that done with digital equipment, old films and the computer?"

"Yes sir. That was the technique used all right."

Boring started laughing. "I'm thinking about that part of the movie where President Lyndon Johnson asked Gump to show him where he had been wounded in the buttocks. Wasn't that hilarious, Mr. Light?"

Laughter rippled through the courtroom. I noticed that Carl Krippendorf was gripping his hands together tightly. His face was pale. Both of us knew that Boring was skillfully picking Light and the video of the attack to pieces.

"Now, Mr. Light. President Johnson was not actually in that movie, was he?. I mean, he didn't ask Gump to pull his pants down and show him his buttocks, did he?"

"Well, no, he didn't."

"Once again, it was digital magic, old films, and the computer, wasn't it?"

"Yes," Light answered.

Boring turned serious and solemn. "Mr. Light. You've perpetrated some magic for us here in this courtroom today, haven't you?"

"What do you mean?" Light asked. He shifted uncomfortably in his chair. His shoulders had tensed up. He stared into Boring's face and rested the point of his chin on his balled fists.

"All of those shadowy figures whose faces we couldn't see stopping in front of Bedford's house. Exiting their cars. Firing automatic weapons, running up his driveway and across his lawn. Falling dead. Being picked up and thrown into three automobiles. Men, their faces unrecognizable, dragging two bodies off Bedford's lawn and placing them on the sidewalk. You worked that magic with old films, the computer and digital equipment, didn't you?"

Xerxes jumped to his feet. "Objection, your Honor. The prosecution is engaging in wild flights of fancy without any proof to back up his assertions. He is bullying and intimidating the witness."

"Objection overruled. The prosecution is perfectly in line with his questioning. You may continue, Mr. Boring.

"Thank you, your Honor. Mr. Light. You used a term, let's see. What was it? Oh, yes. 'Perjured testimony.' What you've done here today in this courtroom with your film magic. That's a crime much worse than the words you used to describe DeLong Tolman's testimony. As a prosecuting attorney, I will certainly attempt to see that you have another day in this court room, a day in which you will be the central figure, not just a witness testifying on behalf of someone else."

Boring, a look of disgust on his face, turned towards the table where we sat. "No further questions."

Xerxes rose slowly and with grim determination. He had his pince nez in his left hand. "Mr. Light. This so-called digital magic that the prosecutor referred to. Did you use any of that in putting together this video shown today?"

"I most certainly did not," Light answered. "And I've been insulted by Boring's inferences. They were very clever, but not true. Why should I do that when the actual events that were filmed that night were far more exciting than any I could have found by searching through old film libraries?"

"The footage at the end. The bodies. They were plainly—and painfully I might add—recognizable. There was no doubt of that, was there?"

"No, sir. There was no doubt as to their identity. I'm so sorry that Mr. Bedford and Miss Peel had to see those scenes, but I knew they were necessary to give an accurate picture of what happened at the Bedford home on the night of March 14th."

"In addition to the video film which was shown today, didn't you further testify that you were an eyewitness to everything that occurred before, during and after the attack that night?"

"Yes. There was no lone car that came to the house that night before the arrival of Karim and his henchmen in their three cars. No two men got out of a lone car, stood on the sidewalk and died from bullets fired by Bedford and his son. That's the plain truth, regardless of the testimony of DeLong Tolman."

"Thank you, Mr. Light. No further questions."

I looked at the faces of the twelve jurors and wondered if they believed what they saw. I could not tell about Wright Talbert. April Stuart's smile? Was that the pleased smile of a girl who'd found an engagement ring nestled in a dozen red roses? No, I decided. We've lost her. I could not tell about the others. Even Alice Rinker's face did not reflect her feelings.

CHAPTER 33

There was no jubilation around the big, oval dining table at Bedford House that night. Emotions were subdued. Each of us seemed lost in our own worlds.

"I'm not too certain we came out ahead on the showing of Morris Light's video today," Carl said at dinner. "Not certain at all. Boring hit us where it hurts most. And he hit us hard." He swirled the contents of his brandy glass gently. "That Boring is clever. You have to give him credit for that."

"Ah—h-h," I sighed. "I'm depressed as hell, and I don't mind admitting it. That bit about Forest Gump and the digitalized special effects which had Lyndon Johnson talking to Gump and inspecting, as Forest says in the movie, 'my buttocks.' That could create doubts in the minds of the jurors. Had I myself not been in the middle of the action captured on the video, I probably would be doubting the credibility of what was shown."

"Damn," Xerxes said. "We need a break. The weight of evidence is definitely on our side, but getting those stone-faced jurors to see and believe it. That's a horse of a different color."

"And perhaps the fault likes with the two of us, Xerxes," Carl said.

"Yes,", Xerxes said. "I don't feel too good about our performances as defense counsel. Believe me, I haven't been sleeping too well the last couple of nights. But, what's missing?"

I held up my hands to stop their depressing soul-searching. "It's the times we're up against, not your performances. The whole country is trying to reach an accommodation to the withering garlands of guilt being hung around the white man's neck. The press is giving a voice to the blacks which they've never had before. It's as if whites have been brow-beaten into public confessions of guilt over what we are told should be our sorrow over racism."

"And it does no good for any of us to proclaim that we're not racist," Carl said. "The finger of scorn is pointed at us and the blanket of condemnation smothers our cries. 'Me thinks', as Shakespeare says, 'he dost protest too much.' "

Julie, deep in thought, was shaking her head, slowly. "As Mr. Bedford points out, it is the times we're living in," she said. "The convoluted, distorted philosophies being rained onto us, the powerful sources outside home and family that preach the molding of different values, the overwhelming cynicism of the average person."

Absent mindedly, she was using her spoon to stir the ice cream melting in the dish in front of her. Each of our faces was turned towards her. "People don't swallow everything they see nowadays as being true, even though the proof is offered. We keep looking over and under what we see, digging, asking, 'what are they trying to pull on us?' We've been taught to question everything, to be cynical, to disbelieve in man's basic honesty. And even when we see the truth, we suspect it might have been rigged. Or at least slanted in a certain direction to prove a particular point."

"How right you are, Julie." Xerxes' said, his handsome face reflecting deep concentration. "Who could see the video of the actual attack by Karim and his followers that night and still not believe what they saw?"

"You know," I said. "I break out in a cold sweat just thinking about the possibility that we might lose our case. It's my neck that's on the chopping block, and I don't find the prospects too appealing. What if they do return a guilty verdict and sentence me to prison? Or to death?"

It was a hot July night, the kind of Southern night which makes us thankful for air conditioning. I glanced up at the antique chandelier above the polished table. The light glinted like diamonds on the cut crystal tear drops nestled among the twenty-five bulbs. On the far end of the table where Xerxes sat, I pictured my mother sitting there and presiding over one of the glittering dinner parties she and my father loved to stage.

Now, those slow-moving days of grace and elegance were gone forever. Momentarily, I was sad that a time like those of her day, when life seemed more beautiful, more meaningful, had gone the way of many other things. Those days of easy grace and intellectual conversation had been brushed rudely aside by the onrushing currents of madness which now billowed daily through our lives like a dark, malignant fog. We were toy soldiers moving in robotic precision to the sounds of clashing symbols and clanging gongs, our minds surrendered to the baton-waving, manipulative despots yelling stridently at us from the evening television news.

The four of us wrestled the cold facts staring us in the face far into the night. Boring had thrown the tainting acid of incredulity over our defense. We searched for the scrub brushes which we could use to burnish our truths and scour away the disbelief Xerxes had painted onto our efforts. None of us felt confident about our efforts when we gave up and went to bed around midnight.

"The defense calls attorney Roy Bester to the stand," Xerxes said.

Roy seemed highly uncomfortable. His eyes kept darting around the room. He couldn't decide, once he sat down, whether to cross his legs or slide forward in the witness chair in what would appear to be a relaxed position. I partially understood the terrible pressure he was under, knowing the scorn and contempt that would be heaped onto him from other blacks.

"You were graduated from the University of Georgia law school, weren't you Mr. Bester?"

"Yes sir," Roy answered in a strong voice. "And I'm proud of it. I'd never have made it through the university without the generous amounts of money Mr. and Mrs. Bedford gave me each semester."

"Oh. And what did the Bedfords require you to do in return for their generosity.

"Nothing," Bester answered. "Absolutely nothing. Not even a 'thank you' was required."

"Do you consider the defendant a friend?"

"Yes. And a very good friend. I was the attorney for his chain of convenience stores and when he sold them to another corporation, part of the consideration for the sale was that they keep me on retainer as the corporate attorney."

"Did you know about Abdul Karim's plans to attack the Bedford home?" Xerxes asked Roy.

"Yes, I knew about Karim's plans. You see, Mr. Xerxes, contrary to popular belief, there are still thousands of black people all over the United States who haven't been swept away in the tides of hate espoused by the Ayatollah and his crowd. In Forest, there are hundreds of us blacks who want only friendly relationships with our fellow men. That's why it is impossible to keep plans such as those DeLong Tolman and Abdul Karim concocted from leaking out. We decent, more level-headed blacks have our sources of information. We know of such incendiary plans within minutes, and they can't plug those leaks."

"Did you inform Stoney Bedford about the planned attack?" Xerxes asked.

"Yes, I did, Mr. Xerxes. I telephoned him and related their plans in detail, even as to the exact time of the attack. And I told Mr. Bedford that they wanted to make a national example out of him; that they were coming for the express purpose of killing him so that others who might be tempted to stand up to them would be intimidated."

"We've heard witness in this courtroom testify that the defendant had planned to kill black people for weeks. Is that true?"

"No, it is not true. Mr. Bedford never planned to kill anyone. He did plan to try to keep others from killing him. And he almost accomplished that, but there were too many of them attacking his home that night. They came from too many directions."

"Mr. Bedford is specifically being tried for murdering Tug Canton and Alonzo Derrick, Mr. Bester. Supposedly, DeLong Tolman and Norris Cape drove those two to Bedford's home several minutes before Karim and his crew arrived in order that they might resume protest marches up and down the sidewalk in front of the house. Without provocation, Bedford supposedly shot each of them, even though they were unarmed and standing on the sidewalk which is public property. Is this true?"

"It is a bald-faced lie," Bester declared. "Those two were part of the group of twelve who arrived in three black Cadillacs, in convoy, at the same time. When the attackers were finally routed, the four who were still alive, pried the guns from Canton's and Derrick's hands, dragged them from the lawn onto the sidewalk, picked up three more of the original attack group who were dying and carted them away. These three were dumped onto the streets in black neighborhoods to die. Their deaths were attributed to 'drive by shootings.' "

"No further questions," Xerxes said. "Your witness, Mr. Boring."

Boring was obviously angry. "How do you as a black man feel coming here and testifying against your black brothers?"

"All men are my brothers, Mr. Boring. If the shoes were on black feet, I'd do the same for them to try and save their lives. It's the right thing to do, wouldn't you agree?"

"I'm asking the questions, Mr. Bester. What do black people call traitors like you who grovel to white people for favors?"

Roy's voice became cold and knife-like. "I resent that kind of questioning, Boring. It offends me, and it certainly shows your own racial prejudice. Just because I don't go along with DeLong Tolman and Karim in their radical ideas does not make me a traitor. And you know that as well as I do."

Boring was persistent. "Answer the question. What do black people call other blacks who try to forget their own racial heritage and endeavor to act like white people?"

"'Uncle Toms'" Roy said. "It's a derogatory term usually applied to those blacks like me who consider themselves Americans first. People who think like me see that their best chance in life is to adapt to the present system of free enterprise and work within it to gain economic, social and political benefits instead of turning away and condemning the system as being tailored for whites instead of blacks."

"In other words, most black people don't trust these 'Uncle Toms' such as you?"

"They try to have as little to do with us as possible," Roy said. "But I'm not afraid of that kind of bad-mouthing. Such people believe that the government and white people owe them everything, when the truth is, no one owes us anything. Black people need to learn and adopt that philosophy."

"Do you believe that every man has a right to be on a public street, day or night, regardless of the particular neighborhood or who might live in a certain home on that street?"

"Yes. That's a fundamental right of all citizens, Mr. Boring. But Karim's men were killed on the lawn of Bedford's home, not on the sidewalk or street. And when they died, they were charging across that lawn with blazing guns. Before the surviving attackers in Karim's party left that night, they pulled two of the dead bodies off the lawn and left them on the sidewalk. They carried the bodies of their wounded with them and dumped them in black neighborhoods."

"How do we know that you are telling the truth?" Boring asked.

"I'll tell you how you should know that I'm telling the truth, but you won't follow up on my suggestions. Circulate in the black community. Find several of the hundreds of us blacks who try desperately to be just plain, everyday Americans. Listen to our voices, our reasoning. We know that our only hope lies in working within the system the way it is, in the same way white people do. Remember, I told you we had sources for this information. The facts I told you were known to us by 3 o'clock in the morning, shortly after the meeting where Karim and Tolman urged the assault on the Bedfords. That was twenty-three hours before the attack."

"Hmpfh," Boring snorted. "I don't believe any such meeting took place. Why should we? You've admitted to being an 'Uncle Tom.' "

The D.A. hissed the word like a coiled rattlesnake waring away his prey. " 'Uncle Toms.' Traitors to their own people. 'Uncle Toms' are not to be trusted, since they're only trying to save their own skins."

Bester had slipped on his legal clothes to give as good as he got. Boring did not intimidate him. "Did it ever occur to you that people like me, as you sneer, are not trying to save our skins. We're trying to do the right thing, trying to see things the way they are in this world, trying to love all men as brothers."

"Judge Johnson, this witness is uncooperative," Boring said. "I have no further questions."

Carl Krippendorf limped forward with the aid of his cane. "The defense calls LaJuana Tolman to the witness stand."

I found DeLong Tolman's face in the audience and watched his reaction. He straightened up in his seat rapidly. His mouth fell open in surprise. He began muttering under his breath, his lips working. He was clenching and unclenching his hands.

DeLong's wife came through the doors to the courtroom and made her way slowly to the witness stand. Her difficulty in walking, some of us knew, came from DeLong's beatings which he enjoyed as part of the once-a-month sexual trysts he demanded. Poor woman. The light was gone from her drawn and sad face. I suspected that her life had been reduced to hell-on-earth and that she probably used drugs to assist her in facing the bleak days of a dreary existence.

Carl did not spring at her as he had some of the earlier witnesses. He was kind in his approach, his voice low and soothing. "Mrs. Tolman, are you married?"

"Yes sir. I was, until my husband took up with another woman almost a year ago. Now, the three children and I live together in a place that ain't fit for dogs, much less people. We try to do our best to get along. It ain't easy."

"I understand that you have significant information that has a bearing on this case, Mrs. Tolman?"

"Yes sir, but I'm afraid to give it to you?"

"Afraid?, Mrs. Tolman?"

"My life is already hell, Mr. Krippendorf, and if I tell you what I know, I might be killed."

The woman was almost paralyzed with fright. I couldn't figure out why she'd risk coming here to testify, knowing what she was up against. Perhaps it was one last effort to strike back at the man who had treated her so shabbily, a man who beat her in his joyful preparations for savagely assaulting her sexually. She submitted in order to get Tolman to give her the pitiful amount of child support awarded her by the courts.

"Why then, would you come forward to testify for the defense, Mrs. Tolman? Could you tell us, or is that too dangerous?"

Her eyes darted towards Tolman's sullen face like a frightened child who knew that swift, certain punishment would be inflicted on them by the parent who had caught them in a forbidden act. Her words were barely audible. "Telling you all the reasons I'm here to testify would sure lead to my killing," the woman said. "I'm up against some mean folks who might decide to kill me for even telling what I know about the day of the attack, but I decided that I had to."

"The information you have is vitally important to seeing that justice is done in this case, Mrs. Tolman." Carl paused, nodding his head for reassurance of the caged woman there in the witness chair whose furtive glances were seeking a way out of the fires licking at her being.

"Where were you on the night of March 14th when Karim and his men attacked the Bedfords in their home?" he asked.

"I was at home. My husband, DeLong Tolman, was with me that night. He stayed until 6 o'clock the following morning. You see, once a month he comes by to bring the child support money, but, in order to get the money, I have to go to bed with him and have sex all night long. He beats me with his fists when he first comes in the door. Says it helps him to get sexed up. Then, he beats me lots of times during the night. Gets on top of me and yells that it makes him come better. Keeps saying, 'I love beating you up for what you've done to me.'"

"How sad, Mrs. Tolman. A woman shouldn't be subjected to anything like that, shouldn't be beaten into fear and intimidation."

Boring sprung to his feet. "Objection, your honor. The words 'fear' and 'intimidation' describe subjective states of a mind. The defense has no way of knowing with any degree of certainty that the witness suffers from such things."

"Objection overruled," Judge Johnson said. "You may continue, Mr. Krippendorf."

"Thank you, Judge Johnson." Carl turned back to LaJuana Tolman. "Something doesn't add up here. Your husband testified under oath that he and Norris Cape drove the two dead men to Bedford's house that night before they died so the two could march up and down on the sidewalk with protest signs. When Bedford supposedly shot the two men, Tolman and Cape left the scene and drove away hurriedly, fearing for their own lives."

"He didn't do no such thing, Mr. Krippendorf. He was with me all night long, humping me, yelling and coming and beating me. He was there until six o'clock that morning, four hours after them folks shot up Mr. Bedford and his family."

"And that was March 14th?", Carl asked.

"That's the truth. It was March 14th."

"No further questions, your honor. Your witness, Mr. Boring."

From his manner, it was plain that the D.A. was going to attempt to intimidate the witness even more than she was already cowed down just by being in the courtroom. "Mrs. Tolman, how much money has Bedford and his attorneys paid you to get you to come here today and tell these lies?"

"They ain't paid me nothing," the woman said in the same quiet voice. "When I saw on television about my husband lying about March 14th, I felt I had to do something. He just lied. He didn't do what he said he done. He didn't bring no two men to Bedford's house to march up and down with protest signs. People don't march in protest when it's dark. Ain't no use to. Nobody sees you."

Boring pressed his attack. "The pupils of your eyes, Mrs. Tolman. Why are they dilated?"

"If they's anything wrong with my eyes, it's the medicine I have to take to ease the pain of my husband beating me," Mrs. Tolman said. She rummaged in her purse. "Here. Here's the bottle with the pain pills the doctor done give me to take."

Boring looked at the label on the bottle of pills, sneered and handed it back to LaJuana. "Good try, Mrs. Tolman. The truth of the matter is, you're on drugs aren't you? You carry that bottle around with you to hide the fact that you're addicted to crack. Isn't that true?"

Carl shouted, "Objection, your honor. The prosecution has no factual basis for such statements. He's on a fishing expedition and is just trying to intimidate the witness."

"Objection overruled," Judge Johnson said. "The witness is instructed to answer the question."

"That ain't true. I ain't never been on crack, Mr. Boring, 'though I've seen my husband DeLong smoke it. That man has tried to get me hooked on that terrible stuff, but he ain't gonna do it. That's one of the reasons he beats me. He wants me to push the stuff for him in the black neighborhood so he won't have to pay me the $500 a month child support. Tells me I can make a heap a money each day. 'You can get rich, woman,' he says. 'Lots of people spend all day looking for crack so's they can stay high. I can get all you can sell. Easy. And I'll give you half of the money you rake in.' But I've seen what that stuff can do to a person. I'd rather die first."

"I think you are lying," Boring shot back. "It's just like a woman to accuse her husband of things she can't prove. She knows a sympathetic jury might believe her. But we all know that DeLong Tolman is a respected community leader and that you're lying when you say these bad things about him."

"I ain't lying," the woman said in protest. "If you'll check with my Doctor Mac Brodie, you'll find I'se telling you the truth. He's treating me for these two ribs on my left side which DeLong broke last month when he spent the night with me." She put her hands to her left rib cage and winced. "I moves slow because they still hurt so bad."

Boring gave up. "No further questions, your honor."

Xerxes called my neighbor, Bob Smith, as the next witness. It was established that he lived across the street from me, two houses down. He had been unable to sleep on the night the attack on my house occurred. He had been standing in his darkened livingroom looking out of his window at one-thirty that morning.

"Did you see a single car stop in front of the Bedford home around 1:45 that morning?" Xerxes asked. "And hear some shots being fired?"

"No," Smith answered. "I saw and heard Tolman tell that lie on the evening television news. No single car drove along the street and stopped in front of Mr. Bedford's house. At two o'clock, I did see three cars with their lights off drive slowly down the street and stop in front of Stoney's house. We had been tipped off by Mr. Bedford that trouble could come at any time. Frankly, I was up because I had this funny feeling that something terrible might happen."

"Tell us what you saw, Mr. Smith."

"Several of us who live near the Bedfords, had purchased night vision binoculars after we had seen those that Stoney had. I had my glasses trained on the three cars when all hell broke loose."

"All hell?" Xerxes asked.

"It was like one of those battles you see in the movies and on television. A fire fight, I think they call it. Automatic weapon fire lit up the night. You could see the streaks of flame shooting from their muzzles. People yelling and screaming. Men dying. I half way expected Bruce Willis to be running sideways across Stoney's lawn and firing his machine pistol."

"What did you do?" Xerxes asked.

"I was scared to death," Smith said. "I ran to the phone to dial 911. All I got was a busy signal. I tried dialing it three or four times. Still got busy signals. The shooting and yelling was still going on. In ten minutes or less, it was over. I counted five men lying on the sidewalk and lawn. Four men ran back towards the three cars. I thought it strange that they pulled two of the five dead men lying on the grass down to the sidewalk and left them there with protest signs. The other three they picked up and loaded into the cars before they drove off. One or two of them were still alive, because I heard them screaming. In another two or three minutes, the police cars with their lights flashing and their sirens screaming came screeching down the street."

"You're certain that no single automobile stopped in front of Bedford's home around 1:45 a.m., then drove off after the Bedfords shot two of the men dead?"

"Quite certain," Smith said. "There were only the three cars with their headlights off that came down the street and stopped before the shooting started and all hell broke loose."

"What did you do after the police cars came?"

"I ran across the street to see if I could help Stoney. I'll never forget that sight the longest day I live. Three black men inside the house were dead. One of them was that fellow, Karim. Then, I saw William, Mr. Bedford's son, dead on the stairway, close to where Karim lay. I could hear Stoney upstairs crying, 'Help me. Help me.' The police would not let me go upstairs. Later, I found out that Donna Elaine, Stoney's wife, was dead and that Stoney himself had been badly wounded. They hauled him off to the hospital in an emergency vehicle."

"Thank you, Mr. Smith. Your witness, counselor."

"Mr. Smith," Boring said. "You tried to call 911 and got a busy signal? I find that impossible to comprehend."

"Yes, I did dial 911 several times during the course of the fire fight. The next day, I went to the offices of 911 to find out why that happened, since it was so unexpected. I was worried. The 911 system does us no good if you call and get a busy signal. The executive director, a Mr. Wearning, told me that for some strange reason, starting at five minutes before two a.m. in the morning and continuing for twenty minutes, the circuits were overloaded to the point where no calls could get through. Later, I read in the newspaper that a worker at the telephone company had inadvertently helped to disable the 911 system by disconnecting a single wire. I'd be willing to bet that it was not 'inadvertent.' "

Carl leaned over and whispered to me. "Smith's testimony should help our case." Both Julie and I were smiling, something neither of us had often done in this courtroom since the start of the trial.

Boring smiled at Smith. "It's good to have friends, Mr. Smith. And out there in your exclusive neighborhood, all the neighbors stick together, don't they?"

"Yes we do," Smith said. "But we don't find it necessary to tell lies for each other."

"Do you object to blacks being in your neighborhood, Mr. Smith?"

"We object to any group that causes the trouble in our neighborhood that Karim and his crew have caused. And there is no reason to bring their anger and violence to a quiet neighborhood such as the one in which we live."

"How many black people live on your street, Mr. Smith?"

"Objection, your Honor," Xerxes said. "That question is irrelevant."

"The question is highly relevant, Judge Johnson," Boring said quickly. "The people in Bedford's neighborhood all stick together to make certain that black people are kept out of their area."

"Objection over ruled," Judge Johnson said. "The witness is instructed to answer the question."

Smith laughed. "You liberals are all alike, Boring. You don't respect the rights of private property in the United States. You're in mad pursuit of some Holy Grail that you think might assuage your own black-hearted, guilty souls and make you feel more sophisticated and superior at your fashionable cocktail parties. The truth of the matter is, that if you weren't constantly running for re-election to public office, you might let yourself see the ridiculous hypocrisy of the positions you take. I've heard you and your kind in fancy restaurants laugh and make fun of black people, only to be using them thirty minutes later to advance your own positions of power."

"Your Honor," Boring interrupted. "The witness has mounted a soap box and is spouting off racist views. Please instruct him to answer the question."

"I do not see the witness' views as being racist, Mr. Boring. He has a right to express his opinions, as long as he eventually answers your question."

"Thank you, Judge," Smith said. "Anything that doesn't fit your twisted views of our conservative society, Boring, you quickly dismiss as being racist. It's one of your favorite put-downs of us conservatives. Fortunately, people in America still have a right to choose their friends and neighbors, to live where they want to live—if they can afford to live there. The homes on our street sell for well over a half million dollars each and most of us paid cash for our homes. Many people would like to live on our street, but they can't afford the price of a home there. There's nothing wrong with that. It's just the free market economy in America. No, we haven't banded together to keep anyone out of our neighborhood, but we sure in hell don't want total strangers marching up and down the streets with those ridiculous signs and shooting up our homes. Perhaps you should enroll in the university and take some economic, psychology and sociology courses, Boring. Your view of issues certainly needs to be broadened; your understanding is sadly in need of updating."

The District Attorney wisely decided not to tangle further with Bob Smith. "No further questions, your honor."

Carl stood up and said, "The defense rests, Judge Johnson."

You could almost hear the spectators gasp in relieved unison. They knew, as I did, that within a few short hours the case would go to the jury. The long ordeal would be ended, one way or another. The reverberations of voices in the courtroom would diminish to an inaudible level, only to become a forgotten page in the indelible history of a hundred forgotten cases of human drama that had been written here in years past.

"This court is recessed until 2 p.m.," Judge Johnson said. "When we reconvene, closing arguments will be presented. Then the case goes to the jury where twelve good men and women will then decide the fate of the accused."

He rapped his gavel. We rose as he made his exit.

CHAPTER 34

"Carl," I said, after the Judge recessed the court for the lunch break. I reached for Julie Peel's small hand. "Do you think you could arrange for the police to bring your car to the front entrance so that Julie and I could ride into the country for the next hour and a half?"

The request caught him by surprise. "Why . . . why I don't see why I can't," he stammered. He and Xerxes walked across the room and huddled with the contingent of officers.

I pulled Julie to the side. "This just may be my last chance as a free man to see the sunshine and feel the wind in my face for a long time," I said softly. "Perhaps my last chance forever. I'd like to go by the house where Donna Elaine and William died. And then, to the cemetery. Would you mind driving?"

She kissed me on the cheek. Tears welled up in her eyes. "I'd be honored and thrilled to do that, Stoney," Her voice was husky. Her words threatened to break into unintelligible sounds. The watermelon pink dress she was wearing showed off her slender waist and was the prettiest thing I'd seen all day. Her long, brown hair, softly curled at its ends, framed her pale, delicate face and glistened in the light.

The silent words formed in my throat. "William. Dear William. If only you and Julie could have been married. If only . . . "

"It's arranged," Carl said. "The two police officers will take you down the service elevator and out through the entrance used by the police. That way, maybe you can avoid most of the crowds. Anyhow, the protesters and the curious have gone to lunch, too."

"I think we can feel more confident about winning after this morning's sessions," Xerxes said. He had read my face and was trying to buoy my spirits.

"I don't know," I said. "I just don't feel good about what that jury will do."

"Oh, c'mon, Stoney," Xerxes said, and put his hand on my shoulder. "Give those men and women in the jury box credit for having better sense than to swallow the lies they've been hearing. Not to mention their consideration of the things we've presented to prove your innocence."

"I don't know, Xerxes. These are strange days in our justice system. We have the Rodney King affair with its bloody riots. And, the O.J. Simpson verdict. Those two changed America's jury system forever."

"As an attorney, I must believe in the justice system," Xerxes said. "I have faith that it still works."

"Hmpfh," I snorted. "Realistically, these days, verdicts oftentimes are not rendered on the basis of evidence. Achieving social goals, pleasing militant minorities, these things are many times shoved ahead of justice and fairness to the accused. And always, there's the fear of what sullen, angry crowds will do if they don't like the verdict and turn into a howling mob."

"Yes," Julie said. "All you have to do is to look into the faces of that mob outside, screaming and cursing as we try to get through to our car. I believe that the members of that jury have been looking into those faces. Some of the twelve in that jury box are frightened out of their wits."

Carl had been listening intently. "Those things you two have pointed out. They scare me, too."

"I just got to believe that justice will still prevail," Xerxes said. "If we don't have faith, what's left for us?"

"Well, you two better get going," Carl said. "Be sure you're back here by 1:50. At the latest."

Julie and I drove towards my Bayou Road home. I hadn't had the courage to revisit it since that fatal night. Workmen had completed erasing the marks of the fire fight of March 12th I'd been told.

"Stoney, my insides are churning," Julie said. "I haven't been able to keep much on my stomach for three days. I get so angry and frustrated there in the courtroom. All those people. How they can lie with such straight faces is beyond me. Don't they have a conscience?"

"Some do," I answered. "Most people don't. These are the days of situation ethics. Do and say, at the moment, what it takes to accomplish your point without giving little if any thought to what's right and what's wrong. Five minutes later, if you have to make a hundred and eighty degree turn in your expressed beliefs to accomplish another point with another person or group, then do it. What matters to people now is winning. There are no absolutes. No hard and fast rules of what is right and what is wrong. Morals and values are old fashioned. They're out the window. Discarded like old socks."

I breathed in the Georgia air. Deeply. Several times. The sun was almost directly overhead. "It's going to be hot this afternoon," I said. "But, it's glorious. Look at the green of the trees and the grass and the shrubbery. We need rain to wash the dust from the leaves and fill up the small brooks down behind Bedford House. Georgia. My Georgia. . . . 'This is my own, my native land . . .' "

It's a cosmic conspiracy I thought, an enchantment that will dazzle your mind, mesmerize you, rob you temporarily of the power of speech. Unless you're stolid and careful, and there are times I don't want to be careful, times when I don't want to respond to deliberate purpose, times when all I want to do is to drift into the invisible currents around me and be lost forever.

Georgia. My Georgia. Its legends of war, nobility, valor and suffering emblazoned forever onto history's pages and written on my heart by my mother's teachings. Those portraits of my forebears on the wall at Bedford House, their storied pasts, their willingness to stand against the winds of war and sacrifice all.

Sacrifice. Over there. To the left. Down that dim logging road. One of my great, great-uncles died in the Civil War. A general, a college professor and a poet. He was killed as he and his rebel troops attacked a union encampment at daybreak. He, too, had lived and died for a great cause. What had I lived for? Had my living counted for something? And would I die in the execution chambers for something of which I was innocent?

"If the jury finds me guilty," I said, "and I'm sentenced to death, I hope I can be worthy of my blood lines and be brave to the end."

"Death," Julie said. "Last night I reread William Cullen Bryant's 'Thanatopsis,' his meditation on death. '. . . wrap the folds . . . around me . . . and lie down quietly . . .' " She honked the horn at someone in the car that turned left directly in front of us. "Bryant was an anti-slavery advocate who wrote beautifully, but his thoughts about death. I'm not ready for that. At this time."

"More than likely, we'll remember the playwright's words, let's see. How did he put it? Something to the effect, '. . . do not go gently into that dark night. Rage, rage, with all thy might . . .' That 's probably what most of us will do."

"It is if we love life," she said. "What time is it?"

I looked at my watch. "It's 12:20. Sidney Lanier sang songs about the South's soul, its very being. But death? As my Daddy used to say, 'If you're getting up a load to go now, forget about me.'"

The beautiful, willowy woman laughed. "Life and living. William loved life. He often got poetic about the South, the way I've heard you do. When he'd start talking about his love for this land," she waved her left hand towards the distant tree line, "his eyes would blaze, a mystic look would settle onto his face and he'd drift quietly into a different world. It amused me, but I understood him."

"How could our love of this land, our proud heritage, be twisted and distorted into something ugly, something of which to be ashamed? Just look out there!" I waved my hand around in a semi-circular motion. "This is a place, a land you can love unreservedly, unashamedly."

We passed several antebellum homes sitting far back off the highway and almost hidden by the huge, ancient live oaks. Long driveways wound through the trees up to the columned verandas of the two-story houses. Occasionally, a sleek, new automobile would be parked in front. How odd, I thought. Those automobiles. They're almost out of place. Instead, there should be horse drawn carriages with restless horses stamping the ground and costumed liverymen, waiting to assist the ladies of the house up into the carriage. And soon, a lone rider coming hard, the hooves of his fatigued horse pounding the gravel, the rider dismounting in a run, announcing, "The Yankees have fired on Ft. Sumter. The war has started."

Julie steered the car off the highway and soon we were driving along the quiet streets toward my old home. A neighbor, out for his walk, looked up and saw me. Startled, he yelled, "Stoney! How are you? How's the trial going?"

Julie slowed the car. "Okay, Jim," I yelled out the window. "We're on our lunch break. I've come back. For the first time since that night."

"Yeah," Jim yelled. "It's good to see you. We miss you. Hope you're soon back here. Permanently."

"Thanks, Jim. Give the other neighbors my best regards."

"Better check the time, Stoney," Julie said.

"It's 12:27. We won't go inside the house. Right now, I don't think I could stand seeing the exact spots where Donna Elaine and William died."

"I know I couldn't," Julie said. "I've had to take a leave of absence from my job as an IBM salesperson. Maybe, after the trial, I'll feel like working again."

She stopped the car. Both of us got out and walked across the front lawn.

"My God," she exclaimed. "What are those dark splotches on the front door? And to each side of the door?"

As we got closer, the smell told us what it was. "It's human excrement, Julie."

"You mean shit, Stoney. That's what it's called. Plain old shit. I'm grown up. We don't need any fancy words to describe shit. Who'd do a thing like that?"

"Once before, shortly before the night of March 14th, this same thing happened," I said. "William and I heard the sounds of a car stopping out front that night, and in a few minutes the car peeled out. He opened the front door and found human shit in globs across the door and on each side of it. They'd even dropped the plastic bag they'd used. It had holes in the bottom so that when they slung it the shit came out."

"Did you catch who did it?"

"No."

"Why would they do a thing like that?"

"Julie, that night, William and I couldn't figure it out. Since that time, I've had a chance to come up with an explanation."

"Oh," she said, looking at me with that quizzical expression on her face. "And what did you decide?"

"Do you remember the *Snopses*, the characters in some of William Faulkner's works?"

"Vaguely," she said. "As well as I remember from college literary classes, the Snopses were the lazy, shiftless, trashy people who multiplied rapidly and sucked their substance from the labor of others."

"Faulkner was a prophet. The work you see here is the work of the Snopses. It's a thing that only the dregs of humanity would do. Since Faulkner's mythical county of Yonknaphawata—or however you say it—the Snopses have used their love of procreation to multiply to the point where their shit has become rivers. These rivers are sucking people like you and me into their rushing torrent."

We walked into the backyard so we could glimpse the lake behind our home. In the blazing July sun, the mirror surface of the water reflected the patches of white clouds that drifted lazily across the sky.

It was 12:57.

I glanced to my left. The white, wrought iron chairs and table still sat on the patio. How many mornings I had sat at that table, drinking coffee and watching the sun come up. The French doors had been replaced. I glanced up at the windows that opened onto the roof from the second story. They were also new. The factory stickers had not been scraped off the window panes.

Suddenly, I could hear the sound of glass shattering, hear William yelling, "Dad, they've busted through." I remembered running to the closet where Donna Elaine was hiding. She'd killed the attacker who had killed her. An instant later, I had wheeled and blown Karim away with the shotgun. William was sprawled across the steel shield at the head of the stairs, dead.

I took a deep breath and shook my head to clear my thoughts. My watch said the time was 1:02.

Julie touched my arm. "What you said about the Snopses really bothers me, Stoney. It's so true. They're taking over the world, shoving our heads under the surface of the shit stream, and sucking everything we've got from us. We're still subsidizing the Snopses while they fuck us out of house and home and fill the land with Snopses by the thousands. They people the world with their kind. And soon, they'll fuck us out of house and home and own and run our country."

"Funny thing, Julie. There's no stopping their shit stream. Both banks of life's river are lined with millions of Snopses, shitting, shitting, shitting. The river grows larger by the minute. The torrents of shit more powerful."

"Maybe," Julie said. "Maybe, our world is doomed to become Snopsian in its landscape. Maybe people like us are doomed to eventually be ruled by Snopses."

"We've still got time to drive by the cemetery," I said, looking at my watch. "If we hurry." I stopped momentarily in front of the house before entering the automobile, saluted and said, my voice breaking, "Goodbye, old house. You were good to Donna Elaine, William and me. Now, I must leave you."

Cemeteries are such quiet places. As we drove through the entrance and along the winding, black top road towards the graves of Donna Elaine and William, my tired mind played tricks on me. In the dark shadows under the tall trees, I imagined I saw figures coalesce into hooded wraiths in long, dark cloaks. They began to dance a slow minuet to the strains of some sad, Confederate songs.

One night, years ago, near Branson, Missouri, Donna Elaine and I had watched a beautiful woman sitting alone on stage, play the dulcimer and sing slow, sad Confederate songs, In her long, hooped skirt, she became a woman left behind to mourn the loss of the South's husbands and brothers, its heroes. As the shadows in the dark splotches of shade under the trees danced, I heard the woman's sad voice again as she sang.

A single, freshly-cut red rose nestled in a tall bronze holder on my wife's grave. On William's, the bronze holder contained a single, yellow rose.

I looked at Julie. "The roses . . . ?"

"Early each morning I come here. The two of them are so precious we must never let them go, never let them be forgotten. Somehow, the roses still link them to life, to the two of us." A deep, involuntary sob escaped her thin body. I was crying as I reached for her hand.

The summer grass had grown over the graves. I plucked long strands of Johnson grass that was growing over the edge of their markers. Like two lost children, we stood silently, each of us immersed in our own private worlds.

"It's 1:16," I said. "It's time we go."

As we drove along, Julie clicked on the car's radio and searched for the all-news channel. "This shocking news just in,", the announcer said. "Minutes ago, police answered a 911 call and found LaJuana Tolman, estranged wife of city councilman DeLong Tolman, shot to death. One of the officers at the scene said it looked like a drug deal gone bad, that she had been trying to buy drugs and the dealer evidently did not like something he saw or heard. Just this morning, Mrs. Tolman appeared as a surprise witness for the defense in the trial of white racist Stoney Bedford. We'll give you additional details as they become available."

Julie snapped off the radio. "My God," she exclaimed. "That poor woman hinted in court this morning that she'd probably be killed for testifying."

"That poor, poor woman," I moaned. "How could something like this happen? And this soon? Those poor children. How many did she have? Three? Oh, God, have pity on them."

"She was murdered," Julie said, and beat on the car's steering wheel with her fist. "Murdered. It was no drug deal. DeLong Tolman had his own wife murdered."

"We can't prove it, of course," I said. "But you can bet that he arranged for her killing. Why, why, why? Boring pretty well discredited her testimony this morning. DeLong and his crowd didn't need to kill LaJuana." I put my hands over my face. "Oh, Lord. We shouldn't have encouraged her to testify. Forgive us, please. Forgive us. Oh, that poor, poor woman. We're responsible for her death. But we didn't know they'd do this. We didn't know . . . "

Julie beat the steering wheel again in shock and frustration. "It's such a cold-blooded thing, but, I guess, they wanted to warn other black people against turning on their brothers to help white people. You think they'll kill Roy Bester?"

"They just might," I said. "But, they don't have a pre-arranged alibi like they had for killing poor LaJuana Tolman. Roy's strong and well known. I don't think they'd dare murder him."

"Now that his wife is dead," Julie said, "DeLong won't be tried for perjured testimony. She's the only one that could prove he was lying about taking those two men to your house before the attack by Karim and his thugs." The wet stream of tears showed on both her cheeks.

Xerxes was waiting in the covered circle that curved by the entrance used by the police. The moment we stopped the car, he opened my door. "Boy, am I glad you're back," he said. "We were worried that you would be late for the reconvening of court and then, just minutes ago, we heard about Mrs. Tolman. The thought crossed my mind that they'd kill you if they could find you.

CHAPTER 35

The trial was nearing its end. All that was left before it went to the jury were the summations by each side. Now, a new dimension was to be added to my body's already unbearable tension; the certain knowledge that my fate would soon be decided by twelve people, none of whom I knew, and certainly, three or four of them who, I had concluded, were not to be trusted to make objective decisions about my guilt or innocence.

Boring spoke for the prosecution. "Ladies and Gentlemen of the jury," he began. "Alonzo Derkin and Tug Canton are no longer numbered among the living. Some people will say that's not important. They were black. They held no positions of power. Our earth did not tremble when they gasped for breath and died on a public sidewalk, murdered by Stonewall Bedford.

"But you and I know that the life of each citizen in America is as important as the life of any other citizen, be he or she powerless or powerful. That's what makes America great.

"There's a man in this room who doesn't buy into that philosophy, the defendant, Stonewall Bedford. A man lost in another age, secretly living the life of a Confederate general, professing to hear the distant drums and bursting shells at Gettysburg, muttering to himself his oft-repeated desire, "Oh, how I wish the South had won the war. If we had whipped the Yankees, our world would be a far better place in which to live."

Boring was a skilled and effective orator. He knew the pauses, the tones and nuances of voice and facial expressions that added great power to his words. He was a one-man show and the stage, at this moment, was all his. And his presence was commanding.

"I ask you to think for a moment," he continued, "of the times in which we now live. Thank God we've moved so far away from that ghastly period in our nation's history called the Civil War, the period out of which spring the myths and legends which haunt Bedford's present life and living.

"There are no Yankee blue coats out there in front of you and me that is the enemy who must be killed. In Bedford's mind though, he's made a substitution. There are still enemies of his beloved South out there all right.

That enemy of the long ago Confederates, the blue-coated men of the Union army, has been replaced by a new enemy, the hundreds of thousands of struggling blacks fighting an uphill battle to reach the high ground where they can make their way to a decent life.

"These present day blacks are nevertheless at war, charging through an alien land called the South where the occupants such as Bedford, with their fancy education and their considerable wealth, are blinded by racist hatred of black people. The Civil War has never ended for Stonewall Bedford and his kind. They are fighting just as hard against the South's new enemy that must be killed in this new kind of battle if the war is to be finally won—and now the enemy is our black citizens.

"Oh, Stonewall Bedford may wear the same fashionable clothes which you and I wear—if we can afford the price tags. But mentally? Mentally, Bedford is dressed in the gray uniform of a Confederate general. His saber is raised aloft and he's yelling 'Char-r-r-rge! Let's win the day for our Southland.'

"That Confederate flag on the lawn at city hall. That's his flag. Even though it offends black people as a symbol of slavery, what does that matter to people like Stonewall Bedford? Black people, in the minds of Bedford and his kind, are the enemy. But, this enemy cannot be killed in the open fields of battles between opposing forces, as they were in the 1860's. No. Other means must be used to dispose of them."

Boring turned to point at me. "There, on his horse, sits Confederate General Stonewall Bedford. Blacks, who only want a better life for themselves, have assaulted his oppressive, psychotic beliefs in things Southern. That Confederate flag, the monument to General Robert E. Lee, the lost Civil War, slavery, plantations, antebellum homes.

"These heralded Southern beliefs and visions, the myths and legends of superiority, nobility and bravery buried deep in Bedford's mind gave rise to actions on Bedford's part that sincerely motivated the attacks by black citizens with opposing philosophies on the flying of the Confederate flag. The general sitting there was affronted that his views of the way life should be would be attacked. The very idea. These 'nothing citizens' challenged his beliefs and did not give obeisance to his vaunted superiority as a member of one of Georgia's distinguished families. How dare they?

"Motive? General Bedford decided that this enemy out there on the horizon must be cut down with gun fire. He built and armed a fortress inside his home, watched black citizens protest his attitudes day after day by parading back and forth along the street and sidewalks in front of his house in a secluded neighborhood. That was the last straw for Bedford. It spun his psychotic mind out of control

"He had a well-trained army fighting alongside him. He told them and himself, 'The enemy's out there. We must kill them.' He heard the faint sound of bugles and the distant drums at Gettysburg. He held the high ground that night, the second floor of his half million dollar home. 'The enemy must not dislodge us,' he pounded into the ears of his son and wife. 'We must hold the high ground at all costs.' From his fortress, he commenced firing. The first casualty was Tug Canton. With Bedford's first shot, Canton's head exploded. He gave the rebel yell, then killed Alonzo Derkin with a shot through the head. Both men were unarmed. Both were on public sidewalks.

"DeLong Tolman and Norris Cape, two highly respected black citizens who had earlier transported Canton and Derkin to Bedford's house, fled as Bedford commenced firing, leaving behind the dead bodies of Canton and Derkin. That is the only battle we are concerned with here in this courtroom. There was another battle a few minutes later. Each side suffered grievous casualties, but the grand jury indictment of Bedford is not concerned with the later battle. Nor is this court. Bedford was indicted for the murder of Canton and Derkin. That is the issue before you jurors.

He consulted his notes briefly, then made a great show of looking off into space as though pondering what to say next. He raised his right hand to signal that an idea had just triggered words, then caught himself, stopped and looked at his notes again.

"I'd like to remind you members of the jury that this is America," Boring said. "The law prescribes harsh penalties for murderers. Bedford had decided several days before he opened fire that the black enemy must die for daring to challenge his psychotic beliefs. As he said, 'He was out to kill himself a few niggers.' The deaths of Alonzo·Derkin and Tug Canton cry out for the law's severest punishment."

He swept his right hand towards the evidence table. "There, on that table, are the weapons of war used by General Bedford and his deadly army. Bedford was trained from early childhood in the skilled and expert use of such weapons. So was his son William. He and his troops practiced the plans and strategy they'd mapped out for killing blacks."

He walked over and seized one of the shields. "What an ingenuous idea. Steel shields to protect Bedford, his son and his wife from enemy fire. Night vision binoculars, night vision scopes for the rifles and pistols, huge stores of ammunition. Funny thing. Canton and Derkin did not go to Bedford's house to wage war. They went to engage in the right of every citizen, peaceful protest on a public sidewalk. They had protest signs, but they were not armed."

Boring held up a spent rifle cartridge. "The general and his troops wasted very little ammunition. Bedford killed the two unsuspecting protesters with rifle shots through the head. You've heard a ballistics expert testify that the bullets that killed Canton and Derkin came from his rifles. You heard DeLong Tolman, respected member of the Forest city council, testify as to having carried the two dead men to Bedford's home to renew their peaceful protests by picketing in front of the General's house."

Boring lowered his head and dropped his voice. He extracted a handkerchief, fluffed it out, then wiped at his eyes. It was his pose of a man in great sorrow. "Another terrible thing has happened as a result of this trial. In a way, Bedford's army has claimed another victim. LaJuana Tolman is dead.

Some members of the jury emitted audible gasps. Helen Rinker, the Methodist activist's mouth had fallen open in dismay and unbelief. April Stuart was determined not to let her face show any surprise. Wright Talbert, the Unitarian minister, had his right hand over his mouth. The still, unsmiling faces of the black jurors showed no emotion at all.

Boring continued."Yes, Mrs. Tolman is dead. DeLong Tolman, at this moment, is at the funeral home, making preparations to bury his wife who was here this morning to testify for the defendant, Stonewall Bedford. She tried to get this court and you jurors to believe that Tolman could not have taken Canton and Derkin to Bedford's home on the night of March 14th because he was spending the night with her at her home.

"But members of the jury will not be fooled by this poor woman's testimony. Sadly, she was addicted to crack, the most potent cocaine derivative of them all. Her eyes were opened far too widely; her pupils were dilated. The pain of going too long without a fix plainly showed on her face and in her walk. She went straight from this court to a drug dealer to get more crack, but something went wrong. The drug dealer killed her. As the police say, 'It's a drug deal gone bad.' And who would believe a drug addict?. I wonder how much money Bedford's emissaries paid her to testify? When they found her body, she had over $1,000 in her hand bag, yet while testifying, she led us to believe that she was practically penniless."

Boring paused to drink cool water from one of the glasses next to the plastic water pitcher on the prosecutor's table. "Oh," he said, as an after thought. "You saw a video that purported to be actual film of the attack on Bedford's house on the night of March 14th. Sadly, an angry Karim with some fellow fighters for freedom did attack Bedford's home that night. And they had great cause if you followed the evening news on TV and read the news stories in the local newspaper that detailed Bedford's verbal assaults on minority citizens.

"But, this trial is not concerned with that attack which occurred after Canton and Derkin were murdered earlier by Bedford. DeLong Tolman and Norris Cape drove those two men to the sidewalk in front of Bedford's house where the General killed them at 1:45 a.m. on the day in question.

"This video was used in an effort to show that the two murdered men were part of Karim's group. It showed dark figures, none of them recognizable, falling onto Bedford's lawn. Before the attackers drove away, two of the fallen figures were dragged from the lawn and deposited on Bedford's sidewalk, or so the producer of the film would have you believe.

"Morris Light has been in the business of making TV documentaries for over twelve years. Under questioning, he frankly admitted that the magic of the digital process could make even former president Lyndon Johnson, many years after his death, show up at a Medal of Honor ceremony at the White House and inspect Forest Gump's buttocks."

Laughter rippled through the spectators. Several members of the jury smiled broadly.

"Yes," Boring said. "It is amusing. But the digitalized version, the doctoring of film to make it show almost anything you wish—that's what you saw on the video which the defense showed you in this courtroom. It's as believable as Snow White and the Seven Dwarfs.

"Then a neighbor of the accused. Let's see. What was his name. Oh, Bob Smith. Good American name, Smith. He came here in efforts to convince us that he couldn't sleep the night of March 14th and that he watched the proceedings through night vision binoculars which he had purchased on Bedford's recommendation. He testified that no cars came at 1:45 a.m. that morning, that only Karim's crew in their three black Cadillacs came down that street and stopped in front of Bedford's house. If you listened carefully to what Bob Smith said, you'd have to conclude that he's of the same mind set, the same cultural attitudes as Bedford. He hates blacks, too, doesn't want them in their exclusive neighborhood. Thus he easily lied to protect his good neighbor, Stoney Bedford.

"Oh, the documentary maker, Morris Light. and his assistant, said they hid behind neighbor's fences and saw the same thing Bob Smith saw. Naturally, I suppose they'd say that. A documentary is supposed to represent the truth, but remember, these are the same two people who can use the digitalized computer process to make dead people come alive years after their funerals. It is magic, but magic doesn't belong in Stoney Bedford's trial for murder. Only truth.

He whirled and pointed to the jury box. Whom do you believe? Respected citizen, DeLong Tolman, his drug-addicted wife who was paid handsomely to come here to testify against her husband, the biased, racially prejudiced Bob Smith or two men who admit to knowing how to make dead men come alive and perform in movies? I'll leave that to you, the members of the jury to decide whom to believe.

"You have seen the evidence; heard the witnesses; watched the vaunted airs of superiority assumed by Stonewall Bedford and his two attorneys. Even to this day, the killing of black citizens is an inconsequential thing to them, a mere inconvenience to be side stepped so that tomorrow Bedford and his kind can again hike the dimmed, glorious and alluring trails of the gone-with-the-wind, Southern way of life.

"This trial is not just another trial of a white man in a small Southern town indicted for killing two black men, the news of which, in days past, was usually buried in two small paragraphs in the back pages of Southern newspapers—after the jury found the white man innocent. Every element of this trial, the summation of the testimony of witnesses, the psychological profiles of the accused and each member of the jury—each day the news is flashed around the world by satellite. Fortunately, the dreams of Martin Luther King and the Civil Rights Acts passed by the U.S. Congress have at last made it possible for black people in the South to have their day in court and receive equal justice.

"I remind each of you members of the jury of the grave responsibility which is yours. Each day of this trial, the angry, sullen crowd outside this courthouse grows larger and more explosive. Remember Rodney King and the riots, the burning buildings and the killings in Los Angeles because the black people knew that justice had not been served. Those angry people outside this building—and out there in the fartherest reaches of our

THE LAST CONFEDERATE FLAG

globe—will be waiting and watching to see if justice is done. I pray that it will be. Grave consequences rest upon your decision.

"The law must remove Bedford from the ancient trails of treason he is following by judging him guilty of the crime with which he is charged. First degree murder."

Boring was pleased with his oratorical ability, with the pictures he had invoked in the minds of the members of the jury; with the way he had led the jury to, he hoped, see that I lived by a mind set that led me to plan to "kill some niggers" and that the deaths of Canton and Derkin were the natural result of such a philosophy. Thus, I was guilty of first degree murder, as charged.

The district attorney could not believe that I was innocent, but then, his job was to prosecute those the grand jury indicted. He looked around the courtroom as though he expected cheers and applause. He lifted his right arm towards the ceiling, then let it fall to his side to indicate that he had finished his summation.

Carl Krippendorf, graying, limping, somber, walked to the section where the twelve jurors were seated. Though he had prepared in depth for this moment, he carried a heavy weight on his shoulders. He did not take it lightly.

Carl placed both of his hands on top of his cane and made certain to look each juror in the face, one by one. Shafts of late afternoon sunlight fell across the left side of the jury box, painting an interesting canvas of light and shadow. I couldn't help but notice the gleaming, ruddy face of one man whose size stood out above the others.

"Ladies and gentlemen of the jury. This is not a routine murder case by any stretch of the imagination, but not for the reasons the prosecutor has offered you. This is a political trial; the defendant is a political prisoner. Indeed, George Orwell's 'Age of Big Brother' has arrived in America with chilling consequences. 'Big Brother' is watching each of us, even you ladies and gentlemen sitting in the jury box. When 'Big Brother' does not approve, when he is angered, we all suffer the consequences. Who knows who will be next?"

The ruddy-faced juror, strangely, had his right fist clinched. The pleasant expression vanished from his face. One of the black women in the box was shaking her head, slowly. One of the immaculately dressed white women was glancing at her fingernails.

Carl tapped his cane on the wooden floor, like a school teacher trying to gain the attention of a room full of students. "'Big Brother' There in his castle on the Potomoc in Washington, D.C. The trial of Stoney Bedford is a powerful political move by the United States government to carry out the persecution of a citizen on trumped up charges to satisfy unrelenting political pressure from militant groups.

"It represents the heavy hand of government trying to crush any citizen who does not fall into mindless, robotic lock step as acknowledgment of the philosophies of this ruler in Washington that forbid too much individual freedom. 'Big Brother', for this power over citizens, must pay the piper with political pay-offs that elevate certain groups in our society over others. The reason? Their votes will be needed come election day to keep him in power."

Carl changed his tone of voice and shook his right index finger. "Within this framework, you must interpret the basic tenets of the American system of jurisprudence, as well as the traditional American philosophies of individual freedom. The most basic precepts of all in this country is that: Number one, no man's freedom to speak his mind in a forthright manner must be denied; Number two, a man has a right to defend his person and property from all attacks.

"Stoney Bedford, that man sitting there at the defendant's table, dared to speak his mind boldly. He dared to defend his home and person against fierce attackers. And for that, he has been charged with murder? It's ridiculous, and I suspect that each of you jurors know this."

The big man on the jury cleared his throat. In the eerie silence of the courtroom, the sound seemed to startle several people. "Oh, excuse me," he murmured. He tried to sink lower in his seat, but was still a half head taller than any of the others.

"You have heard Dean Craig Weynel of the University of Georgia's Law School outline the gross error in the grand jury's indictment of the defendant. The dean gave sound reasons for his positions. He ridiculed the indictment and this trial as a travesty of Justice. 'Kafkaesque', he called it, reminiscent of that pioneering work *'The Trial'*. Kafka's work preceded the further refinement of a picture of today's central government gone mad in its effort to crush individual freedoms, George Orwell's book *1984*.

Carl smiled. "We've had amusing incidents in this trial—as well as the sadder moments. Do you recall the testimony of that coke-snorting psychiatrist? He clothed his wild imaginings in the lurid, fancy dress of psychological research to make it sound scientific. Out of this psycho babble, he had the effrontery to attempt to explain why Bedford behaved in a certain fashion. To add insult to injury, if I may use a well-understood cliche, he labeled himself 'a citizen of the world who owed allegiance to no government, not even our own.' How can such a man be taken seriously in anything he says?"

Carl's words became slow and forceful "We've had our scary moments here, too. You heard two members of the elite, black power structure openly declare their hatred for anything white and extol the virtues of having declared war on white America. Then, each of them attempted to intimidate everyone here in this courtroom with threats that any of us might be their next victims. I don't know about you, but it made me mad as hell. I don't take any man's threatening of my life and liberty lightly."

He shook his head back and forth. His jaws were clenched. He shrugged his shoulders and sighed. "This is unheard of behavior in a court of law, but then this is 1996, the age of the O.J. Simpson modifications to our justice system. We are sliding downhill very fast. I doubt that we will ever see fairness again in a trial such as the one you are now being asked to rule on. I trust that each of you will reach down deep inside of you to see that justice is given the defendant.

"You also heard outright lies given under oath in this courtroom. The dead Karim's cohort, Mueschle Jabbar, swore that Canton and Derkin were not part of Karim's crew of attackers; that they had gone to the Bedford house at least fifteen minutes before Karim and his crew of murderous thugs stormed a man's home, killing his son and his wife and wounding him to the point of death.

"DeLong Tolman was another in the parade of liars. He and Norris Cape supposedly took Canton and Derkin to the Bedford Home fifteen minutes before Karim's attack, 'for peaceful purposes.' Tolman's wife told us how her husband, Delong, lied to us under oath. On March 14th, the date of the killings, he was spending the night with LaJuana Tolman and sexually assaulting and beating her.

"Don't you find it strange that within hours of Mrs. Tolman's testimony here in this courtroom, she lies dead? She told us that she would probably be killed for daring to come forth with the true story of DeLong Tolman's whereabouts on the night of March 14th.'A drug deal gone bad'? You above all must not believe this imaginative lie. She was killed because she told the truth, because, if you believed her, you'd have to set the defendant free.

"Bob Smith, a neighbor of the defendant, who lives across the street, watched the arrival of Karim and his attackers in three cars, witnessed the storming of Bedford's home, visited the death scene, heard Bedford's cries of 'Help me. Help me.' Smith said; 'No car came to the Bedford home fifteen minutes before Karim and the assault team arrived.' "

Carl's voice was tired and scratchy. He drank water from one of the glasses siting on a nearby table. Then, he shifted his weight to try and rest the stump to which the artificial leg was attached. In his mind, the missing leg was still there, throbbing with pain. Such pain is called "Phantom pain", but to the one who's suffering it, it's quite real.

"Another in the colorful parade of liars," he continued, "was Layla Jenkins. This consummate actress gave perjured testimony that Stonewall Bedford raped her on June 20th, 1975. When confronted with the evidence that such a thing was impossible, since the Bedfords were traveling out West on that date, she, as did several other of the prosecution's witnesses, spouted off her boiling hatred of white people and anything Southern. Though she did not admit it, we know she took a large sum of money from someone to come forth with such lies.

"Abdul Karim was waging a holy war for the Black Muslims and the Great Ayatollah of Philadelphia the night he and other members of his army attacked Stoney Bedford's house. Weeks before the attack, Karim boldly told the Forest city council that the Ayatollah's army was trained, disciplined, dedicated and determined to wage all out war against whites in America.

"The attack against the Bedford home was part of that war. Oh, it was cleverly disguised as an attempt to pull down the Confederate flag from in front of city hall. It was also clothed as an attempt by black citizens to defend their hard won rights to equality in the eyes of the law.

"The cries of blacks to pull down the Confederate flag is merely a noble sounding cover for the continued waging of war by blacks against white Southerners. Pulling down the Confederate flag would not still their clangorous voices. Only when whites in the south—and all over the United States for that part—have been subjugated will their outrage, fueled by unreasoning hatred, be satisfied. Of course, that means a war of genocide and the destruction of those freedoms we hold so dear in America.

"When they have subjugated whites, the war of genocide, which they will have ignited, will make the Holocaust, Somalia, Burundi, Rawanda and

Croatia pale in comparison. I know we don't like to face the inevitable truths, but, for our own sakes, we must. This is a very real world in which we live and to ignore the 'Tiger, Tiger, burning bright, In the forest of the night' is to invite our own deaths."

Carl walked to the water pitcher and poured water into his glass. He took several sips, then made his way back to the jury box. Again, he held both of his hands on top of his walking stick and scanned the face of each juror.

"The prosecution has not proved the defendant guilty of anything, much less first degree murder. Stonewall Bedford was a plain American citizen defending his home, his castle, his person and his property against marauding attackers.

"Despite the prosecution's derision of Morris Light's video of the actual attack, their attempts to dismiss it as computerized, digitalized magic, one would have to see their efforts as pure poppycock. Clever poppycock, I assure you, but nevertheless their efforts have failed to portray what you saw as 'manufactured actions.' You saw Bedford's dead son sprawled across the shield at the top of the stairs in their home; You saw Bedford clutching his dead wife in his arms and crying 'Help me. Help me.' Those scenes were real. There were no dead people brought back to life in those scenes. Sadly, those people are now buried out there in a lonely cemetery.

"But the prosecutor ridiculed the scenes showing the surviving attackers loading dead and wounded men into the black Cadillacs and pulling two men off Bedford's lawn and depositing them onto the sidewalk. Those scenes, once again were real. They were not the result of magic."

Carl was nearing the end of his summation. He straightened his shoulders. changed the tone of his voice and started speaking again, this time, slower and with steely emphasis.

"I say to you that you must find Stonewall Bedford 'Innocent,' as he most assuredly is. It is the verdict with which you can sleep in the nights to come. To find otherwise, is to sentence all Americans to untold thousands of sleepless nights in the future. If I know Americans, they will come to see the necessity to take up arms rather than lie down in surrender to these crazed marauders, drunk on their newly found power. Conversely, once these revolutionists learn that the law's deterrence no longer applies to them, these killers who enjoy the blood of vengeance will be unleashed to mount their attacks against innocent citizens at will. It will be a genocidal war, one where all will lose. There will be no winners. Only losers.

"It is an awesome responsibility."

Carl limped slowly back to the defense's table and sat down. The trial was now ended. We listened to the judge as he instructed the jury. The jurors retired from the court room to deliberate my fate and arrive at a verdict.

As a team, Xerxes, Carl, Julie and I had done all that we could do. Had it been enough to convince the twelve members of the jury? I did not know. Pictures of jury members Alice Rinker, the Methodist activist, and Wright Talbert, the Unitarian, flashed through my mind. My mind refused to see April Stuart's face, for I knew she had no respect for people of my age and status. Or for anything Southern. And there was no clue as to how the minority members on the jury might vote. They were hard to read.

The four of us were escorted to a private waiting room on the second floor of the courthouse to await the jury's decision. We would be called back into court chambers to hear the verdict.

We didn't talk much. Over three hours passed. Darkness was falling outside. I drifted into a strange, tortured world of pain and loss of mental clarity. I suppose it was a way to shrink from the horror of what the jury might decide. I was past the point of reacting to most stimuli.

Food was brought in, but I had no appetite. It had started raining outside. When I first heard the raindrops splatter against the window glass, I rose and walked to look outside. The wet sidewalks below glistened in the dim lights that surrounded the county courthouse. A strong wind whipped the limbs of the live oaks into frenzied dancing. Some of the more hardy of the vigilant protestors huddled in rain-slicked capes under the trees. Even they seemed dispirited.

"Something evil this way comes."

It had been raining on that February day months ago when I drove downtown to city hall for the council meeting that fateful day; the meeting that had launched me into headlong controversy over the flying of the Confederate flag. I remembered how the ancient yellow brick of the four storied building glistened that day in the low light.

Harris Woolford had signaled to me that afternoon to wait for him as he turned into the parking lot. He'd had the same feeling I had, a feeling that something bad was about to happen. Neither of us had any idea what it might be.

"Aw, it's just one of those crazy feelings, Stoney," the professor laughed and tried to wave the thoughts away.

We went upstairs and found the air of the milling crowd strangely hostile. That was the day I first met Abdul Karim.

"Something evil this way comes."

So many things in my world had changed since that day.

A bailiff stuck his head into the room where we waited and said simply, "The jury has reached a verdict. I'm to escort you back to the courtroom."

I looked at my watch. It was 9:37 p.m.

We rose when the judge reentered the courtroom through the door immediately behind his high backed leather chair. From his lofty perch, he peered over the rims of his tiny reading glasses, his face impassive.

The members of the jury filed in and took their seats in the jury box.

"Has the jury reached its verdict?" the judge asked.

Alice Rinker, the foreman of the jury stood up. "We have, your honor."

"Will you read the verdict to the court?"

"We, the members of the jury, unanimously find the defendant guilty as charged."

The judge rapped his gavel sharply. "Members of the jury will return to their individual rooms at the hotel and reconvene tomorrow morning at 9 a.m. to decide the defendant's sentence. The deputies will handcuff the prisoner and lead him away. This court is adjourned."

I was so numbed until I scarcely knew what was taking place. I was instructed to place my hands behind my back. The snapping of the handcuffs around my wrist was humiliating. It soon dawned on me that being locked in a jail cell was far worse than I could ever have imagined. When I was locked away before, right after the indictment, I knew that there was an excellent chance that I'd soon be released. This time, when the jail cell doors clanged shut, I realized that I'd never be a free man again.

Ah, "Tis liberty alone that gives the flower of fleeting life its luster and its perfume. And we are weeds without it."

That night, they took away my clothes and gave me the sad, limp, loose fitting cotton pants and jacket that prison inmates wear. When I protested, the burly, tobacco chewing trusty said, "What you hollering about, old man? Where you going, you ain't never gonna wear clothes like this again."

"But I want them saved," I yelled. "I'll have Miss Julie Peel pick them up."

"Saved?" the pot-bellied jailer laughed. "For what? She can pick them up and give them to the homeless. You've got a permanent home now. Food and clothes and lodging provided. You won't be needing these fancy clothes again."

Then it hit me. Like ice water thrown into my face. He was right. Life in prison or the execution chamber? I'd soon know.

By 9:47 the next morning, I knew. The jury had taken less than forty-five minutes to decide my fate.

I sat at the same table in the courtroom where I'd sat for days, this time in handcuffs. It was painful, because my shoulders were stretched to an angle in back where I could not relax. Julie, Carl and Xerxes were there as the jury filed back in.

"Has the jury agreed on a sentence for Stonewall Bedford?" the judge asked.

"We have, your honor," Alice Rinker said. She handed a folded piece of paper to a bailiff who handed it up to Judge Johnson.

He adjusted the angle of his drug store reading glasses, unfolded the piece of paper, read it silently, then raised his head quickly, as though surprised.

Then he read the words aloud. "We the jury, sentence Stonewall Bedford to life imprisonment without benefit of pardon or parole."

He rapped his gavel. "This court is adjourned. The guards will take the prisoner away."

Pandemonium broke lose in the courtroom. Boring and the justice department attorneys were embracing and jumping up and down like children on a pogo stick. Loud booing broke out among the majority of the spectators in the chamber, booing that drowned out the cheers of Mueschle Jabbar, DeLong Tolman and several others.

A roaring arose from the courthouse grounds outside, swelling and increasing in volume like the rushing winds of a sudden thunderstorm. A great many of the hundreds of waiting protesters were decidedly happy. Now, the centerpiece of their frustration would be no more.

Julie took me in her arms. "Oh, Stoney," she cried. "Stoney. How sad. What a terrible injustice. What can we do? What can we do?"

"Nothing," I mumbled. "The graves in the cemetery. Will you take care of them?"

"Oh, Stoney. Yes, yes, yes. But what about you? There must be something we can do."

"We'll file an immediate appeal with the circuit court of appeals," Carl said.

"I just refused all along to accept the fact that we could lose," Xerxes said."I know you're heart broken, Stoney, and so am I. Kafkaesque. That's what it is. There's no rhyme or reason to what's been done here."

"I thank each of you," I said. "I couldn't have made it this far without you. I hope you'll come to see me once in a while. In prison."

"It's time to go, Mr. Bedford," the guard said, tugging at my shoulder.

"Yes, I suppose it is. But let me walk without your hands on my arm. Please. The cameras. The photographers. Leave me some little bit of dignity."

"I'm sorry," the officer said. "The D.A. gave instructions I was to tug you along faster than you wanted to go. He was thinking about the cameras and the photographers, too."

Epilogue

It's still out there, the Confederate flag, waving gently in the late afternoon breeze. God, it's beautiful. I can see it as I look down through the bars on the windows of my jail cell, way up here on top of the county courthouse. I'm in one of the ten cells on the fifth floor in which they hold sentenced prisoners until they haul them away to the state penitentiary.

In prison, a man has a lot of time to review the things that have happened to him, especially when he knows that he'll be shut up for the remainder of his life. The appeals of my sentence to higher courts have been turned down. The system grinds exceedingly slow, but, it grinds, what there is left of it. It took over two months for the appeals court to uphold the lower court's decision.

Carl Krippendorf and Archibald Xerxes are taking my case to the United States Supreme court. Last week, Carl sat down with me in the visitor's room and showed me the petition seeking review. "If anything can get our case heard, I think the pleadings in here will do it," my friend said. "Dean Craig Weynel of the University of Georgia Law School assisted us in the preparation of these papers."

"Dean Weynel?" I asked. "I like that man. The day he took Tighe Boring apart in the courtroom was funny to me." I handed the papers back to Carl. "You think the court will rule in our favor?"

"You never know," Carl said. "Many times, it's like rolling the dice. But it'd be a sin not to go all the way. I certainly wouldn't feel right about it if we didn't. *And it is a 'land mark case' that will take the court into areas where they've never ventured before.*"

"There are two things I want you to do for me, Carl."

"What, Stoney?"

"Take enough of my assets and set them up in a blind trust to pay $1500 a month to the three children of LaJuana Tolman. The source of the checks must remain forever anonymous."

"What?" he exploded. "Why on earth would you do a thing like that?"

"Children need a mother, no matter how low on the moral or social totem that mother may be. You and I both know that if LaJuana Tolman had

405

not come forward and testified on my behalf, she'd probably still be alive today. Perhaps the money might help the children pull through the worst time in their lives."

"That's . . . Well, that's insane, Stoney. You're not responsible for her death. You and I know that DeLong Tolman had her killed."

"Yes, we're reasonably certain that he did, but, he would have had little reason to have her killed but for the fact that she testified on my behalf. Please do it, Carl. My estate is worth over twenty-five million and I can afford it. Seek Roy Bester's help."

He shook his head in amazement. "It's crazy. But, I'll do it. I owe it to you. And the other thing?"

"Draw up the necessary papers to transfer Bedford House to Julie Peel. She and William were planning to live there after they were married."

"But your heirs?" Carl asked. "How will they react to something like this?"

"The closest relatives I have are some distant cousins," I said. "And I haven't seen any of them in years. I don't owe them anything, and I'll never be able to go back there again. It's what I want done, Carl."

Yesterday he brought the necessary papers to me for setting up the blind trust for LaJuana Tolman's children and for effecting the transfer of Bedford House to Julie. I signed them.

Julie came with him. Julie Peel. Each time I look at her, my heart fills with love. That beautiful, willowy, graceful Southern lady. I could see her walking through the library of Bedford House like my mother used to do. Perhaps some day, she'd have children and she could teach them about the portraits on the library walls, tell them about the Bollings and the Bedfords. Somehow, the traditions and our heritage might be kept alive.

"Stoney, you must not do this," she said, holding onto me and crying. "Some how, it just doesn't seem right."

"It's as right as rain, Julie. I'm doing it for William. He loved you, and so did Donna Elaine and I. Without you these last few months, I don't know what I would have done. And William would be applauding right now, if he were here. I know he's looking down on us from heaven and smiling. Let's just say that Bedford House is his yellow rose to his sweetheart each day as long as you live."

"I . . . I don't know what to say. Bedford House is so beautiful. So beautiful."

"Yes, Julie. And it needs a beautiful Southern lady like Julie Peel to preside over it. It hasn't had one since my mother, Mary Jane Bolling."

The reunion with Julie was tearful and touching. I'd swear that even Carl had tears in his eyes, and that had never happened before in the years that I had known him.

I'm still searching for answers as to how I wound up in a place as dreadful as prison, groping through depression's fog which tries to clutch me to its cold, clammy breast every waking moment. I fight it each day, fight like a guerilla hiding in a forest, waiting for the enemy. It's either fight or die from boredom and lack of hope. I've turned to writing in this journal I've started, describing the things that go on around me, recording flashes of thoughts, feelings and impressions. At least, the writing gives me some reason to keep on struggling through the long days of my life that now drag by, oh so slowly.

Morris Light and his associate were here earlier in the day with their television cameras, filming what he said would be some of the final scenes in the documentary he's been making about me, my family and friends—and the opposing forces—in this eight-month long flag controversy.

Light's a thin, greying man, even thinner and grayer than he was eight months ago, if that's possible. He is still enthusiastic and dedicated, a true professional. "This work," he said, tapping his camera. "It's a great human drama, the best thing I've ever done. And it's real. No writer could have come up with the kind of story this is. It's scope, its subject and the characters, it's jarring ending—they should mark it as one of those stories told and retold over the next fifty years, especially in the Southland."

"Those surveillance cameras you had mounted in several places on the night of the attack, Morris," I said. "I wish the shadowy figures had been identifiable. It would have helped to prove the case for the defense."

"Believe me, Stoney. I've tried every kind of technique I know to bring them into clearer focus. But the action took place in the dead of night. Even the moon was hiding. And the cameras were not focused on specific subjects."

I sighed to show my disappointment. I knew he could see how depressed I was with one look at my face."We both know that Canton and Derkin were part of Karim's attack force that night."

Light scratched the back of his head. "I had high hopes about proving that with the video that day in court, Stoney," he said. "Until I found I could not bring the figures into sharper focus." His face took on a resigned expression. "But, that might not have proved our case. Especially after Boring came up with the Forest Gump/Lyndon Johnson example and that 'digitalized computer process.' He made me look like a con artist. He destroyed the credibility of our video."

"You have to give Boring credit," I said. "He's a tough opponent in the courtroom."

Morris talked as his assistant moved the lights to just the right spot to create the effect the two wanted to portray on film. Morris, camera in hand, continued filming. "I want to show the drabness of this place; give the viewer a feel for how prison destroys a man's reason for living. Especially, a person like Stoney Bedford who wanted only to defend his home against attack."

"You pinpointed one of the most difficult things I have to deal with," I said. "I ask the question each morning, 'Why should I get up out of bed today?' I have to really give myself a pep talk. I tell myself that God still has some purpose left for me, that that's why I am still alive. So, I pray and read my Bible and rekindle what little faith I have left."

He and his assistant repositioned the television floodlights. "Damn," Light said. "Look at that bed you have to sleep on. An inch thick mattress atop a sheet of steel. How can a man sleep on something such as that? Move over there, Stoney, close to your bunk. Ah. that's it. That's just right."

The camera continued to grind away. "That naked light bulb hanging from the ceiling," his assistant said. "Let's show that as part of the drabness of this damned place."

He told his assistant to film the same scene of me standing by my bunk from a different angle, then gradually move the camera up to film the light bulb.

"The ordinary criminal," Light said, "one who's caught and convicted, well, he just decides to be smarter the next time and not get caught. For him, it's just the risk he takes. But an innocent person who knows he's a victim of a system intent on destroying him, such a person—like you, Stoney—he doesn't have the same psychology to fall back on. All he thinks about is that his life is wasting away each day and for no purpose."

The man was sensitive to human feelings, to the death of hope which threatened me. "Regardless of what we did in my trial probably wouldn't have mattered too much, Morris," I said. "The government, especially the justice department, wanted me convicted. I was, and still am, a political prisoner. And you know as well as I do, that the members of the jury read the newspapers before they were chosen for the jury. They brought their own mind set to the deliberations. They heard those crowds outside the court-house each day and were frightened, so they took the easy way out."

"Stoney," Light said. "Stand over by that steel commode without a lid or a seat. Then, when I wave my hand, stand in the middle of the room, extend your arms with the hands open and facing up, and shrug. Let that lack of hope look show on your face. A wistful longing, if you please."

I talked as I followed his instructions. "It's the terrible feeling of being shut up and confined to one small space without anything useful to do that drags a person down. The monotony, the boredom, the knowing that you're shut away from society for the rest of your life."

"The media went into a feeding frenzy after you were convicted," Morris said, moving his camera in for a close up of my face. "You would have thought that Gabriel had blown his horn to signal the coming of a great light. They lunged at each of the twelve jury members after the judge released them and badgered them until it's a wonder they have any sanity left."

"They did the same thing in the O.J. Simpson trial. I see in the newspaper where two of the jurors in my trial already have contracts to write books. Each of them got a million dollars in advance. Editors aren't fools. They know a good story when they see one."

"Yeah," Morris said. "That's a lot of money for a publishing house to pay up front for a book yet to be written. They must think it'll sell thousands of copies." He was looking around, still thinking about the documentary. "Move over by the window and look out at the Confederate flag, Stoney. That's it. That's good." He used a zoom lens to gradually bring the flag into focus through the bars on the window after he'd filmed me in the foreground.

Morris was in a talkative mood. "Like you, me, well, like thousands of Americans across this great land of ours, these strange, new influences on juries disturb me. We might as well face up to the changes that the Simpson trial and the Rodney King affair brought to the system of trial by jury. 'A jury of our peers'!"

He snorted. "Who's kidding who? It's an ugly thing. Jury members now decide verdicts, not on the evidence, but on the sociological and psychological aspects surrounding what happened to bring about the trial.

And then, daily the legal analysts try to explain on television what's going on in the courtroom—and in the minds of those who are caught up in the proceedings. Jurors may be sequestered, but they still know what's going on outside the courtroom. They pay close attention to what the press says should be considered."

"I know, Morris," I said. "It's sad but true."

He began packing up his television equipment. "The editing and narration will take another six months and then I hit the road to market it. One thing I've thought about. It's so good, I might just try to market it to theaters as an independent producer. That's a tough way to go, but I believe that word of mouth will make the film one of those cult items that quietly keep attracting movie-goers year after year for decades."

My spirits quickened. "And then, afterwards, there's the marketing of our story through video stores."

It's a September afternoon and the sun is beginning to make its way towards the western horizon. In a way, since the Confederate flag is still flying, and since they didn't pull down General Lee's monument with their four wheel drive vehicles, I guess you could say that I won the battle, but, I sure in hell lost the war, and far more than the war. Far more.

Almost everything I value was consumed in the conflagration. Ah, Lord! I am wrapped in a million threads of guilt spun from my conscience. The demons of despair hold me as their Gulliverian captive and jab me with their barbed spears of regret.

I still don't understand how it all happened. It's incredulous. This is 1996, not 1865, and I'm not the lord of some huge plantation with hundreds of slaves. The forces that brought me to this present low state are so complex, the swiftness of their convergence on me and my family so unimaginable that it just doesn't make sense.

I stood by the window again, for one more view of the outside world before darkness fell. The Confederate flag. It's so beautiful. If only we could have held the high ground at Gettysburg, we'd have won the war. If only . . .

I turned back to write in my journal.

The pieces just don't fit together, at least, not in my mind. My wife and son didn't deserve to die. It was all so uncalled for, but like any war, once it starts, the forces that keep it blazing are no longer in control of mere human beings. The forces take on a life of their own and rage unchecked.

The soldiers on either side of the war become expendable, their deaths scarcely noticeable.

I'm sorry I'm crying. I do that far too often these days. Pardon me while I wipe the sleeve of my limp, gray prison fatigues against my wet cheeks and then blow my nose into this wad of tissues. I hope you'll understand and perhaps even utter a plaintive sigh, for like most of us trapped in such intolerable conditions, I need sympathy. I know there's little of that for me for I've been blackened by the brush of racial intolerance. And that's fatal these days. The more a Southerner protests his innocence of such charges, the more quickly he's convicted in the public mind. He becomes the straw man for unceasing verbal thrusts by the media and the angry masses they've urged on with their inflammatory stories.

Besides, the world moves on so quickly to other things which break upon the public mind, and soon, people like me are forgotten.

I drew in a deep breath and emitted a long sigh. Nowadays, I do this so often, it's almost as automatic as breathing. I never used to be this way. Not Stonewall Bedford, rough, tough outdoorsman who could give as much as he got and never backed down from a fight. I'm an empty hulk now. Most of the fight is gone.

Two days from now, early in the morning, they're going to handcuff me, put me in a sheriff's patrol car with a deputy as a guard, and take me to the state penitentiary one hundred and eighty-three miles from here. Back in July, the jury took forty-seven minutes to deliberate and decide my sentence, "life imprisonment without benefit of parole or pardon"

.

I heard leather heels clicking against the steel floor of the corridor. That would have to be the jailer. Bedford, I told myself. Straighten up. Don't let him see you down in the dumps like this. I lifted my shoulders, straightened up and even tried to summon a smile to my face.

"Mr. Bedford," the kindly man said. "You've got visitors waiting down the hall. Come with me."

"Visitors?"

"Yeah. Two men. Woolford and Erling."

My spirits quickened. I hurried to follow Jim.

The two were sitting at a battered old table, chairs pushed back, waiting. Woolford had on that damned hat on which the brim was turned down all the way around.

"Love that outfit you got on, Stoney," Woolford said. "It's the latest craze, I understand."

"Go to hell, Harris. You smart ass."

"I hope you can stand him for a few minutes," Able said, rubbing his hands across his expansive paunch. "I've just about had enough of his horse shit."

"It's strange," Harris quipped, "but I seem to have that same kind of effect on lots of people. But, my constituents love me. That's why they keep re-electing me."

"But let me tell you why we came. Something happened to both of us last night," Able said. "Something we thought you ought to know."

"Oh," I said. "You mean you didn't come see me just to bring me cookies? What happened?"

Able looked around to make certain that the jailer couldn't hear what he said. He motioned for me to drag my chair closer.

"Damn, Able," I said. "It must be something really important."

Harris Woolford drew his chair close enough so that our heads were almost touching each other.

"You remember Nelson Withaus who testified in your behalf at the trial?" Able asked.

"Yes, he's been a close friend of mine for years. Why? Did he die?"

"Hell no," Harris said. "Quit being so damned negative. He came to see Able and me last night at Able's house. Said there was something big going on that we should know about."

"He asked me to turn on my computer and log onto the internet," Able said. "I'm not too great on the internet, so he had Harris and me draw up our chairs while he took over, surfing the damned thing until he found the web sites he wanted us to see. He's so skilled at it until I think he lost both of us along the way."

"What we saw was chilling," Harris said. "I've known since July that many sites on the internet were filled with angry comments over what thousands of people call a travesty. That's what they've labeled your trial. 'A travesty.' Night after night, people on the web talk about the unfairness of your trial, about the justice department, Boring, DeLong Tolman, Mueschle Jabbar and the jury foreman, Alice Rinker."

I took in a deep breath. Suddenly, I didn't feel as lost and as lonely as I had a few minutes ago. Thousands of people? On my side? Expressing anger? I wished I could sit down to a computer and search out those sites, read what they said, tell them my thoughts. It would give me more courage, and right now, I needed something to help stiffen my spine. Something more than my own resolve.

"Thousands of individuals, as well as people connected with the dozens of militia groups, from all parts of the country, are really upset about what has happened to you, Stoney," Able said. "Withaus said they'd been expressing their fears and concerns about an all-powerful central government since you were indicted. Things really heated up on the internet after you were sentenced."

"They've picked up that phrase, 'political prisoner'," Harris said. "They're running entire chapters of Kafka's "The Prisoner" on the 'net and putting your name in parentheses each time Kafka describes that poor man in his novel who's the bewildered prisoner. Several days ago they came to the parts of the book where Kafka's prisoner kept trying to find out what he was charged with but never could penetrate the governmental bureaucratic maze."

" 'Watch what's happening now,' Withaus told us as he moved from site to site," Able said. "Harris and I couldn't believe what we read. Person after person kept saying, 'They finally executed the poor son-of-a-bitch in Kafka's book. He never knew what he was charged with. The government killed him. For no reason, except they had the power. Now, they're doing the same thing to Stonewall Bedford, American citizen."

As hard as I was trying, it was difficult for me to comprehend the scope of what they were telling me. Thousands of people in our country are no longer the obedient, uncomplaining citizen who fears the power of a central government. They're more informed, they're more expressive of their anger, they're ready to fight back.

"'Now, let me take you to another site,' Withaus told us." Able's face was grim. "'And the source of these comments,' Withaus said, 'are people who've decided to give as much as the government is giving Stonewall Bedford. On the internet, they're exhorting each other to render unto Caesar what is Caesar's and take an eye for an eye and a tooth for a tooth.' It scared hell out of us."

"You're not serious, are you?" My mind was whirling, trying to follow all of this.

"Hell, yes," Harris said. "We're serious. You don't think we'd make up something like this, do you?"

"What'd the people on the internet say they were going to do?" I asked. "And when?"

"They didn't spell it out exactly," Able said. "The people on the internet are clever as hell. They know how to communicate with others of like mind without spelling it out in detail. That's not all. They go through so many maneuvers and down so many different trails, no one can pinpoint exactly who's saying what and where they might be located."

Harris took his hat off so he could lean in closer. "Something big's going to happen. Shit, those folks on the net are ready to strike back. 'They made an example out of an innocent citizen who tried to defend his home against savage, murdering thugs. Now, we're going to give those kind of people some examples they can think about.' I'm not shitting you, Stoney. There it was, right there on Able's computer screen."

"You should have seen Withaus's face," Able said. "He was almost like a child at a Christmas party. He kept bouncing up and down in my computer chair, hitting the computer keys, going from site to site, telling us to 'watch this. Here's the same thing. It's on over twenty different web pages.'"

I'd never seen Able like this. "Look at my hands," he said. "They've been trembling since eleven o'clock last night."

"I logged onto the internet this morning at 5 a.m.," Harris said. "I found some of the same sites Withaus carried us to. And the words I read have gotten even more strident since last night. It's like some giant virus has infected the minds of thousands of the country's citizens. Sanity has taken a back seat. People are mad as hell and they're going to do something terrible."

"We'd better notify the authorities," I said. "If we have such information and don't divulge it, conceivably we could be charged as accessories if anything happens."

Harris and Able both started laughing.

"The authorities?" Able said. "Man, you must be kidding. Hell, probably three million people or more are reading this stuff on the internet hour after hour. If the authorities attempted to charge us, three million other people would have to be charged as accessories at the same time."

"You're still putting other people ahead of Stoney Bedford," Harris said. "How much can you take before you get mad enough to wish some one else bad luck? We're not involved in this stuff, old friend. Like most people, we found out about it on the Internet. We're not promoting these ideas. We can't be charged with anything, regardless of what happens."

"Yeah," I said. "I guess you're right. I just hate to see any more people die in this controversy. Thirteen have already died. That's far too many."

"One dead person was too many," Able said. "But that's over now. The government is sending you to the penitentiary and you're innocent. That's what these people on the internet are so burned up about. You take Withaus. He's so enthusiastic about what he reads until he doesn't even try to hide his sympathies. 'I hope they kill 'em all,' he said."

"We can't control what other people do if we don't even know them. Or where they live. Or what specifically they plan to do. And to whom," Harris said. "Besides, probably every law enforcement agency in the country, including the FBI, knows what's going on on the 'net. We just wanted you to know, so if anything does happen, you won't have a heart attack and be eat up with the dumb ass."

My feelings were hurt. "I guess sometimes I do act dumb. But, that's just the way my mind works."

"I apologize, man," Harris said. "But, we knew the press would come running to you if anything does happen and we didn't want you getting yourself into deep shit. Just act surprised. Like Able and I will if anything does happen. Don't let on that you even know what's been going on. Tell them you're in jail and are not responsible for anything."

"Yeah," I said. "I don't want to buy any more trouble than I've already got. I see what you mean. It makes sense. O.K. I'll keep my cool."

The jailer stuck his head in the door. "I'm sorry, but you guys have already stayed too long. You'd better go now." He nodded to Harris and Able.

"Stoney," Able said,. sticking out his hand. "We're your friends. You can count on us."

"Yeah," Harris said, tapping me on the shoulder. "We're sorry as hell that you are here. It still doesn't make too much sense. We'll see you again. Oh, we did bring you some cookies." He handed me a decorated container and laughed.

"If you want to see me again, better make it tomorrow," I said. "Day after tomorrow, they're hauling me away to the pen. Early in the morning."

"That soon?" Harris said. "Damn, man. I'm sure sorry." He stood up and reached for his brief case. "I don't know why I carry this damned thing. It's just habit, I guess."

Able had his hands on his big stomach. "What they've done to you, Stoney, ain't right. Nothing fair about it. But then, we don't make the rules."

"The rules," Harris said, putting his hat back on. "People in America don't like a lot of the rules the government forces down our throats. That's the source of this trouble. Rules. Kafkaesque rules."

I wish Morris Light hadn't pointed out how thin my mattress was. That night, after the lights were turned out and I lay down, the steel under the mattress seemed to be right next to my body. My muscles ached; my bones were tired; my nerves taut. I hate to try to sleep feeling like that. The next morning when I wake up, it's as though I hadn't slept all night long.

During my fitful dreams, I was surfing the Internet. My body was the pointer. It was being plunged into the web sites and people were shouting at me. "You've messed up our home page," they yelled. "Get out of here." Then, some of them began throwing rocks at me and there was no place I could hide. They were screaming and cursing me.

Towards daylight, I heard a soft voice calling. "Mr. Bedford. Wake up. It's Jim. I've brought you some fresh coffee and the morning paper."

I shook my head and put my feet onto the floor. "What time is it?" I asked.

"It's 6 o'clock," he said. "But some terrible things have happened I knew you'd want to know about."

"Terrible things?" I don't know why I thought of that face I'd seen at city council meeting that day back in February when Karim was telling us what bad things lay ahead for white people. It was the face of the older man who had said to me, "These folks ought to know that they're pushing us too far, Mr. Bedford. We'll make them pay. Two can play at the same game." I'd never seen him before that day; I'd never seen him since.

"Here," Jim said. "Here's a pot of coffee to help you wake up. Drink some coffee and read this newspaper. Those terrible things. It's all in here." He handed me a folded newspaper.

"What's in here that's so terrible?" I was certain some of it was connected to what Harris and Able had whispered to me yesterday.

"You can read all about it in the newspaper. Last night they killed five people. All the dead are people connected to your trial. Crossbows through the back or chest. A terrible thing. I don't know how to react."

I was stunned. "Five people? Who?"

"It's all there," he said. "In the newspaper. I've got to go back and watch some more of NNC That's all they're talking about this morning." The leather heels of his shoes clicked on the steel floor as he walked away.

I poured coffee into a cup and sipped at it. My mind wasn't quite awake yet, and I was almost afraid of what I'd see in the newspaper. I walked to the window and raised it so that some cool air would rush in. Deep breaths. That's what I needed. Fresh air into my sleepy lungs. The coffee and the air began to work. I went back to my bunk and sat down. For several seconds, I thanked God for another day of life, repeating the phrase, "This is the day the Lord hath made. I will rejoice and be glad in it."

I opened the newspaper. Across the top of the first page, black headlines screamed "FIVE PEOPLE KILLED WITH ARROWS FROM CROSSBOWS."

Five people? Who?

"BORING, TOLMAN, RINKER, JABBAR AND HINDSMITH."

My God. No. Even Alice Rinker and Hindsmith? I didn't want to believe it.

There was a picture of Boring sprawled next to his Lincoln Town car alongside the highway. You could see the arrow protruding from his back. I thought of Tom Farris and the arrow through his back the day they burned the Confederate flag. There were smaller pictures of the other four below that of Boring's body.

"EACH OF THE FIVE CONNECTED TO BEDFORD TRIAL."

The brief, fast reading paragraphs told how each of them had died before twelve o'clock last night. Boring was on his way home from a cocktail party and for some reason had stopped by the side of the highway where he was shot. Rinker had been to a church meeting. As she walked to her car in the church parking lot, the arrow had killed her swiftly and silently. DeLong Tolman had been visiting his girl friend. When he started to leave at a few minutes past eleven, as he walked to his automobile the arrow from a crossbow found his back. Jabbar and Hindsmith had been jogging late at night, Jabbar along the streets of Forest and Hindsmith on a jogging trail in a park in the Virginia suburb where he lived. The silent arrows dropped each of them on the jogging path.

A separate story on the front page told of the connections of each of the dead people to my trial. Another covered the heavy Internet traffic about Kafka, *'The Trial'*, the unfairness of my trial and sentencing, and the 'eye for an eye and a tooth for a tooth' retributions hinted at in the skillfully coded language of veteran Internet users. It included entire paragraphs copied from web sites.

"WHO COULD BE BEHIND THESE FIVE MURDERS?"

This story was filled with speculations as to the identity of the archers. There was a picture of Tom Farris dying in the flames of the burning flag. The story quoted several law enforcement authorities, some of them wild-eyed and disconnected from reality, most of them vague in their reasonings. One was brave enough to say, "The truth of the matter is, no one knows who killed the five. Nor are they likely to ever know. There's one thing we do know now. Thousands of people in the U.S. are not at all happy with our justice system and other government actions."

I could feel my heart racing. My pulse pounded in my ears like some temple gong. I let the paper fall onto my bunk, picked up my coffee cup and walked to the window. The fresh air. Perhaps it would help to clear my head. I knew that Harris and Able were right. The press would be clamoring to see me. They'd try to wrest hasty opinions from me, edit them, slant them into something I'd never said and never meant to say.

The advice those two had given me was sound. Hell, I didn't know anything about the killing of these five, didn't know about the Internet traffic, had no way of knowing the moods of those venting their protest against oppressive government all across the Internet. How could I? I'd been in prison since that ignominious day they'd pronounced me guilty, handcuffed me and led me away. I had no access to television, the newspaper or the telephone. Certainly not to a computer. I wouldn't know how to log onto the Internet, even if I did have a computer in my jail cell.

I walked back to my bunk, poured more coffee and picked up the newspaper again. The first streaks of dawn were beginning to lighten up the sky. I reread the headlines and the stories. None of the murdered people had had an opportunity to communicate a single word to any one. Each had died swiftly, silently.

I remembered the day Harris, Able and I were watching the acne-scarred face of Tom Farris as he leered into the television cameras and described how he would burn the Confederate flag. He'd soaked the huge flag with gasoline, poured a tiny trail in front of him as he backed up from the soaked flag some twenty feet, struck a match, then lighted the vapor trail. The flag burst into flames. The cheers had gone up, and then, Farris had begun stumbling towards the burning flag.

Horrified, the television newsman had stammered, "My God. Farris has been shot through the back with an arrow. He's falling into the burning flag. His clothes are on fire. His hair is ablaze. People are stunned. DeLong Tolman is trying to beat out the flames with his coat. It's awful. Terrifying. I've never seen anything like this in all my years of broadcasting."

The jailer came back down the hall, carrying my breakfast tray. Jim was almost unable to talk. His face was twisted into a mask of sadness. "Wish you could watch NNC news. I've never seen anything like it."

He handed me the tray, backed out and locked the cell door behind him. "Them reporters and TV folks have already started calling. They want to know if you'll see them for a news conference."

I laughed. "No, I won't see them. All I know about what has happened is what I've read in this newspaper you brought me. I have nothing to say to them."

"The sheriff telephoned to say that he's coming up here to talk to you," Jim said. "He told me the news people were running him crazy."

"I don't have anything to say to the sheriff. I don't know anything. He'll have to handle the news people the best he can."

"You don't want to talk to him then?" Jim asked.

"Not if I can help it. Of course, it's his jail. He can certainly go any where he wants to go in this abysmal place. And that includes coming back here to my cell. But I'm not going to discuss these murders with him. Please call my attorney, Carl Krippendorf. Tell him to come up here as soon as he can get here. Tell him I said it's urgent."

"I'll do it, Mr. Bedford. I like Mr. Krippendorf. He's so kind and considerate to every one."

At 7:30, Jim unlocked my door. "Come with me," he said. "Mr. Krippendorf is in the visitor's room."

I followed the jailer down the corridor. Carl stood up as I entered the visitor's room. "Stoney," he said. "I didn't know what to think when I saw the news about the killing of those five people."

"Jim brought me the morning newspaper at 6 a.m. That's when I first learned about it."

"I guess the media representatiaves are screaming for a news conference," he said. "You don't owe them a damned thing. You had no way of knowing what has been going on on the Internet. Tell them to back off."

"That's what I want to see you about, Carl. I've had enough of this shit. I want you to tell them to back off. My civil rights have been violated enough and I want these violations stopped, once and for all."

"I can do that," Carl said. "I'm sick and tired of them beating on you. I congratulate you for your willingness to fight back. It's about time you quit playing 'Mr. nice guy.' "

"And the sheriff says he's coming up to see me. I want you in the room when he comes. He probably sees this as a great opportunity to get himself onto the networks and in the newspapers. At my expense. He is in a re-election campaign you know."

"Yes, I know," Carl said. "We'll see that he doesn't use you."

"I guess the blacks are already raising hell."

"Yeah, Stoney. The minorities have started screaming again, saying you are behind all of this. Either you or your sympathizers. The 'Merciful Ayatollah' has said publicly that you probably planned and arranged the murders."

"That pontificating, sorry, lying bastard," I said, pounding my fist onto the battered table. "I've had enough of him and his kind. I've suffered enough because of his venomous prejudice against whites, me in particular. I'm not going to take it anymore."

"Let me answer the Ayatollah," Carl said. "If any one had to get an arrow through their backs, it should have been that prejudiced bastard. He'll keep on fanning his anti-white theme until it destroys us all. Because we know and have proof that you knew nothing about this, let's sue the bastard for fifty million. Let's cause him some pain. I think we'll win."

Jim opened the door and said: "Sheriff Howe is on his way up. He'll be surprised to see you, Mr. Krippendorf."

"Yes, I suspect he will. I guess Bert has on his white cowboy hat and his pistol strapped to his hip."

"You said it," the jailer smiled. "There's a crowd of fifty or so reporters and cameraman downstairs yelling for him to bring you down. I believe that's what he's planning to do."

"Let me handle this, Stoney," Carl said. "I brought this small tape recorder along. It might be good for us to get what the sheriff says on tape." He turned it on and hid it partially behind his brief case.

420

Bert Howe busted through the door like King Kong roaring out of his tomb of antiquity and squashing the little people as they cowered behind buildings.

"OK, Bedford. Let's go downstairs and see them folks from the media." He looked up and saw Carl for the first time. "What the hell are you doing here?" he snarled.

"Don't address me in such a fashion you big bastard," Carl yelled. "This is America and the last time I checked, you hadn't been elected king."

Howe was 6'8" tall and weighed over 350 pounds. "Listen, old man," he snarled at Carl. "This is my jail and I do anything here I want to do. And, I just think I'll take my pistol and beat you to the floor. I can tell them you attacked me."

He turned to me. "Bedford, it'd be best if you just followed me to the elevator so we can go downstairs and see them folks from the media." He adjusted his white, ten-gallon Texas cowboy hat and hitched up his beige cord trousers. His snakeskin cowboy boots glistened with a high shine.

"My client isn't going anywhere with you, Howe," Carl said. "We were having a private conversation until you busted in like a big ox."

"I told you to stand back, old man," Howe said and placed his hand on his pistol. "Or, do I have to knock you on your ass?"

"Oh, you're going to beat me up? Or shoot me?" Carl laughed. "Don't you know that you are violating not only my client's civil rights but mine as well?"

"Civil rights ain't got nothing to do with it. Bedford owes it to them people to come downstairs so they can question him."

"Question him about what?" Carl demanded.

"Them bow and arrow killings," Howe yelled. "Ain't you seen them on TV this morning?"

"Yes, I saw the news on TV," Carl said. "But what does that have to do with Stoney Bedford?"

"He probably planned them murders and arranged to have them carried out," Howe yelled. "Now, get out of my way, old man. Come on, Bedford." Howe reached for my arm. I drew back.

"Don't you dare touch me, Howe," I said. "I've had enough of you and your kind, bullying and shoving me around. By this afternoon at 5 o'clock, I'm entering suit against you for fifty million dollars for violating my civil rights. The first time I knew about those killings was when the jailer brought me the morning newspaper. Now, get your ass out of here so my attorney and I can finish talking about the suit we're filing against you today."

"I'm going to the D.A. at nine o'clock," Howe said, looking at Carl, "and filing charges against you for obstructing justice."

"Obstructing justice?" Carl and I both started laughing. "I shudder to think that a bastard as ignorant as you is charged with the administration of justice in this county. C'mon. Give us a break."

"Leave, Howe," I said, and pointed towards the door.

"I'll make you both sorry you dared to defy me," the sheriff said. He tugged on his big white hat, hitched up his tan cord trousers, ran his finger tips along his gun belt and stomped from the room.

Carl leaned over and talked into the tape recorder. "This is Carl Krippendorf, attorney. In the room with me is my client, Stonewall Bedford. The time is now 8:17 a.m. Sheriff Bert Howe has been yelling and carrying on like a madman. He is the other person you heard on the tape. The date is September, 18th, 1996."

Carl pressed the button to turn the tape recorder off. "I'm going straight to my office and start preparing the papers for the filing of the suit against that big, dumb bastard. I'm going to join you as a party in the suit. He violated my rights as a citizen also. I'll be back before five p.m. to get your signatures on the papers. We'll have fun with this one. And there's no doubt that we'll win. We've got the evidence on this tape player."

I returned to my journal. For almost an hour I wrote very fast. It was important that I get down my impressions of what was happening.

I refused to allow myself to get caught up in the frenzy which I knew was developing over the killing of Hindsmith, Boring, Rinker, Tolman and Jabbar. I'd ridden the emotional roller-coaster for so long and at such high rates of speed, until I had resolved to never get caught up in such insanity again. Let the media people froth and run around in circles, yelling like frustrated children. They'd not get hold of me again. At least I was in a place where they couldn't get to me, now that we had banished the ambitious Sheriff Howe.

As Carl had said, "We'll have fun with this one," referring to the suit we'd be filing against King Kong Howe. Now, some people other than Stoney Bedford were going to be squirming in some courtroom, except this time, the fellow doing the squirming would be guilty as charged in the suit.

I reread some of the lines I'd written, slipped into deep thought, then wrote again. Things will never be the way they used to be. No use fooling ourselves. Now, millions of our citizens decide what's right and what's wrong on the basis of what answer will better accomplish their goals of the moment. Moral relativism. Fletcher's situation ethics. The '60's and the '70s brought this about. The traditional values and morals that used to guide us have been swept away, never to return. The stress of living in this new world is, to many of us, almost unbearable.

Just eight months ago, I guess you could say that I was one of those "pillars of society." Compassionate. God-fearing. Straight laced. Walking with my back straight and my head held high. Hewing to an unbending moral code handed down through generations of Bedfords and Bollings.

I'd sold my chain of quick-mart, convenience stores nine years before for well over twenty-seven million dollars. Called myself retired. Congratulated myself for having navigated life's treacherous currents so well and arriving on that distant shore of peace and contentment we often sing about down at my Baptist church.

Peace and contentment. I have since learned that the world I pictured was mythical. Those two words have proved to be such hollow words now, burned from my soul by the fires of torture in which I was trapped. Once those who wanted to banish the flying of the Confederate flag threw down the gauntlet there was little else my psychological make up would allow me to do except pick it up. The moment I did, I was launched onto the dangerous path of defending my beliefs and principles against an implacable foe. There was no turning back.

After I sold the business, Donna Elaine and I took a three month cruise and sailed around the world. Stopped in dozens of countries, walked and toured with our maps and tourist folders clutched in our hands, smiling at everyone and using our hands to make signs the natives somehow interpreted, and listening to the babble of foreign voices we couldn't understand.

"A symphony of dissonance," Donna Elaine called the strange sounding voices. "They remind me of an Aron Copeland orchestral piece we've heard the Atlanta Symphony play in concerts."

Eager, questioning, we both had the time of our lives as we traveled. We saw strange and wondrous places I'd read about all my life; ate foods I couldn't even begin to name; walked the crowded streets with the wide eyes of children. But no place could begin to compare to these red clay hills of

Georgia. When we finally got back home, I wanted to fall down and kiss the ground.

Donna Elaine. Oh God, how I loved that gracious and gentle lady. I wake up from nightmares yelling "No, no, no! She's not dead. It's not possible. Why, she was the kindest person you'd ever want to meet. Always doing things for other people, especially the old and sick and lonely and the homeless." Then, I remember. I'm in prison and what I'd been dreaming about was very real.

My wife. That clear, controlled singing voice of hers kept her singing up to the day she died. On Sundays, I'd watch her joyfully singing with other choir members in our church's choir loft. I can still see that expression on her face as she sang solos and knew she was lifting the spirits of burdened people heavenward.

And William? Like my daddy before me, I taught him guns and hunting and spent many a night with him at the hunting lodge on the far reaches of our family plantation that has been in the family for a hundred years or more.

William and his fiancee, Julie, were to be married in July, but instead, on the day she was to become his bride, she put on her wedding gown and went to the cemetery where she placed a single yellow rose on his grave. She's still carrying the torch for him, and it saddens me to the point where I'd just like to curl up somewhere and die.

Oh, they're bring me my evening meal, such as it is. In this jail, things happen at the same time each day. The jailer's all right. He's my friend. Can't say much for the sheriff though.

"Evening, Mr. Bedford."

"Evening, Jim. Good to see you."

"It's good to see you too, Mr. Bedford. I know I've told you before, but most of the folks in Forest, and the rest of Georgia, too, well, they're on your side. They are with you standing up for what many of us in the South still believe in. Flying that Confederate flag don't hurt nobody."

"It has always seemed such an innocent thing to most of us, Jim. It's been flying on top of that monument far over seventy years. Then, all of a sudden, the black people decided it offended them and demanded that it be pulled down."

"Yeah, Mr. Bedford," Jim said. "Ain't that ridiculous? Our flag ain't no sysmbol of slavery. It's just part of our proud history and can't be erased, as bad as they might like to see it done. The Civil War happened. Should we make believe that it didn't?"

The short, stocky man's voice was rising. I could see that his anger about the whole thing simmered just beneath the surface and was ready to spill over at the drop of a hat. He hitched up his gray pants with the black stripe down the outside of each leg and jutted out his chin in a show of defiance against any who dared to assault his deeply held beliefs that were as natural a part of his being as breathing.

I set the food tray down on the small steel table in my cell and picked up the cup of coffee. I sipped on it and watched the graying man who sometimes couldn't find the words to say exactly what he was feeling. The setting sun was still lighting up the cool September day.

"Somehow, Jim," I said. "Together, as people, we must find a way to stop this increasing madness that seems now to have become a separate, uncontrollable force. If we could just learn to let each other be, without trying to cram a different philosophy down each other's throat. A man, any man, is what he believes in deeply, those beliefs that have been ingrained into him by his raising. He can't be any other way. This militancy of the various pressure groups has grown too powerful, their voices too shrill. The voices of reason are drowned out."

I moved to the window again so I could see the Confederate flag waving in the rays of the late afternoon sun. I suddenly remembered a radio announcer who loved the falling of night as much as I do. "God of the dusk hour," he used to say reverently into the microphone each evening. "Reach thy gentle hand out over every hustling city street, Out over little towns and rural lands, and into all the troubled hearts that beat, Put forth tranquility . . . Give to man the peace he would attain if he could."

Jim and I were silent for long moments. The faces of my dead son and wife swam through my consciousness. I miss them so and they're dead because of me. If only I'd let a lifetime of beliefs drain away; if only I'd forgotten my fierce pride in the way we are as Southerners and in my right to live my life as an independent soul; if only I'd recognized that I was one of the last of the mastodons and was doomed to extinction. If only . . .

I don't think I can stand to live with this guilt over what has happened much longer. I don't deserve to still be alive and walking around. I've thought about hanging myself here in the cell, but they've designed this place so that it's practically impossible to do it. Anyhow, I've decided I'm not going to do such a cowardly thing. In the years I have left, I'm going to keep on fighting for the things in which I believe. It's the only thing that keeps me going.

I saw again the face of the older man at the council meeting back in February when Karim and I were going at it. "They ought to know," he said, "that we've had enough . . . "

I'm certain that the swift silent flights of the death arrows last night spring from that feeling that man expressed that day. And Sheriff Bert Howe this morning. Eager, for his own political gain, to drag me right back into the middle of the fire. Carl and I both had had enough, so we faced him down. And got his incriminating words on tape. You can't be too nice in this world. If you are, everybody and his brother slaps you around. Sometimes I forget that, probably because I want the world to be different.

Who knows? Perhaps I'll keep on filling up the pages of my journal until I have enough to write a book about what happened to me and why. One that's powerful enough and rational enough to break through the seemingly impenetrable wall that surrounds the mental fortresses of the liberals and the press—and black people, too. Maybe I could persuade them to quit hammering on people like me just because we're Southerners and happen to be the most readily available straw men on which they can vent their frustrations, hatreds and prejudices.

I don't know, though. People might not buy my ideas. Yet, Harris' and Able's recounting of what they've seen on the Internet leads me to believe there are thousands of other people out there who believe as I do. Considering what happened to those five people last night leaves little doubt about that.

It seems that everybody has to have some person or group they can kick around, and lashing the South is such great sport. It's nothing new, though. They've been doing it for two hundred years. I don't know why Yankees have always looked down their nose at us Southern people. But, if they could see how we feel and think, it might make a difference. Hell. Who am I kidding? They'd probably still laugh and sneer at us. Yell that what I've written is the raving of a bigot.

There you go, Bedford. Pipe dreaming again. Write a book? What publisher in his right mind would dare publish such a book? Why, it just isn't possible nowadays. It's not politically correct to tell the truth about the situation between blacks and whites—how bad it is and how it's getting worse by the day. As a matter of fact, the situation is now almost at the flash point of open warfare. But if someone doesn't try to call off the dogs . . .

I wish I didn't know human nature so well. There'll never be an end to this frenzy. Never. It's too profitable for those who are running us through with their verbal bayonets, too good a story filled with the exciting stuff of controversy and drama that turns the media into the hounds of the Baskervilles.

I chided myself again. Why do you think you're any different, Bedford? In today's climate, the screams of "racism" would rent the air; the breast beating of the enraged liberals and the media would muster the dissenters for demonstrations aimed at making the reading of what I write socially unacceptable. Of course, before it was all over, the author would be branded as a Ku Klux Klan member in a white sheet torching a gasoline soaked cross. It's not true, but who cares about truth these days?

It's the method they've used to intimidate thousands of Southerners and cowered us into fear and subjugation, made us ashamed that we are the people of the South. There's very little, if any, willingness to protest left inside of us. We people of the South seem to have lost this ability. They've made us fearful to assert our sense of independence. They've collared us with a sense of guilt that's worse than the iron maiden, and even more deadly because it's so insidious.

I was up pacing my tiny cell again. How I wished for the hunting lodge deep in the woods behind Bedford House. There's room there for a person to roam and enjoy his freedom. After I was first elected and installed in public office, it was a heady brew. "He's a man of vision," the newspaper headlined after I'd pushed through several council measures designed to solve some of the city's pressing needs.

Vision? That's a joke. If I'd seen what lay ahead for me, I would have run screaming through the night in search of a hiding place. I'd have resigned and faded away. In those heady, earlier days, opposing forces had not yet closed in for the kill, had not yet handed me my sop of bitter brew.

Jim's voice brought me back to the harshness of my prison cell. "Well, Mr. Bedford. I guess I'll say goodbye now. I won't be here in the morning when they come to take you away."

I reached my hand out to him. He clasped it. "Thanks, Jim. For all your kindnesses to me."

"I loved the way you and Mr. Krippendorf put Sheriff Howe in his place this morning," he said, as he turned and walked back down the corridor.

I stood at the window again and looked down at the marble monument over which the Confederate flag flew. A white-haired black workman was lowering the flag just before sunset. Nearby, the stars and stripes of our majestic United States flag was still flying, fifty feet higher than the Confederate flag. On its own tall flag pole. The workman moved to lower it, also. On my amphibious assault ship during the war, I'd often thrilled at the sight of our flag as the German bombers tried to sink us. Through all the exploding of the bombs and the bursting of the shells we used to try to knock them from the sky, our flag was still there, flying high.

I looked at my watch. It was 7:13.

"Well, General Bedford," the bearded young white man in the cell across from me taunted. "I see you still looking at that dammed rebel flag a dozen times a day. Each time, I'm tempted to laugh. Tell me again, what happened to you and your family. Was it worth it? Was it worth trading your wife and son for all this hero worship and a Southerner's dreams of past glory? I mean, your taking on those wild-eyed bastards who wanted to pull that worthless rag down?"

Despite the anger that dripped from his words, I liked Ralph Ainsworth. Rough, unschooled, belligerent, Ralph had killed the man he'd caught having sex with his wife. He didn't do it on the spur of the moment, as most of us would have. No, he thought about it for several days. Premeditated murder. That's why he'd been sentenced to death. They'd be moving him down to the penitentiary tomorrow morning, too.

My voice broke. "No, Ralph. I've lost everything that meant anything to me. No sir. Nothing is worth doing if you have to pay that kind of a price."

"Hell, General. Go ahead and cry," Ralph said. "I would, too—if I was in the fix you've gotten yourself into."

"I know a man's not supposed to cry, Ralph, but I'm just human and can't help it. My life's messed up and there's no way out for me."

"My old snuff-dipping granny used to tell me," Ralph said. "'If you mess with shit long enough, you're going to get some of it on you.'"

He laughed. I guess you could call the noise that came out of his throat a laugh. It was weird. It sounded like a newly started chain saw that sputtered, roared, then died.

"Ralph," I said. "I had to do what I did. I simply couldn't help it. It was a matter of principle. I don't think the truth of what's going on has sunk in yet with too many people across the country. Most of us are too busy drinking beer and watching TV when we get home from work in the evenings to figure out what's happening. Besides, we don't want to know. It's too unpleasant."

"Man," Ralph laughed. "You got things all figured out. Everybody used everybody else in this country. It's fuck or get fucked. I ain't like you. I don't feel that strong 'bout nothing."

The laughter, a different kind, from a cell farther down the hall, startled me. I had learned that in prison there was seldom any genuine laughter among inmates. Laughter here was used to punctuate thoughts and words and telegraph the feelings of inmates. This laugh, like Ralph's, also had an insane quality that could scare a person. As many times as I'd heard it since last Saturday night when they brought the man in and locked him up, you'd think I'd be used to it by now.

It came from a black gang member, a rich drug pusher, who'd fought the police fiercely when they arrested him after he'd gunned down two members of a rival black gang trying to invade his territory. Such encroachment on a drug dealer's territory was a thing that very few would have been crazy enough to try.

"What's so dammed funny, Boom Boom?" Ralph yelled.

"You shit heads are unreal," Boom Boom yelled. The laugh punctuated the meaning of his words. Arrogant, angry, unafraid, vengeful.

"The General. That old racist white bastard who killed eight of our finest young black men over that dammed flag that stands for everything us blacks hate." He laughed again. "But at least, my black brothers killed his wife and son before they died. For the killing of my brothers, General, your wife and son deserved to die."

The piercing quality of insanity that laced his laugh grated on my nerves. He exulted over the killing of my family and expressed it openly and often. The thoughts of "the brothers" killing Donna Elaine and William gave him some indefinable satisfaction in which to glory.

"Fuck you, Boom Boom," Ralph yelled. "You're nothing but a thug. A murderous killer. A drug pusher. You're the one those thugs should have gunned down the night they attacked the General's house. Not Bedford's family."

"Look who's calling who a killer," Boom Boom yelled. "Seems to me there's a fellow out in the graveyard 'cause you stuck him real good with a knife."

"Fuck you," Ralph yelled. "I wish I could get to you in a fair fight. But, I forgot, you don't fight that way."

"Boom Boom."

"Yeah, General."

"Got a question for you. Why do you hate white folks so much? We haven't done anything to you. Except try to help you."

"You fucking well know why we hate your white asses. You fucking honkys made slaves out of us. You raped our women. You keep your foot on the black man's neck. Won't give us no jobs, no decent houses to live in, no money to pay for doctors and medicine when we get sick. So, I push drugs to help my folks forget about their miseries, cause when they're high, they're floating in a much prettier world than the one you honkys force us to live in."

His laugh told me he really believed that whites were the root causes of all the troubles he'd named. I'd heard it all before.

"Yeah," Boom Boom said. "I push drugs. Make a lot of money, too. Got me a Cadillac, fine clothes, lots of women. I'm a big hero in the 'hood. Folks look up to old Boom Boom. Most of the young boys want to be like me."

He was telling it like it was, at least the part about the young blacks wanting to copy the same way of life Boom Boom was living. Blue Combs and Wash Washington had told me the same thing many times.

"In the 'hood, what more could a young black man want?" Wash asked. "At least they can make enough money pushing drugs to live high—as long as they're still alive. Which usually ain't a very long time."

"But Wash," I'd ask. "Why don't they get an education and use the American economic system to work their way out of poverty? That's what many poor white people do And that's also what Asians and Vietnamese do."

"That's simple," Wash replied. "They can't see working their way out the same way you whites do. Success that way is not a part of the black man's cultural heritage. They don't believe they can build a better life for themselves in a competitive society. They don't understand the American, do-it-yourself system in the first place, nor how they can fit into it. That route takes too long for a black to use to break out. They want the same things whites have, and they want these things now. And without having to work too hard for them."

Boom Boom was not through venting his hatred of whites and his frustration with being black. "You white folks don't think you've done anything to us black folks?" he asked incredulously. "If that ain't a fucking joke. We're gonna force you to see how wrong you treated us. The Merciful Ayatollah. Now there's somebody who's done something for black people with his Nation of Islam. The Ayatollah is telling us to stand up tall and fight for our rights. He's the one who's gonna lead us black folks out of the slavery you honkys forced on us."

The laughter came again, emotional punctuation marks for his next words. "There's gonna be war, man. The Ayatollah's boys are training us, arming us, plotting for the war that's coming between us blacks and you white racist bastards. And guess what? We'll win. We'll win."

"A revolution usually consumes its own children, Boom Boom," I yelled. "It would be a war of genocide in which millions would be killed. Like in Rawanda, Burundi and Somalia. And Croatia and Liberia. You want that?"

"No, it won't burn us all, General. Us black folks will win because you honkys don't believe we're serious. Neither do them newspaper and television folks. They think we're just spouting off. Just like you and other whites, they feel guilty about what they've done to blacks and by pushing our cause, it's a way they can make themselves feel a little better."

Boom Boom was laughing convulsively now. "Yeah, General. We want what you white racist bastards have. And we're gonna kill you, take what you have and push you down like you've pushed us down since you brought us here as slaves. You white bastards enjoy kicking us around. You're the cause of all our problems. When we win the war, then we'll raise the flag of the Nation of Islam and burn all the other flags. We don't want no stars and stripes. No dammed Confederate flag. We ain't got no allegiance to them flags. But our own flag? Yeah, man."

No use trying to reason with Boom Boom. His hatred was implacable, unyielding. Sadly, too many people in our country are beginning to see the possibilities that what Boom Boom's saying is already unfolding. They're desperate and running for cover, but there's no place to hide. Nor, is there any end in sight. A war of genocide is not too far off.

The only trouble with this kind of revolution, is that it never solves anything. It only makes things worse. It fans the flames of suspicion, distrust and hatred on both sides to unmanageable levels.

Nevertheless, I for one do not intend to stand idly by and let the revisionists of history continue to boil us Southerners in their cauldrons of hate. A man's got to stand for something, lest he fall for anything. Or else, what's the use of living? I'll not be intimidated into silence and submission.

There are already too many people who are afraid to speak out, afraid of being called racist—or worse—tabbed as ignorant, prejudiced and unsophisticated.

I've got extra compelling reasons why I must speak out against this insanity. Donna Elaine. William. They are asleep now out there in that lonely cemetery, largely because I picked up the gauntlet and waged my fight for the Confederate flag. And tomorrow morning I'll be carried to the state penitentiary. What do I have to lose?

Perhaps, just perhaps, my words might remind people that there are two sides to what's happening. And when people get both sides of the story, who knows what might happen? Is it possible all our voices could become quieter? Or that the fires of racial hatred could be dampened to manageable proportions? Could we as a people learn to live and let live, perhaps even love and respect each other, even though we are of different races?

Boom Boom's threatened war between whites and blacks must never come to pass. It would destroy us all, as well as our country. Freedom's last great refuge, the United States of America, would become a barren wasteland, perhaps even uninhabitable.

Yes, it's a story that must be told, but it's a highly controversial one. The manuscript I write will be sneered at, tossed aside as unworthy in most publishing houses. A Southerner to them . . . well, the space he occupies, in their mind, is usually a dark one. Still, I must try, even though my telling of the tragedy might never see the light of day in published form.

Tomorrow morning, I'll get one more glimpse of that glorious Confederate flag out there, flying high on its flag pole over General Lee's monument. I still hear the faint calls of the bugles at Gettysburg; still hear the distant sounds of the roll of the drums, see and feel the explosions of the bursting shells. I'm charging up Cemetery Ridge with the long lines of valiant men in gray, as my Confederate comrades scream, die, and reluctantly fall back. For a moment that day, we reached the high ground. If only we could have held it . . . if only we had won . . . if only . . .